THE CURSE OF
WHEAL HINGSTON

ALSO BY ARTHUR WALTERS

The Judge's Parlour

www.arthurwalters.com

THE CURSE

OF

WHEAL

HINGSTON

by Arthur Walters

Matador
9 Priory Business Park,
Wistow Road, Kibworth Beauchamp,
Leicestershire. LE8 0RX
Tel: 0116 279 2299
Email: books@troubador.co.uk
Web: www.troubador.co.uk/matador
Twitter: @matadorbooks

ISBN 978 1789018 127

British Library Cataloguing in Publication Data.
A catalogue record for this book is available from the British Library.

Printed and bound in Great Britain by 4edge Limited
Typeset in 11pt Adobe Jenson Pro by Troubador Publishing Ltd, Leicester, UK

Matador is an imprint of Troubador Publishing Ltd

Dedicated to

Patricia Margaret Martyn (Mrs Martyn)
Sunrise 23rd January 1936 – Sunset 9th August 2018

My primary school teacher, my friend
and a gentle lady never forgotten

With thanks to

Charlotte Cunningham
For her always-positive encouragement

GLOSSARY OF MINING TERMS

adit	Horizontal entrance into mine – mainly used for drainage
adventurer	Shareholder in a mine
after bargain	An unattractive pitch sold off at the end of an auction
bal Maiden	A woman mine worker
blowing house	A building used for the smelting of tin
bob wall	The strongest wall at the front of an engine house
bounding	The privilege given to a miner to enter land in the search for tin. The rights differed between Devon & Cornwall
cassiterite	The principal tin ore
cobbing hammer	Small hammer used for breaking up pieces of ore
coinage	A tax on refined tin
core	A work shift, usually eight hours
counting house	Mine office, often incorporating accommodation for mine captain

cross-course	A mineral vein running across the principal lode
deads	The waste from a mine
dressing floor	An area above ground on which the ore was processed (dressed)
fathom	A measure of six foot
flat rods	Horizontal wood or chain 'rods' used to transfer power from the engine house to another location
gad & feather	A cone shaped rod and metal wedges used to break off large pieces of rock underground
gook	A bal maiden's bonnet
grass	The above ground surface of a mine
gunnis	An excavated area open to the surface
hoggan	Forerunner of a pasty
jurate	A stannary representative
kibble	Barrel-shaped iron bucket for hoisting ore up a shaft
killas	Cornish term for sedimentary rock
knockers *(superstition)*	The little people who lived in the mine, so named to explain the knocking sometimes heard in the silence. A miner would leave a small portion of food to pacify them
lander	The man responsible for grabbing the kibble when it came to grass (surface)
lode	A vein of mineral ore
lord's dish	The rent paid in the form of ore by an adventurer to a landowner
mispickel	The principal ore of arsenic

mos'el bag	A bag for carrying food
pare	A team formed by a tributer
pitch	An area of the lode sold at auction
poll-pick	A miner's pick axe
sett	The legal boundary of a mine
setting	An auction of pitches attended by tributers
sollar	Wooden platform in or over a shaft
spalling hammer	The heaviest hammer used to break the toughest pieces of ore
spriggans (superstition)	Another name for 'knockers'
stamps	A machine for crushing ore to fine sand
stannary court	Courts deciding mining disputes
stannary law	Law pertaining to tin miners, giving them special rights
stope	An area from which ore is extracted usually between different levels
towser	A rough hessian apron
tributer	A mine worker paid an agreed percentage of the value of ore extracted from an auctioned pitch
tut men	Miners paid to dig the tunnels (levels) and shafts
winze	Vertical shaft within a mine to provide ventilation, but not extending to the surface

PROLOGUE

It's mid July 2018. It's shaping up to be a warm, dry summer. The four-acre, roughly square, sloping paddock, with its four-foot-high drystone boundary walls, is no longer at its best. The grass, once lush, is now long and wispy, and fighting for light and water amongst the brambles, plantain, nettles, and broad and curled leaf docks. The trees that border the walls are in full leaf; a mixture of elm, sycamore, beech and hawthorn. Their thirty to forty feet heights provide privacy, but nothing is able to grow underneath their low-hanging branches.

Three hundred yards or so from the eastern boundary are the hollowed-out workings of Treworthy Quarry, which is still busy on weekdays and the occasional Saturday. Fortunately, an overgrown bank formed from the waste of an ancient disused quarry, together with an area of scrubland and trees, hide it from view. To the south, is a further seven acres of partially managed, sloping woodland.

Horses used to graze this paddock, but it is now only home to rabbits, deer, and the occasional night-time fox or badger. In one fenced off corner, each spring and summer, three or four pigs were fattened for the freezer, their destiny known from birth; however, save for their galvanised ark, the ground lies empty, the earth still to recover from their continuous rooting and digging.

Having resurrected the field from a neglected state four years ago, twice a year, a contractor would cut the seasonal growth of weed. The thistles that annually rear their purple, bulbous heads high above their unwanted, intrusive competitors were felled with a satisfying crunch as the topper blade slashed through their stems an inch above the ground. Now they have won their battle and stand tall, like sentry-box soldiers.

Often, a pair of buzzards soar in circles, high above the land, hunting their field-mouse dinners in the newly mown areas, undisturbed by the drone of the next-door quarry's oversized dumper truck engines, their reversing alarms bleeping as they move the stone from the workings back to the processing plant.

Occasionally, quarry workers temporarily close the public road which passes the paddock's northern edge. Ten minutes later, a Second World War like siren emits its eerie sound, not to warn of impending Luftwaffe air raids but to inform of imminent blasting. After a further three or four minutes, the ground shakes and the noise of an avalanche follows, as the rock – which has lain undisturbed for many thousands of years – disintegrates and tumbles to the floor. The siren continues for a while longer, eventually coughing once or twice before returning to silence, indicating the traffic can once again flow freely.

Some of the dressed stone is used in the new housing developments infiltrating green-belt land in Cornwall and neighbouring Devon, and also to deliver a surface on which to lay tarmac for peace-giving town bypasses and summer-gridlock-relieving dual-carriageway extensions. Together with the usual array of cars, trucks and farm tractors, tarpaulin-covered quarry lorries rumble and clatter past the field's narrow, concealed entrance, and pulling out onto the road can be a tricky manoeuvre.

In the distance can be seen the tors of Bodmin moor and parts of Cornwall's inner landscape, with the latter marred only by an increasing number of modern-day windmills.

Halfway up the slope on the western side of the paddock are the remains of a copper-mine engine house; its separate, circular chimney is still intact. However, the only other part of the structure now standing higher than ten feet is one half of the 'bob wall'. Built from large blocks of cut granite, this wall had to be strong enough to support the steam-engine-driven, rocking, metal beam known as a 'bob' in Cornwall. The bob provided power for a pump used to remove water from the mine and a windlass known as a whim, which was used to lift untreated ore from the mine's depths.

The engine house's roof slates, unless robbed in a bygone age, presumably lie buried under the fallen stone from the walls, decades-old layers of rotting leaves, and the unhindered spread of brambles and nettles. From the middle of the building, a thirty-foot-high sycamore tree spreads its large-leafed branches, as if providing a shelter for what is left of this once-proud and grand construction.

Although still sporting the majority of its four walls –
like the engine house – an attached stone shed sits roofless,
whilst between these two buildings are the remains of the
boiler house, one gable end still complete. In front of the shed
and bob wall is a flat area of ground the size of roughly three
tennis courts, its once grass-covered surface now given over to
ragwort and various unwanted herbaceous intruders.

A mine shaft is situated on the far side of this ground, its
entrance surrounded by some loose wire fencing, whilst forty
yards further up the slope to the south is a pond – latterly a
summer swimming pool for the pigs – but no doubt once the
source of water for the boiler.

Like many Cornish mines, Wheal Hingston was never
a great success; however, unlike other mines, its failure was
not as a result of fluctuating commodity prices, poor quality
ore, unscrupulous landowners, corrupt adventurers, or badly
treated tributers and tut men; rather, it was attributed to
something less comprehensible.

How do I know this?

Because I researched its history, and, like many before
me, this is where I died.

ONE

14th June 2013

ETHAN

The clock showed 7.02am when Ethan at last managed to focus through eyes that felt thickly caked with dried breadcrumbs. He'd rubbed them until they were sore, but at least he could see, not particularly clearly but enough to read the black digital numbers. His neck felt stiff and he could hear a continuous tapping, like someone practising their drumming technique on the back of his skull; however, realising the noise was coming not from inside his head but from somewhere more like twelve inches away, he let out a loud sigh of relief.

'Hello… hello. Are you okay?'

The voice came from the same distance as the tapping. His neck jarred as he turned his head to the right, and a painful bolt shot through his brain as he attempted to shake his mind into action. The knuckles struck the glass again.

'I said, "Are you okay?" Are you badly hurt? Should I call an ambulance?'

The sun was directly behind the head outlined in the driver's side-window, creating a halo effect. It reminded Ethan of pictures he'd seen of Jesus, on the rare occasions he'd scanned through the illustrated Bible given to him by his parents. 'Sarah?' he muttered.

'I said… "Are… you… okay?"' The staccato words were like an Englishman or, in this case, an Englishwoman trying to make herself understood on a foreign holiday.

Ethan pushed one of the buttons in the door's armrest. The window slid smoothly open. It didn't occur to him that for it to operate, the ignition must still be on and the fuel pump primed to push through petrol.

'Turn off the engine,' said the woman.

'Sorry, what did you say?' asked Ethan. The drumming had stopped, but bells were ringing in his ears.

A bare forearm reached across him and pressed the power button.

'There, that's safer,' the gentle female voice at the other end of the arm reassured him. 'Now then, how are you feeling? Anything broken? Can you move your toes? Despite airbags, people still have their legs crushed in car crashes, you know.'

Car crash? How can I be in a fucking crash? he thought as he held his forehead. His brain had stopped hurting, but he had no recollection of driving a car.

'I'm sorry, what did you say?' He looked into the face. He couldn't make out their colour, but the eyes were large and bright, and the eyebrows thin and well-manicured. The cheekbones were clearly defined, the lips full and the nose cutely petite. Although the merest hint of a wrinkle on the brow and around the eyes suggested this was the face of a woman in her thirties, it still had the innocent beauty of someone much younger.

'Probably the airbag... I mean, the airbag going off probably has affected your hearing. Hopefully, you'll get it back soon. Now, can you move everything?'

Ethan took a few seconds to check.

'Affirmative; it's just my neck that hurts. It feels like I've been the fall guy in a Bruce Lee movie – one helluva chop.'

'That'll be whiplash, silly; it's possibly caused concussion as well,' the voice replied, its tone acknowledging his humour. 'Let's see if we can get this door open; there's nothing blocking it on this side.'

The door open, the woman offered Ethan her hand. Instinctively, he went for the seat belt release – it wasn't fastened.

Sitting on a grass bank beside the gully the front of his car had pitched into nose first, Ethan could see his first thoughts were right. The woman not only had the beauty of a young lady, but also the slender body of one. She was dressed in a pink, short-sleeved blouse; ankle-length, tight-fitting, white jeans; and pale-pink trainers. Her auburn hair was tied in a pony tail and her eyes were deep blue.

'You're sure you're all right?' she asked, leaning against the side of the car. 'It's no trouble to call an ambulance. You've been very lucky.'

Ethan shook his head, immediately grabbing his neck. 'No, no, I'm fine, thanks. Just a bit of whiplash, as you say.' He looked around him. 'Where am I and how did I get here?'

She gave a him a smile; her perfect white teeth unstained by cigarette smoke. 'The second part first – like many people from the cities, you were probably going a little too fast around our country lanes. The odd bend or two can catch you out so easily.' She pointed to the road behind her. 'See the skid marks?'

Two thin, black-rubber trails led into the hedge. Two gouged ruts had been made through a three feet high earthen bank as the car continued its journey in a straight-line before dropping five feet or so into a drainage ditch. One of the back wheels was stuck up in the air. Judging by the creased front wings and the buckled bonnet, even without the aid of a seatbelt, the crumple zone and airbag had done their jobs in preserving life; however, Ethan had definitely forfeited his insurance excess, not that right at this moment it featured high on his list of priorities.

'You were very fortunate it wasn't one of Cornwall's finest grass-covered stone hedges,' she continued.

'And the first part?' Ethan asked.

'Oh yes... Er, you're not far out of St Austell, near a village called Treworthy. I've got a cottage... Well it's a little bit bigger I suppose than a traditional cottage... well actually, it was a mine captain's house. Has all the ivy and things growing up the wall now though, so I called it 'Ivy Cottage'. It's about a mile away.'

'I see... er, Miss?'

'Jenny Woodbury, and it's Mrs. I'm divorced. Kept my married name, though. And you?'

'Ethan Menhennett.' He didn't mention he was a widower. He frowned. 'Um... er... do you mind if I ask how you knew I'm from the city?'

Her response was immediate. 'Locals don't normally hire cars, at least not from a company in Devon.' She flashed her eyes at the Enterprise sticker at the top of the windscreen. 'Most don't wear Ralph Lauren polo shirts and handmade loafers.' She smiled. 'And most don't speak so eloquently, at least not with a slight American accent. Am I right?'

He didn't reply immediately. He hadn't thought about what he was wearing until she'd mentioned it. He looked down at his shirt; it was the only excessively expensive one he owned. He'd treated himself to it the day after the magazine launch.

* * *

'Got to look the part at casual dos,' Claire had said. 'Can't wear suits all the time; not even someone with your black hair and the body of James Bond – the present one that is.'

She wasn't joking about his appearance. He did keep himself fit, even though he no longer had time for any sport. His hair was normally neatly groomed, and his dark stubble gave him a handsome, rugged look. Together with his six-foot-one height, he always attracted the attention of party-going ladies.

He'd met Claire when she'd been backpacking in North America in 2002. When money was short, she'd taken a job for a couple of months in the administration office at the copper mine where Ethan worked as an engineer. They'd become good friends, and, when he'd rang her to tell her his wife had died from cancer, it was Claire who'd convinced him to move to England.

'I'm sure your idea for a magazine focusing mainly on historic mining issues would go down well over here. I don't know of anything similar. I could help you... be your P.A. or something. After all, now you're on your own, it's not as though it'll be a big upheaval.'

It had been a massive decision, but with Claire's experience in publishing and public relations, and her motherly, caring attitude – she was married with two kids under the age of six – it had all been worthwhile and remarkably successful. Despite sharing her time between work and family, she was still able to play squash three or four times a week, something that she said helped maintain her petite body in good shape. She was also a very fashion-conscious dresser, hence her chastisement of Ethan's formal style.

* * *

These were the only pair of loafers and shorts he'd brought with him, and he was sure they'd got damaged or perhaps lost. And wasn't he in a pub? He could feel his head beginning to throb.

'Yes, I'm from London. I live in Harrow, not the posh part, though. Moved there from America in... um... um...'

For fuck's sake, brain, what's the matter with you? He mentally chastised himself before continuing out loud, '... a few years ago. I write for a magazine. Well, I own it actually.' He put his fingers on both temples. 'Look, I'm sorry. I'm confused. My memory's not very clear. Obviously the crash.'

'No need for an apology, although the farmer who owns the field might like one.' She reached towards him and touched his shoulder. 'Look, I'm only just down the road. Why don't you come with me, and have a cup of tea and perhaps some breakfast? It's not as though your car's going anywhere soon, and it's not blocking the road, that's for sure. We'll ring your hire company and they'll sort it out. No one's injured, so we don't have to involve the police. What do you say? Have to walk though, I'm afraid. I'm out for an early morning stroll, you see. Try to do it every day.'

The road to the house seemed familiar, but he couldn't remember why. The pink campions, foxgloves and wilted cow parsley, the narrowness and potholes, it could have been one of a thousand Cornish roads, but there was something different about this one.

'It's much nicer when the sun's out. It's not been very pleasant over the last few days, though it's the first rain for several weeks,' said Jenny as they walked.

'Yes, I'm sure,' replied Ethan, hardly hearing her. His mind was elsewhere, searching for anything to help recall this morning, let alone the last few days. Stopping, he dropped his kitbag he'd recovered from the boot of the car and ran his palm over his shirt. 'Sorry, did you say it hadn't rained much?'

She was a few paces ahead. 'That's right. Up until a couple of days ago, that is. Going to be a ban on hose pipes before long if we're not careful.' She continued walking.

Picking up his bag, Ethan followed. He grasped the hem of his shirt. 'And it hasn't rained today?' he asked.

'Nope. It's been fine since the day before yesterday.' She glanced over her shoulder. 'My, your memory really is in a state.'

Still holding his shirt, he gave her a half-hearted smile. *But I'm sure this was soaked by the rain.* Stepping over a large pothole, he shook his head. *I've been down here.*

7

'There's a pub further on,' he exclaimed. 'I stayed there last... er... er... last...?'

She slowed down, allowing him to catch up. Facing him, she dismissed his comment. 'Think you must be mistaken. There's not been anything down this road for years; well, that is other than the ruins of an old mining village, and that was deserted about twenty years ago. Someone tried to make a go of the pub back along, but it's too far out from civilisation. It was once used as a film set, but it's not habitable.' She gave him a condescending smile. 'No, sorry, Ethan, I think the accident has taken more out of you than we realised. The sooner we get you home, the better.'

She walked on. After a further fifty yards, she pointed to a track leading off to the left, its stone surface rutted and uneven. Weeds and grass grew in the centre. A weather-beaten, 'No Through Road' sign, rose out of the hedge, its red and white 'T' barely discernible.

'This way; not far now,' she said.

Her cottage was as she'd described it. Not really a cottage, more of a substantial detached house with tall, Georgian windows. Built of granite and roofed in thick slate, it was fronted by mown lawns and tended flower beds. To the right-hand side was a double garage and to the left a large orangery. A short gravel drive was secured by unlocked, double, eight-foot-high, wrought-iron gates.

At the front door, she bent down and lifted the doormat; underneath, was a key.

'Never like to take it out with me,' she said, 'just in case I lose it.'

Very trusting, thought Ethan.

'Leave your bag in the hall and make yourself comfortable in the lounge,' instructed Jenny. 'It's those doors there. I'll put the kettle on. Would you like eggs and bacon – both free range?'

'No, I'm fine, thank you, Jenny. Er, perhaps some toast, though.'

He wasn't hungry. After the somewhat scornful dismissal of his mention of a pub, they'd exchanged few words. He was sure he'd driven the road and certain – well, reasonably certain – he'd eaten at a pub, something pretty basic – possibly chips. Perhaps he had, and that's why he'd ended up in the ditch. Too much alcohol, unfamiliar roads and an unfamiliar car. *Hadn't I been in a bedroom, and been with someone... someone dark-haired... someone like... like Sarah?* He screwed up his eyes and pressed his palms against his temples, desperate to wind back his memory. The throbbing increased. He needed to sit down, close his eyes. Gratefully, he flopped on the sofa.

TWO

He was alone when he awoke in the high-ceilinged, expensively furnished room. A clock on the mantelpiece above the open fire struck eleven; the loud chimes resonated through him like an Edwardian dressing gong. He could hear someone talking on the telephone.

'That's right, the first junction towards St Austell from Treworthy... It's a silver-grey Mondeo. A hire car. It's in a ditch beside the road, so you can't miss it... You can?... That's great, Bill. You're a star. I'll ring the hire company; they'll need to sort out collection... Oh, and, Bill... don't mention to anyone you've taken it in, we don't want to involve anyone else and I mean anyone else... Thanks Bill.'

He heard the handset being put back in its cradle and the sound of a door closing.

Unconventional, possibly illegal, but perhaps it's how they do things in the 'sticks', he thought.

However – right or wrong, at this moment – he was grateful for small mercies. At least he wouldn't have to ring the hire company and hear, 'I did warn you about them stone walls. Now you're going to have to pay your collision-damage-waiver excess.'

He was beginning to remember. The short, plump woman had lectured him about the narrow roads and stone walls, like a mother chastising a young child for not heeding her warning about falling over in the mud. He smiled to himself, pleased with his subconscious response.

Huh. It was an earth bank, actually, so not such a smart-arse after all – are we? Gotcha, you stupid bitch. You can't send me to my room for answering back.

Beside him – on a small, wooden drinks table – was a hand-painted, bone china cup and saucer, and a tea plate with two slices of buttered, brown toast. He sat up, gingerly touching the cup – it was cold. He scoffed the toast, barely chewing. The tea followed. He grimaced. Not his favourite drink, cold tea, but, although it was sweet, it was still welcome.

What makes her think I take sugar? Probably thought I needed it. Hot, sweet tea, a guaranteed cure-all.

He got to his feet. His head still hurt, but nothing like it had done. He looked around the room, took in the furnishings: full-length, red-velvet curtains; plain, deep-pile, beige carpet; and two sofa-matching, brown-leather Chesterfield chairs. On the walls were hung paintings: original oils of horses and hunting scenes in walnut and gold frames. Jenny Woodbury clearly had taste as well as money.

The double doors opened into the hall. Like in the lounge, there were more paintings. The floor was wooden, with three or four rugs, possibly Persian. A curved staircase swept up from the end of the hall opposite the front door. From behind the door across the hall from the lounge came the thrumming of a powerful cooker-hood fan.

'Ah, there you are; how are you feeling?' asked Jenny as Ethan entered the stylish, modern kitchen. She was standing in front of a cooker range, stirring the contents of a copper saucepan.

He pulled up a stool at the breakfast-bar end of a charcoal-grey, granite-topped island. 'Much better, thank you. Still a bit groggy, but on the mend.'

'And your memory?'

He impulsively touched his shirt. 'I don't know, but I keep thinking about this shirt. Weirdly, it seems to have some significance, but what... I just don't know.'

'Give it time; it'll probably come back to you,' she replied in her kind, reassuring manner. 'Now, I'm making some homegrown-tomato soup. It's my favourite. Thought it might give you some energy...' She frowned. 'You do like tomato soup, I hope?'

He grinned. 'Only if it contains plenty of Cornish clotted cream.'

'You can be sure of that,' she replied, showing him the empty cream tub as she put the wooden spoon on the draining area. 'It'll be a while yet, so, in the meantime, you can tell me why you were driving a hire car and what you're doing in this part of the world; unless, of course, your long-term memory's left you as well.' She sat on the stool beside him. 'Was it something to do with your magazine? What's it called?'

'*The National Heritage Gazette.* It's about what fuelled the First Industrial Revolution. You know, mining in the

17th and 18th centuries – tin, copper, arsenic and coal; that sort of thing. How hard the life was, where the public can still go and see mines for themselves, and what they can expect. We do bits about steam engines, canals and things, but my main interest is the mines. I worked in one in America. We get a lot of copy from readers' letters. It's very popular in Cornwall.'

'Yes, I'm sure it is.'

His smile told her it was a passion.

She continued, 'And you were visiting a mine here?'

The smile left him. He shook his head. 'No, not really. I was… er… was looking… um… looking for someone – one of our freelance journalists.' He frowned. 'She said she'd heard a mine was being restored and she was going to do a feature on it; however, she never reported back to the office.'

'And this girl was called Sarah?'

Ethan looked surprised. 'How did you know? You haven't met her, have you? The mine was local. It was called… er… oh fuck…'

She returned to the stove and began stirring the soup again. 'Wheal Hingston? And you mouthed her name whilst still in the car before you get any ideas.' The wrinkles on Jenny's face had become more pronounced, not that Ethan noticed.

At the mention of Wheal Hingston, his head dropped into his hands. *Wheal Hingston… Wheal Hingston. Someone else said it. Who? Who said Wheal Hingston?* He looked up. 'The pub landlord… It was the pub landlord. He said it was Wheal Hingston. You see, I did go to the pub, I told you I had. Now do you believe me?'

Jenny dropped the spoon she was using to stir the soup. 'Sod it,' she exclaimed. The spoon bounced once on the slate tiles, before settling face down. She had her back to Ethan.

'I said, "Now do you believe me?"' he repeated, raising his voice.

She turned, all colour drained from her face. 'If it was Wheal Hingston, I'm afraid you may never see your friend again.'

He stared at her, mouthing inaudible words. *What the fuck are you talking about?*

Finally, air flowed over his vocal chords. 'What do you mean? What the fuck are you saying? Are you saying she's dead? I don't believe you. That's a ridiculous thing to say.'

Her eyes bored into him. 'There have been many deaths at the mine – more than make sense.' Her eyes narrowed. 'The mine is cursed; cursed by greed. You should go whilst you can.' She turned away, bent down and picked up the spoon. 'I'm sorry.'

Tossing it into the bowl in the sink, she stormed out, slamming the door behind her.

THREE

Ethan had run after Jenny, but, by the time he'd opened the kitchen door, she was halfway up the stairs. Another door, presumably her bedroom, slammed and he heard the click of a lock.

'Cursed,' he shouted. 'You expect me to believe the mine's cursed and Sarah's dead? You're mad, the same... as... the... pub... landlord.' He grabbed the banister with both hands.

'Well, the mine's got a bit of history; in fact, you could say it's cursed.'

Not only could he hear the landlord's words but also, with his eyes closed, he could see them.

Ethan banged his head against the white-painted spindles, then shook them like a prisoner shakes the bars of a gaol when first realising his loss of freedom.

'Jenny,' he yelled. 'I need to talk. I'm sure I was in a pub last night.'

There was no reply.

'Jenny... please... please talk to me. I need to know what's happened to Sarah.'

There was still no response.

'Jenny, I'm warning you. If you don't tell me, I'm going to knock down the door.'

He stomped up the stairs, desperate for an answer.

'I mean it.'

He banged on the only door that was shut. He tried the handle – it was locked.

'Last chance.'

He hadn't felt this wound up since he'd retaliated during a college football match. He may have left the field with a broken nose, but not until he'd ensured his opponent's jaw would need to be wired up for ten weeks. He'd been banned from playing for three months.

There was no sound from inside.

'Right, that's it.'

He took a couple of steps back, then shoulder charged the door. He ended up lying on the bedroom floor, agony suppressing his anger. Pain shot up his arm and invaded his shoulder. The door had put up a much tougher fight than expected.

'Shit, that hurts,' he blurted out as he massaged his burning muscles.

Getting to his knees, he knelt at the foot of a period, four-poster bed; its plain, dark-green drapes matched the heavy, full-length curtains. A dust-covered, mahogany dressing table with an oval mirror complemented a tall, double-fronted Georgian wardrobe and chest of drawers. Like in the hall, rugs partially covered the lightly stained wooden floor.

'Jenny… Jenny… where are you?'

Once on his feet, he crossed to the window – it was latched by its central, metal handle. He looked around for another door, an en suite or walk-in wardrobe, nothing. He checked under the bed – just dust. He ran out onto the landing and pushed the partially opened doors to three further bedrooms. Save for furniture, they were empty. He pushed the bathroom door; it only opened a few inches, like someone was trying to hold it closed.

'Jenny, are you in there?'

Silence.

Shoving with his good arm, the door gave way. A bathrobe was lying on the floor, the reason for the door's resistance. Disappointed, he picked it up and hung it back on its hook.

'Jenny,' he shouted, 'what the hell is going on?' He smelled burning. 'The soup.' He rushed downstairs to the kitchen. Smoke was rising from the pan. He grabbed the handle. It wasn't his best move.

'Shit, that hurts,' he exclaimed, shaking his hand. Two minutes later, having turned off the hotplate and held his hand under the cold tap, he confirmed he was alone in the house. Feeling sick, his head, shoulder and arm pulsating rhythmically in time with each other, and his hand sore to the touch, he collapsed on the lounge sofa. He was awoken an hour later by the telephone ringing. After eight rings, he picked up the handset.

'Hello… hello… can you hear me?' It was a male voice.

'Sorry.' Ethan yawned. Apart from his shoulder, all the pain had subsided. 'I've just woken up. Who is it, please?'

'Is Jenny there?'

'She's gone out. Who's speaking?'

There was no response.

'May I give her a message?'

'Er... tell her it's done, that's all.'

'Sorry, tell her what's done?'

There was a click – the line was dead. Dialling 1471 yielded, 'The caller withheld their number.'

Ethan stared at the handset.

The office, call the office.

A familiar voice answered. 'Ethan, where the hell have you been? I've been tearing my hair out.'

'Don't ask. It's a long story, Claire.'

'Are you all right? Why didn't you answer your mobile? I've been calling you for the last three days. Why the hell didn't—'

'What do you mean "three days"? I only left the office yesterday and, anyway, I don't know where my mobile is; that's why I'm using a landline.'

'Yesterday?' Claire's voice had lifted an octave. 'Today's Friday the 14th; you left on Tuesday the 11th. So where the hell have you been?'

Ethan took a deep breath, not really understanding what Claire was telling him. 'Claire, I don't know. Everything's a bit odd. I crashed the hire car.'

'You what?' she shouted.

Ethan knew it wasn't rage causing her to raise her voice. She was anxious.

'It doesn't matter, I mean it was insured,' he replied. He couldn't help laughing.

'What the hell's so funny?'

That was rage.

'Nothing. It's just an excess issue, that's all.'

'You've lost it. I'm coming down. Sophie can manage the office.' Claire was back to her concerned voice.

'There's no point; there's nothing you can do. I'll find Sarah, hire another car and be back before you know it.' He wasn't that confident, but he didn't want his colleague to worry.

'You mean you haven't found her? Oh God…' She paused. It was a few seconds before she continued. 'Ethan, she didn't receive an email about the mine.'

'Sorry?'

'We had Fred in – you know, the IT geek; my computer kept freezing. Whilst he was here, I asked him if he could access Sarah's inbox; you know, just to make sure she hadn't got the message confused. There was nothing about a restored mine in there, and nothing in her trash folder either. I was worried. That's another reason I wanted to get hold of you as—'

Ethan interrupted, trying to reassure her. 'Claire, you can delete what's in a trash folder, so that's probably what she did.'

'Ethan, I'm not stupid; I do know that. Don't be so bloody patronising.' Anger was mixed with frustration. 'If you'd let me finish, please. With Fred's knowledge, he was able to do much more; everything's still on the hard drive, apparently. He checked. There was nothing on it. She never got an email.'

Ethan took time to consider Claire's words. His head began its now customary throbbing.

'Are you still there?' asked Claire.

'Yeah, yeah, I'm still here. Trying to make sense of things. I can't find the woman who pulled me out of the car. I'm at her house, but she isn't. And I'm sure I went to a pub, but she said it doesn't exist anymore.' He tried to lighten the mood. 'Must be the Cornish sunshine – maybe I've got sunstroke

— and, anyway, Sarah's a big, strong girl; she can look after herself.'

'Then why did you go down there and who's this missing woman? What are you talking about?' She didn't wait for an answer. 'I still think I should come down.'

'No, no, not yet. Give me another day. Perhaps this geek isn't as clever as he thinks.' He sighed. 'Look, there is something you can do, though. Go through all our reference books and search the internet. See if you can find out anything about Wheal Hingston.' He spelled out Hingston. 'I think it might be the mine Sarah was going to visit. It's near the village of… of… Hingston, but…' He paused, picturing the Mondeo's satnav — he couldn't recall it being on there. 'I think the village is called Hingston,' he repeated, 'but I don't think it came up on the satnav. It's important; could provide the answers.'

Claire still wasn't happy, but at least he was involving her. 'Okay, but only one more day. How do I get hold of you? On this number?' She'd noted it from the caller display.

He breathed a silent sigh of relief. It may be only temporary, but for the moment, he'd managed to keep her off his back. The last thing he wanted was for someone else to get involved, especially a close friend such as Claire. 'I'll ring you at home tonight. By then, I should have something to tell you. I'm going to see if I can find the pub. It shouldn't be too difficult.'

'And then what?'

'I'm not sure.'

FOUR

11th June 2013

THREE DAYS EARLIER

'Oh bloody hell. I suppose I don't have a choice. Find out the time of the next train and book me a ticket, please, Claire. Also, you'd better organise a hire car at the other end. This mine's in some godforsaken place in the Cornish countryside.'

Ethan wasn't in the best of moods. A trip away from the office was the last thing he needed right now. The editorial deadline for next month's issue was just three days away, and he'd been relying on photos and copy from Sarah Jenkinson for the lead article. After all, it wasn't every day the magazine could claim an exclusive. However, the lack of her report wasn't what was really worrying him. It was a week ago she'd said she was going to visit the mine, and neither he nor anyone else at the Gazette, had heard from her since.

Her mobile went straight to voicemail. She hadn't answered the ten emails he'd sent, and her landlady hadn't been much help either.

"Er's often out galivanting and not coming 'ome at night,' she'd told Claire. 'So I never worries. She's old enough to look after 'erself.'

Despite the landlady's lack of concern, Sarah had never missed out on a deadline before, and not being able to contact her was playing on Ethan's mind. He'd thought about calling the police, but stopped short of doing so, feeling that it was probably 'making a mountain out of a molehill'. Instead, he decided to visit the mine himself, get the copy he needed and then make his own enquiries as to her whereabouts.

The next day, five hours after catching the 10.03am from Paddington, he drew up in his rented, silver-grey Mondeo at the gateway leading to where he understood the mine to be.

The drive from Plymouth had taken over an hour. He thought negotiating his way around the overcrowded streets of London to be a time-consuming pain in the arse, but once he'd crossed the River Tamar and left the A38, the narrow Cornish lanes had provided an unexpected challenge of their own.

The uncut hedges – in all their coloured, wild-flower-bedecked glory – may look nice to locals and dithery, sightseeing tourists, but to him they were nothing more than a hindrance. However, he'd been warned to treat them with respect.

'They might look soft and cuddly, with all the grass and flora, my luv,' said the female Enterprise receptionist, 'but just remember, underneath, they're still them drystone walls built a few hundred years ago. You don't want to end up paying your collision-damage-waiver excess, do you?'

Fuck the excess, he thought, as a second tractor driver didn't even acknowledge him. *Arsehole*. Twice he'd had to reverse sixty metres or so to let a 'I live here, so get out of my way', oversized farm vehicle pass.

The uncared-for, five-bar, wooden gate, hanging between two gnarled, weather-worn, four-foot-high, twelve-inch-square, granite posts was overgrown with brambles and stinging nettles. He checked his satnav, then looked at the 1960, inch-to-the-mile, clothbound ordnance survey map, one of a dozen various ones he'd bought cheaply online as a job lot a couple of years ago. The grid reference was the one Sarah had given him.

He twisted the map around, checking he was facing the right way. His eyes followed the line of an old, rutted farm track that crossed a field full of ragwort, thistles and two-foot-high grass, its seed-heavy stems swaying nonchalantly in the gentle breeze. Shading his eyes from the still-high, bright June sun, he could just make out the outline of an old engine house chimney on the horizon. He got out of the car, grabbed the keyless fob from the passenger seat and climbed the gate. Five minutes later, hot and irritated, he stared at the remains of the mine buildings. Sweat soaked his armpits and front of his dark-blue polo shirt. He began rubbing the nettle stings on his legs; perhaps shorts hadn't been the best choice, and neither had the tan, designer loafers, which were now scratched and covered in dust.

He shook his head.

Some fucking restoration.

Whilst the ivy-covered, circular chimney was more or less intact up its sixty-foot-tall tapered height, the binding weed no doubt partly responsible for assuring its survival, the rest of what had obviously once been an engine house and associated buildings were nothing more than a few tumbled-down walls. A flat area in front of the bob wall's end was blanketed in a mixture of tufted grass and dock leaves; like the buildings, its appearance was unkempt and unloved.

His trance-like state was interrupted by a large raindrop falling on the top of his head. He looked up.

The thickening, heavily laden clouds, which had formed as he'd walked up the hill, were now beginning to despatch their payload. Within seconds, water dripped from his nose and chin. Running to the far side of the flat ground, he took what little shelter was offered by the trees.

'That's all I fucking need,' he shouted to no one. 'Bloody Cornish weather.'

Cursing the rain, Ethan couldn't have known that, two hundred years ago, had a man named Tomas Roscarrow and his son still been alive, they would have happily accepted a drenching from cool, refreshing summer rain. Unfortunately for Tomas and Peder, they were sixty feet underground in a tunnel below where Ethan was standing. They'd been found kneeling as they prayed, buried up to their necks in mud and silt.

FIVE

8th June 1749

WHEAL HINGSTON

It was just after five in the morning when Rosen Roscarrow waved goodbye to her family and closed the door of the 'one-up one-down', stone cottage that she and her husband Tomas had finished building the day before their son Peder's tenth birthday. They were one of the few families working at the Wheal Hingston tin mine who were not living in Hingston village. Those living in cramped, rented terraced houses had small backyards and no gardens, whereas the Roscarrows had a quarter of an acre on which they grew their own vegetables and, in good years, some fruit. In one corner of their land was a stone-wall-enclosed area in which lived Peggy, their sow. Come November, she would be slaughtered, providing a ready supply of bacon and ham for the winter.

* * *

The land on which they'd built their house had been empty for some two hundred years or so. The stone Tomas and Rosen used for the walls were the remains of a cottage formerly occupied by the Cotterill family, who – according to the landlord of The Miner's Arms tavern in Hingston – had tragically been almost frozen to death one winter, before they were found to have been poisoned.

"Earsay 'as it that all five of them – mother, father and the three young 'uns – was found sat 'uddled together by the stream what runs through their land. Solid as stone statues, they was. They was trying to make for the village. They brought them to the doctor, but 'twas too late. The doctor found out the silly fuckers was full of some fuckin' venom.'

For a short while afterwards, the Polters and their two children had rented the house and the land from the Earl of Dorwall. Wishing to make a living from tin, they'd continued digging the already partly worked gunnis; however, following a cold, harsh winter and a wet summer, they'd left suddenly, leaving all their belongings behind. The earl assumed they'd emigrated to America as they owed him rent, but a jurate from the stannary court could trace no record of their departure.

Following the sudden disappearance of the Polters, no one would take on the lease, with some saying the land was unworkable due to the presence of the troubled spirits of the Cotterills, whilst others said it was the curse of the spriggans. Despite it being working-class tittle-tattle, generations of young earls who subsequently inherited the land forsook their ownership and announced that, should any tin miner wish to mine the land under the rights of bounding, they would face no challenge to their claim. In addition, they would be asked for neither rent nor a share of the proceeds from the tin, if indeed any was found.

Tomas, being a hardworking, God-fearing man – who'd moved from Penryn after being ostracised for refusing to join his fellow miners in their rampaging theft of corn from good, honest people – had no time for curses or folklore. Hearing of the rent-free land, he'd convinced Rosen that they should not stay in their damp cob cottage in Hingston, but instead, like adventurers before them, they should take charge of their own destiny. However, until such time as Peder was stronger and more capable, he and his son would continue to work for their friend and competent tributer, Jago Pengelly, as part of his pare.

* * *

Turning briefly to wave to her mother, Peder's sister Hedra pulled her white gook further over her head and wrapped her arms around her waist, holding her shawl tightly about her. The sun had yet to make much impact through the sheets of rain as she, her father and brother crossed the field. The walk to the mine was less than a mile, but uphill and the path stony and unforgiving. Blowing into their faces, the wind felt unusually cold. It took just minutes for the long, sodden grass to soak the bottom of her clean, white walking-out apron, whilst her wooden-soled boots, still wet from her previous evening's walk home, did little to keep her feet warm.

Her mother used to work with her, dressing the ore, but – four months ago – she'd dropped her spalling hammer on her right hand whilst breaking up small pieces of rock, and ripped apart two tendons. She'd tried to use her left hand to swing the hammer, but found it impossible to control, resulting in her having to stop working. Unable to give up all her domestic duties whilst her family worked, her hand did not have chance to heal, neither could she improve the power in her left.

Tomas had said little, but – with his own meagre earnings – Rosen knew the strain of her lost income was taking its toll. She did what she could to ensure all four of them ate well, but – due to the continuous heavy rains of the last month – the garden's claggy, clay topsoil was rotting the roots of the veg and had proffered slim pickings. For the last seven weeks, unable to afford meat from the butcher's, their diet had consisted mainly of barley bread and stored potatoes, with the occasional treat of a rabbit or a couple of pilchards caught by Tomas and Jago following a twelve-mile round walk to the bay after the Roscarrow family's attendance at Sunday chapel.

Tomas looked more tired than Rosen could remember, and on more than one occasion she'd eyed Peggy their sow with a longing look; however, Tomas had assured her that the tin lode would improve and their meat should not be slaughtered just yet.

The last three months at Wheal Hingston had yielded slim pickings. The tin lode Jago's pare had been following, from the shaft in their ten-fathom drive, was a cross-course running to the north, back towards Tomas' land. A month ago, it had trickled to just a few inches in thickness. Jago had wanted to change pitches, but had been outbid by others. As a consequence, Tomas Roscarrow and Peder – who was now twelve – had continued their daily eight-hour shift with little reward.

Tomas was in his thirty-second year, and, although still strong in body, he had begun feeling weak in stamina. Digging out the ore from the granite with gad and feather left him drained by exhaustion. At the end of his core, it could take him the best part of an hour to climb the perpendicular ladder back to 'grass', as he would have to stop several times to regain his breath. Peder helped his father as much as he could with the hammering, but sometimes the width of the tunnel left little room for two men to work on the lode. Also, this meant he would fall behind with wheelbarrowing the ore to the kibble, where it would be hauled up to grass. He would soon incur the mine captain's wrath if there was any suggestion that he and his father were keeping back some of the mineral so as to sell it when the price went up.

Peder had thought about joining the tut men so he would receive a monthly wage, but his father had firmly forbidden him from doing so.

'There's no money in digging out shafts and tunnels for others, young Peder. 'Tis hard work and less well respected. This lode will open up soon, you'll see, and then Master Jago will reward us well.'

* * *

As Tomas and Peder prepared to climb into the shaft, Hedra headed for the dressing floor. Here, she removed her white apron and donned her hessian towser, tying it tightly behind her back. She was glad of her shawl, as her calf-length skirt allowed the draughts to whistle around her ankles. Today, she would be breaking up the smaller pieces of crushed ore with her not-too-heavy cobbing hammer.

Hedra was also well aware of her father's health, and several times had asked if she could do an extra core each day.

'No daughter of mine is going to work her hands to the bone by working twice as long. We work together as a family and, despite everything, that is how it will stay.'

Father and son pressed their candles into the lumps of clay on their hats, and – with half a dozen tallow candles tied around their necks, and their tools and 'mo'sel bags' containing their meagre lunch hanging from their backs – they began their descent. Tomas, having lit his candle in the fire, went first, closely followed by his son.

'Grip tightly, Peder, for the ladder seems even more slippery today,' shouted Tomas as he saw the wooden sole of Peder's boot on the stave above his head. 'Us don't want you going all the way to the bottom; there's much work to be done afore us gets there.'

His father's joke made Peder smile. Since he was five years old, he'd always wanted to work in the mine. At night, when his father came home – usually wet, his clothes stained red – he'd listen to every word Tomas said to his wife about his day under grass. Sometimes there would be much excitement due to the quantity of ore that had been dug, and sometimes much grief as he related the death or injury of a fellow miner, but, whichever it was, Peder knew it was the life he desired.

The ladder's staves may have presented a risk to the older man, but to Peder they were just pieces of wood to be gripped more tightly than on the rare occasion when they were dry.

Had it not been for his father slowing his progress, Peder reckoned he could have been working the end of the drive twenty minutes sooner.

Stepping off the ladder onto the wooden boards of the sollar, Tomas pushed his back against the wall of the level's entrance, whilst catching his breath. Roughly ten yards away, he could see the flicker from a candle making its way towards him. It would be Jago and his two sons, Hendry and Merran. Eventually, he made out the blackened face of Jago. 'Mornin' Jago,' he said.

Jago's head dipped. 'Mornin' it might be at "grass", but to us down here…'

Immediately, Tomas knew it had not been a good core for the Pengelly family. Jago's tone was one of irritation as well as tiredness. He also knew that if Jago had let his sons walk the length of the planks over the ventilation winzes without lit candles, then it could only have been because money was tight. As far as Tomas was concerned, Peder's safety came first.

'Us can't go on like this,' continued Jago, 'or else there will not even be barley bread on the table.'

For someone usually so optimistic, it wasn't the comment Tomas would have expected from his friend.

'Cheer up, Jago,' Tomas replied, 'The lode will soon open up. Have faith in yourself; you've never been wrong before.'

'"Tis all right for you, old man,' grumbled Jago, who was but one year younger. 'You have no rent to pay and have funds put to one side.'

In the faint light, Tomas saw him wave a hand at Hendry and Merran.

'They have eaten nothing but potatoes and hoggans for the past three weeks. The nourishment is poor and the unleavened flour does nothing to aid their digestion.'

'Come now, Jago.'Tis not a conversation to be had at such a time. We must not let spirits drop, particularly in front of our children. I, for one, believe in you and I believe in God. He will provide for us.'

'Fuck your God, Tomas. A devout Methodist you may be but—'

'Enough, Jago. You may be one of the few who do not believe in my religion, preferring hard liquor instead, but you will not berate it either,' interrupted Tomas, raising his voice. "Tis you who shares out any profits, but 'tis I, my family and three others what helps you earn them.'Tis I who is also your friend, remember.'

The two men fell silent. It was Tomas' sudden loud outburst of coughing that finally broke it.

'Are you all right, Tomas?' asked Jago, his anger diminished. 'You sound as though you are coughing up the ore itself.'

'I wish 'twere, but 'tis just the smell of sulphur from below. Must be the last blast before the end of the core.'

A second later, a candlelit helmet appeared above the sollar, quickly followed by the head, body and legs of one of the miners working the original lode a level below. He acknowledged the two men and three boys, and then began his climb up the next ladder. Thirty seconds later, two more men appeared. One of them was Denzel Penna, a next-door neighbour of Jago's.

'How do, Jago… Tomas,' said Denzel.

'How do Denzel,' replied Jago.

Tomas nodded whilst making an effort to stifle his cough.

'Doesn't sound good, Tomas,' said Denzel.

"Tis all good, Denzel; 'tis just a reaction to the sulphur,' confirmed Tomas.

'Ah, yes, apologies. 'Twas neither of us three who is to blame, though. 'Tis young tributer Diggary and his friends in the cross-course below you. Still to learn not to blast at the start. Says he be anxious to clear the ore. 'Tis of a good quality and wants to get it to grass, so that it has been smelted in time for the next Liskeard coinage. Mind, there is much water to barrow out first.'

'He has good ore did you say, Denzel?' asked Jago.

'The lode 'tis wide, he tells us, and easy to dig after blasting. It runs towards grass, so should be near to your pitch.'

In the poor light, Tomas couldn't see Jago smile, but he knew Denzel's words would have given him good heart. As Jago and the others disappeared up the ladder, a touch of euphoria filled Tomas' chest and he began to whistle; he was quickly joined by Peder.

Perhaps we will eat well soon, thought Tomas, as he stooped for Peder to light his own candle.

'Come, boy, let's get to the end. Perhaps you and I can put a lengthy smile on Jago's face – one that will maintain his pleasure for days.'

SIX

Tomas and Peder had been working for three hours when Tomas broke into Diggary's lode. He had decided to leave the narrow vein of tin he and the other members of the pare had been following, and instead see if he could find the one Denzel said would emerge from below.

He'd been breaking the granite at floor level when he saw the first sign of the strange ore.

"Ere, young Peder, light me another candle.' He knelt to where his poll-pick had removed a small lump of rock. Holding it in front of him with one hand, the candle in the other, he murmured, 'Well, I'll be bound. 'Tis the work of God. No wonder Diggary was keen to blast.'

'What is it father? What have you found?'

Tomas rose to his feet. He showed the fingernail sized lump of bright, glasslike rock to his son. "Tis not tin, my boy. 'Tis something far more valuable. Take it, I needs another swing of the pick.'

As the point of his pick struck home, the ground below their feet shook violently. A sudden rush of air was enough to blow out the flames of their candles.

'What the devil was that?' exclaimed Tomas. 'Even with his find, surely Diggary is not blasting at such a time.'

'What else could it, be Father?' asked his son, his voice shaky, his expression of fear hidden by the darkness. 'Please God 'tis not the knockers.'

'Don't be silly boy, the knockers be well fed, and therefore there is no need for them to be angry.' But inside, Tomas did not feel so confident. He was too educated to believe in the spirits who allegedly lived underground, but he also didn't believe the shaking had been caused by a fellow miner. The next level should be several fathoms deeper, and, however petulant and impatient Diggary was, to blast out rock during a core would fill the drive with dust and foul air, and prevent any one man from working for a minimum of two hours. And where had the gust of wind come from? The nearest winze was at least one hundred yards back in direction of the shaft.

'We cannot stay here, boy. We needs light and 'twere the blast accidental, then we must check that those below are unharmed. Take my hand. Try to see our path in your mind. There is no need to be afeard, for God will guide us.'

Feeling his way with his free hand, Tomas led Peder slowly back along the level. It was nearly half a mile from the shaft, and several times his head hit granite that had proven too hard and time-consuming to dig out. His resin-soaked felt helmet gave little protection, and, as he progressed, he knew it wasn't water trickling down his face, but rather his own blood.

Relying on carefully placed feet, he took one deliberate step at a time. Every now and again, he paused, listening for any sound that might emanate from a winze dug to the lower level. When he reached the first one, he cupped his hand around his mouth and shouted to those below, 'Is everything well with you?'

Silence.

He shouted again, 'Is anyone hurt?'

Still silence.

There was a strong smell of sulphur.

Single planks, roughly ten inches wide and up to four feet long, lay across the centre of each opening. Like the staves of the ladders, they were wet and slippery. Even in candlelight they presented a hazardous crossing, particularly when pushing a wheelbarrow, and it was not unknown for cocky young miners to lose their footing and cause themselves serious injury. Melor Tremaine, an eighteen-year-old son of a tut man, had fallen to his death whilst showing his friends how he could dance a jig on the board.

'Steady now, boy,' Tomas said to Peder, as his foot touched the end of a board. 'One small pace at a time.' Being too narrow to crawl along, it took great skill to balance as they tentatively negotiated their way across. 'Only one more to go,' Tomas reassured his son after they'd put the first two behind them. 'Us'll be making a mine captain out of you soon.'

After crossing the third winze, Tomas knew they should soon be able to see the slightest hint of light from the main shaft. Even if it was still raining, the sun at this time of year would be nearing its highest and, normally, a few rays would penetrate to at least the first level. However, after thirty minutes, not only did he not see any daylight, but the toe of his boot kicked something solid in front of him. Reaching out, he felt hard rock. The way ahead was blocked, as the roof had collapsed. No doubt it had been this that had caused the ground to shake and the air to blow out their candles.

'What is it, Father? Why have you stopped? Are we not at the shaft? Surely we should have reached it by now, but I can see no light.' Peder's voice was trembling. 'Father, what is it?' he pleaded.

'Peder, do not fret. 'Tis nothing but a roof fall. It cannot be much as the shaft must be t'other side. Us'll rest, then start to dig our way ahead. No doubt the captain will organise others to do the same from t'other side.'

'But our shovels be at the drive's end. Will we need to go back and get them?'

'Perhaps it will be necessary, but first us'll use the shovels God gave us.' He grasped Peder's wrists and raised them up in the air. 'Our hands will be our tools, and only if they prove too weak will we return for the shovels. Now, boy, sit yourself down and regain your strength.'

Doing as he was told, Peder sat down on the damp floor. His father sat close and Peder could not resist snuggling up to him. Until now, mining had been exciting – hard work, but exciting nonetheless. He knew he had to be strong, but if he were honest, sitting in the dark with his clothing soaked through and their only way out blocked by lumps of granite, he wished for the comfort his mother used to give him when putting him to bed, when he'd hurt himself falling over or when he was too ill to get up in the morning. Naturally, he'd rejected these acts of love from the day he'd proudly set off to the mine to join his father underground; after all, he was now a man and it was time for him to do the comforting and reassuring of the women folk. However, as he began to shiver, not with cold but with fear, he would happily have rescinded his masculinity in return for her soothing.

'Come now, Peder, I needs you to be strong and have faith,' Tomas said, sitting his son up straight. 'Whatever would your mother and sister think?'

Rather than encourage, the mention of his eleven-year-old sister brought tears to Peder's eyes. They had grown up close and had always looked out for each other. For the short time their parents could afford to pay for them to have a basic education, Hedra had made sure her brother learned as much as was possible.

'It will help you when you are a respected mine captain,' she had assured him. 'They will not give you that job 'less you be brighter than t'others.'

Picturing her now, looking prettier than all the other bal maidens as she barrowed the black tin or griddled the crushed ore, the tears flowed uncontrollably down his cheeks; however, a moment later, being distracted by the ice-cold water soaking into the seat of his flannel trousers, they ceased. It took a second or two more before the flood water registered with his father, causing him to jump to his feet.

'It must be seepin' in from above.' He grabbed hold of Peder. 'On your feet. Us must make our way to the winze and scramble down.'

The thought that he and his son would not get out never occurred to Tomas. He was confident that – once they reached the winze, with their backs against one side of the roughly hewn shaft and their feet pushing firmly against the opposite one – they would be able to work their way down to the next level. Unfortunately, unbeknown to him, Diggary had indeed ignited another load of black powder: a load that was twice that of a safe amount.

Like Tomas, Diggary had also struck his pick into the glasslike ore and was anxious to release it before the mine captain realised what had been found. As a consequence, the blast had caused not only a rock fall on Tomas' level but also a crack in the floor of the drainage adit below, an adit already bursting at the seams with water. Tomas' plan to climb down the winze and walk to the main shaft and climb to grass was doomed long before the plank across the top of the winze had begun to float. Incredibly, not only was their level flooding, but, unbeknown to him and Peder, so was the whole mine.

At grass, the makeshift roof covering the dressing floor had already lost many slates. The wind had wound itself up to gale force, causing the rain to sweep horizontally across the site of the mine. Cold, sodden and spent, Jan Rowse and Tal Carne were struggling to turn the windlass handles as the water-filled kibble swung frantically to and fro in the shaft, crashing loudly against the shaft's rough and unyielding sides.

Water was forming pools all over the mud and grassed area of the sett. Joss Delaware, the mine captain, considered the site, with his mind wavering between continuing to work or getting the men out.

Flooding had never been a concern. Wheel Hingston's levels had not long been sunk below the water table, and therefore drainage had so far not been an issue. However, the adit had never had to cope with such a massive cloudburst over the soft, clay land that abutted the granite terrain.

The kibble had brought up nothing but water for the last two hours, and water couldn't be turned into tin. Lord

Hingston, the land owner, had only yesterday announced his dissatisfaction with his 'lord's dish' share of profits and had insisted more ore needed to be found. The earnings he had been led to believe would be his had fallen well short of expectation, and he had told Delaware that if production did not increase, then he would happily appeal to the stannary court with a view to asking that the mining rights be given to different proprietors.

Whilst Delaware did not for one moment believe that the court would agree to this request, it would not prevent his own job from being in jeopardy. As he stood, with rain pouring off the three corners of his cocked hat, he thought of his wife. He'd married above himself, something that he'd soon lived to regret. His wife was unable to conceive and had no desire to take on an orphan. So, instead of rearing offspring, she spent her time galivanting with the ladies of St Austell, regularly demanding that her husband provide funds to purchase extravagant gowns and undergarments, and to pay for dinners and entertaining at home.

He'd staunchly objected to her continued spending, but, each time he raised the matter, it instantly drew her venomous tongue.

'Should you not do as I ask, then I will have no hesitation in visiting Lord Hingston, and informing him of your past demeanours at the gaming table and your indiscretions with the harlots in The Miner's Arms. I cannot believe that he will take anything other than a dim opinion.'

Delaware watched Dulgudden, the lander, grab the rope as the kibble emerged once again from below. He watched as he tipped the kibble's contents onto the waterlogged ground, then swing it back over the shaft, and he watched as Rowse and Carne unwound the windlass, sending the kibble back for what he knew would only be water. Despite this, Delaware had to keep the mine working.

'The rain will cease soon,' Delaware told the bal maidens, who were pleading with him to withdraw the miners to grass.

'My 'usband and two sons is down there. Surely it cannot make sense to leave them working?' said one.

'The last core what came up spoke of flooding rising at the bottom, and that were four hours gone,' said another.

'Get back to work,' snapped Delaware, 'or I'll be docking your wages.'

He turned his back and shut the counting-house door behind him. He poured a large brandy into a pewter tankard and downed it in one gulp. Sitting at a table, he held his head in both hands. 'God forgive me if I do any harm,' he murmured.

At that moment, he couldn't have envisaged how much harm his decision would do.

* * *

Hedra had continued working when the senior bal maidens had petitioned Joss Delaware. She was as concerned as all the rest, but she'd fallen foul of the mine captain once before and she had no intention of doing so again. She'd missed a large deposit of black tin in one of the lumps of granite, and, having chastised her in front of all the other women and children, he'd then not only docked a day's wages but had said that if she did it again, her father and brother would not receive their full dues.

Glancing over her shoulder, she watched Delaware disappear into the counting house. Removing her towser, she scurried through the deep puddles to the top of the shaft.

'What be doing?' shouted Jenna, a girl the same age as Hedra. 'If Master Delaware sees 'ee, he'll turn nasty again.'

'I doesn't care,' shouted back Hedra. 'I'm going to warn my father and brother.' She stared into the darkness of the shaft. Undeterred by Rowse and Carne's half-hearted attempts to stop her, she lowered one leg onto the ladder.

She'd never been down the shaft before.

"Tis back luck for a girl or woman to enter the mine, Hedra,' her father had told her. "Tis man's work.'

She was just nine staves below when she caught the toe of her boot in the hem of her skirt. Although determined and strong for her girl of her age, her hands were small and her arms yet to develop strength enough to hold her own body weight. Losing her foothold, she screamed.

Even if one of the windlass men had heard her pleas for help, neither could have done anything to save her. Within seconds her grip gave way, sanctioning her descent in the way her father had joked about with Peder that very morning. Her skull cracked open by the edge of the rising kibble, she was dead long before her body – having at first bounced on the wooden sollar ten fathoms below – slid off its side into the deeper depths of the mine. Like the forty-nine men and boys who also died that day, her corpse wouldn't be found until twenty days later, when the red-stained, mud-laden waters of the flood having subsided and the numerous rock falls dug out.

Tomas and Peder Roscarrow, their palms tightly together, their fingertips firmly against their mouths, were discovered huddled together at the end of their drive, buried several feet deep in thick, slimy sludge – the same muck that kept hidden any evidence of Tomas' and Diggary's valuable discovery.

'Don't worry, boy, 'tis impossible for the water to rise much above adit; it will soon drain away,' Tomas had assured his shivering son.

Had the waters risen gradually, Tomas would have been right. The adit was at least five fathoms below them, and any water deeper down in the mine had been regularly kibbled to it. The mine's deepest level was fifty-two-fathoms, but, unlike many mines in the county, he knew water had never caused any problems in summer. However, this was no normal flooding. The mine had filled in less than an hour.

'Once level has subsided, us'll climb down a winze and soon be out. I'm betting others is already at grass.' Although his words gave Peder much comfort, Tomas could not understand why his fellow miners working below had not warned him of the rising flood waters. He may not get on with all of them, particularly the ones who didn't share his love of Methodism, but miners were renowned for their fellowship and care of their own. However, he could not have known that the thirty-eight men and nine boys in the levels below had also been hemmed in by roof falls and were already dead, long before he and Peder succumbed to suffocation.

* * *

A month after the flooding, Joss Delaware was tried at the Blackmore County Court in Lostwithiel, found guilty of gross negligence and hanged. Because of continuing roof falls and a fear of flash flooding, Wheal Hingston was abandoned. The shaft was boarded over, and the planks covered in rubble and turf.

Those miners who hadn't been working a core at the time of the flood found work at Wheal Chilsley, as did the majority of the bal maidens and tut men. For most, it was an eight-mile walk to work, as – due to a fall in the price of tin – nearby Wheal Hussey was winding down and was already shedding some of its workforce. It may have meant a long walk, but it also meant their families would eat.

Sadly, Rosen Roscarrow – heartbroken and with no income – was eventually admitted to the asylum in Bodmin following her arrest in The Miner's Arms. She was accused of prostitution, but the magistrate took pity on her and recommended she be committed rather than imprisoned. Her hand withered, she died in solitary confinement aged thirty-five years.

Over tankards of ale, those miners not attending chapel on a Sunday would instead spend many an hour in The Miner's Arms discussing the flood that had taken so many lives.

''Twas an act of they chapel lot's God, I'll be bound,' said one. 'They must have upset him by their lack of attendance the Sunday previous.'

'Don't be daft,' said another, ''Twas the knockers. They weren't fed proper by the night core and they took their revenge. I swear I 'eard 'em when I finished the evenin' before. I was climbing the ladder and—'

'Twaddle,' said a third. ''Twould have been the cracking of the rock unsettled by the heavy rainfall and we all knows it.

Nowt to do with God or spirits.'

'Ah, but I 'eard before 'e was 'anged,' said a fourth, 'old Delaware, the sod, insisted four skeletons was found on top of poor Tomas and Peder. Said they must 'ave fallen in from above. 'Parently, all had blades in their chests. Said 'twas definitely the work of the spriggans.'

'Balderdash,' challenged the third. "Twas just his way of trying to relinquish the blame. 'Ad he pulled out those below grass when the rain started, then none would have perished.'

'Then there would 'ave been fewer jobs for us at Wheal Chilsley,' said the first, grinning from ear to ear. 'So 'twas definitely an act of somebody's God. Shame it didn't wipe out all they what worship.' He got up from the table. 'Right. Who's for another?'

* * *

Whatever they chose to believe, Wheal Hingston was left abandoned until, in 1878, four tut men driving a deep adit to the north from the revitalised Wheal Hussey, discovered two exceptional copper lodes close to the Wheal Hingston workings. Before the adit broke out into a valley below Wheal Hingston, a small tin vein was also discovered. Unbeknown to either workers or mine owners, the tin ran to the surface where, in the early sixteenth century, it had been worked by a tinner called Ely Polter. It was also unknown that Ely and his family had been murdered in an act of revenge by a paid associate of a local widow called Maud Chechester.

Even with the price of copper at a barely profitable level, the then-owners of Wheal Hussey — J. Pendeen Esquire,

G. Trethorne Esquire and T. Pollick Esquire – decided, at the company meeting on 3rd April 1879, to build an engine house and associated buildings on the former sett of Wheal Hingston. The shaft would be reopened to service new drives. Regrettably, due to their excitement at the prospect of easy pickings, they did little research into the location, direction and depth of Wheal Hingston's original levels. After all, it wouldn't be them working underground and, with two generations since the last mining took place, tales of the flooding were long forgotten. It was a decision that was to have dire consequences.

SEVEN

14th June 2013

ETHAN

After ending his conversation with Claire, Ethan made himself a ham-and-cheese sandwich. Whilst not exactly ravenous, he thought he should eat something, even if the bread wasn't fresh; toasting it earlier had proved to be a wise move. Jenny's fridge was well stocked, which suggested that – although she'd managed her disappearing act – it probably wasn't pre-planned. He downed fresh orange juice straight from the carton and took a handful of digestive biscuits from the stone jar by the kettle. In a wall cupboard, he found a packet of supermarket-branded Ibuprofen tablets. He swallowed four, washing them down with more juice.

The front door had a traditional lock with a large key and keyhole. He opened the door and stepped outside. Locking the door behind him, he paused.

You fucking stupid idiot.

He unlocked the door, went back in and ran up the stairs. He looked at the lock on the door of the bedroom he'd broken into – like the front door, it needed a key. There wasn't one on the inside, so the chances were that it had been locked from the outside.

She never came in here you stupid prat… but you did, didn't you? The crafty so and so. She was in another room, and must have slipped past you when you were down. My concussion must be worse than I thought. But why run away?

Leaving the house once more, he slipped the front-door key under the doormat; surely Jenny Woodbury would reappear. At the end of the lane, where it joined the potholed road, he turned right, as he wanted to check if he'd left his mobile in the car. At the junction, the skid marks were still there, the gouges in the bank were still there, but the Mondeo had gone.

He suddenly remembered the telephone call, and the voice saying, 'Tell her it's done.'

The painkillers began to kick in as he made his way back; however, on reaching the turning to Jenny's house, he continued to walk straight ahead, hoping to find the pub. About eight hundred yards past the turning, he came to a ford or rather what had once been a ford. The river it served may have been shallow enough at one time to negotiate with a horse and cart – or, in later years, a car – but now its three-foot depth would stifle any attempt to cross, unless in a specialist vehicle. It was obvious to Ethan that he couldn't have driven through it and nor could he wade through it now. However, convinced this road led to the pub, he decided to find an alternative place to cross.

Following the river downstream, he saw it continued at a width and depth that made crossing difficult and possibly dangerous; however, after half a mile, it narrowed as it flowed into what struck him as an old gunnis, the open tin works long abandoned. After a further fifteen yards, Ethan could see an opportunity to jump across. He scrambled down the side of the bank, his feet loosening stone dug out centuries ago. On reaching the river, he cursed. The sole of his right loafer had detached from the upper.

'That's all I fucking need,' he said aloud. He sighed.

Deciding there was little point in pursuing his search for the pub without suitable footwear, he looked for an easier place to climb back up. After walking another thirty yards downstream, the gunnis ended and the river began widening. However, just before it did so, two wooden planks – each approximately a foot in width and four feet apart – had been laid across from one bank to the other. A track on the other side of the river led off into the start of a conifer forest. On Ethan's side, he could just make out faint wheel tracks leading up to what he immediately recognised as being the open end of an adit. It was roughly six feet high and three feet wide.

He considered the uneven, hewn-out rock floor of the tunnel's entrance. Loafers and the lack of a torch meant exploring it would have to wait. He also reminded himself of his purpose for being there.

I'm meant to be finding Sarah, not undertaking a mining expedition.

He contemplated the entrance. Unable to resist temptation, he stepped inside, stooping to avoid knocking his head, as the ceiling wasn't smooth enough to accommodate a six-foot-one-inch tall American. He couldn't see more than a few yards in, but it was far enough to spot the pale-pink trainer. As his eyes became accustomed to the darkness, several feet further in, he saw another.

* * *

The key was still under the mat when Ethan got back to the house. Having found the trainers, he'd been eager to investigate the adit, but common sense told him that, without light, the risk wasn't worth it. As he'd walked along the riverbank and road, his mind was in turmoil. He was no nearer to finding Sarah, no closer to recalling his whereabouts during the last three days and, now, he also had the added complication of why Jenny Woodbury's trainers were in the adit.

Why the hell had she gone there?

Why take off her shoes?

Where the fuck is she now?

On a sideboard in the dining room, he found what he desperately needed. He poured a large measure from the unopened bottle of Laphroaig into one of the half-dozen cut-crystal glasses sitting on a silver salver. He gasped as the whisky caught his throat. It wasn't his Scotch of choice, but it didn't matter – he downed another. Before he had chance to pour a third, the phone rang.

He stared at the handset in the hall. What the hell? He'd answered it earlier so why not again? He walked into the hall and picked up the receiver.

'Hello,' he said.

'Ethan, is that you?'

'Claire. I thought I'd said I'd ring you.' He'd wanted to have some good news before speaking to her.

She ignored his comment. 'Have you found Sarah?'

He didn't reply.

'You haven't, have you?'

'No.'

'Oh my God.'

'I will Claire. Don't be such a drama queen. Like I told you, I just need more time. If you—'

'Ethan, four people went missing there two years ago.'

His knees felt weak. He lurched into the seat attached to the telephone table. He screwed up his eyes and tried to remember.

'Ethan… Ethan… are you still there?' She was beginning to panic. She shouted, 'Ethan, answer me.'

'It was four Americans,' he mumbled.

'That's right. Two couples. The tabloids suggested it was murder, but no bodies were found. The police said there was another possibility and that they'd "done a runner". They discovered their hire scooters dumped in a river. I came across it by accident when I googled Hing…' She paused, taking in what he'd just said. 'But, hang about, how the hell did you know?'

'I don't know, Claire.' He was still mumbling. 'I honestly don't know.'

'Ethan, you're scaring me now.'

Hearing the trembling in her voice, Ethan tried to be more positive. 'I'm not joking. Honestly, I can't remember, but, anyway, it was two years ago, Claire; that's a long time.'

'But if they were killed, the murderer hasn't been found. It means he could still be out there. He could have…' She took a deep breath. 'He could have killed Sarah.' She began to sob.

'Look, it's fine. You know what Sarah's like: always out partying. She probably overdid it somewhere and is still recovering at a friend's.' As soon as he said it, even he knew he was talking out of his backside.

'Don't fuck around, Ethan. Call the police. Perhaps you should have done so long before now.'

He heard her blow her nose.

'Claire, I promise you that I'll find her. Once I've found this pub, I'm certain things will be a lot clearer. If they aren't, then I'll call the police.'

'If you don't, I will.' She swallowed hard and let out a breath. 'Oh, I also found some information about Hingston village and the mine. It was in one of the "to read" second-hand books you bought recently. It's in front of me on your desk. Six villagers suffered a pretty horrendous death at the hands of some psychopathic woman executioner from London. It was really vicious. Rumour had it that, afterwards, the land around was cursed.'

Ethan didn't tell her that Jenny Woodbury had mentioned the curse before she fled from the kitchen, nor that he was certain he'd also heard it broached by someone other than her.

'Wheal Hingston,' continued Claire, her sobbing under control, 'was never a success despite two attempts, one in the eighteenth century and another in the nineteenth. It flooded both times, killing a total of one hundred and twelve men and boys, and one girl. Some even said it was the girl's fault, as, according to superstition, she should never had entered the mine. Reckoned they'd found silver, but none was ever brought to the surface, just copper and tin. The land where Wheal Hingston's engine house was built doesn't appear to be owned by anybody – nothing on the Land Registry. I've got a friend who works there. She contacted a colleague in its Plymouth office.

'Anyway, that's about it so far. Oh, other than the fact that the village was abandoned some twenty years ago. Several residents had died unexpectedly, something to do with an unexplained illness, and nobody was interested in buying their properties. The village is often cut off by flash floods, apparently; the same as the mine I, suppose.' She laughed, if a little half-heartedly. 'Or perhaps they were afraid of the curse.'

Feeling relieved she was sounding a little happier, he decided not to mention that he'd found Jenny Woodbury's trainers. The last thing he wanted Claire to think was that there'd been another murder.

'Well done, my love, you've worked hard.' He glanced through the doorway at the clock on the lounge mantelpiece – it was 6.25pm. 'Time you went home. I'll give you a ring there as soon as I can. If I haven't found Sarah by the morning, I'll call the police.'

'You'd better.'

Once they'd said their goodbyes, Ethan poured another Scotch. Although it was time to find the pub, the adit and trainers were playing on his mind. He pulled his jeans and own trainers, out of his kit bag that was still lying in the hall. He smiled to himself, raised his glass and proposed out loud, 'Here's to the curse – the reason for everything.'

Warming to the iodine tang, he emptied the contents and refilled.

'The curse, the curse, the blessed curse.'

EIGHT

In a drawer in the kitchen, Ethan found three torches: two rechargeable and one with ordinary batteries. They all worked.

Must get a lot of power cuts down this neck of the woods.

He took the ordinary one. The clock on the cooker showed 7pm. He still had probably three hours of good light, but the pub might be an hour or so away and he had to get back again.

Reaching the spot where the two planks lay across the river, he couldn't resist taking a few steps inside the adit. Jenny's trainers still lay there. He picked them up, subconsciously examining them.

Nike, nice. Money no object. He turned them over. *Size eight – bigger than I would have thought.*

He placed them back on the ground, not as he'd found them, but neatly together. He shone the torch above him. Like the floor, the roof was roughly hewn. Shining the light into the tunnel, the beam petered out after about twenty yards.

Just a little bit further.

It was as if more than just professional curiosity was sucking him in. To begin with, the ground was dry, but, after

54

he'd progressed about one hundred yards, he could see water lying in puddles ahead of him.

Perhaps that's why Jenny took off her expensive footwear, he joked to himself.

Stooping uncomfortably and keeping as far to one side of the tunnel as possible to avoid the worst of the pools of water, he continued deeper into the adit. It reminded him of the potholed road to the pub and it reminded him it was where he was meant to be heading. More importantly, it reminded him of Sarah.

'Sorry Jenny, I've got someone else to find first,' he called out as he was about to turn to leave. 'Be back for you late—'

Fuck.

Spotting a bright light in the distance ahead of him, his sense of humour abruptly evaporated. Shining his torch straight at it, it immediately disappeared.

'Is that you, Jenny?'

No reply.

'I said "Is that you Jenny?"' he repeated, raising his voice.

Despite his assertiveness, the lack of a response was causing his composure to weaken. His mouth was dry, as though lined with sandpaper. The longer he stood in silence, the coarser the grade of paper became. A cold shiver ran from the rising hairs on his neck to the base of his spine. Swallowing hard, he eventually tried a different approach.

'If you're not Jenny, then who... who are you?' he asked, his tone much softer.

Silence.

'Stop playing games.' He wanted to say please.

His palms were sweating. What if it wasn't Jenny? He bent down, feeling around for a rock or anything he could use in defence. All he could find was water.

Shit.

Ethan's heart was thumping, ramming rather than pumping blood through his arteries.

He decided attack was safer than defence. Not wanting to broadcast his approach, he turned off his torch. With his left arm stretched out in front of him as though fending off a tackle at rugby, he edged forwards, keeping his head low, trying not to splash or stumble. The torch was in his right hand, level with his shoulder. He was certain that even a rubber-cased blow would do some damage if the person refusing to identify themselves came on the attack.

Guessing he must be within a couple of yards of where he'd last seen the light, Ethan tilted the torch from vertical to horizontal and switched it on. Instantly, the beam reflected straight back at him. He shook his head in relief.

'You bloody idiot,' he muttered, blowing out through his lips. 'What the hell's wrong with you?' He picked up the clear-glass bottle from where it was resting on a ledge created by a small piece of projecting rock. His hand was shaking.

Pull yourself together, man. Just a reflection, that's all it was. Just a reflection.

In spite of convincing himself the light was no more than his own torch shining back at him, he was grateful to return to the evening sunlight. He couldn't be sure how long he'd been in the adit, but, regardless of the time, he still had to try to find the pub. Deep inside, he was convinced it had something to do with him being unable to remember what had happened between Tuesday, when he'd visited the mine, and today, when Jenny had helped him out of the car.

He followed the other side of the river back to the ford and then carried on along the road. Its tarmacked surface was broken by even larger potholes than those before the ford. Just like the lane to Jenny's, grass and weeds grew along its centre. After a mile, silhouetted against the distant sunset, he saw what looked like a possible pub. As he approached, the piles of brick and stone rubble at intervals on either side of the road confirmed it had once been part of a deserted village, presumably Hingston.

Outside this lone building was a ten-foot-high post, on top of which was an empty, wooden frame, no doubt originally bearing the name of the pub.

Ethan eyed the boarded-up windows. Several lengths of guttering were hanging loose, and there were gaps in the thatch where it had worn and fallen away.

Surely this can't be it. Perhaps Jenny was right.

Crossing to the front door, he instinctively looked all around, checking he wasn't being watched. He was surprised when the tarnished brass knob turned in his hand. After glancing over his shoulder, he pushed the door open. Switching on the torch, he stepped into a small foyer. Faded, white writing on the door to his left said 'Public Bar', whilst on his right was the entrance to the 'Lounge Bar & Restaurant'. He chose the public bar.

Outside, the air had been warm, the light from the setting sun serene and comforting, whereas, inside, the atmosphere was dark, cold and unwelcoming.

The low, oak ceiling beams caused him to stoop. A large, stone fireplace, the hearth full of soot and ashes, faced him as he entered. To his right and behind the open door, an L-shaped, oak bar counter supported three traditional beer-pump handles. Thick cobwebs filled the space between them. A few dust-covered pint glasses and tumblers sat on low shelves behind the counter, whilst seven empty optics were attached to the front of a higher shelf. Tables and chairs were scattered haphazardly. More cobwebs hung from anything onto which the spiders had managed to gain a foothold.

Whilst it was obvious that this couldn't be the pub Ethan felt he'd visited, nonetheless, there was something vaguely familiar about it. He recalled Jenny had said it had once been used as a filmset.

Could be I've seen the film, I suppose. Alternatively, I've got it all wrong.

The small amount of light finding its way through gaps in the boards covering the windows began to dwindle. Realising the sun must have gone down, and feeling despondent, Ethan concluded there was little point in staying any longer. Once back at Jenny's, however reluctant he was to do so, he knew he would have no option but to call the police and report Sarah missing. Regarding his own lost time, he could only hope that his memory would return, as it had with fellow players who'd suffered concussion in college football. As to the whereabouts of Jenny, God only knew. Why had she run away from him? And why run into the adit?

Flashing the torch around in order to take one final look, something on the floor under a table caught his eye. It was a twenty-pence coin.

'*That'll be two pounds eighty, please.*'

The words bombarded his mind.

Change… change from three pounds. I gave her three pounds and she gave me twenty pence change. But who did?

He thumped his forehead with his free fist.

Who for fuck's sake?

He wanted to scream. He guessed it was how a dementia sufferer felt. You know it's in there but it just won't come out.

Bollocks.

But it wasn't only his memory that had caused him to swear – the light from the torch was beginning to weaken.

* * *

By the time Ethan got to the planks across the river, the torch had just about drained the batteries. However, it was a clear night and he had no problem in negotiating his way back to Jenny's. As soon as he got there, he would ring Claire and then the police. As he entered the gates, he saw lights coming from the downstairs windows of the house.

She's back; this could be fun.

The key was no longer under the mat; the door was locked. He rang the doorbell, immediately setting off a deep barking.

'Quiet, Dylan,' shouted a woman's voice. It wasn't Jenny's. 'I'll get it.'

The door opened about four inches – it was held back by the door chain. Through the gap, Ethan could see the wrinkled face of a woman – probably in her sixties.

'Hello?' she said. It was a question as much as a greeting.

'Er, hi. Um… er… is… er, Jenny in?' replied Ethan, struggling to say anything at all. On seeing the lights, although hoping for an apology, he'd also prepared himself for an argument. Being greeted by an unknown face hadn't been a consideration.

'Jenny? Jenny who? There's no Jenny here. I'm sorry. Now if you'd be so kind as to leave—'

Ethan jammed his toe in the gap.

'The kitbag in the hall is mine.' His words had the desired effect. The woman shouted to someone, presumably her husband.

'Roger, there's a man here who says the kitbag belongs to him.' The barking started up again. 'I said quiet, Dylan.' Once again, the barking ceased immediately.

The bald head of a man, with reading glasses perched on the end of his nose, replaced the woman's wrinkled face.

'And who are you?' he asked, his tone terse and unwelcoming.

'Ethan… Ethan Menhennett. I was here today with Jenny. I had a car accident at the end of the road and she helped me. She brought me back here for tea. That's why my bag's here.'

'Menhennett, you say?' queried Roger, adjusting his glasses, as if to thoroughly examine Ethan's face. 'Just a moment,' he instructed.

The door closed. Ethan could hear muffled voices. After a few seconds of conferring, he heard the chain slip off and the door opened.

'You'd better come in.' Once in the hallway, the medium-height, portly, headmasterly looking man introduced himself. Like his grey-haired wife, he was in his sixties; however, he was taller and not as fat as her. 'I'm Roger Jones, and this is my wife, Linda. This is our house. We've been here for nigh on eleven years, ever since we both retired. My wife has lived in Cornwall most of her life. However, as she has already told you, there is no one called Jenny living here.'

'But I was with her... she had auburn hair tied in a pony tail, and her eyes were deep blue.' Ethan could still see her, looking at him through the car window, concerned for his well-being. 'She was wearing a pink blouse and white jeans. You must know her,' pleaded Ethan. 'It was her who called Bill at the local garage to come and collect my car.'

The husband and wife exchanged lingering, supportive looks. The wife's eyes began watering.

'I think you must be mistaken, Mr Menhennett,' said Roger Jones. 'The nearest garage is twenty-odd miles away. There was someone there called Bill; in fact, he towed away...' Seeing his wife shaking her head, he paused. 'Um... er... but I understood he died a few months ago.' He pointed to the kitbag still sitting where Ethan had left it after changing. 'So, that's yours. Threw us – didn't know what to think. Having found nothing but old clothes in it, we thought squatters had moved in or a burglar had left it behind. I was going to call the police until we realised there was nothing missing or damaged, other than the saucepan. Was that you?'

Ethan shook his head. 'No, that was Jenny. She was making soup.'

A tear ran down Linda's cheek. 'What sort of soup?'

A weird question. Does it really matter? thought Ethan. 'Tomato. Is it important?' he replied.

A tear ran down Linda's other cheek. 'No, not really.'

Ethan took a deep breath. 'Look, I know this must seem strange, but if it helps, I'm just as confused as you. Perhaps if I could sit down and explain.' His head was beginning to throb. 'A bit much to ask perhaps, but I don't suppose there's any chance of a cup of tea.'

Linda looked at her husband. 'I think that's probably a very good idea. Go and sit in the lounge.' She forced a smiled. 'Presumably you already know where that is?'

'Thank you, I really appreciate it.' Stopping in the lounge doorway, Ethan noticed the time. It was just after 11pm. 'I know it's late, but may I use your phone? I promised to ring a work colleague. You see, we're both worried about someone – someone called Sarah. We think she's gone missing. She was visiting Wheal Hingston.'

'Go ahead,' said Roger.

'And may I have your email address, please; I want my colleague to send me a picture… you know, so I can show it around?'

Roger wrote it on a faded A5 notepad next to the telephone. The paper was headed:

Roger Jones & Co.
Dispensing Chemists

It had an address and telephone number in Surrey.

'Thank you. Oh, this is yours, I believe.' Ethan passed him the torch. 'The batteries need replacing I'm afraid. I used it to explore the adit down by the river. I found Jenny's pink trainers in there.'

The torch fell to the ground. Roger's face had lost all colour. 'Linda, get the tea.'

* * *

'Still looking,' said Ethan, keeping his voice low.

When Claire had answered, she had asked the obvious question.

'Then call the police like you promised,' she prompted.

'Yes, yes, I will, don't worry. It will help, though, if I have a photo to show them – can you look one out for me, please?' asked Ethan. 'There's several in that magazine you still keep on your coffee table. The one in her running gear's probably the best.' He remembered it vividly, wished he'd kept a copy. 'Her hair's tied back and it shows her face really well. Scan it or take a picture. It'll be a start.'

Not only had Sarah had an article make the front page of a tabloid, but a feature about her had been run in a Sunday newspaper supplement. Claire enjoyed showing it to her friends.

'She also writes for us as well, you know,' she would tell them over a gin and tonic.

Ethan gave Claire the email address of the Joneses – it didn't have their names in it.

He didn't tell Claire about the pub and he didn't tell her Jenny had taken him to a house that, seemingly, wasn't hers.

* * *

His telephone call finished, Ethan joined the Joneses in the lounge. He sat in an armchair. Roger's colour had returned, and there was an air of composure about him as he spoke slowly and calmly.

'It was a year ago now. We will never forget it,' recounted Roger. 'We heard the police and ambulance sirens going along the top road. It was at exactly the same junction where you say you crashed. She was turning right, to come down to us. The police think the sun may have been in her eyes, but, whatever it was, we were told she couldn't have seen the thirty-tonne contractor's lorry. They tend to be in a hurry to collect from the quarry and get back again. The more they do in a day the more they earn, I suppose.'

'The quarry's just along from Wheal Hingston, about five hundred yards past it,' explained Linda. 'They supply crushed granite for new roads, building sites and that sort of thing. We're not the only ones to complain about how fast all the traffic travels, but the police can't do anything unless they're exceeding the limit.' She wiped her eyes with a tissue.

Roger touched her arm. 'It hit her full on the passenger side,' he continued for her. 'Squashed the car to half its width. She was killed instantly, they said. We were advised by the investigating officer not to see the body nor the crash scene. Jenny was badly disfigured and... and...' He looked at his wife, 'she was decapitated. She was only thirty-three; no children; divorced a year before.' He stared at the floor. 'Such a waste.'

Linda got out of her chair and opened a drawer in the sideboard. Lifting out a framed photo, she passed it to Ethan. 'Is this the girl you say you saw?'

The auburn hair wasn't in a pony tail. Instead, it was hanging – shiny and wavy – just off her shoulders. It was parted to one side; however, there was no doubting those deep-blue eyes staring back at Ethan. They seemed so familiar. He nodded.

'And she was wearing a pink blouse and white jeans?' asked Roger.

'And pink trainers; the ones I found in the adit,' replied Ethan.

'Excuse me.' Linda left the room. He heard her go upstairs. The two men sat in silence until she returned. She was carrying a pair of pink Nike trainers. Ethan looked at them and then at Linda.

'She had more than one pair?' he asked.

'No, only the one. She was living with us when she died – she had been since her divorce. She bought these the day before her accident. We kept them, as a sort of keepsake, something… something… something unsoiled from the moment she died.' Pointing at the photo Ethan had put on an arm of the chair, she smiled ruefully. 'I've never been one for photos – they make me feel old.' She passed him the trainers.

Ethan turned them over. The moulded soles showed they were size six.

NINE

'How could you do this to us? Are you some sort of sick pervert? Can't you see what it's done to my wife? It's brought it all back.' After showing him the trainers, Linda had sunk back into the armchair and started sobbing. The atmosphere had changed, as if with a click of the fingers. Roger Jones was pacing up and down in front of the fireplace. 'What is it you want?' he demanded of Ethan. 'Money?'

'No, I don't want anything from you. I came here to find Sarah, not to play games. If it wasn't Jenny, then I don't know who the hell it was. I can only tell you what I saw and what was said.' He sighed. 'I honestly thought they must have been her trainers. How was I to know they were the wrong size.'

He remembered Linda's reaction when he told her what soup Jenny was cooking. 'It was her favourite wasn't it?' he exclaimed. 'Tomato soup was her favourite. That's why you asked me, wasn't it?' His comment drew a loud sob from Linda. 'How could I have known that?'

'You could have met her, been in a restaurant at the same time or anything,' snapped Roger.

Ethan closed his eyes, his face in his hands.

'I'd never seen her before, let alone met her. I swear,' he mumbled through open fingers. He lifted his head. 'Look, all I can tell you is that I came searching for Sarah. I went to the mine. It rained heavily. I… I think I went to a pub, but I can't be sure, and then – apparently three days later – I woke up in a car that had run off the road and a person – whom I believe to be your daughter, but obviously can't be – helped me out, brought me back here and then ran away. I found what I thought were her trainers, and now you're accusing me of blackmail.' He shrugged. 'If I were going to try to extort money, I promise you that I would have found a much easier way to do it.' He linked his fingers behind his neck. 'For God's sake, you've got to believe me.' He yawned; the events of the day were taking their toll. Perhaps that's why he didn't dismiss Linda's next comment as pure bunkum, and, bearing in mind the way he was feeling, he was happy to believe it – if only until he could come up with a better and more credible explanation.

'It's the curse, Roger. I told you we should have moved when those four people went missing, but you wouldn't have it, would you?' She'd stopped sobbing and was now full of vitriol against her husband. 'All that poking around in the adit and the old mine. You've stirred it all up again.' She got to her feet. 'Mr Menhennett, there's something about you that says I can trust you. In the morning, I suggest you ring the police and see if they can help find your friend; however, I would not hold out much hope.' She didn't explain her reasoning. 'In the meantime, I'm off to bed.' She turned to her husband. 'I'll change the sheets in the guest room; Mr Menhennett can have that tonight. You'll have to make do with the single, instead – it won't do you any harm.' She stormed out, slamming the door behind her. Within seconds, it reopened. 'And don't forget to let Dylan out for a wet.' The door slammed for a second time.

Roger sat down, avoiding eye contact with Ethan.

Despite his tiredness and the awkwardness of the situation, Ethan wanted to learn more. 'Are the missing people the Americans?' he asked.

Roger looked across at him. He nodded.

'And why did your wife say not to hold out much hope?'

'She blames the police for not making the lorries slow down,' Roger replied with a deep sigh. 'She has no faith in the local constabulary, not that you can call them local anymore. They closed the Treworthy police station last year.'

'Can you tell me what happened… to the Americans, I mean?'

Roger stood up and took the couple of steps to the sideboard. 'Whisky?' he asked, his back to Ethan.

'Please.'

'I assume it was you who opened this?'

'Yes, I'm sorry. I'll replace it. I was desperate.'

Ignoring Ethan's offer, Roger poured two large measures. He handed a glass to Ethan. They both took a long pull. Leaning an elbow on the mantelpiece, Roger took time to study the ceiling. After clearing his throat, he confronted his uninvited house guest.

'Unlike my wife, Mr Menhennett – assuming that is your name – I am not so trusting of strangers. Why you are saying you saw her late daughter is because…' Having seen Ethan's puzzled look, he paused. 'Sarah was my stepdaughter; Linda was married before.'

'Ah, I understand, thank you.'

'Now, as I was about to suggest… I can only imagine you suffered concussion in your accident, made your way here, somehow got in, perhaps saw the tomatoes on the window sill and started cooking yourself a meal.'

'And how do you explain my car not being where I crashed?'

Roger shrugged. 'You're confused; it's probably at another junction.'

'And the girl – there was definitely a girl. I didn't come here on my own.'

'God only knows.' Shaking his head, Roger sighed. 'Look, I have absolutely no idea what or who you saw, other than it definitely wasn't Linda's daughter…' He stopped to think, then continued, 'We have a cleaner, a girl from the farm a mile away towards St Austell. I suppose she's broadly similar in looks to Jenny and she didn't expect us back until tomorrow. Perhaps she thought she was being helpful by bringing you here. She's not particularly bright – she possibly realised she was doing wrong and ran off. She's not due in until Monday, so I'll give her a ring in the morning – it's too late now. I'll ask her if it was her.'

'Thank you.'

'That's all right. For the moment, I shall give you the benefit of the doubt. However, also unlike my wife, I am not a believer in the ridiculous curse that is supposed to affect anyone who tries to extract ore from the land hereabouts.'

'This is the curse uttered by six people before they were executed?'

'You are obviously well informed. According to hearsay, they cursed the land in the name of Cavall, a legendary dog belonging to King Arthur. It's all total rubbish, of course, but some locals still believe it was responsible for the loss of many men and boys. In the eighteenth century, a tunnel was dug from the original Wheal Hingston mine that reached the land where the six were accused of having stolen tin. During a prolonged period of rain, the mine flooded, killing all those below ground. Despite the flood receding, the mine closed until towards the end of the nineteenth century, when three men joined forces to start working it again. In building a tunnel that was intended to act as an adit for Wheal Hussey, which is situated further up the hill, two previously undetected veins of copper were discovered near Wheal Hingston. You see, an adit is used as an entrance and a natural drainage outlet amongst other...' Frowning, he paused. 'Ah, I forgot. You used the word adit a while ago, so are you familiar with mining terms?'

Ethan nodded. 'I publish a magazine about mining. Sarah, the girl who's missing, writes for it.'

'I see,' acknowledged Roger.

'And she told me she was visiting a restored mine, which I understand is Wheal Hingston.'

Obviously amused by this comment, Roger tutted. 'Restored,' he sniggered. 'The mine's not been touched for years – it's not even known who owns the land.'

'I'm aware of that now; that's why I'm worried about her. I'm afraid someone lured her here – someone she'd upset enough to want to kill her.'

Roger sipped his whisky, savouring its flavour. 'Hmm, you think that's likely?'

Ethan stared into his glass; he didn't want to contemplate the possibility. He avoided giving a direct answer. 'Could the Americans have been murdered?' he asked.

Roger looked at him intently for a moment, then went back to the sideboard. He picked up the whisky bottle. 'Top up, Ethan? I assume it's okay for me to call you that.'

'Of course and, yes, please.'

After refreshing Ethan's glass, Roger sat down in an armchair. He pursed his lips, taking time out before answering Ethan's question. 'I'm confident that they were murdered, but not for any reason you might imagine and certainly not due to any curse made by six transgressors of former stannary law.' He huffed. 'Not that everyone agrees it no longer exists – stannary law, that is.'

TEN

27th February 1520

THE MINER'S ARMS, HINGSTON

Two weeks after learning that the Cotterill farm was unoccupied, Father Rowland Worsley, priest of the parish of Hingston, and Edmund Folsham, Justice of the Peace, were sitting at a table in the bar of The Miner's Arms enjoying the landlord's ale.

At thirty-two years of age and of good breeding, Edmund was seen as cocky and arrogant, a demeanour he upheld both in or out of court. He always maintained a high standard of dress, even when strutting along the precarious, unmade village paths. However, although negotiating ankle-deep mud whilst attired in half-length leather breeches, a dark-brown tunic with ruffs and fancy leather shoes was considered somewhat ridiculous by all who knew him, few, if any, were prepared to openly criticise his choice. Should a punishment need to be dispensed for a minor felony, being admonished by Folsham as magistrate was far more preferable to being put in front of Judge Fredricks, the High Court's travelling Lord Justice. At least with Folsham, any miscreant had a chance of escaping with body and soul intact.

'Drink up, man, 'tis your turn to pay. She'll be closing soon,' Folsham said loudly, half his attention on Elizabeth Ansty, the barmaid-come-stablehand. The magistrate took great pride in having an intimate knowledge of the majority of the young, attractive females in the locality, but, so far, he hadn't had any joy in discovering whether or not Elizabeth remained intact. He was therefore eager to determine an answer and consequently grabbed any chance to summon her presence in the hope of slipping a hand under a skirt.

Worsley gulped down the remaining contents of his pewter tankard and thumped it on the table. 'There you go, boy, fill the fucker up,' the priest demanded, his Sunday sermon voice echoing off the limewashed walls and flagstone floor. Drunkenly, his bloodshot eyes managed to focus on Elizabeth. As she leaned over to toss more logs on the large, open fire in front of them, both he and Folsham admired her still unwrinkled bosom, lovingly forced up by the tightness of her bodice. Worsley reached out and pinched her buttock as she carried empty tankards back to the bar. She was half expecting such a gesture and showed no physical reaction. However, it was fortunate for her that the priest could not read her thoughts, nor see her contemptuous expression, else it was likely he'd ensure she'd end up in the heinous Lostwithiel gaol for contemplating his murder.

'Two pints of your finest, please,' ordered Folsham, waving his empty tankard.

'I'll be with you as soon as I can. I've got someone to attend to in the snug first.' She disappeared through the door to where tired travellers ate their evening repast.

'Why, the impudence of the girl! I'll see that Hyde dismisses her at once,' slurred Worsley, shaking his head. He belched.

'I think that highly unlikely,' responded Folsham, his open hand vigorously flapping away the smell of alcohol and half-digested meat exhaled by his companion. 'There'd be no one to look after the horses nor pot wash. Her guardian would be lost without her.'

'Guardian, my arse. He's her father all right and the Chechester woman's her mother, you mark my words. Just because she bears the name Ansty doesn't mean to say she wasn't his doing. Why else would he have been so keen to raise her?'

* * *

Elizabeth's mother had allegedly died giving birth. However, gossip had it that she had come from the womb of Maud Chechester, the wealthy widow woman whose husband Rewan had died four years ago from pleurisy, nineteen years after Elizabeth's birth. He had been a highly regarded yeoman and tinner. Loyal to King Henry, at the time of his wife's supposed confinement, he was away suppressing the rebellion by his fellow Cornishmen, and he had gone to his grave still unaware of the rumours abounding his spouse's infidelity.

Under stannary law, wives of tinners could be imprisoned for betraying their husbands, so Maud had said Ruth Ansty, her housemaid, had fallen to One-Tooth Tom, who visited annually. However, not wanting to be burdened by a servant's child, Maud had supposedly appointed the inn's landlord and his wife as godparents, on the basis that the child would eventually work in the inn. Ruth Ansty's body had been buried in the churchyard after being examined by the St Austell doctor, the same doctor who'd delivered the baby and administered the arsenic doses to her purported, unfortunate bearer.

'It's obvious. Her heart gave out. The birth was too much,' he'd declared as the coffin was lowered into the grave.

It was a declaration no one was prepared to challenge in public, although the priest would certainly have been able to do so. Whilst the deceased woman had lain prone in his vestry, awaiting burial, he'd been intimate with her and was aware, from her tightness, that no baby had passed from her loins.

'A dead body doesn't protest,' he'd joked many times with his creator whilst inebriated from drinking the Eucharist wine.

* * *

'You want to be careful what you say about young Elizabeth, else you won't be given any more ale,' chastised the handsome, rugged Folsham. 'Even your God won't be able to get you out of that one. I can't imagine you without your daily fill.'

Worsley ran his hand through his long, straggly, fair hair. Together with his six-foot height, it gave him a commanding stature as his voice boomed out from the pulpit. His lowly parishioners hung on his every word, emptying their pockets into the collection box lest he should pay them an unannounced visit at home. It had been one of these visits to the house of the unmarried twenty-year-old Agnes Laken that had led to providing the village with the alcoholic labourer John Laken.

In complete denial, the priest swore to Agnes that God would not have allowed such a conception between a young woman and a man nearer fifty than forty, and therefore had taken no part in his child's upbringing. As a consequence, poor John had grown up unloved and illiterate. Maud had felt sorry for the lad and, on many occasions, had treated him as her own. He found work at the various farmsteads, and, although unable to read or write, he could recite the names of all the pubs in the parish and beyond; the hanging picture signs granting him knowledge.

Folsham was disappointed when William Hyde, the landlord, brought their tankards to their table. He'd taken over, having sent Elizabeth to the kitchen, a pile of dirty pots needing attention.

'Good evening, gents, I trust 'ee fares well?' enquired Hyde, picking up the coins Worsley had thrown on the table. ''Tis a very cold night.'

'That it is, William,' acknowledged Folsham. 'But your fire and your ale are keeping us warm.'

'Not as warm as your goddaughter would keep me if her legs were wrapped around my groin,' retorted Worsley, stroking his short-pointed beard as he licked his tongue suggestively round his lips.

The bearded, bald-headed Hyde glared at the priest. He had no fear of him despite his holy status. Since his wife had died unexpectedly some eight months ago, Hyde worshipped no religion, a choice frowned upon by several of the village's do-gooders. Although some six inches or so shorter than the obnoxious, supposedly righteous Worsley, and a year or two older, Hyde had no reason to be concerned, as, like Folsham, he knew the priest was addicted to the inn's ale and would not endanger its loss by handing out physical punishment. He also held the upper hand when it came to renting out rooms at the inn.

"Ee keep thy hands off 'er; 'er's not a fresh piece of meat to be fondled by the likes of 'ee."

The priest jumped up. 'How dare you speak to me, a man of the cloth, in such a manner? I shall have you—'

"Ave me what, Rowland Worsley?' replied Hyde. "anged?' he sneered. 'Who then would provide 'ee with ale and the occasional room for thy use? Where would 'ee entertain the desperate women and young men that comes to 'ee in the night begging forgiveness? In thy 'ome?'

Worsley slumped back in his chair.

'I thought not,' continued Hyde, taking much pleasure from his verbal assault. 'Thy 'ousekeeper would readily gossip and tell of the sick pleasure 'ee gains from the arse as well as the cunt. P'raps the church, then?' Hyde shook his head. 'Nay. Even with an offer to suck 'ee dry, 'twould be too cold in there for 'ee to get your tiny pintel out from under thy robes.'

During this exchange, Folsham had remained silent and shown no surprise at the landlord's outburst. However, whilst he himself had no need to worry about how he spoke to the priest, he knew that once Worsley sobered up, Hyde's tirade would not be forgotten. However, Worsley dared not risk losing his source of liquid and physical pleasure, and therefore, for the time being, would leave well alone.

'Come, gentlemen,' chirped Folsham, deciding it was time to lighten the mood. 'Let us forget the harsh words and drink to an early spring.' He gave a wry smile. 'The Cotterill's land is now untenanted, and rumour has it there are easy tin pickings to be found. The law of "bounding" opens it up to others.' He raised his tankard. Half-heartedly, Worsley responded, not immediately latching on to Folsham's reason for mentioning the Cotterill's demise. Hyde merely nodded, poked the fire, then returned to the bar. He was already aware of the lode Edward Cotterill had discovered shortly before the snows had come in, and he also knew Folsham was prepared to exploit it.

* * *

Although no longer physically involved with each other, Hyde and Maud Chechester remained close, and had discussed the undug tin a couple of times when they'd dined alone together in the inn's kitchen after Maud attended Sunday church. Unfortunately, as the Earl of Dorwall owned the land and would soon allocate a new tenant, any attempts to dig it would have to be with his permission, which was something that Maud doubted would be forthcoming. However, she merely saw this as a slight hindrance and, with the right person on their side, something that could be easily overcome.

'Tis a terrible thing to have happened to the Cotterills,' said Maud on the Sunday before last, as she and Hyde enjoyed the pork he'd cooked fresh for her that morning.

'That it is, Maud,' he replied smiling. 'They should have drunk only my ale and mead, rather than that arsenic infected water of theirs.'

'Come now, William, show some sympathy,' snapped Maud, frowning. 'I understand their deaths were slow and painful. They could not have known that the mispickel they threw back into their spring would cause such terrible digestive problems and trouble with their breathing. They were all gibbering wrecks in their beds before they finally went. They had to be tied down, by all accounts. 'Tis said that, when the surgeon opened them up, their organs were vile and stunk of garlic.'

'Then perhaps us should have offered their offal to that bastard of a priest; 'e'd be too drunk to tell it was neither good venison nor beef, but no doubt 'e'd have enjoyed the flavour matching the stench of 'is breath.'

Hyde had had little time for Edward and Amice Cotterill and their three children: Larkin, Megan and Ralf. As far as he was concerned, anyone who welcomed the loathsome Worsley into their home deserved to die. Also, Edward was an abstainer, and – despite earning a reasonable income from tin and farming – he never spent any of it in Hyde's establishment. When Hyde had heard of their deaths, he'd quietly hoped they'd offered Worsley pitchers of water when visiting and that the arsenic would strike him down as well.

'William, that is neither the words of a devout Christian nor a decent-minded non-believer,' chastised Maud. 'Were this pork not so good, I would be tempted not to share my secret,' she added, before forking a large slice into her mouth.

Hyde's eyebrows rose. 'Secret? What secret be that?'

'Ah.' She put her hand to her mouth, indicating it was full. Hyde waited impatiently. Besides being a well-read woman, Maud was also well up on the local gossip from the gentry – the ones who sat in the inn's snug away from listening ears. Her secrets were usually worth hearing and, on the odd occasion Hyde had imbibed sufficient alcohol to loosen his tongue, worth sharing. Eventually, she finished chewing.

'I thought that would change your snide demeanour.' She swallowed some wine. 'Now then, as we know, the Cotterills had exhausted the supply of ore in the stream and intended to dig the shallow lode as soon as the winter had ended and spring was in the air.'

Hyde nodded. 'But that be no secret and, anyway, us knows the earl will only give rights to 'is tenants.'

'Dorwall is in Italy for the winter and will not return until April ends. With a couple of helpers, in his absence, we could remove sufficient ore to see us comfortable for the rest of our lives.'

'But others would talk if we trespass,' objected Hyde. 'And if they makes Folsham aware, 'twould be 'is duty to report us to the stannary court – our lives would not be so comfortable then.'

'Ah, but what if we had Folsham on our side, for he would challenge the earl's opinion about who can and cannot dig for tin?'

'Folsham?' scoffed Hyde. 'Why does 'ee think 'e'd be prepared to 'elp?'

'Because of my little secret.' A wry smile lit her pretty but weather-beaten and wrinkled face. She sipped the fine red wine Hyde kept hidden in the false cupboard in the rear of his cellar. 'I hear he has had a slight problem with one of the ladies he met at the Bodmin brothel. She is draining him financially dry.'

Hyde leaned forwards, his head cocked to one side. 'For what reason? And how do 'ee know such a thing?'

Maud passed him her empty glass. He obligingly refilled it. She took another sip. 'Our local magistrate has some peculiar habits involving leather, rope and small animals, of which he wouldn't want others to know,' she replied.

'And 'ow 'as this got back to 'ee?'

She sniggered. 'Let's just say that the St Austell doctor still receives a small fee to keep me informed of surgery scandal. It is he who continues to treat Folsham for the pox.'

Wide eyed, Hyde stared at her in disbelief. He glanced around the kitchen for fear Elizabeth may be listening. Content they were alone, he chortled. 'The pox, you say? Well, I never; old Folsham, the filthy bastard.'

Maud put her finger to her lips. 'You must not breathe a word to anyone, not even Folsham himself. Leave any negotiating to me.' She finished her wine. 'Now, I must take my leave; I have much to attend to. I need to check on young Laken. He's a hard worker, but constantly requires instruction.' She rose from her seat and thanked Hyde as he helped her on with her cloak.

'There be one thing, Maud.'

'Which is?'

'You say to see us all comfortable. But what of 'ee? 'Ee has much land and a good working farm, so why should'ee need more?'

She smiled. 'Dear William, but I thought you knew everything about me. Did I never mention my late husband, God rest his soul, enjoyed the dice too much in the years before his death?'

Hyde shook his head.

'Regrettably, he was a born loser when it came to gambling; he never knew when to stop. It started when he came back from fighting his fellow Cornishmen. He carried much guilt and regret. It was fortunate that we had the land as collateral and... I... I had a body that offers much appeal to the earl. I would very much like to repay his lordship's generosity with something more tangible and – now that I am older – in my opinion, far more enjoyable than the pleasures of the flesh.' She crossed to the back door. 'How do you think I found out the earl would not grant permission, dearest William. Unfortunately, not even my comforting moistness and bosom, which once pleased you, would change his mind.' Pulling up her hood, she smiled. 'We will talk some more another day, but, in the meantime, consider what I have had to say.' The solid oak door closed behind her.

* * *

'And what of the tin? Are you intending to claim it?' enquired Worsley. The thought of sharing a couple of ingots had had a sobering effect on the priest.

'As we are both aware, the earl is away; he will not return until the weather is fair,' replied Folsham. Tolerating Worsley's stinking breath, he lowered his voice and leaned closer to the foul holy man. 'One or two good men could do a lot in that time; certainly enough to sustain them for many a year.' He saw the look of interest in the priest's eyes and continued. 'I myself could do with an extra income. There has been little reason for me to sit in judgement of late, and my share of fines has fallen dramatically.' He had no intention of mentioning he was being blackmailed. 'And you, dear priest, you must surely receive little income from your church, and, although I have known for some while in whose pocket your collections are put, much of it I am certain disappears on ale, those women and…' He paused and gave Worsley an exaggerated wink. 'The young men Hyde mentioned. No doubt you have to pay him for his furtiveness in bringing them to your room in the inn.'

Worsley swallowed hard as he gulped from his tankard.

'Ah.' Folsham knew he had the priest by the bawbels and had no intention of letting go. 'And you thought none apart from Hyde knew of your unholy sexual-gratification needs. How naïve of you, Worsley. Your parishioners may live in fear of you, but that does not stop them talking behind your back. Probably the only one who remains unaware of your depravity is your bishop, although it is rumoured he enjoys the company of young boys also.' Taking a pull on his ale, Folsham smiled haughtily at the priest.

* * *

It wasn't his bishop's retribution that the priest feared; as Folsham had suggested, he was probably no more 'holier than thou' than Worsley himself. Instead, it was the Earl of Dorwall – a philanthropic, discreet bachelor and respected Cornishman who had served his county and country since inheriting his title twelve years ago.

He was the Lord Warden, the head of the stannary officials, which was a role that he carried out enthusiastically and diligently. It was this diligence that had seen numerous tin miners, or even their families, serve a term in Lostwithiel's prison for the most trivial of offences. More serious ones often received a penalty of death by hanging; the accused occasionally tortured or slaughtered before being granted a fair trial.

Presumably, having heard rumours about Worsley's unsavoury behaviour, the earl had instructed his staff to keep an eye on the priest, a fact Worsley learned after overhearing a conversation between two of Dorwall's coachmen as they relieved themselves under the vestry window, whilst waiting for the earl and his wife one Christmas morning.

'A real dirty fucker is that holy bastard,' one had said to the other. 'Earl says 'e'll hang 'im if 'e catches 'im with 'is cock in one of they village kids. I ain't seen nuffin yet, but 'e says us must both keep our eyes skinned.'

Fortunately for Worsley, the earl's nagging and relentless cough, which had driven him to his bed a week after the turn of the year and had subsequently persuaded him to winter in a warmer climate, meant he still had time to enjoy his pleasures without fear, if only temporarily. There was little doubt that the earl would punish him the same as a miner, should he know of the parish priest's sexual preferences.

* * *

Worsley observed Folsham closely. 'But why would a man in your position wish to risk his reputation? Penance fees may not be so lucrative at present, but surely you have a good income from your sheep and cattle?' he asked. 'And is it not right that you are wishing to stand for Parliament, though it is said you have little chance of success.'

Folsham shifted uncomfortably. The priest was correct. He was keen to make progress within his political calling, but he had many opposers. Also, he was not poor — at least not yet — but, should future winters follow the course of the present one, his often-neglected stock may not provide for his commitments. In addition, the Bodmin prostitute was not the only female to be draining him of income; there were several other women in adjoining parishes with whom he'd practised his carnal desires. They were not extracting money from him by blackmail, but they had borne his offspring, and he felt an inbred loyalty towards them or, more accurately, a devotion to buying their silence.

'You are right in what you say, Worsley, but I am in need of excitement and the thrill of the chase, for tin beckons me like it does many others.' He glanced at Hyde. The landlord had busied himself collecting empty tankards and clearing plates from the tables, whilst the clergyman and magistrate had their dialogue, but he had overheard every word; a fact that Folsham suspected, so much so that he was invited to join them at their table.

'Sit down, William. I have a proposition to put to you and possibly your young ward.'

Regrettably for Folsham, including Worsley in the discussion that followed would have fatal consequences.

ELEVEN

15th June 2013

ETHAN

Ethan lay awake, his thoughts overriding his body's desperate desire for sleep.

He tried to convince himself that, in a few hours, he'd wake up in his own bed, go to the loo and make coffee in the kitchen of his one-bedroom apartment, his nightmare few days being just a dream. However, being able to see the unfamiliar surroundings of the Joneses' guest room in the dim light stifled any hopes of this desire being anything more than wishful thinking.

He'd wanted to shower but, feeling too tired, decided it could wait until morning.

* * *

When he and Roger had walked upstairs together, his host had pointed to the guest room.

'You're in there, and – at my darling wife's behest – I'm in here tonight.' He shrugged. 'I've been exiled for several years now. Quite prefer it, if I'm honest. I can read as long as I like without disturbing her. Unlike my wife, I'm a bit of a heavy sleeper and I snore a lot too, apparently.' He waved his hand at a fourth door. 'That's Jenny's bedroom. We keep it locked, so I don't go in there very often; I leave that to Linda – it's bit of a shrine I suppose.'

It was the bedroom Ethan had broken into when searching for Jenny. Fortunately for him, there was no visible damage to the lock or door frame.

Roger shrugged. 'I still miss her you know.' He managed a hint of a smile. 'The bathroom's there, although your room does have an en suite. You should have everything you need – my wife's very particular about that sort of thing – likes to impress, you see; she's very hospitable. Now, unless there's anything you want, I'll bid you goodnight.' He opened the door to his room and stepped inside. The latch clicked loudly as it closed behind him.

* * *

In the semi-darkness, the red LED display on the bedside digital alarm clock showed 2.39am. The curtains left undrawn, Ethan could see through the window. The sky was cloudless, and, unlike at home in London, the stars shone as bright and clear as the reflected light in the adit.

Recalling his conversation with Roger, as Ethan's resistance to sleep eventually began to wane, an image of Sarah's prone and bloodied body lying faceup on the floor of the adit filled his mind. Her throat had been ripped away, and rats were gnawing at the exposed flesh and bone.

Why the hell didn't you ask me to go with you?

There was no answer.

Stubborn woman.

Eyes closed, he slipped into a nightmare ridden slumber.

* * *

'It was Luke Davis, a retired GP, who found the scooters,' Roger had told him as they sat drinking the Scotch. 'He was walking his dog by the river when it jumped in the water and got out the other side. Must have picked up on a scent and wouldn't come back. Rather than use the small bridge, Luke decided to try to cross on some rocks on the edge of a deep part.' Roger laughed, obviously imaging the situation. 'Silly bugger fell in. He's not the fittest of men, despite spending years of telling everyone else to lose weight and give up smoking. Anyway, to cut a long story short, he stumbled on two scooters: Vespas, apparently. He called the police. They were identified as being hired in Newquay by two American couples who were holidaying in a cottage on the north coast. It transpired that they'd left all their belongings and their return tickets were never used.'

'And the police suspect they were murdered around here somewhere?' asked Ethan.

Roger nodded. 'That's what their enquiries pointed to, although no one recalled seeing them since leaving the hire company's office. However, the police also thought there was a possibility that the four might have wanted to stay in

England. Apparently, one of their group had jumped bail in America for a drink-driving offence. If he returned, he would have been arrested.'

'So they faked their own disappearances?'

'That's what was suggested.' Roger gave a wry smile. 'It would have solved the case for the local constabulary and left it with immigration, or whatever its fancy title is now, to deal with.'

'I take it from your sarcasm that you don't believe it?'

'Correct, Mr Menhennett.' Roger's friendliness had momentarily dissipated.

'So, what do you believe?'

'What I have already said. They were murdered.'

Lightly tapping the rim of his glass against his chin, Ethan eyed the man sitting in the armchair. He obviously knew more than he was letting on. He leaned forwards in his seat. 'How can you be so sure?' he asked.

Roger held Ethan's stare for a moment before answering. 'Because they found out.'

Ethan shook his head. 'Sorry, found out what?'

Roger sighed deeply. He got out of his chair and looked away from Ethan. 'I've said too much. I don't even know you. You come wandering into our house, tell us you've seen Linda's dead daughter – my stepdaughter – and now you're asking me to tell you everything. How do I know you're not working for one of those depraved tabloids? I mean, you said you were a journalist.'

'Oh, for God's sake! Is that what you really think?' Ethan was finding it difficult to hide his frustration. 'So, first of all I'm a blackmailer and now I'm a gutter journalist?'

'Possibly.'

Drawing a deep breath, Ethan glanced at the ceiling. Shaking his head, he exhaled through pursed lips. 'Okay, you're right, I am a journalist, but I'm here to find a colleague not trawl up information about a past murder case.'

Roger's eyes narrowed. 'I'm not just talking about the past.'

Ethan's mouth fell open. He studied Roger's stern expression. 'You do, don't you?'

'Do what?'

'You think Sarah may be dead as well?'

Slowing finishing his whisky, Roger's cold, grey eyes met Ethan's.

'There is... probably... no "maybe" about it.'

'What are you saying? How do you know?' There was panic in Ethan's voice.

'I don't – not for certain, that is – but there are... there are, shall we say, some people who don't forget.' He looked at his watch and then, just as quickly as Roger's demeanour had become unexpectedly threatening, it just as rapidly abated.

'That's enough for one evening. We'll perhaps talk again another time.' He lifted the whisky bottle. 'Now, one more for the road?' He didn't wait for an answer. 'Not worth leaving that little drop.' His definition of 'little drop' wasn't Ethan's – it half-filled his tumbler. 'Should help you sleep, Ethan. Makes a change from the cocoa Linda normally makes me every night. By the way, may I get you something to eat? A sandwich maybe?'

This time the 'maybe' was of the friendly variety.

Ethan reluctantly accepted their conversation was over, at least for the moment. He hoped 'perhaps' meant tomorrow.

'No, I'm fine, thanks, Roger. I don't like to eat after about 10pm – else I suffer a bit from indigestion.'

'Fair enough.' Roger nodded towards Ethan's glass. 'Get that down the hatch and I'll show you where you're sleeping.' He got to his feet. 'Oh, there is one other thing.'

'Go on,' replied Ethan, his glass empty.

'My wife has early onset Alzheimer's – it started after Jenny's death – so it's unlikely she'll remember this evening's conversation in the morning.'

TWELVE

The morning

Roger Jones was sitting at the breakfast bar and his wife was standing by the cooker when Ethan entered the kitchen. Having showered, Ethan had changed into a pale-green t-shirt, the only other one he'd brought with him. He had on the same jeans. A black Labrador lay in its basket, totally disinterested in the stranger's entrance.

'Ah, there you are, Ethan,' welcomed Linda. 'Bacon and eggs?'

'Thank you, that would be very nice,' he responded.

She poured him a cup of coffee. 'Milk?'

'Please. No sugar, though.'

If the atmosphere before Linda went to bed last night could at best be described as tense and condemning, then, this morning – as Roger had told him to expect – was completely the opposite.

'Did you sleep well?' enquired Linda. 'Bed comfortable?'

'Fine, thank you. It's a very nice room, Linda.'

'It's kind of you to say so,' she acknowledged, placing a plate with two fried eggs and three rashers of bacon in front of him. She put the cup of coffee on a coaster. 'I'll do you some toast if you'd like some.'

'That will be lovely.'

'Is brown okay?'

'Fine.'

It was surreal – like another world; there was no sign of the upsets from the night before.

'There is one thing, Roger,' said Ethan tucking into his breakfast. 'Would you see if you've received an email from my colleague?'

'I already have, and, yes, there is,' Roger replied. 'I took the liberty of opening it. Apologies, but we wanted to see if we recognised the girl.'

'And did you?' Ethan hoped that Claire hadn't said anything more about Jenny.

'I'm afraid not, Ethan, but there is one thing.'

Oh God, what has Claire said?

'What do you mean?'

'Take a look for yourself.' Roger fetched the laptop from the work surface behind Ethan. It was similar to the one Ethan used in his office: a top of the range Apple Mac. As soon as he saw the picture, the one he'd suggested Claire send, it was obvious to what Roger was referring. He felt his stomach tighten, and the undigested eggs and bacon threaten to rebel.

Sarah was standing, with her hands on her hips, in a mint-green and light-grey, loose-fitting tracksuit. Even without makeup, she was still the stunningly attractive, dark-haired girl he'd danced with a few weeks ago at the publishing conference in Leicester. However, it wasn't her beauty that made him feel sick – it was what was on her feet. Like the ones he'd seen on Jenny, or rather the girl he'd thought was Jenny, Sarah was wearing pink trainers. The picture was so clear, he could even make out the Nike symbol on the side. He had no idea what size feet she had, but – as she was five foot ten, something he'd asked her when smooching at the conference disco – he knew there was a good chance of them being size eight. There was no text, just a couple of kisses.

'Are you all right?' asked Linda. 'Would you like more coffee?'

'No… I'm okay, thanks. I would like to use your phone again though, please. I need to speak to Claire: the girl who sent the photo.'

'I'm sorry,' replied Roger. He sounded genuinely apologetic. 'It's not working. They're replacing one of the poles, apparently. Linda was told last week. She …er… she forgot to mention it to me. It means I couldn't ring our cleaner either. It's lucky your friend got the email through exceptionally early this morning; it came in just after 5am. The broadband's obviously down as well now.'

'Do either of you have a mobile?' He was desperate to call Claire to ask if she knew Sarah's shoe size.

'Sorry, I don't believe in them. They don't work around here anyway, so not much use.' Roger took a moment to think. 'There is a phone box in Treworthy – you could possibly try there.'

'You'll be lucky, Roger,' chipped in Linda. 'That's not worked since it was vandalised months ago. British Telecom said it wasn't worth mending, what with most having mobiles. Now, if you'll excuse me, I must hang the washing out. It's such a lovely day, so it should dry quickly.' She lifted the blue-plastic washing basket with both hands. 'Will you open the door, please, darling?' she asked, sounding faintly irritated. 'I've only got one pair of hands, you know.'

'Sorry,' said Roger. He opened the double-glazed back door. 'There you go.'

'I'll go straight out with Dylan then – I could do with some fresh air,' she said as the black lab followed close behind her.

'Okay.' Roger shut the door firmly behind her.

Ethan was becoming impatient. *Sod the domestic chores,* he thought.

'Look, I've got to ring the police as well,' he said. 'Please can you drive me to St Austell? There's bound to be a phone I can use or I can even buy another mobile.'

Roger sucked in air through his teeth. 'It could be difficult, I'm afraid. The car was playing up – that's the reason we came home from our short break yesterday. I tried to start it once we got back and it was having none of it. I was going to call the RAC this morning. I'll have to wait now, though, I suppose. Tell you what, Ethan, why don't I go down to the adit with you? I can lend you a pair of wellingtons – I suspect we've got a pair that would fit – and we can search for your lady friend, not that I think she'll be in there. It'll put your mind at rest. When we're finished, the phone should be back on. How does that sound?'

What the fuck is going on? thought Ethan. It was as though they didn't want him to ring anyone; however, what choice did he have?' He could walk to St Austell, not that he knew how far it was, but that would waste time that could be spent on searching for Sarah. Reluctantly, he agreed to Roger's suggestion.

'Okay. I'm size eleven, but if the phone's not working when we get back, then I'll walk into St Austell if needs be.'

'Ah, that's lucky, you're the same size as me,' acknowledged Roger. 'I'm sure the phone will be working by then; Linda said that whatever they were doing would only take the morning. It's ten miles to St Austell, so I'm sure you'd rather call from here.'

* * *

'They were here. I picked them up and put them together. Somebody must have moved them,' Ethan said as he shone the torch into the adit. 'They were… really they were.' He rubbed the top of his head. 'I suppose you don't believe that either.'

When he and Roger had walked to the adit, they'd made no mention of their previous night's conversation. They had exchanged words, but only about Sarah and Ethan's magazine. Ethan had gained the impression that, although Roger accepted he wasn't after money, he still thought he might be after an article and was merely humouring him until he left. It came as a great surprise, therefore, when Roger turned to him and said, 'On the contrary, I do believe you, Ethan.'

'You what?'

'I can accept there's a chance your friend Sarah's shoes were here and that they've been removed.'

'But why? Last night I felt you thought me to be a… a… a snooping guttersnipe.' He saw Roger smile.

'I did, at least at first – rather a harsh judgement, for which I apologise. However, having spent what little time I've had in bed, I realised what you told me had some ring of truth about it, particularly running your car off the road. As we turned off the main road yesterday evening, I saw there were skid marks at the junction that weren't there when we left a couple of days ago.'

'They might not be mine.'

'True, but there's a strong chance they could be.'

'And what about Bill, the one who towed it away?'

'I'm not sure. There was a Bill who collected Jenny's car for the police after she was… was killed, but, as far as I know, he's dead.'

'So… who took it?'

'They did.'

Here we go again, thought Ethan. 'And who are "they", Roger?'

Blatantly ignoring the question, Roger chose instead to surprise Ethan with his next comment. 'Also, your story about visiting a pub—'

'You mean you think I may have stayed in one?' interrupted Ethan impatiently. He was amazed by the man's change of heart.

Roger stepped outside the adit's entrance, carefully scrutinised everything around him and then pointed to some large rocks beside the river. 'Come and sit down, Ethan; I think there's a few things I need to tell you.'

* * *

Fifteen minutes later, Ethan knew he wasn't going mad after all; that is, providing Roger had been telling the truth before he died.

'It all started a month or so before the disappearance of the four Americans. Although I'm usually a heavy sleeper, occasionally I have nights when I get virtually no sleep at all. It's usually after I haven't had anything to eat and drink before I go to bed. I lie awake worrying that I'd made a mistake with a prescription and harmed someone – I was a chemist, you see.'

'I saw the old notepad.'

'Yes, quite. I retired sooner than planned… well, the business actually got bought out. There's not much room for the small boys, especially ones who are finding keeping up with things a little challenging, shall we say? I had a lot of stationery left over. Anyway, I digress. On a couple of those sleepless nights, I've heard a vehicle travelling down the lane at about 3am. It's got a noisy, old diesel engine and heavy tyres. The wife takes sleeping pills, so she's out cold. I thought it must be a courting couple in a company lorry… but then I never heard it come back. There's nowhere to go other than Hingston.'

'But there's nothing there,' said Ethan, 'except the old pub.' He frowned.

'Exactly,' acknowledged Roger. 'It's the only building remaining anywhere near intact.'

'And what do you think?' A modern version of *Jamaica Inn* came to Ethan's mind.

'I'm not sure what I think. I've been out there several times, but...' Roger shrugged, 'it's just a rundown building.'

'But Jen... sorry, somebody said it had been used as a filmset, although – as you say – when I had a look it was just a...' He remembered the twenty-pence coin. 'Is it possible it's being used for something?' He resisted saying wreckers' pilfered goods.

Roger shook his head. 'I don't know. Getting there is nigh on impossible; the river is usually too deep to cross, although a heavy truck or a modified four-by-four could probably get through – perhaps even an ordinary vehicle if the level dropped.'

'Due to lack of rain?'

'Exactly,' confirmed Roger, nodding his head.

'And you think I could have driven there?'

'I don't know, Ethan.' He sighed deeply. 'But it fits. Until a few days ago, we hadn't had rain for several weeks.' He got to his feet and began to pace around. 'Your friend's trainers weren't the only items to be found in the adit. You see, I began to hunt about; took more of an interest in my surroundings, so to speak. It annoyed my wife; she said I'd stir up the curse, bless her.'

'It upset her last night.'

'Indeed, but – as I told you – she is mentally unwell. She remembers things from the past, but sometimes struggles with short-term memory, and can't always differentiate between what is real and what isn't. Makes her quite... quite angry; a totally different person.'

'I'm sorry,' empathised Ethan. 'However, you said you found something in the adit.' He was eager to learn more.

'That's right…' Roger hesitated, observing Ethan closely. Finally, sucking in his lips, he continued, 'This is strictly between you and me, and – for your own safety – must go no further.'

Bit dramatic, thought Ethan before encouraging Roger to keep going. 'Go on.'

'There's evidence of silver.'

Perplexed by Roger's comment, Ethan began shaking his head. 'But neither silver nor lead was mined in this area. At least…' However, as he spoke, he recalled what Claire had told him:

'They reckoned they'd found silver, but none was ever brought to the surface, just copper and tin.'

'… silver wasn't,' he continued. 'I know there was some silver mining in North Cornwall, Marazion and even Harrowbarrow near Callington and possibly some other small mines but I'm not aware of anything local. Are you sure?'

Roger's expression told him that he was.

'From what I learned at university, and from what I've since read about mineral extraction and the colour of oxides – yes, I'm sure. I've done some tests of my own from water I've taken from deeper in the adit,' confirmed Roger.

'But I don't understand. What's that got to do with murdering the Americans?'

'Because, like I said last night, they must have found out.'

Ethan was becoming frustrated. 'Look, Roger, it's one thing you doing tests and recognising what's in there.' He pointed to the adit. 'But it's another thing for tourists to recognise it, especially as silver's often mixed with lead. I mean, I used to work in a mine, for God's sake, and I'm not even sure I'd be able to spot it.' He shook his head. 'No, I'm sorry, Roger. And, anyway, even if they were able to tell, why are you so confident they were murdered?'

'For crying out loud, Ethan, isn't it obvious?'

Ethan looked at him blankly.

'They don't want others to know about the silver—'

'Who doesn't, for fuck's sake?' snapped Ethan interrupting. 'Who doesn't want anyone to know?'

'And also, my wife hasn't told you that—'

But Roger never had chance to either tell Ethan who didn't want anyone to know or what his wife hadn't told him. The bullet that entered his right temple and ripped a large chunk of flesh from below his left ear as it exited killed him instantly. Blood spurted like projectile vomit as his lifeless body fell forwards into Ethan, knocking him off his perch as the second bullet thudded harmlessly into the valley bank at least two metres above Ethan's head.

'Shit,' exclaimed Ethan. 'What the fuck?' His instinct was to rush into the adit, but his brain overruled. *One way in, one way out equals trapped*, it shouted at him.

Instead, he started to run in the direction of the ford, his stride limited by his wellingtons. To his relief, it appeared that their aggressor didn't fancy a moving target. After three hundred yards, he ducked down behind a four-foot-high granite boulder. Panting, he scanned the sides of the valley. Nothing. He wondered if the Americans, the four from his homeland, had indeed suffered the same fate as Roger.

THIRTEEN

27th May 2011

LOS ANGELES
AIRPORT, AMERICA

'C'mon, Mason, you fucking prat. We'll miss the fucking check-in. Shouldn't have drunk so much fucking beer.'

'Shouldn't have let him, Charlie. He's your kid brother. You know what he's like when he's not working.'

'That's easy to say Lily, but I thought he might at least lay off hitting the booze too heavily – after what's happened – until we get to England.'

'Fat chance of that, asshole,' said Grace, laughing as Mason tripped over his own suitcase. 'I think you'd better give him a hand, Lily. Threaten him with no sex unless he's sober. If he's anything like Charlie, you'll get an immediate response.'

Twenty-seven-year-old Charlie White and his brother Mason were both lifeguards on Playa Del Rey Beach. Although two years younger than Charlie, Mason was the same six-foot-three height; and had the same shoulder-length, bleached, blond hair, blue eyes and ripped, suntanned body. It was what had attracted Grace Brown and Lily Taylor, two nurses from the East Hills Medical Center, to them fifteen months ago.

'Look at those gorgeous hunks,' Lily had said over the top of her mojito glass, with her sunglasses pushed back on the top of her short, red hair. 'Let's see if we can pull 'em.'

Both in white bikinis, with figures the envy of any woman, they had little trouble in achieving their objective.

The four met for drinks the same evening. Lily, twenty-seven, paired off with Mason and twenty-six-year-old Grace with Charlie. A month later, despite Mason showing a tendency to over indulge his taste for alcohol on occasions, all four were still dating. In April, the girls moved out of their nurses' accommodation and into a shared apartment, and – over a few beers at Christmas – the four of them planned a four-week surfing holiday in Cornwall.

'Nothing like we have over here, but we could make those Brits look silly on the waves. You can't beat a bit of Brit bashing, I say,' said Charlie. He shared a rented two-bedroom house with his brother, or rather Mason had moved in with him after his girlfriend at the time had kicked him out, which was not long after Ellie, Charlie's partner of three years, had dumped him.

'But I thought Ellie was from England?' queried Grace.

'She was,' replied Mason with a big grin. 'It's his way of getting his own back.'

The four had booked a cottage near Newquay, and, whilst they were there, Charlie was keen to visit the village where his and Mason's great, great grandfather had owned a mine before emigrating to America.

* * *

Sitting up in bed the day before she died, their mother was thumbing through an old photo album left to her by her father and to him by his father. One of the pictures was of three proud and astute men dressed in double-breasted overcoats and top hats, standing in front of a stone building with what looked like a metal arm projecting out at right angles, two-thirds of the way up the wall.

'That's Josiah Pendeen, my great grandfather, on the left,' said their mother, 'Towards the end of the nineteenth century, he was joint owner of Wheal Hussey and Wheal Hingston, two Cornish mines. That's a Cornish engine house behind him. I've always wanted to go and see what, if any, remains are still standing, but it's too late now.' Aged fifty-seven, Pamela White – née Pendeen – had been diagnosed with breast cancer, and, in September 2010, had been told it was unlikely she would see another Christmas. Unfortunately, the specialist had been right– she died in November 2010.

Growing up closer to his mother than Mason, Charlie had sworn to visit the remains for her.

* * *

'Is this it? Is this what we've come all this way from Newquay to see?'

'For fuck's sake, Grace, stop moaning. You know it was always my intention to visit both mines.'

'Yeah, but not when the sun's out and the surf's up, bro,' contributed Mason. 'We could have come another day. It ain't California. Just 'cos they haven't had any rain for a while, doesn't mean it'll stay dry forever. We should make use of the good weather whilst we can.'

'Look, we're here, and you know I promised mum,' argued Charlie, just as agitated as his brother. 'If you want to fuck off you can, but I'm going to find this other mine, full stop.'

'Okay, fair point, I suppose. But if we don't find it soon, I'm going to find a pub instead. My throat's parched.'

The four had hired two Vespa scooters for the day. Wheal Hussey had been easy to find – in fact, the remains of its engine house had been restored; however, finding Wheal Hingston had proved more difficult. There was nothing marked on the map they'd bought on their arrival in Newquay.

'Perhaps it's down here,' suggested Lily when they stopped at a T-junction, unaware that the entrance to the field containing the mine was just a few yards back the way they'd come.

'It's possible, I guess,' agreed Charlie. He shrugged. 'There's nothing to lose. Might be someone about who could give us directions.' He twisted the throttle grip. 'This way, Mason,' he shouted as he accelerated down the lane.

* * *

'Shit,' exclaimed Mason. He'd tried kick starting the Vespa at least ten times. 'Why the fuck didn't we hire a car or something?'

'Because you said scooters would be more fun, and, anyway, it's your fault for going through the river so quick,' replied Grace.

'She's right, bro – we're gonna have to let it dry out. There're no spanners, so no other choice.'

Mason lashed at his scooter's seat with his crash helmet. 'Fucking Italian crap.'

'Careful,' exclaimed Lily, 'or we won't get our deposit back.'

Mason put his helmet down gently on the ground. 'Ah, fuck it; I need a drink. Perhaps there's somewhere down here.'

'It's worth a try,' said Charlie. 'We can leave the scooters and helmets here. As long as we take the keys, it's unlikely anyone will pinch 'em. And if there is a pub, we can ask where Wheal Hingston is.'

Unlike Mason, who – with feet in the air –had attempted the crossing at somewhere around thirty miles per hour, Charlie and Grace had taken it slowly and made it through the ford.

After walking the best part of half a mile, they reached a metal sign, one end of which was hanging loose on the ground, as the fixing on its mounting post had rusted through.

'Hingston' the sign had no doubt announced proudly in the past, before the once-black letters on a white background had deteriorated and faded to a dark grey.

'Wasn't on the map,' said Lily, sheepishly, having protested that they were wasting their time when making the decision to leave the scooters and walk.

'Typical bloody woman,' sneered Mason. 'Can't fucking map read.'

'That's unfair, you bastard,' she responded angrily. 'How can it be my fault if it's not marked?'

'Probably had it upside down, you—'

'For God's sake, you pair,' interrupted Charlie. 'There's no point in…' He stopped. 'Shit, where did that come from?' He looked up at the sky – it had started to rain. 'Christ, that's bloody heavy.'

'C'mon,' shouted Grace, just as a thunder clap boomed in the distance. 'There must be somewhere to shelter, even if it's not a pub.' Holding her lightweight rucksack over her head, she started to run.

'I know I read that council road-maintenance budgets are tight in England, but you would have thought they could have done better than this,' remarked Charlie as he jumped over a pothole roughly a metre in diameter and already filing with water. 'Just as well we didn't bring the scooters.'

After a further half mile, the girls attempt at running had fizzled out to a fast walk. Unlike their boyfriends, their jobs didn't involve regular runs along the beach. Thick cloud was now blocking the sun's warmth, and what light managed to penetrate them was dull and wintry.

As they hurried past a building on the right, they saw its cream, rendered walls were flaking and crumbling. Various brick-built bungalows and stone cottages on either side of the main road, looked tired and run down, the gardens neglected and paintwork peeling. In addition, all windows were boarded up, as were those in what had once been a school.

It was beginning to seem as if the place were deserted.

'The war memorial looks pretty neglected,' commented Lily. The three-metre-high granite cross on a three-stepped base in the middle of the crossroads was covered in grassy moss and thick, white, invasive bird droppings. Its base had sunk on one side, tilting the cross to a forty-five-degree angle.

Two hundred yards further on, the ends of a flat, solid-looking metal bar had been bolted into the stone blockwork on either side of the wooden, double entrance doors to what must have once been a village hall. Together with iron bars on the windows, a thick chain and a prominently placed padlock securing the wrought-iron front gates, gaining entry was clearly prohibited.

A 'KEEP OUT, TRESPASSERS WILL BE PROSECUTED' sign tied to the gates with thick, brown string, confirmed the restriction. Many of the roof slates had slipped off, exposing rotting, wooden rafters.

Grace crossed the road to where a glass-fronted noticeboard stood on two wooden legs. Rain running down her face, she attempted to read the paper posters, two of which had fallen forwards and were 'hanging on for dear life'.

'They're all so faded. They must have been here for ages,' she reported.

They continued their walk in silence; it was Mason who spotted the sign. 'Is that a good old English pub I see?' he shouted enthusiastically.

'Yeah, you could be right you fucking smart-ass,' replied Charlie, wiping his eyes. 'And what's more, there're lights on. C'mon, first round's on me.' He strode off ahead of the others, but, on reaching the pub, he came to an abrupt halt. He was staring at the sign hanging in a frame on top of a tall pole. 'What the…?'

'Charlie, what's the matter?' Grace slipped her hand into her partner's.

'The sign...'

The other three followed to where his finger was pointing.

'Oh my God, that's disgusting,' exclaimed Lily.

'You're not wrong, Lily.' Mason pulled her in tight. 'Who the hell would paint a sign like that?'

'Calling it that is one thing, but illustrating it with a dismembered corpse showing its insides hanging out is sick,' stressed Grace.

The rain running off the sign's surface did little to disguise its detail and bright colours. The pub's name encircled a picture of a simple gallows, the sort used when playing the game Hangman. However, hanging from it wasn't a 'stick man', rather it was a naked male corpse, its generous genitals still intact, but minus its arms and legs. The torso had been split open, exposing its bright-crimson guts and intestines. Lying on the emerald-green grass below the body could clearly be seen a vivid-red heart still attached to pinkish-grey lungs by its light-blue pulmonary arteries. The darkened eye sockets were empty. Perched on the drooping head, was a shiny, black crow, in its beak the intact former contents of one of the sockets.

Although only a painting, it caused both girls to turn away and retch.

'Must be someone's idea of a joke,' suggested Charlie.

'That's one bizarre sense of humour, if you ask me,' replied Mason. 'Still want to go in?'

Charlie looked at Grace and Lily who were wiping their mouths with tissues.

'Ladies?' he enquired.

Grace and Lily shook their heads. However, in addition to being soaking wet, Charlie was feeling hungry and thirsty

– he made it clear he wouldn't be put off by the females' lack of enthusiasm.

'We might not be able to get food anywhere else and at least we can shelter until the rain passes over. Have a look in the window; it's probably all right inside.' He took a couple of steps and peered in. He turned, his face beaming. 'Have a look for yourself. There's quite a few people in there and some are eating. The sign doesn't seem to have discouraged them.'

Thirty seconds later, the two females were sitting at the table just inside the public bar's door, whilst their respective partners – both needing to be aware of the low beamed-ceilings – headed to the counter of The Hung, Drawn & Quartered.

FOURTEEN

15th June 2013

ETHAN

For twenty minutes, Ethan remained motionless, save for the overwhelming shaking of his body. His heart punched his ribs, as though on a mission to force itself free. During his time working in mines, he'd taken many risks, but those risks were calculated and understood. Being shot at was different. He had no control, no influence and no idea of what to do next. Eventually, he made the decision to move.

Keeping low, he dodged between rocks, bracken and brambles, using any cover he could find regardless of whether it would stop a bullet. Every few steps he stopped and scanned the horizon in every direction. On reaching the ford, he felt a sense of relief. No further shots hopefully meant that Roger's killer hadn't followed him. It was now that he thought about Roger, and how if he had fallen off his stone in a different direction and not knocked Ethan over, the second bullet most likely would have found its intended target.

Ethan felt guilty he'd left Roger, but what could he have done if he'd stayed? People don't survive one side of their head being blown off. He was obviously dead. There would have been no point in them both dying. He had to tell Linda. What would she say? She would blame Ethan, the journalist who said he'd met her dead daughter: a daughter who'd died in a car crash.

He had to tell the police that Roger had been murdered. As he half ran, half stumbled, he considered how he would tell them and more importantly, would they believe him?

Well, Officer, it's like this. We were sitting beside the river having a chat when, for no apparent reason, someone blew Roger's brains out, but fortunately missed me. No, I don't own a gun and, no, we hadn't had a row. Well, yes, I did turn up on his doorstep yesterday having never met him before, and, yes, I did tell him and his wife that his dead daughter had helped me out of my crashed car – a car I can't even remember driving that day. Oh, by the way, I stayed in a pub that closed down years ago. I spoke to a lot of people there, but you see you must understand that, as I'm from London, it's all perfectly normal… Oh, you want to know why I've come all this way.

His thoughts turned to Sarah – a girl who'd been missing for over a week and nobody had bothered to inform the police of that fact.

Well, you see, Officer, she was a bit of a free spirit; liked doing her own thing… What's that? Wasn't I worried? Well, not to begin with then… then I realised she meant more to me than I had at first appreciated, so, rather than tell the police, I came looking for her. Didn't want to trouble your over stretched resources, you see.'

Imagining the conversation did little to reassure him.

He reached the house. His first knock drew no response, neither from Linda nor a bark from Dylan. His second and third also went unanswered. He lifted the coir doormat – the key was there. He unlocked and opened the door, and went inside. It didn't take long to establish that the neat and tidy house was empty. He picked up the telephone handset – there was no dialling tone.

Bollocks.

Leaving the house by the front door, he ran to the garage – the lift-up door was unlocked. Inside was an elderly, medium-sized Vauxhall saloon. There was no key in the ignition. He rushed back inside.

Keys, where are the fucking keys?

He found them on a rack behind the kitchen door.

He ran back to the garage, opened the car and got in. Turning the key in the ignition, the engine fired into life, then spluttered to a halt.

C'mon, c'mon.

Three times it started, and three times it stopped. He recalled what Roger had said: the car was playing up; the reason they came home early; he was going to call the RAC this morning.

Fuck. He thumped back against the head restraint.

Where's Linda? Perhaps she's walking the dog and will be back in a minute.

Twenty-five minutes later, she still hadn't appeared.

Shit, shit, shit, shit.

He climbed out, shut the garage door and the front door, and headed down the lane to the potholed road. Two hundred yards from the junction where he'd crashed, he heaved a sigh of relief.

Thank God for that.

Coming towards him was a police car. He stood his ground, waving his arms. The car drew to a stop. Through the open driver's window, Ethan blurted, 'A man's been murdered… down there, next to the stream. He's been shot in the head.' His voice was two or three octaves higher than normal.

The policeman turned off the engine. After pulling on the door handle, he pushed the door slowly open, forcing Ethan to take a step back.

'You've got to do something,' pleaded Ethan.

The crewcut, cap-less policeman hauled his six-foot frame out of the car. By the way his stomach bulged over the top of his belt, he hadn't chased a criminal in years, or if he had, it was unlikely he'd caught them. He patted the air.

'Now then, calm yourself down, sir – one thing at a time.'

'I was on my way to call you. It's the man who lived in the house down there, Roger… Roger Jones. His wife is called Linda. Roger's been murdered: shot. I managed to get away.'

'Hmm, I see. And when was this?'

'About an hour ago.'

'Hmm, I see.' The policeman stroked his chin. 'And where was this?'

'I'll show you. You can drive part of the way.'

'And your name is?'

'Ethan Menhennett. I'm a journalist from London.'

'London, eh? You're a long way from home.'

Ethan had heard of the Cornish word '*dreckly*' and now he was learning how frustrating it could be.

'Yes, London. I came down here looking for someone.'

'Anyone in particular?'

For fuck's sake, does it matter? was in Ethan's mind, but he managed to keep it there. 'Yes, it was someone who worked for me. Now, may we get on?'

The policeman stroked his chin again. 'Well, if he's dead, he's unlikely to be going anywhere wouldn't you say? Perhaps you just need to take things a bit steady.'

Ethan could feel his chest tightening. He took a deep breath.

'Look, Officer. I saw a man shot and another bullet just missed me. Wouldn't you be a little wound up?'

The policeman looked at his watch. 'Fair enough, I s'pose.' He pointed to the car. 'Better get in then, sir.' Ethan walked around to the passenger side and climbed in. After manoeuvring into the driver's seat, the policeman started the engine. 'Down here, is it?'

'That's right. Down to the ford and then we need to walk.'

* * *

'Looks like he wasn't dead after all.'

The policeman was dabbing his brow with a white handkerchief. He'd started sweating profusely within a few yards of the ford. When they'd arrived at the spot where Roger Jones' body had been, it had taken him a while to catch his breath. Still panting, he sat on the rock Ethan had unceremoniously vacated earlier.

'But he was here.' Irrationally, Ethan began searching around. He checked the river, a few yards into the adit, further downstream, the other side of the plank bridge, in a thick clump of bracken. 'There's no way he could have moved. Half his skull was missing.'

'Chickens still run around minus their heads,' suggested the policeman, without the slightest hint of a smile.

Ethan glared at him. 'Are you being serious?'

The policeman sniffed his armpits. Pulling a face, he glanced down at the ground and then all around.

'Well, based on the fact that there's no body anywhere to be seen, I would say that my comment holds as much water as you saying that someone had their head blown off, and then apparently got up and walked away.' He smiled. 'Would you not agree, Mr... er, sorry, what was it?' he asked, his tone full of sarcasm.

'Menhennett. And he was here.' Getting down on his knees, Ethan searched for any signs of blood; less than a minute later, he had to concede there were none. 'I don't understand it.' He sat on the grass, his head in his hands.

'Perhaps you've had too much sun sir.' The policeman heaved himself to his feet. 'Tell you what, if it makes you feel any better, let's go and see if by any chance Mr Jones managed to get home safe and sound.'

'But I've already been to the house, so what's the point,' protested Ethan. He was tired and confused. Apart from curling up in a heap on the ground and closing his eyes, he had nothing more to offer; reluctantly, he accepted the policeman's proposal. If Linda was at home, she could at least confirm Roger wasn't.

* * *

'Well, thank you Mr and Mrs Jones, you've been exceptionally helpful. We won't trouble you any longer. Goodbye; look after yourselves.'

In the rear seat of the police car, tears began rolling down Ethan's cheeks.

'I think it might be worth a visit to the hospital in Bodmin, don't you, sir?' The policeman wasn't expecting an objection to his suggestion, nor was Ethan likely to give him one. The handcuffs making it difficult to wipe away his tears, he continued to sob like a child.

FIFTEEN

Two days later

ETHAN

'Sarah, is that you? Thank God you're alive. I've been so worried.' Ethan held out his hand, caught hold of the warm, soft hand offered by the woman sitting on the edge of the bed. 'Where were you? I looked everywhere for you.' His eyes began to focus more clearly. He sat bolt upright. 'Claire,' he exclaimed, 'What the hell are you doing here? Where's Sarah?'

The gentle, blonde-haired mother of two touched his shoulder with her other hand.

'It's all right, Ethan. Take it easy.'

'Is Sarah okay? Have you found her?'

Claire shook her head. 'No, not yet, but I'm sure we will. In the meantime, you need to rest.' She encouraged him to lie back.

'Where am I?' he asked, his voice meek, his eyes beginning to close.

'You're in hospital in Bodmin. They said a policeman brought you in. They said he'd found you sitting at the roadside, appearing to be drunk as a lord and shouting abuse at all the cars and lorries.' She frowned as a mother might frown at a naughty offspring. 'Whatever were you doing, Ethan?'

He stared through her. 'I don't know – it doesn't make sense.' He glanced around the room, studied the medical equipment; none of it appeared to be switched on. 'What's going on? Why am I in here... on my own?'

'When you arrived, they said you were dehydrated and undernourished. They put you on drips and monitors but disconnected them this morning. It's now 3.30pm. They said you seemed fine, other than that you were rambling about some couple... someone called Jones.'

Ethan's eyes lit up. 'Linda and Roger, but Roger's dead. Shot in the head; missed me. Then a policeman picked me up... took me to their house. Roger was there but he wasn't the same.'

Claire was shaking her head in exasperation. 'What are you going on about? It must be the sedatives they gave you... making you confused; I mean it's not the first time in the last few days, is it?'

Ethan looked at her. 'You don't believe me, do you?'

She met his eyes, tapped her steepled fingers against her chin and took a deep breath. 'I don't know what to believe, Ethan.' She took his hand in both of hers. 'See it my way, Ethan; you came down to Cornwall to find Sarah, I hear nothing from you for three days and, when you finally make contact, you don't know what's happened over that time, although you say you've been to a pub, you crashed your car, a strange woman helped you and you ended up in her house and now you're in hospital having been shot at. Worst of all, Sarah's still missing.' She sighed. 'So, can you understand why I'm lost?'

All the time she spoke, he couldn't look at her; he just stared at the ceiling. However, as soon as she'd finished, he sat up.

'I've got to get out of here... got to find Sarah.' He swung his legs over the side of the bed.

'Have you listened to a word I've said?' She wanted to scream at him, relieve her frustration, but, inside, she understood. 'Wait. Whatever it is you intend to do, I'm coming with you.'

'No, it's too dangerous.' He found his clothes in the bedside cabinet, pulled a face as he held up the shirt. 'I can't wear this, it's filthy.' Rummaging through everything he'd been wearing, he chucked it all on the floor. He sat back on the bed. 'You'll have to get me some more. I've still got my wallet, so I can pay you.'

Claire stood up and walked around the bed. Confronting him, she said, 'You may think you're my boss – and I suppose, in the office, technically you are – but just one thing, Ethan fucking Menhennett, if you want me to run around after you, then you'd better change your attitude and that change starts right now.'

It was a school-mistress-like side of Claire not seen by Ethan before, and her chastisement had the desired effect. His head drooped. 'I'm sorry, Claire. You're right... again. I'm totally fucked up.' His hands behind his head, he looked up and smiled. 'How did you find me?'

'Luck, really,' she replied, sitting beside him. 'I drove down. Got lost after leaving the A30, I think it was. My satnav told me there were delays due to roadworks and suggested I try a different route. It was then that I saw a sign for Bodmin Hospital. Instinct or something told me to check that you hadn't ended up in here – you know, suffering from concussion. It seemed a sensible idea and – bingo – it was.'

He put his arm around her shoulders. 'I love you, Claire, but don't tell your husband.'

'I won't, but only if you tell me what's going on, and, by the way.' She grinned. 'I only take cash and it'll cost more than just the twenty pounds I see in your wallet.'

He nodded. 'Okay. I'll start with the Joneses.'

* * *

'Up here is it? This lane?'

'That's right, Officer. It's at the end.'

The policeman pulled up outside the Joneses' house. Knocking on the door, he beckoned Ethan to join him. A dog began barking as the door opened.

'Oh.' Startled, the woman took a step back. 'What's wrong?' She spotted Ethan standing behind the policeman. 'And who's this?'

Ethan was about to jump in with both feet and say, 'What do you mean, who the hell am I?' when he remembered her dementia.

'I'm Ethan Menhennett, Linda. I stayed here last night and went out for a walk with Roger this morning; don't you remember?'

She frowned and shook her head. 'I think you must be mistaken, Mr Menhennett. Roger's been with me all morning. He's in the back garden at the moment.'

'No… no, he can't be. I saw him sh—'

Before he had time to finish, the policeman stepped inside the hall. 'Mrs Jones?' he asked.

'Yes.'

'I'm Police Constable Fraser. May I have a word?'

Regaining her composure, she led the two men into the lounge. Instantly, Ethan noticed something different – there were four framed photographs on the sideboard. One was of Linda and a man, sitting on a low wall, with a bright-blue sea and sky behind them. Another was of her and the same man sitting at a table, wine glasses and wine bottles in front of them. The man was in a dinner jacket, whilst Linda was wearing a black evening dress. The two other photos were of the same couple: one was of them in a garden with a white-and-brown spaniel, and – judging by Linda's basketwork hat and the man's suit – the fourth was presumably taken at a wedding. Based on Linda's appearance, all were probably taken a few years ago. He picked up the one of them at a wedding. The man looked familiar, but it wasn't the man he'd seen killed by a bullet.

'This isn't Roger,' he protested to Linda.

'Of course it is. What are you suggesting?' she snapped back at him, 'That I don't know my own husband?'

'But—'

Again, PC Fraser interrupted him. 'All in good time, Mr Menhennett.' He turned to Linda. 'Now then, Mrs Jones, this gentleman is concerned that your husband may have been involved in an incident earlier today.'

'Incident? What sort of incident?' She was shaking her head.

'Well, that's what I'm trying to find out.' Fraser wiped his brow with his handkerchief. 'It's a little warm, Mrs Jones; do you mind if I sit down?'

She smiled. 'No, of course not. It was rather remiss of me not to invite you to do so.' She pointed to the sofa. Fraser made himself comfortable. Linda sat in armchair – Ethan chose to remain standing.

'Now then, Mrs Jones, about your husband; you say he's in the garden?'

'That's right – has been since breakfast. Much needs doing since the rain; everything's shot up and needs cutting. It was quite a dry spell we had.'

'Yes, indeed: too warm for me,' acknowledged Fraser before continuing with his questioning. 'And he's not been anywhere else?'

'No, definitely not, Constable. I would have known if he had. He doesn't just wander off without telling me. Anyway, he came in for a coffee not long ago.'

'I see.' Fraser glanced at the photos. 'And that's your husband?'

'Yes. On holiday, at a... um... er... the annual dinner of an organisation my husband belongs to, a friend's wedding and in our garden with a previous dog; it died a while ago. We have a different one now,' replied Linda.

'Hmm.' Fraser scratched his chin. 'I wonder if you wouldn't mind asking him in.'

'No, of course not.' As she got up, she glared at Ethan. 'Perhaps then this gentleman will come to his senses.'

Ten minutes later, Fraser was ready to leave. A bald-headed man, no more than five-foot-eight tall, with a neatly trimmed, black beard, had apologised to him for not shaking hands. In the flesh, he looked a few years younger than in the photos. He'd also grown a beard since they were taken. Ethan was sure he'd met him before.

'Sorry, Constable, my hands are a bit sweaty. It's rather warm out there.'

Ethan didn't recognise the voice.

'No problem, sir,' replied Fraser. 'You're Roger Jones, Mrs Jones' husband?'

'Yes.' He nodded towards Ethan. 'Linda has already told me that this gentleman says I accompanied him on a walk this morning, but I can assure you that, in the first instance, I have not left the house other than to go into the garden and, in the second, I have never seen this man before.'

Ethan stared at him, his mouth wide open. 'But you're not Roger Jones. I was with Roger this morning when he was shot.'

The man laughed loudly. 'Shot… out here? This isn't the big city you know. We don't have murders in this part of the world.'

Immediately, Ethan came back at him. 'Murdered… how did you know he was murdered?'

Again, the man laughed, a condescending smile ending his obvious amusement. 'I don't, but I sense that was what you were implying, was it not?'

Frustrated, Ethan tugged at his hair with both hands. Irritated by the man's manner and superior diction, he glowered at him. 'Okay, if you're Roger Jones, tell me what Jenny's favourite soup was.'

Frowning, the man replied, 'Who's Jenny?'

'Your stepdaughter... the one who was killed in a crash just up the road. You told me about it last night. You said a lorry hit her car and rendered her unidentifiable.' Ethan was shouting. 'For God's sake, what's the fucking matter with you?' He grabbed the man by the shoulders, intending to shake the truth out of him; however, before he could do so, Fraser stepped in.

'That's quite enough, Menhennett, or I'll have to arrest you for assault.' He pulled Ethan away. 'Sorry about that, Mr Jones.'

Jones smiled. 'No problem, Constable. As a retired psychiatrist, I'm used to these sorts of outburst, although I would prefer he kept his blasphemy and profanities to himself. Obviously, Mr... er... Mr Menhennett has been upset by something serious and, in my opinion, requires immediate medical help. I would recommend you take him to—'

'Fuck your recommendations, you pompous git,' yelled Ethan. 'I'll prove I was here.' He rushed from the room. Running up the stairs, he shouted, 'My kitbag – I left my kitbag here. I'll fetch it from the bedroom.' After a short while, Fraser helped him up from where he was sitting at the top of the stairs, sobbing.

'Now then, Mr Menhennett, I'll just put these on you – for your own safety, you understand.' The handcuffs clicked shut. 'Right, let's get you out of here.'

On the way to the hospital, Ethan heard Fraser talking on the radio.

'Yep, I've found him... I'm taking him straight to the hospital... I think he's had a breakdown... He's not committed a criminal offence as far, as I can see… The Joneses didn't want to press any charges – they're a nice couple… Apparently it wasn't them who reported seeing somebody on the old road to Hingston wandering around and looking drunk.' There was then a long silence before Fraser said, 'Well, if that's what the chief wants me to say, then who am I to argue, I suppose?'

* * *

'But the nurse said the police found you on the side of the road?' queried Claire.

Lightly tapping his front teeth with his thumb nail, Ethan looked straight at her, through narrowed eyes, whilst he considered what she'd said; it began to make her uncomfortable.

'Ethan, what is it? Are you all right? Should I call the nurse?'

He didn't answer, but just kept staring.

'Ethan… Ethan… I'm going to call the nurse.' She made to get up. He grabbed her arm.

'That's it. He's in on it. That's why the copper said I was sitting beside the road. He was told to.'

'Now you're beginning to scare me. You're not well.' He tightened the grip on her arm. 'Ethan, you're hurting me. I mean it, I'm going to press the call button.'

Ethan looked down at the hand clasping Claire. He gave her a faint smile, then released his hold.

'Sorry… I'm so sorry, but don't you see?'

'See what?' she replied, rubbing her arm. 'There'll be a massive bruise in the morning, you animal, that's all I can see.'

'Sod the bruise, Claire – we've got to go back. The man who said he was Roger, I've seen him somewhere before.'

'The only place we're going,' said Claire, dismissing his comment, 'is to the police station. We should have reported Sarah missing days ago. If any harm comes to her, it'll be our fault.'

Ethan shook his head. He drew a deep breath, then blew it out slowly through pursed lips.

'I just hope it's not already too late,' he whispered.

SIXTEEN

3rd June 2013

SARAH

Sarah Jenkinson sat crossed legged on her bed. It was 10am. Still in her check-print, favourite-colour-pink M&S pyjamas, she hastily devoured the slice of buttered toast and slurped her mug of black coffee. She'd been out until 3am and had woken with more than the slightest hint of a hangover. On reflection, doing shots with her friend Lucy probably hadn't been the best of ideas.

Sitting in front of her on the bed was a box file containing her late father's notes and photos of the Cornish mines he'd visited during the thirty odd years before he'd passed away from a heart attack three months ago. Joan, her stepmother, had telephoned to say Eric had died after complaining of a shortage of breath following his return from exploring a mine in the St Austell area; he was just sixty-four. His death had been totally unexpected and came as a massive shock to all who knew him. His work and underground exploration of mines meant he kept himself physically fit for a man of his age, and, each week, he would run at least ten miles. Unlike his daughter, he hardly ever drank and had never smoked.

The post-mortem found no untoward contributory factors, and the coroner returned a verdict of 'death from natural causes'.

At the funeral, Joan had told Sarah that she was putting the matrimonial home on the market and would be returning to Caerphilly in South Wales. She hadn't shared her husband's love of old machinery and Cornish mines; her interest was political history and she could study that surrounded by the neighbours and friends she'd left behind when she had moved to Cornwall.

After graduating from university with a degree in land management, as a lover of all things mechanical, Eric had forsaken his hard-earned qualification, preferring instead to make a living as an agricultural engineer. Although he earned enough for him and his second wife to pay their way, he'd lost much of his capital when his first wife Sheila had divorced him. She'd blamed Eric for putting his hobbies before her, and, like many in the same situation, she had found an alternative love interest. Sheila still kept in touch with Sarah by email and the occasional phone call, but, as she was yet to forgive her mother for leaving, Sarah rarely saw her.

Joan had met Eric whilst she was on holiday. Like many tourists, she'd decided to visit the Levant mine. Eric had been repairing a ride-on lawnmower used to maintain the gardens, they got chatting and, after a six-month courtship, had married. Joan had bought a house in St Agnes in her name only; hence, there was only the agricultural tools and well-used equipment for Sarah to inherit. The auction was arranged for a month's time at the industrial unit Eric had rented.

Having nothing planned for the day, Sarah thought it a good opportunity to go through her father's file. She needed to find subject matter for an article for Ethan's magazine, not only because he'd asked for some copy but also because she had a bit of cashflow issue. Since her damning front-page article concerning the married male celebrity and his male lover, she'd found it difficult to get interviews. It was suggested, by a tabloid editor, that she use another pseudonym and gain the trust of showbiz agents, perhaps writing nice things for a while. However, in the meantime, it was back to her 'bread and butter'.

On top of her father's printed reports was a sheet of A4 lined paper, with a rough map on the front and handwritten bullet points on the back:

Unnamed remains of an engine house and associated buildings. Didn't pick up on it at the County Records office.

Discovered it researching Wheal Hussey for Percy at Parish Archives (mention of new engine shaft and building 1880) to mine copper and to service the adit running from Hussey to a valley near to the derelict village of Hingston.

Extent of drives not known.

Entrance to adit located downstream from an unusable ford – too deep for normal vehicle crossing. See sketch map for location.

About half a mile into adit, evidence of lead and silver deposits.

Water underfoot began to deepen – decided not to go any further without waterproof clothing and headgear. Also began to feel unwell – fresh air must have been restricted.

Return next weekend.

3rd March 2013.

Sarah stared at her father's notes. An unrecorded mine and the mention of silver deposits – what a find. He may not have been able to go back, but she could. She was certain he would want her to – it would be his legacy. She could explore the adit, the remains of the engine house, then write an exclusive for the magazine. She could dedicate it to her dad. Ethan was bound to pay her extra for something like this. They could keep the location secret and… Her excitement faded. And nothing really.

She looked at the hand-drawn map. It was between Treworthy and St Austell. Her hangover forgotten, she hurried to the bathroom to shower.

Standing under the square showerhead, the warmth of the water washing away last night's stale sweat and smell of kebab, she had a thought.

If Dad's wrong and everybody already knows about the mine, Ethan will say it was just an eccentric old fogey's imagination and he won't cover my taxi fares.

Her car was in for repair, or rather it had been repaired, but she hadn't the money to pay the three-hundred-and-fifty-pound bill.

After getting into debt three years ago, she'd cut up her credit card, swearing not to borrow so stupidly again. She'd cleared the outstanding balance and ridiculous amount of interest with what she'd been paid for the 'front pager', but it meant she now survived from article to article. Fortunately, she'd paid her rent a month in advance.

It was as she was towelling her hair that she came up with the idea of the false email.

He can't refuse an expense claim if I was following up a third-party lead. It wouldn't be my fault if it turned out to be a lie, especially if I say it's from a keen supporter of the magazine. She chuckled. I might also say it's an admirer – that'll make him jealous.

Cheating an employer wasn't her normal way of working, but she was confident what she'd find would be of real interest, and, anyway, she knew Ethan quite fancied her and wouldn't quibble at giving her a few bob.

Happy this would work, she dialled Ethan's mobile. However, had she known about the reaction her father had received when visiting the archives, she may not have been so keen to follow in his footsteps.

SEVENTEEN

3rd March 2013

ERIC JENKINSON

Eric Jenkinson drew up outside the local visitor centre in Treworthy. It had taken him almost two hours from St Agnes in his fifteen-year-old Daihatsu Fourtrak. It was a great vehicle for towing a trailer loaded with garden machinery, but not particularly fast on the open road. However, speed wasn't a major concern for Eric – he was never in a hurry, and was more than happy working or travelling at *dreckly* pace! It was something that frequently annoyed Joan, as he was always last to get ready when they were going out.

'You'll be late for your own *angladd*,' she'd tell him, partly in Welsh, when he'd finally be putting on his jacket. However, she'd certainly not expected to be burying him so soon.

The visitor centre was an impressive-looking, semi-glazed, two-storey building, with a flat roof, and wood-panelled sides and back walls. Stretching his legs and arms as he got out, he yawned loudly, scratched the top of his head through his wispy grey hair and headed for the entrance. He was dressed in clean denim jeans and a blue checked shirt, far removed from his usual greasy, brown overalls he virtually lived in at home and at work.

'The archive department is up they stairs over there,' the jolly female receptionist told him. 'Careful how you goes – we've not long washed the floor.' It was 10.30am and the centre had opened at 10am. 'We do all the cleaning ourselves, you see – us is all volunteers.'

Eric thanked this woman, who was probably in her forties; with short, dark hair; and wearing a loose-fitting, black jumper and a full-length, lilac-coloured pleated skirt.

He was greeted on the landing by a middle-aged lady, smartly dressed in tight-fitting black slacks and a short-sleeved, red blouse. Her wavy, fair hair immediately reminded Eric of pictures he'd seen of women in the fifties. He vaguely remembered his mother looking like it.

'Good morning, I'm Beverly; how may I help you?' she asked, with a beaming, welcoming smile.

'Eric.' He thought about shaking hands, but somehow it didn't seem right. 'I understand from a young gentleman at the County Records Office in Truro that you have some... er... how should I say... interesting information about Wheal Hussey copper mine.'

Beverly's smile disappeared. 'When you say "interesting", what exactly do you mean?'

'Well, not exactly the usual thing like... um... depths of the levels or amount of ore produced; you know, that sort of thing.' He shuffled uncomfortably from one foot to the other. 'You see, I was talking to a friend – well, we were having a pint, actually – and he said he'd heard Wheal Hussey had some history to it.' Embarrassed, he took a deep breath, followed by a sigh. 'Look, basically, I understand that, years ago, people who tried to mine the tin in the land surrounding what eventually became Wheal Hussey came to a bit of a sticky end.'

Beverly clasped her hands in front of her. 'I see,' she said, pursing her lips, 'and why would you be interested in such things?'

"Er, I'm not, but my friend is and he can't leave his ironmonger's business in Penzance during the day – well, not for the next few weeks – so I said I'd come for him. You know… see if I could help him out. He's a social historian and wants to write some Cornish folklore tales; something a bit different to the usual – particularly stories that include mysterious deaths.'

'Hmm, I see,' she repeated. 'And what makes him think Wheal Hussey has anything to hide…' She grimaced. 'Er, I mean, has unexplained deaths attached to it?'

'Not sure, really, other than he also researches Manorialism…' Seeing Beverly's quizzical look, he explained, 'It's to do with lord-of-the-manor land ownership and control of the peasants who worked it, or that's what he told me. Bit out of my league these days, to be honest. Anyway, he discovered that the Earl of Dorwall and his subsequent heirs lost interest in land hereabouts following the death of four tenants. According to Percy, that's my friend, hearsay has it that the land is cursed by the spriggans; you know, the spirits—'

'Yes, yes, I know what spriggans are,' interrupted Beverly, impatiently. 'I've lived in Cornwall all my life.'

'So?' queried Eric.

'So, I'll need to see what the manager says.'

Her curt manner, particularly after her welcoming demeanour, was making Eric feel as though he'd asked to take the crown jewels out of their display case.

'Have a seat by the table.' She indicated with her hand. 'And I'll be back in a moment.' Turning on her heel, she exited through a door marked 'Staff only'. As instructed, Eric took a seat at the round, glass table and started thumbing through an old copy of *Country Life*.

It was four minutes before she returned, perhaps just enough time to finish the cigarette he could smell on her breath. She was carrying an A4 sized, manilla document folder.

'I'm sorry, but this is all there is.' She handed him the folder. 'Apparently, everything else was lost when we moved here from down the road, several years ago.' She didn't look him in the eye. 'Before my time, I'm afraid. I apologise if your journey's been wasted.' The phone rang in the manager's office. 'Excuse me, I'd better get that – the manager's rather busy.' She disappeared into the office again.

The file contained a report by a mining expert regarding the land surrounding Wheal Hussey. Eric thumbed through it half-heartedly, disappointed by Beverly's lack of information, not only for Percy, but also for himself. Whilst Eric's real interest was exploring old mine tunnels, the occasional bit of historical tittle-tattle was always welcome. He was just about to close the file when he noticed a subheading – 'Wheal Hingston'.

He'd not heard of that one.

He read on: 'Although not mentioned in any popular publications, when preparing this report, I unearthed details of a new shaft, along with an engine house and associated buildings, which was sunk in 1880 to the north of Wheal Hussey to explore two copper lodes discovered when an adit was driven from Wheal Hussey. It appears that the adit's exit is located in a small valley below what is now the road between the town of St Austell and the village of Treworthy.

'The remains of these buildings are in a state of continued decay and are not visible from the aforementioned road.'

'Well, I'm buggered,' muttered Eric, 'perhaps my journey's not been a total waste of time after all.'

Tidying up the file, he headed to the manager's office. He could hear Beverly talking.

'That's right… He said he wanted to look into the deaths… No, he didn't say he had any interest in the mine itself… What do you think I am? Of course I didn't say anything; I just gave him the archaeological report… No, he doesn't want to explore the adit… No, nothing was mentioned about the rumours on what's in there…'

From the breaks in the conversation with no audible replies, Eric realised she was on the phone. Eager to get on, he knocked on the door and turned the handle, intending to return the folder to the manager.

'That should keep him quiet… He'll probably just go back to…' Beverly stopped her conversation stone dead as Eric walked in. Her jaw dropped and her face reddened.

'Oh… er… sorry,' sputtered Eric. 'Didn't mean to interrupt.' He glanced around the room – Beverly was alone.

Sheepishly, he placed the folder on the desk in front of her, nodded his thanks and left.

There must be another exit somewhere, he thought, as he closed the door behind him.

Excited about the news of the unlisted engine house, he didn't give the overheard conversation another thought. His mind was purely focused on locating the engine house and, more importantly, the adit. Investigating tunnels could lead to all sorts of things. Percy's interest in folklore and mysterious deaths, a distant memory.

* * *

Back in the Daihatsu, he opened up his map.

North of Wheal Hussey, the note in the folder had said.

EIGHTEEN

17th June 2013

ETHAN
BODMIN HOSPITAL

'Not a bad fit – thank you, Claire.'

'My pleasure, and, remember, you still owe me.' She got out of the bedside seat. 'Now that you're clothed, can we get to the police station? I've had enough of not doing anything.'

'Okay.' Ethan smoothed down the packaging creases in the sleeveless, black, checked M&S shirt. Running the black-leather belt through the hoops on the blue denims, he smiled. 'I could do with someone like you to be my personal dresser.'

'No chance, I'm afraid. I have enough to think about looking after Neil and the two girls.' She picked up the bag with his old clothes. 'Right, may we get on?'

He slipped on his navy-blue deck shoes.

* * *

'I see,' said the duty sergeant. 'She's been missing since the 4th and it's now the 17th. That's a long time to leave it, wouldn't you say?'

'I know, but Sarah – the girl who's missing – is a bit of a party animal. So, for a while, I just thought she'd gone away somewhere and was having a good time,' replied Ethan, knowing full well that he'd been a total idiot in not reporting it sooner.

'Hmm. So when was the last time you tried to contact her?'

'I … um… er…' sputtered Ethan.

Claire quickly jumped in. 'This morning, Sergeant. I rang her landlady, who said there was still no sign of her; she was worried. It was the longest she'd ever be away, other than on holiday.'

'I see,' said the sergeant. He looked over Claire's shoulder, as the glass front door of the station swung open. 'Ah, Fraser.'

PC Fraser walked up to the hatch. 'Sarge?'

'Weren't you looking into the report of a missing girl?'

'I was, Sarge, but she turned up this morning. I haven't filed my report yet. Found her at Exeter Airport with her boyfriend, or should I say man friend? Thirty-five years older than her, the dirty bastard. She's only thirteen. They were trying to catch a flight to Barcelona. The woman on the—'

'The girl we're looking for is twenty-seven,' interrupted Ethan, his patience stretched.

'Ah, a different one then,' acknowledged the sergeant.

Fraser looked Ethan up and down. 'Mr Menhennett,' he said. 'Are you feeling better?' Fraser turned to his sergeant. 'Had a chat with this gentleman a day or two ago. Had a bit of sunstroke, I reckon. Didn't bother troubling you, Sarge, not with the workload you're carrying.'

'What?' exclaimed Ethan. 'I told you I saw a man shot, but you wouldn't believe me. And why did you tell the hospital you found me beside the road?'

Half looking at his sergeant, Fraser replied, 'Because I didn't want the hospital thinking you'd been imaging things. Far better for you they just thought you'd had a few difficulties. I did it for your own good.' He looked dejected. 'Sorry if I've dropped you in it with your missus.' He smiled politely at Claire. 'So, who's missing?'

'A girl, or a woman, really. Sarah Jenkinson,' Claire informed him. 'She did some work for our magazine in London.'

'Ah. That's right. Your husband did say something about being from London and searching for another woman. But, see, we get a lot of men – and women, come to that – who come to Cornwall looking for love 'cos their other half don't want to know them in bed anymore. Not a big county, so can't satisfy them all, I'm afraid.'

'He's not my husband,' said Claire indignantly. 'And, anyway, that's got nothing to do with it.' She cold shouldered Fraser and spoke directly to the sergeant. 'Are you going to take a description and get your officers to help find her, or am I going to have to go to Truro and speak to someone more senior?'

'Now, now, miss, no need for that. We can handle it from here. Do you have a photo?'

* * *

'Tell me I'm not going mad, Claire.'

'You're not, Ethan, and nor am I. It's a different world down here – no urgency.'

'No urgency? It's as if they don't want to know, full stop.'

'Look,' said Claire, 'they've taken her description, it will be circulated and he said enquiries will be made – we can't ask for any more than that.'

'But what about the shooting and the different Roger?' protested Ethan. 'They weren't interested in that.'

Claire sighed. 'Ethan, let's be honest. There was no body and then, when you went to the Joneses' house, Mrs Jones – whom you recognised – introduced you and the policeman to her husband. Can you really blame the sergeant for not taking you seriously?'

Ethan pressed the switch for the electric motor on the front passenger seat of the white Range Rover Evoque and dropped it back to the horizontal. He could do with the seat turning into a psychiatrist's couch and for Claire to start analysing him. He felt alone. If Claire didn't believe him, and he was certain she didn't, then who else could he turn to? Waking up in the morning after a heavy drinking session and being unable to recall the previous night's events was one thing, but losing days was something different. He had to convince Claire he hadn't imagined meeting the dead Jenny, had to convince her he'd witnessed Roger being shot and, even more importantly, he had to find Sarah.

'I've got to go back,' he said.

'Go back where, Ethan? London?'

The seat smoothly returned to the upright position.

'No, Claire. I've got to go back to the adit and I need to go back to the pub. I'm sure they have something to do with

Sarah's disappearance, and I'm sure the guy who said he was Roger was taking advantage of Linda Jones' dementia – you know, covering up in some way for killing him.'

Claire shook her head. 'I don't know what to say, Ethan. I'm beginning to think whatever it was that happened to you during the days you say you can't remember has had one hell of an effect on you. Perhaps—'

'Will you take me back or not?'

'Ethan—'

'Yes or no, Claire. If you won't, then I'll take a taxi or… or… hire another car. I don't care how I get there.'

Claire smiled condescendingly. 'And how will you pay a taxi driver when you've got very little cash?'

'By card. Or there's bound to be an ATM here; they can't have shut all the bank branches in Cornwall ye…' He stopped; his mouth fell wide open. He looked at Claire; his furrowed brow told her that his own internal Google was rifling his brain. Eventually, it obtained a result. 'That's it – they didn't take cards; I had to go out in the rain to the car to get some change. Claire, how much is a pint of beer in Cornwall?'

'How the hell should I know that? I don't drink it.' She touched his arm. 'I think it's time to go home. The police have got my number. We can come back once they find something. Sophie and I will be fine whilst you have a break.'

Ethan pushed away her hand and wrenched the door release.

'Ethan, where are you going?'

Stooping to speak through the open door, he exclaimed, 'To The Red Lion.' He pointed to a pub across the road; it's rundown façade suggested it was a drinking house, not a quasi-restaurant. 'I won't be a minute – I need a beer.' The door slammed. Avoiding two cars, one of which had to brake to miss him, he disappeared through the pub's front door. Three minutes later, he was back beside Claire. He was ecstatic.

'Three pounds sixty, and he reckoned they were the cheapest around.' He slapped Claire's thigh. 'There, that proves it. Now you've got to drive me back to Hingston; no question about it. Has this thing got four-wheel drive?'

'Have you just drunk a bottle of Scotch or something? And, yes, it's top of the range, but what's that got to do with it?'

'Just drive, Claire, and I'll explain.'

The lost days were beginning to come back to him.

NINETEEN

11th June 2013 – Six days earlier

ETHAN

Making his way back to the car from the mine, the nettles had seemingly taken even greater pleasure in dispensing their poison. Grateful that he'd brought an overnight bag, Ethan changed his polo shirt for a t-shirt, its logo extolling his love of steam railways and real ale. His shorts were swapped for a pair of jeans and his shoes for white trainers.

Climbing into the car, Ethan looked at his bare legs. A bright-red rash had formed around his shins and calves. The desire to scratch was overwhelming, but he knew from past experience that it would only add to the discomfort. In an effort to take his mind off the temptation, he tried to imagine what Sarah would have done when she'd arrived at the site of the mine, only to discover that the invitation was one massively sick joke.

It was obvious Sarah had been fooled by someone, perhaps someone who had been riled by last month's editorial in which

Ethan had questioned the feasibility of any Cornish tin mine ever being viable enough to reopen. He'd received a number of comments on social media from various 'anoraks' calling themselves diehard descendants of Cornish miners, none of whom had suggested they had the slightest comprehension of profitability or practicality. He'd wanted to reply, telling them to put their money where their mouths were, but had thought better of it; after all, its circulation figures barely kept *The National Heritage Gazette* afloat and he couldn't afford to upset any more readers. Without the Cornish postcode subscriptions, the magazine would have folded months ago.

Sarah had sounded so excited when she'd told him about the mine restoration. 'It's not one I've ever heard of, and I can't find it on any map or in any of the reference books. It must be a mine that was virtually buried in someone's field somewhere and forgotten. Perhaps it wasn't open very long and was of no importance. Anyway, just think, your magazine will be the first to reveal it, it will get you loads of publicity and you'll be able to pay me loads of money.'

All she had given Ethan was a grid reference, which she said was contained in an email sent to her inbox at the magazine, together with a short message: 'Sarah, be the first to see our working, fully restored nineteenth-century engine house, reopened shaft and levels.' She said it was signed 'An avid reader and admirer'.

He'd thought it odd and told her to tread carefully. There was no reason why anyone wouldn't restore an old engine house. In fact, there were several around the county that had been made into private dwellings; however, they didn't normally include the underground workings. He also hadn't liked the word 'admirer', and – although it had sounded only moderately stalker-like at the time – with hindsight, it now sounded sinister and threatening.

He had no access to her inbox.

During his train journey, a deep feeling of guilt had embroiled his thoughts, and he'd been unable to complete the article he was writing about the consequences of the 1984 Coal Miners' Strike some twenty-nine years later. Instead, he'd gazed out the window, not seeing the countryside and urban expanses, but instead constant reflective images of Sarah tied up by some sick and drooling pervert.

He should have told her not to go, at least not alone. He could have taken the time to join her. Okay, so he was up to his neck in putting the issue together, balancing the accounts and preparing for his annual meeting with the bank to review the firm's overdraft, but a break from routine would have done him good. However, having Sarah readily available and located in the county meant it was easy for her to follow up the invitation. He would simply cover her expenses, pay her normal fee and the cost to *The National Heritage Gazette* would be minimal. But he hadn't chosen to go with her, and he now felt culpable for her apparent disappearance and possible kidnapping – or something much worse. Immediately, he tried to convince himself that he was overreacting, but the thought she'd been murdered wouldn't stop pecking at his conscience.

However, if – on the other hand – she'd found the culprit who'd sent her on a wild goose chase, Ethan knew she'd be angry and in no mood to accept bullshit responses to questions she wanted answered, however personal and probing.

* * *

She'd proved her tenacity when carrying out her other role in journalism. Under the pseudonym Jenny Jenkins, she also undertook assignments for a Sunday tabloid to interview some of the celebrities who either lived in or had expensive second homes in Cornwall. It was a far cry from mines and archaeology, but she'd told Ethan that she loved learning how the other half lived, particularly the ones who – in her words – had dubious backgrounds. Her outwardly innocent, West Country approach got her into places others couldn't, but, once in, her bite was much worse than her bark. She'd recently made the front page when she'd reported on how she 'accidentally' stumbled in on a well-known, married pop singer performing a sexual act with another male as they lay beside his swimming pool. The celebrity had threatened to sue, but her photos didn't lie.

'I got very well paid for that,' she'd told Ethan.

'I'm sure you did,' he'd replied, 'but mining doesn't gain quite the same public interest!'

Nonetheless, she was still happy to contribute to *The National Heritage Gazette* on a regular basis. She'd submitted a couple of impressive articles 'on spec', after which he'd agreed to employ on a freelance basis and pay her a monthly retainer.

Sarah had a degree in archaeology, and it was her late father's love of old machinery that had influenced her interest in mines. At twenty-seven, she was ten years younger than Ethan, but – like him, at least since the death of his wife seven years ago – she was single and, at after-conference parties, was always up for a laugh. 'Up for a laugh' was all it had ever been, or at least that's what Ethan thought. However, he was beginning to realise that perhaps it wasn't simply guilt that had made him get on the train.

* * *

Apart from Sarah being angry, Ethan also guessed that she would be peeved enough to need a strong, calming drink. A pub might 'kill two birds with one stone': firstly, it would definitely provide the alcohol and, secondly, it would possibly provide a landlord and local residents with answers.

A search of the Mondeo's satnav returned no mention of a nearby pub, but, on his map, he saw the village of Hingston was just a couple of miles away and marked right in the middle of it was a 'PH' for 'public house' symbol. Assuming a small hamlet was not worthy of inclusion on modern technology, he pressed the start button on the dashboard.

TWENTY

In the same way as he'd stood motionless staring at the ruins of what he'd expected to be an intact engine house and buildings, Ethan stared at the pub sign swinging violently back and forth in the strengthening wind. He shook his head, his jet-black hair sticking to his forehead as he watched the unrelenting rain – like surreal blood – running in torrents off the sign's smooth surface. It began to sting his eyes and he quickly lowered his head, but not before he noticed the pub's exterior looked tired, and in need of some paint and render.

The journey down the narrow valley road from the mine had needed his full concentration. There were many potholes, and one in particular that he'd been powerless to avoid. Fortunately, he'd spotted it early and managed to slow down, so his tyres and suspension remained intact. There had been a shallow ford to negotiate, and he'd winced as he'd heard the car's sump, followed by the exhaust, scrape something solid as he'd entered and exited. The car radio had lost the signal not far from the mine, and, despite selecting all the presets, he was unable to find either local or national stations.

Walking into the public bar, the six-foot-plus American ducked to avoid the low beamed-ceilings, just as his fellow countrymen had done two years before him.

Between the old, irregular shaped beams, only the coating of nicotine appeared to be keeping the bowed, plastered ceilings from dropping. The walls were half-panelled with dark, ebony-coloured wood, whereas – like the ceiling – the plaster of the upper part was stained a sickly, yellowish brown. Various pictures of hunting scenes hung haphazardly between low-wattage candle wall lights. A large, stone fireplace with a granite lintel and a pile of ash in the hearth took pride of place on the end wall of the sixteenth-century building. Ethan approached the L-shaped bar, the front also dark ebony and the counter two slabs of thick, but well-worn, polished, light oak.

'Welcome, what can I get for you?' This curt, but strangely soothing, greeting came from a slim, blue-eyed, young barmaid with shoulder-length, dark hair, dressed in a white blouse. As he leaned on the counter, he couldn't help but notice that her tight, above-knee, black skirt revealed slim thighs and shapely calves; however, there was no hint of a tan and they were almost as white as her top.

Perhaps she's had little time for leisure or simply doesn't enjoy the sun, he thought. Out loud, he said, 'Well, actually, I was wondering if you've seen a young, dark-haired girl in here recently?'

The barmaid smiled and pointed to the customers behind him. 'If you look closely, you'll see one or two sat over there. Perhaps you'd like to take your pick.'

Ethan's face reddened. 'Sorry, silly question.' He grimaced. 'Um… er… I guess I really meant to ask have you seen someone… um… whom you haven't seen before?' He wished he'd taken the trouble to find a picture of Sarah before he'd left the office. There was bound to be one included next to a past magazine article.

The barmaid smiled. 'You mean a stranger?'

He nodded.

She took a moment to think then shook her head. 'Nope, sorry, I can't say I have. You see, we don't get many new customers in here since…' Glancing at a bearded man standing watching her from one of the tables, she stopped abruptly. 'Sorry, it's not important.'

Ethan begged to differ. 'Go on, since what?' he encouraged.

'Oh, nothing. Now then, are you sure I can't get you a drink? We only have one cask ale, but I'd thoroughly recommend it.' She'd obviously read his t-shirt.

'Okay, I'll try a pint.' He had no intention of leaving until he knew the reason for her sudden reluctance to continue.

Holding a sleever glass under the swan neck of one of the three handpumps, she pulled twice on the handle in quick succession, then placed the frothing, overflowing beer in front of him. She appeared agitated.

'Er… um…' She shrugged. 'Two pounds eighty, please.'

Business rates must be a helluva lot lower down here! thought Ethan. He offered her his debit card.

'Er, sorry, sir. I'm afraid we can't take cards. There's no broadband connection or mobile signal, you see.'

He pulled a twenty-pound note from his wallet, the only cash in it.

'You don't have anything smaller do you?'

Bloody 'sticks'.

He smiled. 'I do in the car. If you'd like to hold on a moment.'

On his return, she was serving another customer: one of those who'd been sitting at the table where the bearded man was still standing.

'There we go,' said Ethan loudly, as he offered her three one-pound coins.

The barmaid hesitated, looked at the coins, then reached under the counter. Ethan heard her rifling through some change. Eventually, she handed him a twenty-pence coin. There was no till.

'Your change, sir.'

Prepared to bide his time, he wandered towards an empty table by the door and sat down. He took a sip of his beer. Attempting to put the twenty-pence coin in his pocket, he caught his finger on the table edge and the coin fell to the floor. Before he had chance to bend down and pick it up, he was startled by a man's voice.

'Tristan Mawgan, at your service. Landlord of this fine establishment for what seems like a hundred years. Nice to meet you.' He was well-spoken, without any discernible accent.

Standing up, Ethan shook his hand. It was cold. He had a firm grip; it was almost too firm. Had he held on to it for much longer than twenty seconds, he was sure it would have cut off his circulation.

'Ethan… Ethan Menhennett. Pleased to meet you too.'

* * *

Claire had listened intently to Ethan as he'd related the story of his visit to The Hung, Drawn & Quartered. It hadn't explained his lost days and neither did it explain why Roger Jones, if indeed it was Roger Jones, had been shot; however, it had helped Ethan regain his confidence.

* * *

'Just passing through, are we? Not a particularly nice day to see the sights; that is, if you can call this pub a sight. In centuries past, it used to be a popular inn for the tin merchants from London and abroad. They stayed here before each 'coinage day'. Most stayed at the inn in Lostwithiel, but the nervous ones didn't like the old prison nearby… thought it was haunted. Nasty place, especially when an old boy from London oversaw the courts. They said he wasn't as harsh as judges in Devon, but history says different in my mind. You see, we were in the Blackmore Stannary and—'

'Yes, yes, I'm sure,' interrupted Ethan. A lesson in stannary history, particularly one he was reasonably familiar with, wasn't something he needed right now. 'Look, before you say anything more, I'm here because I'm looking for a friend – a lady in her twenties. She's a slim, attractive girl with short, dark hair. Tall… about… er… nearly six feet. You haven't seen her, have you? She was visiting the old mine up the road.'

The landlord's eyes narrowed. He leaned towards Ethan. His voice fell to a whisper. 'You mean Wheal Hingston – the one with the old engine house.' It was a statement, not a question.

'Yes, of course. How many other mines are there around here?'

'Plenty, if you care to look, but none now with a building at "grass". The landlord straightened his shoulders, the index fingers of his clasped hands tapping his chin as he considered the man standing opposite him. The silence that followed was too much for Ethan.

'Well, have you seen her?' he snapped.

'Short, dark hair you say?'

Managing to control his frustration, Ethan nodded. 'And pretty with it, so I'm sure she would have stood out. She was told the mine had been restored.'

'Restored?' The landlord smiled. 'I think someone's been winding her up – on a bit of a whim, you might say.'

'If that's meant to be a joke, I don't think it's very funny. She's been missing since last week.' His own lips pressed tightly together, Ethan could gladly have grabbed hold of the man's throat and shaken him. However, he guessed the locals might not take too kindly to a stranger assaulting their purveyor of alcohol, not that they seemed to be taking much notice.

Sensing Ethan's anger, the landlord apologised. 'Sorry, that was a bit out of order.' He took a couple of moments, then shook his head. 'Nope, I can't say that I have… seen her, that is. Shame you haven't got a photo. That would have made things a lot easier.'

Disappointed by the response, Ethan shrugged his shoulders. Releasing a loud sigh, he took a long draw on his beer. He glanced at where the customers sat. 'Perhaps one of them might have seen her?'

'You can ask, but I doubt it. You see, we don't get many visitors in here, so – when we do – everybody tends to pass comment. That's what we were doing when you walked in.' He crossed to the window and watched the drops of rain run down the glass.

'We used to, mind,' continued the landlord, his back to Ethan, 'but after the great storm of two years ago… well, let's just say that things changed.' He stroked his beard. 'Hmm, I haven't seen rain like this for a very long time. The ford is probably already impassable.'

Unaware the road with the ford – the one that he'd driven down – was the only one in and out of the village, the landlord's comment meant nothing to Ethan

'How do you mean "changed"? And what's it got to do with my friend's disappearance?' asked Ethan.

Once again, the landlord's voice fell to a whisper. His eyes pierced Ethan's. 'If she was at the mine, then it could have a lot to do with it.'

Ethan wanted to say, 'What the fuck are you on about?', but the landlord's intense expression told him he wasn't talking to the village idiot. He felt sweat begin to trickle down his brow. He took a sharp breath, trying to quell the painful pounding in his chest.

Still whispering, the landlord added, 'Well, the mine's got a bit of history; in fact, you could say it's cursed.'

TWENTY-ONE

June 24th, 1520

THE TRIAL OF THE SIX

The dank stench of the dungeon filled the nostrils of all those incarcerated in the depths of Lostwithiel Prison, a square tower in The Stannary Palace, built during the thirteenth century to house men, women and even children found guilty of breaking stannary law, the laws that governed forestry and tin mining in the counties of Devon and Cornwall. In 1508, King Henry VII had pardoned the Cornish for rising against him in 1497, and he agreed that anyone with a connection to the Cornish tin industry was protected by stannary law.

Stannary law overrode the laws of the land and meant that the individuals governed by them enjoyed privileges not offered to the common man; however, should a tinner steal, kill or injure, the penalties were punitive. Punishments imposed by the stannary courts could often be more severe than those of the Westminster Parliament. Whether the accused was found guilty or not, the infamous travelling Judge Fredricks took great delight in handing out hideous sentences, perhaps feeling he was striking a blow for those who had to abide by and respect the individual ownership of land and payment of national taxes.

Many prisoners would be held in custody for several weeks; the more serious offenders were chained to the walls and rarely released regardless of their toiletry needs. Some would be heard shouting for forgiveness, some pleading their innocence, whilst others cried for their anticipated sentence of death to be sooner rather than later – life's end being preferable to their futile existence. Whatever their situation, all were starving, as the rations of grain and water – with the occasional addition of rotted vegetables – were insufficient to meet their daily needs.

* * *

It was two hours past noon on the 17th June when the sound of the metal bolts sliding back disturbed some of the prisoners. These were the unfortunate ones who had been unable to drift into semi-consciousness; the lucky ones having found solace in comatose sleep. As the heavy, wooden door creaked open, the sudden brightness of the gaoler's flaring torch caused the roused interned to blink painfully, their eyelids scratching the dry surface of their corneas. Despite their pupils being slow to respond, they would turn away, desperate to avoid focusing on the gaoler for fear he would strike them with the cudgel strapped to his side. However, they did not need eyes to know where he was heading, for the foul smell of stale urine and sour, alcoholic breath accompanied him wherever he went.

Crossing to the far side of the black hole of a prison cell, he cuffed the face of a half-sitting, half-kneeling twenty-year-old man, the chains tying his arms above his head ensuring his total discomfort. Not for him the luxury of a piss-soaked and faeces-stained straw mattress.

'Come now, young Joshua Pentille,'tis time for 'ee to meet the judge. Us doesn't want to keep 'im waiting, does us?' As the emaciated man rose slowly and awkwardly to his feet, the gaoler landed a solid, wooden-soled boot to his groin. Joshua Pentille fell back down, his cries of agony echoing around the uncompassionate, bare, stone walls.

'I said, come now,'ee fucking bastard.' The gaoler crashed a fist into the side of the snivelling man's head. 'Or else t'will be me who's put on trial.' The gaoler undid the manacles and hauled Pentille to his feet. A further cuff across the back of the head encouraged him to make his way to the door. As the gaoler pulled it to, he snarled at the remaining incumbents. "Ee won't be seeing this little runt again, I'll be bound.' The door was slammed behind him and the bolts thrown across.

The gaoler cajoled and dragged Pentille up the stone steps leading from the unlit passageway to the upper floor; the prisoner's legs too weak to cope. He struck Pentille several times with his fist, before finally heaving him into the large hall that doubled as a courtroom. Minor offences were dealt with by local magistrates, such as Edmund Folsham, but every quarter day the king's appointed High Court judge, Judge Fredricks, would attend to the more serious ones. This meant that those awaiting trial could spend up to three months in the dire, inhospitable dungeon before being found guilty or, on exceptionally rare occasions, innocent.

'Stand there, 'ee little bastard,' instructed the gaoler.

Sitting opposite the prisoner, in a throne-like chair behind an oak dining table five yards long, was a man dressed in a full-length, bright-red coat, his thick, tightly curled, black hair resting on narrow shoulders. He had a long, almost-pointed nose and his stern expression made him appear older than his thirty years.

Sitting on less-regal, high-backed, wooden chairs were four male jurates, two on either side of the judge. All looked weather-beaten and weary, their ages much higher than their superior.

To the judge's right, at the far end of the table, stood the clerk, resplendent in his dark-blue doublet, the wide shoulders and full upper sleeves making him seem stockier and more arrogant than his five-foot-nothing frame would have otherwise suggested. He wore a soft, flat, black cap, which he removed as he read from the book lying open on the table in front of him. Like Fredricks, he sported a dark, tidily trimmed beard, giving him an air of authority and superiority.

'Joshua Pentille, you are charged with attempting to sell tin containing many impurities with the intention of passing it off for your own financial gain and greed.' The clerk looked up, his eyes fixing on the bedraggled man who was only managing to remain standing with the assistance of the foetid-smelling gaoler. 'How do you plead: guilty or not guilty?'

His head drooping, Pentille replied, 'Guilty, m'lud, but we was desperate. My kids was starving and our barley had failed. I had to do—'

There was a loud thud as Judge Fredricks brought his palm down hard on the table. 'Enough, man, I will not listen to any excuses. You have admitted your sins, and it is the way of the Lord and of stannary law that you should be punished accordingly.' He glanced to either side, acknowledging the nodded agreement of his four jurates. 'Therefore, the ore that you used to deceive will be smelted and a tankard full poured down your open throat. Should you survive, you will be a free man.' He turned to the gloating gaoler. 'Take him away and deal with him accordingly.'

'Yes, m'lud.' He grabbed Pentille's matted hair. 'Come, my lad, that's sufficient fresh air for one day.'

It had been a long time since such a punishment had been handed out, and it was one that delighted the gaoler. The muffled screams as the molten ore filled a victim's throat and lungs aroused him, and he would enjoy pleasuring himself as he watched his sadistic colleague administer the judge's instructions. Pushing Joshua Pentille down the stairs, he guided him through a door opposite the entrance to the dungeon. The floor of the room was covered in reasonably fresh straw, and set in the middle was a small blacksmith's forge and a set of bellows. Standing over it was a second gaoler, whose appearance was no more appealing than the first.

Various chains and ropes hung from the walls, together with three fire-blackened pokers of differing lengths. An iron vat, about the size of a leather pail, lay on its side on the floor.

Shoving Pentille into a corner, the first gaoler turned to his colleague. "Ere's a bit of good news, Isaac; this one's got to drink his own stinking tin.' He looked at Pentille, who was now a gibbering and shaking mess; his arms were wrapped around his knees as he huddled in the corner. 'The judge said he was to be given a tankard full, but I reckons two would make it more fun.' He licked his lips, with the anticipation of hearing the victim's fading, gurgling screams causing his already semi-erect penis to grow even harder. He always aimed to come as the tortured wretch gave his or her last gasp. He didn't always time it right, but, if he did, then watching his blood-infused semen trickle down the helpless criminal's face and slide over a reflexive outstretched tongue, gave him far more satisfaction than Annie the village whore ever managed with her toothless mouth or pox-ridden cunt.

'Thank fuck, Solomon,' replied Isaac. 'Another unpaid taxes punishment and I'd be losing me mind. No fun in knifing some bugger's 'and to a stake. Takes too long, and I ain't got time to sit and watch the fucker suffer. Don't fucking care if it stops 'em from ever working with two 'ands again. Should be like me; I can still gets off with just one.' The two gaolers broke into spasmodic, compulsive laughter.

'Right,' said Solomon, coughing up phlegm disturbed by his convulsions. 'Time to fetch the next lot. Judge should have finished 'is afternoon jug of digestive wine. 'E says it 'elps 'im keep a benevolent demeanour.'

'Better get 'em up quick I reckons. Weather's turning foul and 'ee knows that lot upstairs don't like working if they flashes in the sky gets too much. They'll be across to the inn quicker than 'ee or I can tighten a noose.'

'Won't take long,' acknowledged Solomon, wiping the snot from his nose and lips. 'They'm all as guilty as fuck and they knows it. T'will be funny to see that bastard Folsham receive some of his own medicine, the tosspot.' He pointed to the quivering Pentille. "Ere, and don't 'ee go starting on 'im before I gets back. Haven't had a good pull since old Joseph got drawn and quartered. Managed two good uns all over his liver before he stopped breathing."

He hurried out of the door and lifted a hatch in the passageway. Peering into the darkness below, he bellowed, 'Right, me pretties, out 'ee come; Judge Fredricks is eager to meet 'ee.'

One by one, the six climbed up the wooden ladder out of the pit. Only the most serious of offenders were imprisoned in its partially flooded and rat-infested interior. The six had only been in there less than two months, but being rarely fed and having to drink the water in which they stood or sat, they were gaunt, withered, and covered in scabs and boils. Much of their clothing had suffered at the teeth of the rats and what little fabric remained, hung loosely from their shoulders and waists. The two women's bodices barely covered their breasts, something that didn't go unnoticed by Solomon.

'Don't mind if I has a grope, do 'ee?' he said, stretching out his hand towards the younger of the two. "Aven't felt a firm tit like that for some time.'

Immediately, Elizabeth Ansty covered her chest with her hands.

'Go away, you filthy scum,' she warned him, 'or I'll—'.

'Or 'ee'll what, you brazen 'ussy? Those pair of peaches ain't going to be any use to 'ee once the judge has finished with 'ee, so you might as well let someone as loving as me have one last feel.' He grabbed her arms and wrenched them away. Reaching for her breasts, he failed to see the swinging arm approaching from his right. It wasn't Edmund Folsham's best punch, he was too weak for that, but it was sufficient to put the gaoler on the floor.

'Why 'ee fucking turd,' responded Solomon as he rubbed his chin. ''Ee'll pay for that, 'ee—'

'Feel these if you must,' said Maud Chechester, cutting short his threat, at the same time, stepping in front of Folsham and ripping apart the shreds of her bodice. 'They might not be as fresh, but do to them what you will.'

Getting to his feet, the gaoler stared into her eyes. He saw no fear and immediately his erection abated. He shrugged his shoulders, his foul breath causing Maud to turn her head. 'Huh, 'ee don't think I'd fancy that pair of wrinkled walnuts does 'ee? I's not that desperate. Anyway, I 'as to get 'ee to the judge.' He shoved Rowland Worsley in the back. 'Get a move on priest, thy God ain't going to save 'ee now.'

Slowly and feebly, as many had done before them, they climbed the stairs to the courtroom; Maud Chechester covered herself as best she could. There was a large clap of thunder as they entered the room and heavy rain could be heard rattling on the tiled roof above. A flash of lightning lit up the narrow, deeply-splayed, round-headed window at one end of the hall. The six were manoeuvred into a line in front of the judge and his jurates. An empty pewter jug and five goblets were on a tray at the opposite end of the table to the clerk. The judge eyed the accused curiously, and smiled briefly as he gazed upon Edmund Folsham, the man who normally occupied the adjudicator's chair. The clerk read from his book.

'Father Rowland Worsley, priest of the parish of Hingston; William Hyde, landlord of The Miner's Arms; Maud Chechester, widow; Elizabeth Ansty, stablehand and barmaid; The Honourable Edmund Folsham, Justice of the Peace; and John Laken, labourer and drunkard; you are all charged with trespassing with intent to mine tin on land owned solely and absolutely by his Right Honourable, the Earl of Dorwall. How do you plead?'

The six exchanged glances, but gave no response.

'I will ask you again, how do you plead?'

Still no response.

The clerk turned to Judge Fredricks. 'Your honour?'

Fredricks sat back in his chair. He whispered to the four jurates. They all nodded. He turned to the six.

'In that case, I will assume your guilt, for which you are all sentenced to death.' A flash of lightning – more intense than the previous one – caught his attention as it tore past the window, lighting up the dim, candlelit room. It was immediately followed by a crash of thunder, much closer and louder than before. The judge stood up. 'In view of the inclement weather, I will leave the choice of execution to our friend the gaoler. He will decide how you die as punishment for your misdeeds.'

He walked out of the room. His four jurates followed him to the door, leaving the clerk to finish tidying up his book, ink and quill. Once the items were secured in a leather satchel, the clerk summoned in four gaolers from their position outside the hall. In contrast to the foetid-smelling clothes worn by Solomon, they were respectably dressed in clean, white, linen shirts; leather tunics; and breeches. As they entered, Solomon – having had the choice of execution bestowed on him by the judge – was now beside himself. Rubbing his hands, a gruesome smile contorted his face, revealing one yellow incisor, bordered by the remains of two broken and decaying canine teeth.

Appreciating the status of two of the six individuals, one of the gaolers spoke quietly and without disfavour.

'This way, please.'

Despite their impending punishments, their heads remained high as they followed the gaoler to a windowless antechamber, lit by five candles. It was no more than ten-foot square. The walls were bare and covered in slimy, green mould. Two wooden benches provided seating for four.

'You will remain 'ere until your time to serve the will of God is carried out. You is welcome to a final meal of bread and water. Can I get some for you?'

Maintaining their silence, the six shook their heads.

'Then I takes my leave.' About to close the door, he studied the priest. 'May your own God forgive you.' The door closed.

* * *

On the floor below, Solomon having returned from the courtroom, the two wretched gaolers were supping mead, laughing and joking as the heat from the fire in the forge began rising. Every now and again, the terrified face of Joshua Pentille was lit up as one of the gaolers pumped the bellows, causing bright-orange and yellow flames to flare a foot or so high. Still huddled in the corner, Pentille was mumbling and begging forgiveness.

His offer of a share of future tin earnings had gone unheeded by his two sadistic aggressors. The little they earned was enough to keep them replete with ale and mead. The prison supplied them with meat and some fresh vegetables, along with their rations of bread, cheese and onions, and their quarters contained dry straw beds. Neither was interested in bribes and promises of a better life outside; their rewards came from administering the sentences handed out by Judge Fredricks, plus the occasional extra-special ones thrown in by themselves. Their fathers had been gaolers before them and neither had known their mothers. Now in their thirties, prison life was comfortable and the only one they both understood.

"Ere Solomon, I thinks the fire's 'ot enough now,' said Isaac, his hand a good half-yard above the forge. 'One more pump and us can get to work.'

Solomon put his leather tankard on the floor and picked up the vat. He held it up in front of Pentille. 'Won't be long now, me boy; us'll soon have that thirst of yours quenched.' He grinned and tipped the empty container over the head of the quaking and gibbering man. The scream was deafening. 'It's empty, boy; calm down now, 'ee got nothing to worry about.'

'Not yet there ain't,' added Isaac. 'Won't always be so.' He picked up a piece of rock from the floor, where it had been thrown along with several other lumps, whilst the six were receiving their sentence. He examined it in the light from a flickering candle. 'Not much shining in 'ere boy, 'ee should be ashamed of thyself. No stannary keeper was likely to have stamped thy ingot.'

'Sounds like 'ee's about to get what 'ee deserves, in that case.' Solomon took the rock and dropped it into the vat. 'Right then, let's see what us can get out of this.' He hung the vat on a hook above the forge and began to furiously pump the bellows. Sweat dampened both gaolers' unwashed hair as the heat filled the already humid and squalid room. Eventually, the ore started to liquify. 'Not long now, old chap,' he informed Pentille in an attempted imitation of Edmund Folsham's posh accent. 'Us'll soon have 'ee as right as rain. Thy throat will give 'ee no more trouble after this medicinal dose.'

His words caused Isaac to double up with laughter, followed by his customary retching and sporadic relief of thick, green mucus. Solomon thumped him hard on his back. 'Come now, dear Isaac, you'll have none of that; you'll upset young Mr Pentille.' Solomon's continued imitation did nothing to help Isaac; it was another five minutes before his coughing ceased and he was ready to wrench their victim from his squat in the corner.

'Let's be 'aving 'ee, boy; 'tis time to receive thy refreshment.' He dragged Pentille to the middle of the floor. The petrified man left a light-brown, glutinous trail over several stone slabs, as his bare feet spread the excrement released by his unrestrained bowels.

"Ee'll 'ave to clean that up after 'ee, 'ee dirty, little fucker,' chastised Isaac. 'Don't want that sort of thing in our workplace. Now, on your back boy and open wide.'

It took a few punches to Pentille's head and ribs before he finally took up the required position. Solomon knelt astride him. With one knee on each of his victim's upper arms, the fingers of one of his grubby hands forced open the young man's mouth, whilst the other tugged at the lace on the front of his own trousers. He pulled out his cock, already erect, his foreskin covering an unwashed, purulent glans. He eased back the skin and tilted forwards.

'Fancy a suck of this lovely beauty before we starts?'

The pitiful Pentille, his fate sealed, stared into his aggressor's bloodshot eyes. Summoning up the last of his will and strength, he broke free of Solomon's fingers. Lifting his shoulders, in one swift movement he spat into the gaoler's face, before drawing the abscess-infected cock into his mouth.

Too late, Solomon realised the prone man's intention. Squealing like a pig at castration, he fell back, blood squirting out of his rapidly deflating cock, an inch of which was now hanging by a thin piece of gristle. Still screaming, he grabbed his broken tool and lay on the ground, writhing from side to side.

"Ee bastard. What has 'ee done?' he shrieked, the high-pitched sound enough to wake those whose lives he'd taken in the past. He received no reply, for having watched his close friend's suffering, Isaac had lifted the vat off the hook and was now pouring the molten contents over Pentille's face. Instantly melting his eyes, any instinctive cries of agony were stifled as the liquid ran into his mouth and filled his nostrils. His body arched and shook, then, as if full of lead, sank back unceremoniously to the floor.

Had he survived this heinous punishment, Pentille would have no doubt taken pleasure in the knowledge that not only had he inflicted a wound on Solomon from which he would bleed to death within the hour but, in Isaac's haste to help his friend, he'd not taken time to put on the thick, leather gauntlets before lifting the vat. Isaac's severely blistered fingers would eventually become infected, the subsequent gangrene causing his life to expire before the end of the month.

Regrettably, Father Rowland Worsley, priest of the parish of Hingston; William Hyde, landlord of The Miner's Arms; Maud Chechester, widow; Elizabeth Ansty, stablehand and barmaid; The Honourable Edmund Folsham, Justice of the Peace; and John Laken, labourer and drunkard would pay the price for Pentille's attack on the two gaolers. For, the next day, Judge Fredricks temporarily appointed his close friend Martha Guildeforde, the only female overseer and persecutor of satanic heresy in the country, to replace them. Her sadistic tendencies had been nurtured and developed by Fredricks when he mentored her in London, and he had every confidence that she would ensure no convicted criminal ever repeated Joshua Pentille's act of retribution.

* * *

Nine weeks had passed since Worsley, Folsham, Hyde, Maud Chechester, Elizabeth Ansty and John Laken had been dragged by the feet from the gunnis near the Cotterill's house, by six of the Earl of Dorwall's best bred shires.

Like Hyde, Maud had been pleasantly surprised how little persuasion had been required to convince Folsham to join forces. Without the need to resort to blackmail, her secret knowledge about his love life could be saved for another day. With him on board, she'd firmly believed his authority would offer them protection against any arrest.

Once Folsham had pledged his commitment, Worsley had little choice but to accept the magistrate's 'invitation', as refusal would have meant the instant exposure of his unholy misdeeds.

Elizabeth had initially been unwilling, but – after much cajoling from her 'godfather' – she had reluctantly agreed to manage the carthorses. As for John Laken, he'd smiled his toothless grin when Hyde had offered him a free tankard of ale every evening for a year in return for his muscle. Whether he would receive a share of the proceeds from the tin once smelted, John Laken didn't care. A promise of ale was worth more to him than a few bits of old rock and ore.

Their plan had started without problem. Laken did most of the digging, following the lode and loosening the rock. Folsham and Hyde then transported it by horse-drawn cart to Maud's land, where they washed away the unwanted decomposed granite. It was her responsibility to take it, with Elizabeth's help, to the blowing house where they claimed it was dug from her own mine. It was good quality ore, and word soon got around that Maud Chechester was a widow of much repute and probable future wealth.

It was sharing this suddenly found wealth that indirectly led to their downfall. Worsley, whose sole function was to keep paper records of the amounts dug and to oversee the stannary keeper's stamping of the ingots as agent for Maud, knew only one way of spending his share. Still inebriated from an evening supping Hyde's finest brandy, rather than his much cheaper ale, he failed to hear the post-communion gossip concerning the earl's declaration by messenger that new tenants had been appointed to the Cotterill's land. Within days of them taking up residency, the presence of the trespassers had been reported by Ely Polter to the Lord Warden, who in turn instructed his militia.

Folsham's insistence that, under the rules of bounding, they were entitled to dig for tin regardless of whether they had the landowner's permission or not fell on deaf ears.

'You might t'other side of the Tamar, but not in this county, you doesn't,' replied the captain of the militia.

Now, as they sat in the antechamber awaiting their fate, it was Folsham who broke their allegiance to silence.

'Nothing we could have said would have saved us from the wrath of that evil man,' he conceded. 'At least by maintaining our silence, it removed the temptation to beg for forgiveness.'

Elizabeth glared at him through the dim light. 'It is fine for you to say that, Edmund, but you have at least lived some years. For my part, I have not had the chance to enjoy similar pleasures to the ones that your early gained wealth bestowed upon you.'

"Ee cannot blame Edmund, girl; it was thy decision and thine alone to join with us. 'Ee knew the risk 'ee were taking,' scoffed Hyde. 'Should us have gone undetected, 'ee would surely have left the village and no doubt spent thy money on the finer things.'

'How can you say I had a choice? Had I not accepted your invitation, life in the inn would have been much worse than hell.'

'Come now, Elizabeth, what point is there in making complaint now? We are condemned to death, and death it will be.' If Maud's factual chastising was intended to offer comfort, her words fell on deaf ears.

'No doubt you wish me to thank you for protecting me from the hands of that repulsive gaoler,' retaliated Elizabeth, 'but perhaps if I had let him use his grubby fingers on my breasts, he may have ensured me a quick and painless end.'

'I only did what any mother should do.'

She looked at Hyde, who immediately turned away. Embarrassed by his own lack of interference, he was fully aware his face had reddened.

Sensing conflict, the priest – whose stay in prison had ensured his sobriety – intervened.

'Perhaps I should offer a prayer. After all, the Lord is the only one who can forgive us now.'

'Stuff thy fuckin' Lord and stuff the fuckin' day 'ee told me of thy plan, for if I'd known 'twas anything other than proper, I would have told 'ee to shove it up thy arse.' It was John Laken.

To a man, the others gaped at him with wide-open mouths. It was the first time anyone present had heard such an outburst from the labourer.

'And that includes 'ee, Rowland Worsley, the man who passed on the part of 'is brain what desires an excess of drink,' he continued. ''Ee may be a father to all they who comes reluctantly to thy church on Sunday, but 'ee's never been a father to me, 'ee wasted fuckin' soak.' Laken barely felt the slap Worsley administered to the side of his face. He looked around the still gaping audience. ''Ee didn't know, did 'ee?' he sniggered. 'Well, 'ee does now.' He looked Worsley in the eye. 'As for 'ee…' he spat in the priest's face. 'That's what I thinks of 'ee.'

Before Worsley had chance to come back at his illegitimate son, the door swung open. It was the gaoler who had shown them to the room.

'I've got some good news for 'ee 'eaps of shit,' the gaoler said. A wide grin revealed his lack of front teeth. ''Ee's 'ad a reprieve. 'Ee's all free to go... back to thy pit.' A loud guffaw followed as his three associates entered. 'Been a slight 'itch with the lovely man who was going to ensure 'ee each died slowly... 'is cock's fallen off.' The four gaolers took great delight at this comment, and laughed heartily as they pushed and shoved the six towards the stairs. 'Gunna be looked after by a lady instead. I 'ears er's pretty nifty with a poker.' He'd directed this to Worsley. 'Not adverse to a bit of arse poking are we, 'specially the young village boys?'

The priest's anger and embarrassment rapidly abated as he and the others were hurried down the stairs.

Opening the hatch, the gaoler pointed through the door at Pentille's body lying on the floor beside the forge, his head still smouldering. 'At least you won't be getting what he got, kills 'ee too quickly I's told. Now then, in we all goes. 'Er ladyship won't be with 'ee for some days, 'as to travel from London I 'ears, so best make thyselves comfortable.'

TWENTY-TWO

1st July 1520

ROOM NINE, THE COACH & HORSES, LOSTWITHIEL

'Not too tight I trust, my lord?' Martha Guildeforde tied one end of the last piece of rope to the remaining free post of the bed, the other end of which was securely knotted around the left ankle of her naked mentor and lover.

'A little,' he replied, 'but the pain adds to my excitement.'

The delight he was enjoying was clearly visible. Even before she had finished tying the first length of rope to the carved-oak four-poster bed, her subjugate partner was in a state of much arousal, something that excited her also. Not only was Judge Fredricks renowned for his harsh court dealings, but also for his generously sized member. It was longer and thicker than anything Guildeforde had ever sadistically teased and coaxed to hardness before inflicting punishment on her guilty victims. As she began to lick and suck its head, she knew she was moist and ready to receive.

On her arrival from London, a journey of six days by a not particularly comfortable coach, she had been welcomed by Fredrick's open arms and passionate embrace. After barely time to partake of a goblet of wine and a plate of cold beef, he'd whisked her away to his bedroom, undressed her, and fondled and caressed every part of her taught, small-breasted, boyish, twenty-three-year-old body. She stood a little shy of six feet, three inches taller than him, but it was this dominant height that had first attracted him to her. She wasn't the prettiest of women in his London court, but he admired her long, red hair and she always favoured him with a noisy orgasm, something few of his other lovers could guarantee.

Moving her attention away from his cock, she knelt astride his face and pushed her soaking cunt against his mouth. Without hesitation, he slipped his tongue inside her and explored as deeply as this deft muscle would allow. She threw her head back, moaning as she squeezed and stretched her own sensitive nipples. Withdrawing his tongue, he drew her clitoris into his lips, and alternatively sucked and licked its solid tip. It was enough to cause her to gush and he drank in the taste of her female ejaculation as she screamed his name and pulled at his hair.

He bit her inner thighs and she tugged harder, eventually pushing his face away with the palm of her hand. Sliding back the length of his body, she pressed against him, ensuring he felt every last drop of her female cum on his chest and stomach. He writhed underneath her, but she was strong and intent, holding him down with one hand, whilst the other playfully, but firmly, teased the length of his tool. Finally, with him begging her for forgiveness, she raised her buttocks and easily slid her opening down his desperate shaft. She rose and fell like a ship in a storm, and it took just a few strokes before he shot his load in perfect unison with her second orgasm.

For many women, it would have been sufficient, but, lifting herself off, she grabbed his rapidly failing cock, took it into her mouth and encouraged it to give for a second time. Her lover responded, but not with a cry of delight, but instead one of pain as she forced his remaining semen to release. Satisfied she'd pleased him sufficiently, she bit both his nipples, then lay contented by his side. Eventually, releasing one of his arms from the bedpost, she snuggled into him, safe in his limited embrace.

That night she slept well, the expectation of the first of the six executions ensuring she stayed damp between her thighs.

Over a breakfast of hard-boiled eggs and salted fish, Judge Fredricks discussed the crimes of the six awaiting their deaths. The order and nature of their demise he left to her, requesting only that each individual punishment should be agonisingly slow. He would attend, but he insisted she later give him a full description of how they responded as their lives slipped away – particularly the two women, one of whom was young and bore a good figure. Martha Guildeforde, executioner and temptress, assured Judge Fredricks, Lord Justice and lover, she would whisper every detail in his ear as they bedded together at night.

With breakfast done, she returned to their room and donned her men's black-leather breeches, black-leather tunic and knee-length, brown boots, for this outfit made her feel powerful and respected in the eyes of her God, whose blessing she would silently request before the final breath left each pathetic soul.

Martha Guildeforde took great delight in planning the death of the six. Eager to please her lover and mentor, she decided to leave the two women until last; it would mean her stay in Lostwithiel would end with every lingering detail clear in her mind.

Her superiors in London had insisted that she return to her regular employment as soon as possible, so – apart from what she had gleaned from the judge and the four gaolers – she had little time to learn much about the individuals. However, what she did manage to learn was sufficient for her to choose the way they would die.

Neither of the women had pleaded guilty to witchcraft, but, nonetheless, she would close her display of contemptuous slaughter by burning the older of the two at the stake; her victim's screams and nostril-engulfing smell would excite her every sense. She would light the faggots late in the evening, so that the brief gap 'twixt life's final shriek and her own shared bed would ensure that the utmost enjoyment would be gained from the judge's lovemaking. In the morning, she would set off to the capital, leaving her master exhausted but satisfied.

It would not be long before the judge's duties would be fulfilled in this goddamned outpost of the country, permitting them to rekindle their shameful affair in the comfort of their own boudoir, whilst his wife contentedly subsisted in inebriated, joyful ignorance.

Before examining the tools available to help her administer pain and suffering to others, she scrutinised the bloodstained straw on the floor in the dungeon. She'd been told that the gaoler Solomon had writhed in agony, his partially severed cock liberally spouting his thin and infected blood over the face and torso of the guilty Joshua Pentille. Pausing, she bent down and ran her hand over the stubbly covering, sniffing her fingers and running them over her lips as she straightened. She smiled, aware she would soon smell the scent of something much fresher.

She selected a poker, the longest of three hanging on the wall, its two-foot length guaranteeing the utmost discomfort. Being the implement of torture to least gratify her, she would use it to probe the labourer, a waster and alcoholic by all accounts. The poker would be heated until smoke curled from its glowing end. This would not only inflict much discomfort, but, more importantly, having heard one of the warders describe how 'loose' Laken had become during his stay in prison, the immediate cauterising would ensure his orifice was incapable of shedding any pox-ridden gaoler's fluid.

Resting on the top of the central forge was a butcher's knife. She ran her thumb along its twelve-inch blade; it was perfectly bent and blunt. His wrists tied to the ceiling, his spread-eagled legs held firmly by two gaolers, she imagined the high-pitched screams of the naked magistrate as she unhurriedly removed all of his manhood. It was an appropriate death for the alleged philanderer.

She would also use the knife on the inn's landlord, but it would not be his genitals spilling onto the floor. Once his torso was split from throat to groin, encouragement and persuasion would ensure his entrails departed the sanctity and comfort of his abdomen. It would be fair recompense for the mouldy and contaminated offal it was rumoured he had served to his travelling guests.

His young maid, the one who was also the stable girl, would die from the driven spikes of her own pitchfork, the points penetrating her virgin parts.

That just left the priest, the one who regularly abused his holy position. She crossed to a corner of the room where a length of coiled rope, a noose at one end, lay damp and covered in mould. She lifted the noose, passing it over her head. It felt exhilarating and stimulated a warmth in her breasts. She pressed her hand against her crotch. Had her judge been with her, no doubt he would have wished to indulge in the anticipation of the pleasurable fulfilment it offered, but, for now, she threw it back to the floor. She would order its collection when the time came to hang the priest by his neck, with his toes just touching the ground. Not for Martha Guildeforde was the clean break of bone; gasping suffocation was what moistened the lips between her thighs.

She would commence God's will at ten of the clock the next day. Orders were given for the gibbet to be erected in the prison's courtyard close to where the bonfire was already being built around the foreboding, ten-foot-high wooden pole.

Hangings were commonplace in the town of Lostwithiel, but it had been many years since the inhabitants had witnessed the burning of a witch. As word spread, an air of excitement began to grow, and, on the instructions of their husbands, women packed baskets with rye bread, cheese and bottles of mead. Torches would be lit, and an evening of merriment planned.

TWENTY-THREE

3rd July 1520

LOSTWITHIEL PRISON

The following morning, having risen early and sought God's sanctification of her forthcoming day's work, Martha Guildeforde entered the prison gate just after 9am. Dressed in her leather outfit, her red hair tied back in a ponytail, she was accompanied by Judge Fredricks, attired in his long, green cloak with ermine trimmings and a cowl. In the dungeon, one of the gaolers had already lit and bellowed the forge.

Naked and barefoot, John Laken was dragged in by two gaolers. He showed no fear or emotion. A wooden table, some three feet square and three feet high, had been placed by the forge. Two manacles were fastened to the middle of the table top. Guildeforde pushed Laken's head down and locked his wrists in the iron bracelets. She kicked his legs apart.

The judge stepped forwards, his eyes meeting Laken's. 'Have you anything to say John Laken? Repenting for your sins now will make your life in hell less painful.'

Lifting his head, Laken stared at him, his eyes unblinking. 'May 'ee go to 'ell thyself. I has done nothing wrong but to have been led by others. I curse the land we dug, and I curse 'ee, Judge Fredricks, likes I curse a dog that has shat on my shoe.'

Laken was unable to wipe away the blood from the split lip the judge inflicted with the back of his hand, but it mattered little – for, within a moment of receiving the slap, his mind was distracted as he felt the heat and searing pain induced by the red-hot poker entering his rectum. However, no screams nor cries of agony left his lips, even when Guildeforde pushed and twisted the iron into his bowel. The judge shook his head, astonished by the man's silence. He glanced at Guildeforde. She shrugged and pushed harder, but – try as she might – there was still no reaction from Laken. However, a few seconds later, Laken's pain threshold was broken. Having held his head high throughout his ordeal, there was a sudden, sickening, squelching sound as his nose bone crunched, his face having smashed down hard on the table. Guildeforde withdrew the poker and plunged it into one of Laken's eye sockets. He gasped, as – still hot – it burned its way into his brain. Restrained by the manacles, his knees fell forwards, his lifeless body seemingly in prayer.

'I don't understand,' said Guildeforde. Like the judge, she was dismayed and disappointed that there had been no pleas to stop, no begging for mercy. It had a strange effect on both of them. 'Perhaps the pain rendered him dumb,' she suggested, 'as though I had cut off his tongue.'

Her companion didn't reply. Instead, he beckoned one of the gaolers to him. 'My mouth is dry; fetch me a pitcher of wine this instant,' he snarled at the gaoler. He wiped the sweat from his brow, as a cold and uncomfortable sensation caused him to shiver. It was a feeling he would experience four times again that day. Guildeforde waited patiently until his thirst was quenched.

Edmund Folsham, Justice of the Peace, was next.

As the magistrate hung naked from the ceiling by his arms, his legs held wide by two gaolers, Fredricks asked if he wished to repent his sins.

Folsham looked down at him, his expression one of contempt. 'Go to hell, Fredricks.'

Seeing the judge's rising fury, Guildeforde began working the blunt knife into Folsham's scrotum. Blood spurted over her face. She wiped it off with her sleeve.

His voice increasing in pitch, Folsham yelled, 'I curse the land we dug, and may you join the pack of wild dogs, Fredricks, and be cursed forever. How you can order this to be done to a man of my standing...' He stopped. Having removed his testicles and thrown them to the nearest gaoler, Guildeforde had clenched his cock in her fist and was slowly drawing the knife back and forth across its base.

Before applying the first hack, she'd momentarily studied the flaccid length of flesh, but, now – as the blood ran over her hands and arms – any admiration she'd felt for it vanished. Stretching it taught, she pressed harder and more fiercely. A sharp knife would have made a clean cut, but this one found the gristle and tissue difficult to breach. Fortunately for Folsham, the pain and the shock had taken his life long before she triumphantly held up the bleeding, dismembered appendage.

'Looks like our honourable friend has been dipping this somewhere unclean,' she said with a smile, before tossing the ulcer ridden tissue onto the forge.

Fredricks was shivering incessantly. He pulled his cloak tightly around him.

'What ails you, my love?' enquired Guildeforde, looking up from the searing piece of shrivelling meat. 'Even after the wine, you do not seem refreshed.'

'It is just the stench of this dungeon; I will be much better once we are outside,' he replied, swallowing the last of his drink. 'May we dispense with the younger woman in the fresh air? I am certain the sight of her nakedness will restore my zest.'

Elizabeth Ansty did indeed have a beautiful body under her torn and sullied clothing. Although suffering from malnutrition, and displaying several festering sores plus one or two boils on her slender neck, her fair hair; small, firm breasts; slim waist and round hips, enhanced by shapely legs, still aroused desire in the judge. Had she not been sentenced to death, he would most definitely had requested she be scrubbed and brought to his bedroom, following Guildeforde's return to London.

With each limb held on the stone floor of the courtyard by the four gaolers, Fredricks watched desirously as Guildeforde knelt beside the naked girl and caressed her pert, smooth breasts. She knew it would excite the judge, as did her gentle fingering of the younger female's tight and virtuous cunt. Elizabeth gave no objection, knowing resistance would only annoy her executioner and make her forthcoming death more painful. However, as Guildeforde got to her feet and raised the pitchfork high in the air, Elizabeth spat at the judge.

'I curse the land we dug, and may you rot in hell with the dogs, Judge Fredricks, for I have done nothing but guide the horses.'

Riled by her outburst, Fredricks kicked the girl's head. 'Do it,' he urged, his voice rising several octaves. 'Do it now, for she does not repent.' There was a sense of panic in his urgency.

Fortunately for Elizabeth Ansty, she passed out as the prongs broke through her skin and into her womb and uterus.

Not waiting to watch the several more thrusts that were to follow, Fredricks rushed towards the inn. 'I need sustenance,' he roared to Guildeforde, who – with one foot on Elizabeth's shoulder – was now struggling to pull the pitchfork out of the girl's chest. 'Prepare the gallows and send for me when all is ready.'

He hurried away, his demeanour distressed and awkward. He felt as though he was suffering from the fever; his skin itchy and his bowels loose. He needed to be away from this place, but was aware he would be seen to lose face if he was not present come the main event of the day. He knew from chatter in the inn that a large crowd was expected at the burning and, should he not be there, the villagers would think he was regretting the sentence handed out to the respected Maud Chechester. Conscious that she was one of the Earl of Dorwall's favourites, he did not want to appear to be in fear of the stannary warden.

Despite her concern for Fredricks and the lack of remorse shown by her victims, Guildeforde was still finding the executions gratifying and needed no respite from her duties. Instead, she ordered that William Hyde should be brought to the gallows. He was not to die by the rope, so she instructed that his wrists, not his neck, be strung to the gibbet. Kicking away the small stool on which he had been standing, she watched as Hyde's body dangled loosely, his bound feet hanging a foot or so above the ground. For a few minutes, he raised and kicked his legs, before fatigue finally possessed them, and they hung still and limp.

Guildeforde did not rush, for she hoped for the judge's return; however, after an hour had passed, it became evident that he was to remain at the inn for some time. Ordering the butcher's knife to be brought from the dungeon, she held it close to the landlord's face.

'I was not an instigator, just a helper,' screamed Hyde as the point of the knife made contact with his throat. 'I curse the land we dug, and may your lover find no solace with the dogs he will forever run with.' His screams turned to a gurgle as the blade struck home.

Keeping her eyes fixed on her victim's, and with both hands on the handle, Guildeforde yanked and twisted the knife through his chest and stomach. It took all of her strength to cut the entrails free, but, eventually, the guts hung loose and slack in front of Hyde's groin. Ignoring the stench from the intestines, she stood on the stool and freed his bonds.

The lifeless torso slumped to the ground. The point of the blade having torn through his heart, Hyde had died long before it had reached his stomach, but, even so, Guildeforde's task was not yet complete.

Wiping away the sweat from her face with a hand still dripping with blood from the knife, she shouted to a gaoler. 'Bring me the axe and make sure it's honed.'

As she swung at Hyde's limbs, the gaolers fell silent. They had seen many acts of quartering, but none carried out with such gusto. Having sliced easily through each joint,

Guildeforde shouted a further instruction. 'Pull his hair firmly, so I may get a clear strike.'

With Hyde's neck taught, the axe cut cleanly. Guildeforde screamed manically as what blood remained poured from the severed arteries.

'Give me that,' she ordered, grabbing Hyde's head from the gaoler. Laughing hysterically, she held it close to her face. 'You won't be serving anymore jugs of ale and stealing another man's ore ever again, you bastard.'

She pitched the head back at the gaoler. 'Hang it from the gibbet once I am done here. It will be a lesson for others to learn from.'

Regaining her composure, she stepped back to admire her work. A pang of disquiet rippled through her muscular physique. It was only now that she wondered why each of her patrons had uttered a canine curse before meeting their God. It wasn't something she had experienced before when punishing others, irrespective of their guilt or innocence.

She shook her head, challenging the thought, but it would not disappear. None of the four had struggled and, though they gave their reasons for their involvement, not one had begged for mercy. It was as though they'd accepted their fate, perhaps believing they were going to a place far better than either the earth on which they had already lived or the hell they now deserved. She called a temporary halt to the proceedings. Sitting on the grass in front of Hyde, his body like that of a gutted animal carcass, she summoned the brightest of the gaolers.

'Did you allow these scum to consult with a wise woman, for they appear to show no fear of their death?' she asked, assuming this to be the cause of their silence.

'No, madam, I is not aware of any such connivance,' he replied, refusing to meet her eyes.

'Do not lie to me, you repulsive excuse for a man, for I can see it in your face. Tell me, did they have such an encounter?' As she spoke, she got to her feet.

The gaoler, some five inches shorter, began backing away. 'No, I swears on me father's grave.' His cheeks crimson, he began trembling uncontrollably. For a tall woman, Guildeforde was agile and nimble; even so, had the gaoler not stumbled, he may have avoided the slash of the knife. Falling backwards, his attempt to dodge her swinging arm proved fruitless. With his blood pumping from a shredded jugular, he straightened and his eyes stared into hers. Although all life had left his understanding, he remained upright for a few seconds before his buckling legs deposited him unceremoniously onto the ground.

Guildeforde swung round to face the remaining three gaolers, who were in no mood for a further confrontation. 'Well?' she snarled. 'Who was this woman who provided them with strength and hope?'

The three looked at her, but proffered no answer. She took two paces forwards. 'I said, who was she? Answer me or you will suffer the same fate as your hopeless friend.' She pointed the knife at the twitching body behind her, its hands covering its bleeding throat in an instinctive but futile effort to stem the flow. The knife then moved in the direction of the smallest gaoler, the one who had admitted to buggering John Laken. His diminutive physique was no match for this woman and he cowered submissively as she approached. 'Tell me, or I shall see to it that you never enter the arse again.'

"Er was… was… from Bod… Bod… min, some six miles away," he sputtered, his hands held in front of his face. "Er said 'er'd been sent for."

'Sent for?' queried Guildeforde, prodding the knife towards the pitiful man. 'Who sent for her?'

'Us… us… doesn't know. But 'er said 'er was rewarded 'andsomely and shared some of 'er silver…' He glanced at the other two. 'With all of us.'

'I see.' Guildeforde lowered the knife. 'And what did she tell them?'

There was no response.

Raising the knife, she asked again. 'What did she tell them, or you'll be joining your friend in hell, with or without your shit-stained cock intact?'

The gaoler turned towards the body of his fallen colleague. It lay prone and still; the pool of blood surrounding its neck drying rapidly in the warm sunshine as it soaked into the grass. He could feel his bladder beginning to empty. He looked back at Guildeforde, but still he did not answer her question. She grabbed him by the throat. It was enough to draw a response from one of the other gaolers.

'All us 'eard was that they was to remain strong and bonded, and to make sure they cursed Judge Fredricks in the name of Cavall,' he replied. 'But it meant nothing to us. Us just thought 'er wanted 'er silver.'

'Cavall? Who the fuck be Cavall?' Although still determined, Guildeforde felt some of her confidence drain from her. She had no idea what the reference to Cavall meant, but – for some reason unknown to her – it had an unsettling effect in her gut.

'I's sorry madam, but I's no idea. 'Er just came said 'er words and then went.' It was the gaoler who'd spoken first. He no longer felt the need to stay silent.

One of the others then added, 'Beggin' your pardon, madam, but 'er also said they'd been wronged, for if the land be empty, then the tin belongs to no one. It was untenanted, and so they was entitled to dig it. Just 'cos it belonged to 'is lordship the earl, 'tweren't 'is right if he didn't dwell on it. 'Tis stannary law, apparently.'

Guildeforde did not know the law and, even if she did, she had no intention of challenging Judge Fredricks. 'And did this so-called wise woman say anything else?'

'Only that justice would be done and they would return.'

The comment from the third gaoler caused Guildeforde to drop the knife. She did not believe in witchcraft, but as the four executed thus far had shown no fear, she could not dismiss the fact that somehow this woman had instilled a belief in the six found guilty of the theft of tin – a belief that was stronger than death itself.

Her thoughts were interrupted by a voice from behind.

'Is everything all right, my dear?' It was Judge Fredricks and he seemed in finer fettle than when he'd left. He scrutinised the headless corpse of William Hyde and then briefly examined the body of the dead gaoler. 'It would appear that not all has gone smoothly.'

Guildeforde bent down and picked up the knife. 'All is well, my lord; it was just a slight disagreement to which I have attended.'

'Hmm, I see.' The meat pie and ale had invigorated the judge. He considered Hyde's dismembered torso again. 'They don't look so troublesome without their limbs and head,' he snorted. He turned to the gaoler. 'Scrape him together and throw him with the others.' He looked at Guildeforde. 'No doubt you will be displaying the head, my dear.'

She smiled. 'Already taken care of, my love.'

Two gaolers gathered up Hyde. There would be no burial, for the guilty did not deserve a holy send off. Instead, the corpses were thrown over the low wall onto barren ground behind the prison's courtyard. Here they would be pecked at by the crows, and torn apart by foxes and the wild dogs that roamed the untamed parish forests and the deep valleys of the nearby gorge. The third gaoler lifted his dead comrade and carried him on his shoulder into the prison's keep; he would be buried once a new priest was appointed.

Judge Fredricks rubbed his hands together. 'Well, are we ready for Rowland Worsley?' He had no intention of referring to him as a priest, for that title had expired when he was found guilty.

'Yes, my lord, but I think I should tell...' Abruptly she curtailed her desire to recount what the gaoler had said about the wise woman. She knew the judge wouldn't have any time for such idle tittle-tattle, and she didn't want him to think less of her.

'Tell me what, Martha?' pressed the judge, his curiosity roused.

"Tis nothing, my lord, that cannot wait until we are in our bedchamber.' She smiled. 'I will delight you with William Hyde's demise then.'

Fredricks acknowledged her mirth. 'I shall look forward to it. Now... the hanging.'

Sober and upright, Worsley shrugged off the grip of the two gaolers escorting him.

'In my condition and with my years, is it likely I shall chance to run away?' he demanded. They accepted his request and followed one pace behind as he strode as purposefully as his weak and decrepit body would allow. He spat at the judge's feet.

'Damn you, Fredricks, for all I am guilty of is recording and observing, not theft.'

The judge resisted retaliating, for he did not wish to sink to the unwholesome level of this disgraced so-called holy man.

'You are as guilty as the next man, Worsley, even if you did not trespass. I trust you will take your punishment in a righteous and dignified manner, for there is already a crowd gathering?'

At least thirty or so men, women and young children were standing either side of the prison's gates.

'Of course, but not without cursing you and the land we dug.' Worsley sank to his knees, his palms held together in front of him. 'Oh Lord, I do not ask for your forgiveness for I knew what I was doing, but…' He glanced up at Fredricks, who – with eyes half closed – had curled back his lips exposing large yellow teeth. 'Please grant my prayer that this man standing before me is spared no mercy and will spend the rest of his life dogged by those he so ruthlessly committed to their deaths, for it were not for—'

Fredricks resistance had waned. Wrenching the knife from Guildeforde's hand, Worsley felt the full force of the handle as it struck his skull; the crack of bone splitting drew a loud groan from the crowd. He fell sideways, the speed of his fall increased by the sole of Guildeforde's leather boot.

'Get up, you bastard excuse for a priest, for I have not finished with you yet,' growled Fredricks. He grabbed what was left of Worsley's rat-bitten collar. As he started to lift the pitiful and semi-conscious man, Guildeforde's hand came down firmly on his.

'No more, my lord, or there will be no hanging,' she said.

Fredricks paused. Peering over his shoulder at one half of the crowd, he realised she was right. Some of the men were already jeering, and if he angered them further, they might start baying for blood – his not Worsley's. He was well aware that, unlike London, small prisons such as Lostwithiel were not protected by the king's soldiers, but by militia men employed by the local peer. It was not uncommon for them to neglect their duty when faced by a mob. He let go of the collar, allowing Worsley to fall back to the ground. He turned to the gaolers. 'String him up now,' he yelled, 'before I lose my patience.'

'Yes, my lord,' replied the one who had been threatened by Guildeforde. Five minutes later, the stool having been kicked from under him by Guildeforde, Worsley was hanged by the neck, his feet just touching the ground beneath him. Blood ran freely from the wound on the side of his head. A loud cheer rose from the crowd. As it began to die down, Rowland Worsley gasped his last breaths, but not before he'd managed to wheeze his final words. 'Go to hell, Judge Fredricks, where I promise you will find no peace for centuries to come.' His body fell limp.

Noticing Fredricks was rocking from side to side, his arms wrapped about him, Guildeforde offered him comfort.

'Ignore him, my lord, for it is just a dying man's desperate threat.'

But Fredricks took no relief from her good intention. Worsley's threat had genuinely frightened him, and – together with the lack of fear shown by all those who had died so far that day – paranoia about his own mortality was beginning to creep its way in.

'Bring forwards the burning of the witch,' he instructed Guildeforde, 'for I wish to retire early.'

'But, my lord, the crowd is not yet full. There will be dissatisfaction if the townspeople should miss it,' she protested in reply.

'Fuck the townspeople and fuck this town, for in the morning I will be returning to London with you. The king will have to find another judge to carry out his good work.' Running his hand aggressively through his hair, he began pacing two steps to either side. 'You heard me woman, get started. The sooner it is done, the sooner I can leave the grounds of this godforsaken prison.' He gazed up at the building's front wall. Doused in bright afternoon sunlight, the two upstairs windows and large, ground-floor, wide-open door gave it the visage of a grinning court jester – a jester who was laughing at him. He pulled his hood over his head.

However, the next day neither Judge Fredricks nor Martha Guildeforde left the town of Lostwithiel.

TWENTY-FOUR

The evening

ROOM NINE, THE COACH & HORSES, LOSTWITHIEL

'My lord, what is wrong?'

Judge Fredricks was lying fully clothed on the bed. He was shaking and whimpering like an anxious puppy. He looked at his lover, Guildeforde. 'I have been taken by a malady, my dearest Martha. It causes me much irritation and discomfort. I believe it to be this town. It has turned against me.'

'But how can a town turn so quickly?' She sat on the bed beside him and stroked his forehead. 'You were only doing your duty, my lord, and dealt appropriate punishments.' She was confident in her reassurance. 'For my part, I gave the miscreants what they deserved.'

'But you saw them; you saw their demeanour. They were not scared and felt genuinely wronged.' He sat upright, staring at the fireplace. 'Perhaps I am the one in the wrong;

perhaps I misunderstood these ridiculous local laws and have interpreted them falsely.'

It was the first time Guildeforde had heard him doubt himself. Whenever she had worked with him, he had been forthright and well read. His punishments were harsh but justified. He was never popular with those he judged, but his masters thought highly of him and supported his findings.

The final execution had gone well, at least until the judge's departure.

* * *

Maud Chechester held her head high as, bare-breasted, she crossed the courtyard to where the bonfire had been built. The last remnants of her bodice had been ripped from her by one of the gaolers as he attempted to rape her whilst dragging her to the stairs from the dungeon. It was only a well-aimed kick to his groin and her uncut finger nails scraping his cheek that had driven him away. He'd slapped her face twice – the second blow breaking her nose – but she'd felt no pain, for her body and soul were numb.

Before Maud reached the bonfire, she nodded to a cloaked man in the crowd who was standing next to Ely Polter – he nodded back. He had been a close friend of Maud's late husband and, like him, a trusted yeoman. Since her husband's death, Maud had enjoyed this man's intimate company on several occasions, and, during one such liaison, he had sworn to protect her from anyone who bore her malice. Unfortunately for Maud, his promise had fallen short; however, although unable to save her from the stake, he could ensure that her informer and his family would also not profit from the tin.

Without hesitation and in silence, Maud climbed up the crude wooden steps onto a narrow platform about three feet off the ground. She placed her back against the coarsely hewn pole. Seizing his opportunity to reap his revenge, the gaoler, with dried blood covering one cheek, stripped away the remains of her skirts, then forcefully wrenched her arms behind her. The popping sound of her shoulder dislocating from its socket provided him with satisfying pleasure.

Maud grimaced, but stayed silent as the leather thongs that her antagonist needlessly overtightened behind the pole cut through to the undernourished bones of her wrists.

The tautness of a firmly secured rope around her waist drove a two-inch remnant of a sprouting branch into her injured shoulder. She took a deep breath and forced back the tears that were threatening to expose her distress.

Still proudly holding her head erect, she was conscious of the three gaolers piling the faggots evenly below her feet. She wanted to screw up her eyes and shut out the world, but – resisting any show of fear – she watched as the short staff with a tallow-soaked rag bound to one end flared up in the cast-iron fire pit. Holding high the torch that would initiate the downfall of Maud Chechester, the gaoler passed it to Guildeforde. She cast an eye at Fredricks.

Despite his desire to have done with the guilty woman as quickly as possible, reluctantly, the judge accepted the crowd, which had now risen to at least sixty in number, needed to see him to be fair and equitable. Looking up at Maud Chechester, he asked, 'Do you repent your sins?'

She scowled back at him. 'I curse the land we dug, and, as for you Judge Fredricks, go to hell where you will join the other dogs of your evil vocation. I have been wrongfully accused and tried, and for that I will seek revenge, not just for me but for—'

The judge's ranting drowned the rest of her sentence. 'Light the fire, Guildeforde,' he shrieked at the top of his voice, 'for she has spoken too much.'

Guildeforde lowered the torch into the faggots, paused until they were well alight, then moved around and lit several other bundles. As the flames flared, the skin on Maud Chechester's bare thighs, chest and face began to bubble and peel. Although her eyes declared her agonising suffering, her screams were withheld deep inside. Passing out before her flesh was engulfed and roasted, her head rolled to one side, facing the judge and his executioner. Her sickly, ingrained smirk was that of the prison wall's jester-like smile: mocking and defiant. Fredricks turned away and – ignoring his status – ran to the inn, his flowing robe dragging in the grass and mud. With his hood falling back onto his shoulders, he pushed to one side anyone who got in his path.

As the remaining bodyfat on Maud Chechester ignited and began burning fiercely, the crowd shouted and yelled their approval. No one had taken much interest in Fredricks' departure, save for, that is, the woman with a black, woollen shawl wrapped tightly around her head and her face. Through a small opening for her eyes, she watched him leave, pleased that his conduct was one of panic and fear. The wise woman of Bodmin patted the head of her beloved Cadan, descendant of Cavall, the legendary boar-slaying dog of King Arthur.

Turning, she left as inconspicuously as she'd arrived, her wolfhound close to her side. She smiled, happy in the knowledge that Fredricks, the judge who'd ordered the death of her son, Joshua Pentille, had only a few hours to live.

* * *

'I think you worry unnecessarily,' Guildeforde said as she tugged at the lace of Fredricks' tunic with one hand, whilst the other rubbed his groin. 'Here, let me soothe you.' He knocked her hands away.

'No, not tonight. I cannot take anymore. We must sleep and rise early. A full breakfast will put us in good heart for the journey.'

Surprised by his response, for it was most unusual for Fredricks to turn down the offer of a wet cunt and a sucking of his cock, Guildeforde crossed to the pitcher on the washstand and poured some fresh, cool water into the large pewter bowl. Her face and hands washed, she removed her bloodstained clothing and climbed naked into bed. Fredricks was still fully clothed. She eased close to him and began whispering in his ear.

'Did you see the fine body that the young maiden, Ansty, had? Such lovely breasts and rounded hips. I imagined her sitting astride you, pumping your cock with her cunt as I stand watching, exciting myself by fondling my breasts and my nip—'

Before she could utter another word, Fredricks was upon her, slapping and punching her head and her abdomen. He was screaming hysterically, shouting words in Latin that were unintelligible to his lover. She looked up at him, her expression one of terror and dread. She covered her face, but it wasn't the part that needed protecting.

He arched his neck backwards. What had once been a mouth was now a long snout, its jaw stretched wide open, its canine teeth dripping with saliva. His shouts and screams had become the soulful howling of a dog. His claws pressed down hard into her shoulders, scratching and tearing at her uncovered flesh. Guildeforde wriggled and struggled for release from this hideous, repugnant creature, but – trapped between its legs – she was powerless and weak.

Try as she might, she was unable to repel this vile and vicious assault. Any hope of survival she had held swiftly disappeared, as – with an ear-splitting cry – it sank its teeth into her throat, ripping and shredding like two foxes disputing a rabbit. It was over in three seconds, and ended with the blood-soaked pillow supporting the bone-exposed neck of Martha Guildeforde.

* * *

In the bar directly below room nine, Henry Hyde – the landlord of The Coach & Horses and the second cousin of William Hyde, the former landlord of The Miner's Arms – had been drinking with several locals. Sitting around laughing and joking, the din from their banter had done much to hide the noise from above; however, when he rose from their table to refill the tankards, the commotion became abundantly clear.

"Ere lads, what the 'ell is that?' enquired Henry.

'I doesn't know, 'Enry,' replied Josiah Gubbings, 'but, as sure as fuck, 'twere not the wind.'

The two rushed up the bare, wooden stairs, the noise from their boots echoing around the whitewashed walls. At the top of the stairs, they turned right; Henry was in front. After two more paces, Josiah cursed as he clattered into the back of his companion.

'Why does 'ee stop, 'Enry?' asked Josiah, rubbing his nose. However, he didn't have to wait for an answer, as – over Henry's shoulder – he could just make out the reason. Running towards them, along the candlelit and mouldy smelling corridor, was a repulsive monster, the size of a fully grown sow, but with the elongated and hairy snout of a massive lurcher. Thick strands of saliva hung from its muzzle. Its head swayed from side to side, blood from its drooling jowls splattering the walls.

'Out t'way; it ain't going round us,' shouted Josiah. Pressing themselves against the wall, the beast brushed by, its moist jaws drenching their stockinged knees.

'What the fuck 'twere that, Josiah?'

'Fucked if I know, 'Enry, but – more pressing – where's the bugger gone?'

It hadn't turned down the stairs, but had uncannily disappeared as it entered the corridor on the other side of the stairs. Josiah was the first to react. Pushing past Henry, he made his way cautiously towards room nine, the palms of his hands working their way along the wall, like a mime artist on an imaginary pane of glass.

The door to room nine was open, the curtains drawn. Although the flickering light from the candles on the mantelpiece barely lit up half of the bedchamber, it was sufficient to reveal the gruesome work carried out by the revolting canine.

On the bed lay the naked remains of Martha Guildeforde. The exposed vertebrae of her neck glistened in the pale-yellow light, whilst blood from the flesh torn from her torso, arms and legs soaked unimpeded into the sheets. Her eyes were staring at the overhead drapes, a look of horror and disbelief etched on her face. It was more than Josiah could take. He spewed the last three tankards of ale into one corner of the room. Henry had a stronger constitution, as – other than this being human flesh – it was nothing he hadn't seen before when butchering the deer poached from the Earl of Dorwall's estate; even so, it caused him to retch and swallow hard.

'Where be Judge Fredricks?' Josiah eventually managed to ask. "E were sharing with this woman of torment, were 'e not?'

Henry nodded. 'Perhaps that rabid dog devoured 'im before slaughtering this evil bitch, but whatever 'as 'appened 'ere, I feel 'tis only decent we covers this vile woman's body with a sheet, for there is no priest to do so and a maid would surely break down should she walk in on such a scene.'

His head turned to one side to avoid looking at the mutilated corpse, Josiah helped Henry pull the edges of the folded-in sheet out from under the mattress. Carefully, they threw it over Guildeforde before wrapping her up tightly.

'What now?' enquired Josiah, relieved that the dreadful sight was hidden.

Henry rubbed his stubbled chin; it was a full minute before he replied. "Tis quiet, Josiah, 'twould be a good time to dispose of 'er.'

Josiah looked at him in amazement. 'But, surely, us should report this, or else us will feel the anger of the earl and his militia.'

Henry laughed, shaking his head. 'And 'ee think they'd believe us if us tells them 'er was killed by a dog the size of a pig?'

Josiah's expression told him he clearly agreed they would not.

'I thought so,' Henry continued, 'And what of the judge? What does us say 'appened to him? That 'ee were eaten? No, us must clear this room of all belongings and throw the dead woman over the wall with t'others from the prison.'

'But the judge – how does us know 'ee's not still alive?'

'Because I see'd him go up the stairs to the room, and I never see'd him come back down. Us will tell them who ask in the morning that they both left on the dawn coach. There is two in the bar who can vouch for this, as they was there when Fredricks gave his instruction that they would be leaving earlier than planned. If anyone misses 'em, there will be no signs 'ere.'

Henry was relishing every moment. Bizarrely, he was not interested in finding out more as to what had happened. Being happy to believe it was some rabid dog from the village that they both saw run past them in the corridor, he had no intention of asking more questions. His only thought was of revenge for his cousin. He would take great pleasure in tossing Martha Guildeforde's remains away, in the same way that she had taken great delight in taking away the lives of others, whether guilty or not. He wasn't the brightest of men and, being God-fearing, he was prepared to accept that Judge

Fredricks' disappearance was due to the curse from the six executed that day, particularly the priest's.

'Right, Josiah, first us must return to the bar, tell 'em that's there 'twere just a disagreement between the judge and 'is woman, and that us quelled the commotion. I will then provide free ale and, once they is done, 'ee and I will carry the dead woman to her final resting place. Provided us puts her under some of they that has preceded her, no one will know.' Seeing Josiah's look of doubt, he tried to reassure him. 'Come now, good friend, surely 'ee is not afeard?'

"Tis not fear of the dead, 'Enry, but the fear of the curse, for I believes 'twere that what 'as caused this.'

Henry was relieved Josiah shared his belief.

'The curse 'twere not for us, dear Josiah, but 'twere for the judge and 'is woman. They is now both dead, and therefore us 'as nothing to fear. The curse will 'ave died with 'em, will it not?'

Josiah looked at Henry, pursed his lips then shrugged. 'I 'opes 'ee's right, 'Enry.'

TWENTY-FIVE

4th June 2013

SARAH

'If you head for Treworthy, I'll talk you in from there,' said Sarah.

Sarah was sitting in the back of a taxi. She'd rung Ethan, told him what she was doing and where she was going, and he'd confirmed he'd cover her expenses.

'You won't see much change from a hundred and twenty quid,' she'd told him, 'but I'm sure it'll be worth it.'

After an hour and half, they pulled up in front of the ford.

'That's it, miss; it's too deep to go any further. Sorry about that,' stated the taxi driver.

'No… no, that's all right. I hope you haven't damaged your car on those potholes.'

'It'll be fine. It only causes problems if you hit 'em too fast.' He looked at the meter. 'Call it fifty quid, bearing in mind you want me to pick you up later.'

She gave him two twenties and a ten, all of which she'd borrowed from her landlady. 'I'll be able to pay you back with next month's rent, if that's okay,' she'd virtually begged. She had enough of her own for the journey back, plus a tip, and for some food at a nearby pub, which she was sure there would be – not that she'd bothered to look thoroughly at a map of the area.

'Thanks again. I'll meet you at the top of the road when I'm done; I'll give you a ring, as there's bound to be a signal up there,' confirmed Sarah.

She closed the door, swung her rucksack (with her miner's helmet attached) onto her back and headed to where her father had written the adit was to be found. She'd go to the mine after.

'Nice one, Dad,' she said to herself as she sat on the grass, 'Always precise and accurate with what you did.' Undoing the flap of her rucksack, she tugged out her wellies and rolled-up, lightweight anorak, and undid the chin strap of her helmet and head lamp.

'I don't want to get these little rascals wet,' she murmured as she squeezed her trainers into the space left by her boots and waterproof. After checking she had her waterproof torch in the side pocket, she got to her feet. Rolling her shoulders a couple of times to ensure the rucksack was comfortably positioned, she tightened the straps. Clicking the light switch on the helmet, she eased it onto her head. It was slightly loose, but – as always, as she was afraid it would totally flatten her hair – she didn't bother to tighten the adjuster. At full brightness, the battery would last for six hours, more than enough time.

She was glad she'd brought her wellies rather than her walking boots. Like her father had noted, the further into the adit she went, the deeper the occasional water underfoot became. In places, the adit's width was no more than two feet, and she found herself removing her rucksack and turning sideways to get through. Occasionally, the roof dropped low enough for her to have to duck, her helmet taking the impact when she didn't stoop low enough.

Coming to yet an even narrower part, she decided to ditch the rucksack. Undoing the straps, she took out three chocolate bars and shoved them into a leg pocket of her cargo trousers – the same pocket where she always kept her mobile phone. The floor here was dry.

I'll pick it up on the way back, she thought.

As she squeezed past the jutting rock, behind her, the unfastened rucksack fell on its side.

A few yards further on, she came to an abrupt halt.

'Christ!' she exclaimed. 'Just as well I saw that.' On the ground in front of her was an irregularly shaped hole, the full width of the floor and at least seven feet in length. Unless she was an accomplished long jumper, there was no way she could get past it without lying across a plank or a ladder.

Gingerly, she shone her lamp into its darkness. The beam reflected off water no more than two yards below the level of the floor. Minimal depth had certainly been left between levels.

Lying on her stomach, she unclipped the lamp from her helmet. Her arm at full stretch, she held the lamp into the hole. Immediately, she realised she was looking into a 'stope', which had been dug out to such an extent that the roof was no more than a foot thick. Directly below, she could see a pile of loose rock rising from the water.

Let's hope they weren't pumping water into the adit if this lot collapsed whilst men were still working, she thought to herself.

She stared at the pile. There was a gap of a yard between its top and her hand. A twinge of excitement ran down her spine.

It could be interesting. Dad didn't mention it, but he must have seen it. Perhaps he didn't get this far or it's only just caved in. I haven't seen any sign of silver, though. It has to be recent. I could be the first to explore the level – even more to tell Ethan.

Refixing the lamp, she sat on the edge of the hole and lowered herself onto the rockpile. Instantly, some of the stone moved from under her feet.

Steady, old girl, don't want to upset it too much.

Careful not to lessen the height of the pile any further, she climbed down its side and tested the depth of the water with her foot. It just covered her instep. With both feet on the ground, she scanned around with her lamp. A low and narrow tunnel led off in the same direction as she'd been going in the adit. Stooping, she entered the tunnel; after two paces, she had to crouch. A second later, she screamed. In front of her were the remnants of a pair of leather boots. But it wasn't the sight of them that had caused her to cry out. Ahead of the boots were the tattered remains of a pair of trousers and ahead of them were a small, skeletal torso and a partially helmeted skull.

Desperate to get away before she threw up, she swung her head around, dislodging her untightened helmet. The lamp smashed against the tunnel wall, cracking the glass and the bulb.

She screamed again, but this time in darkness. Panicking, she crawled on her hands and knees to the open space of the stope, the water filling her boots as their loose-fitting tops scraped along the rough, waterlogged floor of the tunnel. Occasionally, her knees thudded against what she guessed were the rusted bits of tramway rails. She patted her pockets.

'My torch… where the fuck's my torch.' She remembered it was still in the rucksack. 'Fuck.'

She felt around with her hands and found the rockpile. She began to scramble up, frantically clawing at the stones as they came away in her hands. After twenty seconds of scrabbling, she finally accepted that not only were her boots full of water, but their toe caps were constantly sliding back onto the flooded floor below. She did her best to calm down.

'Come on, you stupid bitch,' she shouted. 'Take it steady. There's no need to freak out. You've just got to be careful… no need to rush. Go back to the adit, find the rucksack, get the torch and, bingo, I'm home and dry.'

But there was not be a full house for Sarah Jenkinson. However stealthily she tried to reach the top of the pile, her efforts simply loosened more of the chunks of rock and gravelly fragments. Exhausted and in tears, she leaned against the side of the stope.

'Don't worry,' she told herself. 'The taxi driver will wonder why I've not called, and will come back and look for me.'

Unbeknown to Sarah, the boot and trousers belonged to Jory Tregunna, one of several boys to have died in 1883 when Wheal Hingston flooded for the second time.

TWENTY-SIX

10th February 1883

WHEAL HINGSTON

Iron-oxide-stained water from the roof of the stope had been dripping on Kevern Tregunna's face for the last hour. It wasn't something Kevern had anticipated when he took the pitch. Being new to Wheal Hingston, he'd had to take the mine captain's word at the 'setting' that water had caused few problems in the levels at the depth Kevern and his sons were working. However, having originally perceived Captain Pendogget to be fair and equitable, he'd soon learned that Pendogget was under much pressure from those who employed him. Selling every pitch regardless of safety or price was essential to the mine's continued existence, as it was one of few in the area still working.

"'Tis an old tin drive us discovered when digging the adit from Wheal Hussey,' Pendogget had told him, 'but 'twas never worked out. She should prove plentiful once you moves on.' What he hadn't told him was that, in order to follow the lode, the level dug out by the tut men sloped gently upwards, thereby narrowing the gap between it and the adit above.

* * *

The Tregunna family lived in a rented mine cottage in Hingston. It was damp and, with two children, very cramped. The not-too-distant arrival of another child would make living conditions more difficult. Money was tight, but they were managing. Tegen was a good housekeeper, and Kevern was grateful for how well she managed what little was left over after paying for – amongst other things – candles, black powder, fuses, and the cost of raising and dressing his ore. He already had credit with the mine's shopkeeper; the goods were vastly overpriced, but – like most miners – Kevern had no choice but to buy from him.

It was a was a two-and-a-half-mile walk to Wheal Hingston, not unpleasant on a fine spring day, but with the ground frosty and slippery, in winter it could take its toll. The last week had seen heavy snow falls, and the fields were covered in wet, slushy snow. Many a time, Kevern wished for the ten-minute walk he had enjoyed to Wheal Penandrea in Redruth, although – on his days off in summer – the countryside around Hingston ensured the dust and blasting fumes of the mine could be forgotten, if only for twenty-four hours. Unlike many of the workers at Wheal Hingston, he did not attend Sunday chapel nor did he drink heavily. He loved spending time with Tegen and the boys, often splashing around in the river between the mine and the village.

Prior to its closure, at his previous mine in Redruth, thirty-five-year-old Kevern had gained much knowledge working for his cousin, an experienced tributer. However, Wheal Hingston was his first taste of forming his own pare with his two sons – Davith aged thirteen and Jory a year younger – and bidding himself for a pitch. He had been unable to find others to join him, so although the three of them worked more than a normal length core, not unexpectedly, the last month had yielded little tin for the Tregunna family. Kevern had known the pitch he'd successfully bid for was unlikely to be one of the best, as it was one of the 'after bargains' no one else particularly wanted, but it was better than nothing and would at least get him started. Once his sons had learned their trade, then he would join others, bid for more rewarding pitches and hopefully acquire some savings; perhaps even taking a job at grass and rebuild his health.

* * *

Women and young girls were already hard at work, hoping an early start would earn extra wages, when Kevern and his sons arrived at Wheal Hingston on the morning of the 10th February. The older women acknowledged Kevern, and, in return, he doffed his helmet.

'Hurry along, Tregunna,' instructed Pendogget from the doorway of the counting house. 'There's no time for niceties when there's ore to be mined.' Pendogget had little interest in chatting; the mine's owners would be there later that day to go through the accounts, and he wanted to ensure they would see that, despite the poor production, he had complete control of the operation.

The engine house was situated fifty yards from the shaft. As the man and two boys approached the collar protecting the edge of the shaft, the tapping of the women's hammers was quickly replaced by the pulsating racket from the flat rods driving the pump, together with the continuous, loud pounding of the power-driven stamps crushing the small particles of rock. However, once they had descended the first few rungs of the metal ladder attached to one side of the six-and-a-half-by-four-foot shaft, it was the sucking and wheezing of the pump rods removing the unwelcome water that filled the ears of the Tregunnas.

These pump rods, together with the guiding track for the truck used to bring the rock and the ore to grass, left little room for human manoeuvre; however, even Jory was now adept at reaching the twelve-fathom level without a slip. Fifteen minutes after stepping off the ladder, they were ready to start their day's work.

Whilst Kevern normally had Davith with him at all times, he was alone when the water dripping from the roof above him increased to a trickle. It being slightly overloaded and too heavy for Jory, Davith had agreed to help his brother push and pull the wagon they used to take the rock and cassiterite ore to the shaft.

The passage was narrow and so low in places that even the two boys had to crawl to get through.

'If there's no tin, then 'tis pointless for the tut men to dig out more rock than they needs,' Kevern had told them on their first day in the mine. However, now he was wishing they'd made it much wider. Saving effort was one thing, but it also meant slower progress for the wagon; his two sons were yet to return.

Had they been there, he would have been able to use one of their flames to relight his candle, which had been put out by the water, rather than having to scrabble around looking for the small, metal box containing his lucifer matches and sandpaper, which lay on the floor. He also would have been able to see where the stope's roof was starting to split.

* * *

That morning, as Kevern had pulled on his coarse flannel trousers, loose-fitting flannel shirt and a leather waistcoat, he'd had a feeling of unease. At the end of yesterday's core, the last strikes on his gad with the flat of his poll-pick had produced an odd, hollow sound. He'd intended to finish with blasting the drive's end, but had decided against it until he'd explored further by hand. He'd heard of other reopened mines blasting into old levels, only to discover they were flooded. Lives had been lost, and he didn't want himself and his sons to add to the numbers.

'You doesn't look so hale this morning, Husband,' said Tegen, his seven-months-pregnant wife. 'Are you suffering, m'dear?'

"Tis not my health, sweet Tegen, but I is worried 'bout today's work. I fears the worst, but the mine captain says 'tis fine.'

'Then why shouldn't it be so?' asked Tegen, her brow furrowed. 'Surely he would not say all is well were things not right.'

Kevern took her hands in his. 'Sweet Tegen, you is so trusting.' He smiled. 'And probably right. 'Tis I who frets too much.' He kissed her lips. 'Now, us must be going. 'Twill not do to be so late that I in particular upsets the Captain.' He called his two sons, who were outside in the yard feeding the chickens.

* * *

'Boys... boys... is you there?' shouted Kevern. He could feel the flow of the water increasing. If he didn't find his matches soon, they would be sodden and useless. He heard Davith's muffled reply.

'The wagon has come of it's rails. 'Tis too heavy for us to lift. Us needs your help father.'

'Leave it, for I needs to light my candle. Water is dripping in.'

A few moments later, the shirtless Jory appeared, his face in shadow under the brim of his helmet. 'Davith is stuck behind the wagon. The passage is too narrow for him to pass,' he said.

'Do not fret; I will help him, but I must relight my candle. The water comes from above. I is not aware of any drive over us, but I does not believe it comes from an adit either.' With his candle relit, he pulled it out of the clay and held it towards the roof.

'See, boy.' He pointed with his finger. 'The killas is splitting and letting in water. We must get out of here. Pick up your bag and tools. I will go first and help Davith.'

Jory had only managed two steps before the roof of the stope collapsed. Once the cascade of mud-filled water from the flooded adit above had engulfed the hollowed-out area, it immediately pursued the three fleeing miners. Jory drowned first; the thick, lung-clogging liquid instantly ceasing his breathing. Kevern, who had been unable to pass the wagon, drowned next. Davith was on his hands and knees crawling as fast as he could when the tsunami-like wave swallowed him up. His father had shouted a panic-stricken warning, but – even if he'd received it one minute earlier – it would not have saved him nor any others underground from their fate.

In all, forty-six men and seventeen boys died that day as the flood overwhelmed all the levels, causing numerous rockfalls and blocking the drives, including the one the Tregunnas were working. Their bodies were never recovered.

'Tis too dangerous to dig out. Us cannot risk anymore loss,' declared Pendogget.

Unbeknown to him, the melting snow on the downs around Wheal Hussey had begun flooding the adit the evening before, and, unbeknown to Kevern Tregunna, he was only working a yard underneath it. His last strike on his gad had weakened the rock, and the weight of the water had done the rest.

On the 30th September 1883, Pendogget along with J. Pendeen Esquire, G. Trethorne Esquire and T. Pollick Esquire were tried at Truro Stannary Court, the Lostwithiel Court buildings having been sold to local tradesmen. The three mine owners denied negligence, and blamed Captain Pendogget for not taking greater care in researching all existing drives before allocating pitches. His Lord Justice, Judge Abrahams, found in their favour and the case against them was dropped. However, Pendogget was found guilty and, on the 1st December 1883, was publicly hanged.

Pendeen, Trethorne and Pollick ordered all machinery at Wheal Hingston to be sold, and the shaft sollared over and covered in soil. Wheal Hussey continued working until in 1885, when it was deemed no longer profitable. It was then that the three owners, together with their families, emigrated to America with the intention of using their capital to explore other mining opportunities.

TWENTY-SEVEN

4th June 2013

SARAH

Regardless of how optimistic and possibly unrealistic her expectations of busy taxi drivers were, if nothing else, the thought that hers would come looking for her provided temporary comfort. She tucked into one of the chocolate bars. As a newly discovered tin or copper lode may have lifted the spirits of a miner, the naturally occurring chemicals in the cacao seeds hitting Sarah's brain gave her a momentary elation. Savouring the smooth, delicious taste, she recalled the book about the thirty-three miners in Chile who survived two thousand odd feet underground for over two weeks on barely an ounce of food before being rescued after sixty-nine days. Like them, she would be fine. She had a supply of water, perhaps not the most palatable, but at least it would keep her alive, for days if necessary.

Unfortunately, as the effect of the chocolate wore off, so did her optimism. She remembered that, once they were found, the Chileans had food sent down a narrow shaft to keep them alive, and she was alone in the darkness, whereas they'd had light and also each other. Perhaps, most importantly, they had families and work colleagues who knew they were trapped, not just a taxi driver, who – common sense now told her – would probably assume she'd found her way home by alternative means. She began to sob.

'Why didn't I tell Ethan everything I was up to, including the adit?' she whimpered. Then, as if trying to make herself feel better about her stupidity, she mumbled, 'Even if he was to come looking for me, he might just go to the mine, see it wasn't restored and think I was winding him up. Probably go back to London in a huff and end my contract.'

She let out a big wail.

'Oh, why didn't I just tell him the truth about my father's notes?' Her back against the wall, she slid slowly down. Unaware of the water soaking through the backside of her jeans, she hugged her knees. Rocking back and forth, her eyes closed, for a moment she began to accept that – like for many in centuries past – dying in a Cornish mine was to be her fate.

However, as the cold water started numbing her buttocks and thighs, she yelled out, 'No, it's fucking not going to be,' followed by, 'My phone… the torch in it. Thank God.' Pulling it out of her pocket, she pressed the 'home' button.

The screen didn't light up.

She pressed again… and again… and again. Finally, she threw it at the wall.

'Fucking useless bit of South Korean crap. Why didn't you make the fucking thing waterproof?'

It's fine, I don't need light.

Determined not to give in, she got to her feet.

'No fucking Cornish tin mine's going to beat me, you fucking bastard,' she shouted at the walls. Emptying each wellie of its wet, sludgy contents, she continued, 'I'm going to get out of here and you're not going to stop me.' It was as if the mine were alive. She made another attempt at climbing the rockpile, but – like old-style tent canvas in a downpour – once it had started to leak, there was no way of stopping it; the loosened stone had become a miniature avalanche. A large lump of granite struck her knee.

'Fuck that hurts, you shitbag.'

She took a deep breath. 'Right, plan B,' she said quietly, as if she didn't want the mine to hear. With her hands in front of her to feel her way, she searched for the tunnel entrance. Twice she knocked her helmet where the wall jutted out, before finding what she hoped would be her means of escape. Stooping but not quite crawling, she prepared herself for the climb over the body of the dead miner, a body no bigger than that of a young boy – a boy she had never met and had never known.

A loud crack told her she'd probably stood on part of the skeleton's trunk, perhaps breaking a young, partially grown and calcium-deficient rib cage. She swallowed hard, trying to ignore the thought of what she'd done.

She forced a laugh. 'He died a hundred years ago,' she said, keeping it impersonal. 'He ain't going to be bothered.' However, when she tripped over the feet of Kevern Tregunna and landed on top of his body, her self-induced sense of humour rapidly deflated. Fortunately, his much stronger bone structure had broken her fall.

Putting out a hand to push herself up, she instantly jerked it back.

'Oh my God,' she shrieked. Breaking a bone with the sole of a boot was one thing, but feeling the smooth, roundness of a human skull with her palm was quite different. The undigested chocolate bar shot out her mouth.

Wiping her lips with the back of a grubby hand, she crawled forwards, eventually clearing the oldest of the three Tregunnas. Staying on her hands and knees, she tentatively continued until her lowered head collided with something solid, jarring her neck. She'd made contact with the metal chassis of an ore-carrying wagon. Sarah rolled onto her back. If her life hadn't depended on getting out, she would happily have closed her eyes and drifted into an eternal, defeated sleep.

'Must go on,' she muttered, attempting to stand up. Before she'd reached a stooping position, the back of her helmet struck the roof.

She cursed aloud. 'Fuck, fuck, fuck.'

Despite her helmet both times absorbing most of the shock, she could still feel the onset of a splitting headache. Once again, keeping as low as possible without crawling, she explored the sides of the wagon. Fortunately, but unbeknown to her, when the mine flooded in 1883 – drowning the Tregunnas and those in all levels below – the force of the water had pushed the wagon further off the rails. Had this not happened, there would have been no way past. As it was, the slight gap between wagon and wall was barely wide enough for her to squeeze through; however, fuelled by desperation and adrenaline, after two minutes of manoeuvring her body lengthways whilst lying on her side, she emerged breathless, her anorak scraped and torn. Having had to leave her helmet behind, its hard shell refusing to give or bend past the wagon, her hair was now tangled and matted with mud.

Taking time to catch her wind, she sat motionless. The level of the water had fallen to less than a half-inch deep on the other side of the wagon and, here, it had virtually ceased altogether. Had this been a planned exploratory outing, Sarah would have turned off her lamp and soaked in the atmosphere, imagining what life would have been like for those working by candlelight eight hours a day or more in the cramped and (at times) damp, uncomfortably hot, airless confines of a mine, risking their lives for little reward. However, despite being in darkness, she had no desire for reflection; she had one objective and one only – she had to get out. Getting up on her knees, she felt above her head; the roof was inches above her. Continuing to crawl, within a few yards, she encountered the third Tregunna. There was no swearing no revulsion, just the acceptance of pulling herself over the prone remains of another unknown miner, sacrificed for the successful economy of a country that, at times, had shown little support for the tin and copper industries of Cornwall.

Once over Davith, she avoided bumping into the walls by running her hands gently along the remnants of the rails, hoping to feel any rusted, sharp edges before they tore into her fingers. After roughly five yards of progressing in this way, her senses told her the tunnel had heightened. Cautiously, she got to her feet and felt above her – she could just touch the roof with her fingertips. After continuing for another fifteen minutes, something sharp caught her shin.

Rubbing her leg with one hand, she fumbled in front of her with the other. The object she'd struck was angular like a box, its surface smooth in places, rough in others. On one side of the box she felt a round, hinged lid. It reminded her of a porthole on a boat. The hole it fitted into was lined with floppy rubber. Exploring it with both hands, she found two knobs.

'Yes,' she cried out. 'Thank you, God.'

TWENTY-EIGHT

2nd June 2011

THE AMERICANS
THE HUNG, DRAWN &
QUARTERED

'Welcome, gentlemen, what can I get for you?'

Mason and Charlie responded gratefully to the warm greeting given by the petite, blue-eyed, twenty-something barmaid with long, auburn hair. The chatter had ceased the moment they'd walked in. Her question broke the tension.

'Two pints of your best English cask ale and two lagers please,' ordered Charlie.

'Certainly.' She reached for a pair of pint glasses on a shelf behind her. 'We only have the one ale now, I'm afraid,' she apologised.

'No worries. As long as it's wet,' said Mason. 'It might be raining, but my throat's like the Mojave Desert.'

It was obvious from the barmaid's expression that she had little knowledge of America's geography.

'Sorry, ignore him,' apologised Charlie. 'He's just an asshole... sorry... I mean...'

She smiled. 'That's all right, I work in a pub, not in a convent.'

She placed the two beers in front of them. 'And two lagers?' She glanced at where Grace and Lily were sitting, busily scanning through a handwritten menu. 'Is that pints or halves?'

'Pints, please; they're pretty dry on the inside,' confirmed Charlie grinning. He frowned. 'Does it always rain like this in England?' he asked; his native drawl was less pronounced than his brother's.

'It's the first rain we've had in ages. I shan't be a moment; the lager's in the other bar.' She disappeared through an open archway behind her.

Mason was peering cautiously around. Conversations had started up again amongst the dozen or so people sitting at tables. 'What the fuck?' he whispered to Charlie.

'I know. It's weird, bro. What with the pitted road and the emptiness of the village, and yet...' He nodded at the customers, 'how did they all get here? There's no cars outside.'

'Parked out the back?' suggested Mason.

'Possibly, I suppose, but...' Charlie stopped as the barmaid returned with the lagers. She put them on the counter. 'Would you like to start a tab? I see your friends are absorbed in the menu.'

'Yes, please, we could do with some brunch... I mean food,' Mason replied.

She huffed. 'I may live in the sticks, but I think most people know what you're talking about,' she said, unimpressed by his patronising. 'Excuse me.' Another customer was holding a menu and seeking to order. She tutted as she turned away. 'Americans.'

It went unheard by the brothers.

After carrying the drinks to the table, the brothers pulled up two stools. Before either of them had time to express their thoughts about the beer, Grace thrust a menu in front of them.

'Look at this,' she instructed. 'Look at the choice of food; it's crazy.'

Mason read aloud. 'Cheddar cheese ploughman's. What the fuck's that?'

Grace thumped the next line on the menu with her index finger. 'Hot or cold homemade Cornish pasty, and not much else unless you like ham and salad.' She took a long draw on her lager. 'Somebody please tell me this is a dream and...' she grimaced, as her taste buds had registered the flavour. 'And the English call our lager gnat's piss. Who the fuck drinks this?' She slammed her glass on the table. 'C'mon, I've had enough; let's go.'

As she stood up, she looked around at the other customers. Those who were eating appeared more than happy with their pasties, or their cheese and granary bread on a plate.

'Calm down, Grace; it'll be fine,' reassured Lily, touching her friend's arm. 'You're getting worked up over nothing. If you like, I'll get a dash of lime in your lager and at least let's have some nuts, if nothing else.'

Lily's comforting words had the desired effect, and – three-quarters of an hour and three pints later – they'd all relaxed. The quality of the cheddar ploughman's had surprised even Grace.

'Not bad for a bit of bread and old cheese.' She smiled. 'Okay, I admit I overreacted, but I still don't feel right. Something is a little bit weird.'

'Weird, my dear? What do you mean by weird?' They hadn't seen the short, wiry, bald-headed man with the tousled beard approach their table. Although – judging by his time-wrinkled face – he was probably in his fifties, the black hair of his beard and his piercing, blue eyes suggested someone much younger. He was carrying three chutney-soiled, plain-white plates, cutlery and used, bright-red napkins, so Charlie guessed he was the landlord.

'Er, hi.' Charlie sensed his face had turned the same colour as the napkins. 'We, um… well, we were a little surprised at the name of the pub.' He didn't feel the lack of food choice was the right topic for discussion at this awkward moment. Although the man had spoken softly, his serious expression and rigid posture implied he might not be the sort to upset. However, much to the four's relief, Charlie's comment extracted an immediate encouraging smile.

'Oh, that; I thought you were talking about me.' A hearty laugh followed. 'That was my idea after trade virtually ceased overnight. More intriguing than The Miner's Arms, don't you think?'

Their expressions told him they didn't.

'Ah, well, not to worry.' His shoulders visibly relaxed. 'Anyway, Tristan Mawgan at your service.'

'May I ask why you chose it?' enquired Grace, less unperturbed than the others by the landlord's presence. 'I mean, it's not very tasteful, if you don't mind me saying.'

He laughed again. 'You're welcome to say what you like, my dear. As far as I know, it's still a free country, same as yours, I expect. American, aren't we?'

Charlie nodded.

'Thought so. We don't get any visitors these days. We're too far off the beaten track.' He turned back to Grace. 'Look, I'm too old and thick skinned to be upset by a simple question to which there is a simple answer.' He nodded at the empty, hoop-backed, black, wooden chair at the end of the table. 'Mind if I join you? I'll explain everything.' Not waiting for an answer, he put the plates on the bar counter and sat down. It was now after 2pm, but, as yet, none of the other customers had left. Before the landlord had time to speak, Grace noticed three of the male customers had lit up and were openly smoking roll-ups. She immediately let the landlord know her feelings.

'Why are they smoking? I thought it wasn't allowed in your country. Are you going to have a word?' As an only child, she'd been used to getting her own way, and if there was something she didn't like, then she expected it to be dealt with.

Glancing cautiously over his shoulder, the landlord dragged his seat closer in. He leaned towards them and spoke in lowered tones.

'It's all right, nobody from the council or whatever enforcing authority's responsible ever comes out here to check whether we're smoke free or not. If you ask me, it's a load of old rubbish, anyway. It used to do more harm to your lungs walking up the village street and breathing in all those exhaust fumes.' Once more, he enjoyed a hearty laugh. Holding up the palms of his hands in front of him, he shook his head. 'Sorry... sorry. There I go again. Moaning about the traffic. Perhaps I should have been a traffic cop.' He sensed his new customers weren't amused. 'Look, I'm sorry if you don't like the smoke, but if I banned everyone from enjoying a cigarette or two, I'd lose a load of my regulars.'

'It's that bad?' asked Charlie. He was quite taken by this cheerful, welcoming man.

'There's no need to feel sorry for me, young man; we manage all right, thanks. We don't offer much, but what we do offer we do well...' He paused, hoping to receive their agreement. It came from Lily, Mason and Charlie, but not from Grace, who merely shrugged. 'Oh well, more important things than happy customers,' quipped the landlord, untroubled by her reaction. 'Now then, where was I? Ah yes, I was about to tell you why trade fell so rapidly.'

His voice dropped to a whisper.

'You see, it all began about twenty years ago; strangely enough, after the village experienced one of the worst storms in its history, much worse than today's and I should know. Until then, the village was buoyant and received far more than its fair share of tourists, or at least ones who couldn't understand a thirty mile an hour speed limit wasn't a target.' He roared with laughter. 'Sorry, I shouldn't keep going on about my bugbears.'

Controlling his outburst, he continued, 'The river flooded, giving rise to our water supply becoming contaminated via a broken pipe. The utility company took three weeks to replace it, then allegedly made a horrendous error: it poured a chemical – some sulphate, or something or other – into the filtration unit, which caused no end of health problems. The council tried to keep it quiet, and, of course, the company said people would recover and there were no long-term effects, but it appears it might have been wrong. Elderly residents died and kids grew up deformed. Houses became empty, as nobody wanted to buy them, and then... well, properties deteriorated until eventually only the pub survived. The village became a tourist attraction – a bit of a curiosity – and trade was good.'

'And then?' asked Mason. 'You said trade fell overnight.' He was fascinated by the landlord's story and was eager to learn more.

The landlord's head cocked to one side. As if trying to read their minds, he studied each of them in turn. After a few seconds, he added, 'But then the curse took hold.'

'Oh, here we go,' interrupted Grace, sitting back. 'The good old "dreaded curse", probably medieval and guaranteed to bring people in.' She didn't make friends easily; something Charlie had needed to learn to deal with and accept.

'Grace, don't be so damn rude,' snapped Lily, embarrassed by her companion's lack of respect.

The landlord held up his hand. 'That's all right, my dear; I'm not offended. I don't expect your country's civilised history is old enough to have such things,' he said sarcastically. 'All I can tell you is what has been passed down through centuries, from one generation to the next. You either choose to believe or you don't; however, whichever choice you make, the ending's the same.' He lifted an arm towards the other customers. 'Does it look as though the curse is inundating us with business? Steady? Yes. Inundated? No.'

'Where do your customers park?' asked Charlie, a question

he'd been desperate to ask. 'I mean there's no cars outside.'

Any sign of a smile immediately disappeared from the landlord's face, being replaced instead by half-closed eyes and partially clenched teeth. His expression caused Lily to hunch her shoulders and she felt a tiny release of wee. She could never have known that, in a few hours' time, her whole bladder would uncontrollably empty.

The landlord stood up. He looked out the window, studied the water splashing and bouncing back off the windowsill. Without turning, he said, 'And you also have no car?'

'That's right,' replied Lily. 'We came by scooter looking for Wheal Hingston. We had a slight—'

'But we left them the other side of the river,' interrupted Charlie, cutting off Lily deliberately. 'We thought it best, just in case we couldn't get them back across.'

'Very sensible, young man. If the river floods, then nothing can get through. It's the only road out of the village, you know.' His manner had lost all of its friendliness. He stroked his beard, with his back still towards them. 'Wheal Hingston, you say. Why would you want to go there?'

'Mason and I are related to one of the nineteenth-century owners... er... Josiah Pendeen.'

The mention of the Pendeen name caused the landlord to raise his eyebrows. 'Pendeen, you say... hmm, interesting.'

'And we'd like to see where he worked,' continued Charlie. 'Can you tell us where the mine is?'

'Oh, yes, I can tell you, but I think it best you don't visit.'

Grace had taken enough of the landlord's strange demeanour and was ready to leave. Also, the continuous dripping from the blocked gutters was beginning to irritate her, as was the smoke, which had seemingly formed an opaque, milky fog around their table. 'Why?' she asked.

'Because it was badly affected by the curse. Men and boys died there. Tunnels were flooded.'

'What, you think it's going to kill us as well?' sneered Grace. 'Don't be so ridiculous.'

'Yeah, it sounds like just the sort of place,' agreed Mason. 'Might try and see if we can find the shaft – imagine looking down that.'

The landlord swung round. All the time he'd been talking, the barmaid had been watching him from where she was sitting on a barstool on the public side of the counter. He caught her eye.

He picked up their empty glasses. Lifting the counter flap, he nodded to the barmaid and then took his leave through the open door. A few seconds later, the barmaid followed him.

'I've had enough of this crap,' snapped Mason, pushing his chair back and knocking it against the wall. 'I'm going to the john.' He stormed off in the direction of the gents.

Just as he reached the bar's rear exit, the landlord returned. He was calm and spoke quietly. 'The rain's still heavy, and there's been a couple of flashes of lightning. The weather forecast on the internet says it's set in for the rest of the day and night. It's not going to improve until the morning.'

Mason shrugged. 'So?'

'So, young man, you and your pals are welcome to stay here tonight – free of charge; that is, provided you pay for an evening meal. There's a wider menu in the evenings.' He flashed his eyes at the ceiling. 'Room nine's free, as is room five. I might as well have someone in them keeping them aired, rather than left empty.' He started unloading the tray of washed glasses he'd brought in from the lounge bar.

Mason studied him suspiciously. 'I'm sorry, but why would you do that?'

'It's up to you. No skin off my nose, whatever you decide.' The tray empty, he made his way back to the lounge. 'Let me know,' he shouted as he disappeared.

Mason changed his mind about visiting the gents. The offer had struck him as generous – having the chance to spend a night free of charge in a pub didn't come along often. He glanced around the room. People were still drinking, some smoking, but none taking a blind bit of notice of him. *Oh well*, he thought, *I'd better let the others know.* He walked back to the table.

'And you think he was serious?' asked Grace.

She and Lily looked a lot more relaxed. When Mason had headed to the gents, they'd asked Charlie to get them another drink. He was about to get up.

'I think so.' Mason grinned. 'One catch, though.'

'Which is?' asked Lily.

'We have to pay for an evening meal.' He saw Grace's face drop. 'There's a more extensive menu apparently, so it's not all bad. What do you think, Charlie?'

'Might as well,' he replied. 'There's no point in getting soaked.' He looked at Lily. 'Are you up for it?' He pointed to the window. 'It's pretty dark out there. If it carries on like this, it'll be a helluva ride back.'

'The landlord said the weather's in for the night. There'll be more lightning as well,' added Mason. 'Anyway, whilst you think about it, let's get those drinks.' Charlie got up to give him a hand.

'What can I get you?' asked the barmaid.

'Er, two pints of bitter, please, a pint of lager and lime, and…' He turned to Lily. 'What are you having, love?'

'Gin and tonic, please; a large one. I feel a bit queasy – the quinine might settle my stomach.'

'More likely the gin will numb your stomach,' chortled Grace. 'Tell you what, Mason, I'll have one too, please.'

'Cancel the lager, please, and make it two large gin and tonics with lime.'

'Sorry, sir, we don't have any fresh limes or lemons. We have cordial or cucumber though.'

Mason's eyebrows shot up. *Really? What sort of pub do you call this?* Fortunately, the words didn't leave his mouth. 'Okay, cucumber's fine, thank you.' Out of the corner of his eye, he saw Charlie also looking somewhat puzzled. The barmaid set two pints of beer in front of Mason, and vanished into the other bar carrying two tumblers. Mason glanced up at the half full Plymouth Gin bottle on the optic. 'Why couldn't she had used that?' he muttered to Charlie.

'God knows. Perhaps the better stuff's in the other bar.'

'Shall I put them on the tab?' she asked when she came back with the drinks. 'I understand you're staying with us tonight.'

'Um… well… er, yes. We haven't actually decided,' replied Charlie.

'Well, I'm keen, Charles me old boy, and I'm sure once the girls get these down their throats…' Mason picked up the two tumblers, 'they'll be just as keen as well.'

'Well, that's decided,' said the barmaid. 'I'll tell cook so she can ensure there's something special on the menu. 'Oh, and you'd better take these.' She dusted off two, small Schweppes tonic water bottles with a cloth bar mat. 'Sorry, we've only got slimline, I'm afraid. I hope that's all right.'

'I'm sure it'll be fine, thanks, and, yes, please put them on a tab,' confirmed Mason. Placing the tumblers on their table, he returned for the mixers.

'That's different… nice though.' Grace was the first to take a sip of her gin and tonic. 'I wonder what gin it is.'

'I can't help, but will ask when we have another,' replied Charlie. 'So that's it, we're all agreed we're staying then? Lily and Mason in room nine, and Grace and me in room five?'

'Cheers.' Mason raised his glass. 'Here's to a dry night, on the outside that is.'

Grace was twiddling her empty tonic bottle around in her hand as she responded. 'Cheers,' she said. Taking a large pull on her drink, she frowned. 'That's strange.'

'What is darling?' asked Charlie.

'The best-before date on the tonic bottle is June 2009: two years ago.'

'It's only a guide, Grace; it's not going to poison you.' Charlie had downed three-quarters of his pint and was now in the mood for a party.

'I didn't say it would, but two years out of date?' queried Grace.

'Perhaps they got stuck on the back of the shelf,' suggested Mason. 'Anyway, not to worry. As we're staying, how about a couple of shots to give us an appetite?'

'It doesn't seem like the sort of place to serve them, a bit straight-laced if you ask me.' Grace nodded towards the other customers, who were still supping, despite never seeming to buy more drinks. 'They're all on bottled beer or wine by the looks of it.'

'I'll ask,' acknowledged Mason.

The barmaid flashed Mason an apologetic smile. 'Sorry, sir we don't have any shot glasses. I could put some vodka in small sherry glasses if that would do.'

'Sounds good,' he replied. 'Oh, by the way, do you have free Wi-Fi, as I can't get a mobile signal?'

She shook her head. 'Sorry, again. We used to, but after a recent storm we lost the connection and the landlord never bothered to get it sorted. We weren't really using the internet anyway.'

'Okay, not to worry. Just wanted to catch up on the tide times – we're big surfers, and we wanted to plan for tomorrow; that is, assuming we ever get out of this place.' He saw her quizzical expression. 'The weather, I meant; provided it stops raining. It is England, after all.'

'Yes, of course.' She looked relieved. 'I'll get your drinks – oh, and I'll need you to sign the register.'

* * *

They'd had a couple more shots and then decided to have a break before dinner, the effects of the alcohol beginning to raise their voices. Even so, none of the other customers had shown any irritation or annoyance.

The girl had given them their keys and led them to their rooms.

'Dinner's at seven. You're the only ones in tonight, so if

you're happy to eat then, it would help us.' As she prepared to close room five's door, she asked if there was anything else she could get Charlie and Grace.

'No, we're fine, thanks,' replied Grace, Charlie having already headed to the loo. She glanced at her watch; it said 5.30pm. 'See you in an hour and a half.' The door closed.

The room had a four-poster bed. The fresh, white walls and ceiling; bright-red, velvet curtains; and red, plush Axminster wool carpet all added to the cosiness offered by the antique, feather-mattress bed.

She switched on the television mounted on a swing bracket on the wall and swung the screen towards her. After fiddling with the remote for a few seconds, she shouted to her boyfriend. 'Will you come and look at this, please? I can't get a picture.'

Charlie appeared from the en suite wearing just his grey Calvin Klein underpants. 'What's the matter?'

'I told you, I can't get a picture. It's like a snow scene.'

'Perhaps the aerial's not plugged in.' He checked the wall socket. Pushing the silver plug he announced it was in as far as it would go. 'Here, give me the damn control.'

Sitting back on the bed, he pointed the remote at the TV. 'It's probably broken, judging by all the dust on these buttons.' He pressed each one. Although the screen flashed a couple of times, no picture or sound resulted. He threw the remote on the floor and patted the bedding.

'C'mon Grace, there's something much better to do than lie here watching TV.' He laid back, his hands behind his head. 'You know how much I like it when you're drunk.'

'I don't know. My head feels a bit weird; too many shots.

The gin hit me like a logging truck; it went straight to my legs.'

'You don't need legs if you're on the bed.' Charlie felt inebriated and, if he were honest, would also have said his head felt weird, as if he'd smoked one helluva spliff. However, it hadn't stopped the front of his pants bulging. He patted the bed again. 'I'll do all the work if you want. You can just lie there and think of England, as the Brits say.' He grinned. 'C'mon, you know you want to.' He slipped off his pants. 'Look at this bad boy. He's been very naughty and could do with a good seeing too.'

She pulled her blue t-shirt over her head, with her raised arms lifting what Charlie called her magnificent breasts. She may only measure thirty-four inches around her chest, but a good part of that measurement was taken up with boobs and outstanding nipples. Dropping her shirt on the floor, her sports bra maintained its support as she lowered her arms and eased her thumbs under the elasticated waistband of her shorts. As soon as she stepped out of them and stood at the end of the bed in her briefs and bra, her sexual desire overruled any feelings posed by her woozy head.

'Okay, but I'll dictate what we do.' She knew her comment would make Charlie's erect cock twitch. He loved her taking control.

'Yes, miss, whatever you say, miss. I promise not to move; at least, not just yet.'

'Spread your legs,' she ordered.

As Charlie stretched them as far apart as comfortable, she reached behind her back and undid her bra. His cock twitched again, desperate for some attention. Charlie's half-closed eyes were fixed on hers as she rested one knee on the bed. Slowly lifting herself up on the other, she eased forwards. He saw the dampness on the front of her panties, and he wanted to touch her, to explore her, but he knew that, until she said otherwise, feeling her was not permitted. Licking her lips, she lowered her mouth onto his cock. He gasped as her tongue licked the back of the glans.

God, she is so damn good, he thought to himself, fighting the desire to fondle her breasts.

Pushing down gently, she took him deeper, working up and down the length of his shaft. Once she sensed he was on the verge of coming, he knew she would finally allow him to touch her body. He wouldn't enter her immediately, but would caress and enjoy her moistness. She would tell him when she wanted him. He wasn't massive, but his technique of controlled, side-to-side thrusting was more than enough to bring her to multiple orgasms. However, today, their lovemaking wouldn't reach the penetration stage.

Her teeth gripping him tightly, he screamed. Grabbing her shoulders, he pushed her away. 'What the fuck are you doing?' he yelled. 'Are you trying to bite my cock off?'

'I'm sorry.' She knelt back on her heels. 'I don't feel very well… I think I'm going to pass…' Head first, she fell backwards off the end of the bed, the thickness of the carpet breaking her fall.

* * *

As soon as Lily had entered room nine, she'd began giggling and kissing Mason's face. Mason had been a hardened drinker from the age of thirteen, and, whilst alcohol made him noisy and clumsy, it would take far more than what he'd drunk to lose total control of his mind.

He gently loosened his girlfriend's embraces.

'In a minute, Lily; I need time to think.' He lay on the bed, his hands behind his head. It wasn't a four-poster, but – like Charlie and Grace's room – the walls were painted white, and the carpet and curtains were bright red. 'I'm sure he said, "According to the internet," and that "Rooms five and nine are empty," as if… as if the others were taken. And yet the barmaid said, "The internet's broken," and when she showed us the room she told us, "Dinner's at seven. You're the only ones in tonight, so if you're happy to eat then, it would help us."'

Lily had no interest in what had been said. She jumped on the bed beside him, and began undoing the buttons on the front of his shorts. He didn't resist, but his mind was elsewhere. Unlike Grace, Lily was usually happy to let her boyfriend take the initiative, but – right at this moment – she felt remarkably horny and wanted him inside her. Also, unlike Grace, she didn't need any sort of bra – let alone a sports bra – to keep her breasts from swaying side to side, and bouncing painfully up and down when they'd negotiated the potholed lane on the scooters. Her pale-yellow polo shirt was hauled in an ungainly way over her long, blonde hair; she lay on her back, before lifting both legs in the air. Once she'd manoeuvred her matching shorts over her hips, down her thighs and calves, and kicked them off with her feet, she stood over him.

'Mason, look at me; don't you fancy some of this?' She

was cupping her breasts in her hands, attempting to make them jiggle. At last, she got through to her partner. He shook his head and smiled.

'I think you need a lot more than that to get a wobble on; perhaps you should try wearing some tassels.'

'What, and stick them onto these pert little things?' She'd pushed her breasts together and was tantalizingly squeezing her nipples; they were hardening and so was Mason's cock.

'Come here, you gorgeous hunk of womanhood.' He reached up towards her, just as she collapsed on top of him. 'Get off; stop playing games.'

Lily didn't move.

'I said get off, Lily – your tit's in my face, and I can hardly breathe.'

Still she didn't move.

'Lily… Lily… are you okay?' Mason managed to shift her to one side. He shook her.

'Lily… Lily… wake up.' He shook her harder.

'Holy shit, Lily.'

Kneeling up, he put his ear to her chest. She was breathing. 'Thank fuck for that.'

Tears welled up in his eyes. He shook her again, then decided she was best put in the recovery position, something he'd done with many a surfer and swimmer.

He saw her bladder had emptied. 'I knew I shouldn't have let you drink so much, you… you stupid bitch.' He wanted to pull off the sodden duvet, but he was too tired. He kissed her forehead and stretched out beside her.

* * *

Mason was lying on his stomach when he woke up two hours later. Feeling groggy, he put it down to blood sugar levels sent haywire by the beer and vodka. The unfamiliar bed didn't help. Lily was still asleep beside him.

Rolling gently over onto his back so as not to wake her, he rubbed his eyes.

'Shit,' he exclaimed, checking his watch. 'Dinner.'

He swung his legs over the side, shook his head and unsteadily got to his feet. He could hear the rain pounding the window. Intending to draw the curtains, he noticed a heavy goods truck parked outside. Three men were loading a beer keg into the back of the truck, whilst to his left another man was on a ladder removing the swinging pub sign. From the porch entrance a woman, whom Mason recognised as the barmaid, emerged carrying empty, blue-plastic bread trays. She passed them to one of the men in the truck.

What the…? He thought.

Pulling the curtains across, he turned to Lily – she was still asleep. He opened the bedroom door.

The narrow corridor was empty. The only light came from the top of the stairs, some six or seven yards to his right. Opposite was the door to room eight and to his left, the end wall of the pub. He stepped out onto the wooden floorboards. Room five was no more than eight paces away. He walked over to the door.

'Charlie,' he whispered. 'Open up… it's me.' He knocked lightly. 'Charlie… Grace.'

Bastards must have gone down for dinner without us.

He tried the brass doorknob – it turned. He didn't need to push the door fully open to see that his brother and his girlfriend hadn't decided to eat without them; Grace lay in her underwear on the floor at the foot of the bed, whilst Charlie was naked on his back on top of the covers. Dried blood covered his groin.

What the hell?

His life saving training had taught him not to panic, but his immediate natural reaction was to yell for help. However, before any sound had chance to leave his mouth, he remembered what he'd seen out of the window.

It's them who's caused this. They've drugged us. Didn't want us to see what's going on.

He knelt down beside Grace, checked she was breathing. Once he'd confirmed they were both still alive, he sat on the edge of bed. He thought about wiping the blood off Charlie, but, as it had already congealed, he decided to leave it until he could clean up the wound with a sterile wipe.

There must be a first aid kit downstairs, probably in the kitchen.

Mason cautiously opened the bedroom door just far enough to check he was still alone. It was also just far enough for the fist belonging to an unseen assailant to strike him squarely on the chin; his legs having no time to inform his brain they'd been rendered incapable of providing support, Mason crashed to the ground.

TWENTY-NINE

4th June 2013

SARAH

Certain the metal object that she'd bumped into was a washing machine, her spirits had immediately lifted. Also, running her fingertips over the casing and finding only a small area was rusty, lifted them even higher. She had reached the shaft, but not only had she reached it, the rubbish that had been dumped in it over the years had filled it to her level. The lack of rust on the washing machine must mean it hadn't been there long, which in turn must surely mean that – please God – the top of the shaft must still be open.

Keeping her head low, slowly but deliberately, she clambered over the machine. Standing on what she guessed were other bits of worn out appliances and scrap metal, she tentatively stretched up. Her hand made contact with nothing but air. She wanted to shout, but it was too soon to celebrate. Even if she was in the shaft and not in a stope, there was no guarantee that the top was open. Standing on something soft, she closed her eyes, then unhurriedly bent her neck backwards as far as she could without losing balance. Her palms pressed together, she opened her eyes.

'Please, please, please. Please let there be light, God,' she whispered, as if in church.

There was, but it was the smallest of specks. There was no way she could tell whether it was small because it was shining through a tiny hole not many feet above, which in her heart she knew was most unlikely, or whether it was small because it was tens of yards away. However, whichever it was, it was light and it gave her hope: hope that she would get out, hope that she would live to party and hope that her story would be a big hit with a tabloid. It could be so good that they might even let her write her own headline:

EXCLUSIVE
GIRL CHEATS DEATH IN CORNISH MINE
BY SARAH JENKINSON

Needs more work, she thought to herself, *but it's a start, and think of the money.*

However much she might get paid, it was utterly pointless unless she got out.

'Right, Big G, I now need a ladder that's still fixed to the wall and has few rungs missing – can you help?' she said quietly.

* * *

Sarah had never considered herself religious. At her mother's insistence, she'd had to go to Sunday school until age eleven, but after that her parents had told her it was up to her to decide whether she continued to go to church as a teenager. Fortunately for Sarah, neither her mum nor her dad were bothered when she opted out. Five years later, when her parents split up, her mother told her the real reason she'd insisted on her only child's regular Sunday school attendance: it meant she could spend time in bed with her husband. Sarah hadn't found this confession funny at the time, but – as she grew up and explored a sex life of her own – she often looked back and had a good laugh. Now, in the darkness, opting back in to enlist help from the only being she thought could save her seemed perfectly natural and guilt free.

* * *

Yes, you little beauty.

Still fixed to the inside of the shaft were the remains of an iron ladder. She gave it a hard tug – it stayed firm. Stretching to the highest rung she could reach, she pulled herself up – it supported her weight.

Easy does it, girl; there's no rush. The adit can't be far above. Even if I only get that far, it'll provide a way out.

She'd failed to notice that the level along which she crawled had sloped down towards the shaft. Had she done so, she would have known the depth between it and the adit above would have steadily increased; the adit's incline being opposite to that of the level.

She raised her right leg and felt for the rung with the ball of her foot. Once located, she lifted her left foot onto the rung above. Gradually, she started to climb. The ladder was perpendicular; scaling it in the dry jeans and thick jumper she'd worn for warmth would have been difficult enough, but – like the miners before her – sodden clothing and a tired body made it far more challenging. After just a dozen rungs, she put an arm through one and used the crook of her elbow to support herself whilst she rested.

She was tempted to kick off her wellingtons, as their open tops kept catching, but her socks would have provided little or no protection against the rusted sharpness of the ladder's slimy metal. She allowed herself roughly five minutes before continuing. She looked up; the speck of light appeared no nearer.

Got to keep going… mustn't give up… it's the only way.

Another ten rungs, another rest, then another six before she screamed as she fell backwards down the shaft. The ladder had pulled away from its fixing.

'Oomph,' she cried as the air exited her lungs. 'Oh my God, that hurt.' It wasn't an attack on her 'hoped for' saviour. Whilst the majority of her body had landed on the same soft material she'd stood on before starting her bid for freedom, her ankle had struck part of the dumped machinery. Immediately, she realised she couldn't move her toes. She burst into tears. A minute later, she passed out.

* * *

When she was awake, she was determined not to give up, not lie back and die, but whilst asleep the reality of her situation filled her dreams. She saw the unlikelihood of an escape, and foresaw her death, her destiny decided by someone much more powerful than her: someone who'd ignored her plea for help.

When she woke, not knowing whether the speck of light above was from the sun or the moon meant nothing to her. The only thing that mattered was how she was going to get out. She sat up and began taking off her right boot. Ignoring the tears running down her cheeks, she eventually managed to ease it free, as the swollen ankle had resisted its release. She didn't need to work in the medical profession to tell the break was serious – the fingers of her right hand were sufficient for that. She mouthed the words, 'Oh fuck.' Two seconds later, she repeated the same words; however, this time they reverberated in the mine's atmosphere.

Sitting with her legs out straight in front of her, she'd put her hands on the ground behind her for support. One of them settled on something round and like a tenpin bowling ball, it had holes for the fingers. It didn't take long for her to discover it also had teeth. Turning onto her side, she scraped the damp, soft material from around the skull and found it was still attached to a neck and shoulders. An hour or so ago she would have screamed and ran; however, even if she had been able to use her legs to get away, she was now numb to further emotion and over reaction.

Scraping the skull free, she recognised that what had provided her soft landing was earth, possibly earth that had been thrown down to cover the body and hide it from the most powerful of search-party torches shone from above.

It occurred to her that the same might happen to her; not as a deliberate act of concealment, but one of the innocent dumping of garden rubbish, old tyres and worn out machinery, meaning her lifeless body may never be found. Trying to put the thought out of her mind, she rubbed the skinless, bald head of what she believed to be her only companion.

I wonder why it's here?

She sniggered.

'It'; I'm calling it, 'it'. How rude and remiss.

'Sincere apologies, sir or madam,' she said to the skull. 'You are not an it, you are a she like me or a he like... like... Eth... Ethan.'

Why the fuck didn't I tell him where I was going?

Her eyes began to well up, but, before a tear had chance to start its journey, she began screaming hysterically.

'No, no, no God; no, no, please, no,' she yelled. On top of everything that had happened to her, she was now confronted by her biggest, and perhaps only, phobia. 'Please, please, no.'

A rat had run over her bare ankle. She knew it was a rat; she could tell from the way its clawed paws felt on her skin. It was the same feeling she'd had when the Treherne twin boys had held her down when she was seven years old, and their older sister had put her pet rat on her face. She'd fought tooth and nail to knock it off by shaking her head, but the rat had clung on, as if it, too, was enjoying the bullying. Finally, it had lost interest and scooted away, but – although released by her assailants – she'd remained motionless on the tarmac surface of the school playground, traumatised, her pants wet. Scared of being picked on again, she'd told her teacher she'd fallen over. She didn't mention she'd wet herself, so by the time she got home, the tops of her thighs were chafed and sore. What wouldn't she give for it to be chaffing this time and not a broken ankle?

'Get off... get off, you fucking bastard. Haven't I got enough to cope with?' she bawled, tears flowing freely. Fortunately, the rat didn't belong to the Treherne girl and, as quickly as it had appeared, it was gone. Her eyes closed, her palms together, she turned once again to her unseen saviour. 'Thank you, but please tell me what I do now.'

There was no reply.

THIRTY

2nd June 2011

THE AMERICANS
THE HUNG, DRAWN &
QUARTERED

'So, what do you suggest? We can't let them go,' said the man, with the hood of his full-length, shiny, black, satin cloak covering part of his face.

'I don't know. I was not the one who said that benzodiazepine and strong alcohol would knock them all out and destroy their memories,' said the second, his face also partially covered by the hood of a black cloak.

'Which is what I was led to believe,' admitted the third hooded figure, 'so I could not have known that, for one of them, the dose would not be strong enough.'

The generator having been switched off, the three were sitting in candlelight at a table in the public bar of The Hung,

Drawn & Quartered. Apart from the four bound-and-gagged bodies still unconscious upstairs, they were alone, all other 'guests' having left on the lorry.

'They must be disposed of – we have no choice. If the one who woke up reveals our purpose, then all will be lost,' said the man who had spoken first.

'He may not have seen anything,' said the second.

'We cannot take that risk,' said the third. 'Nor can we allow them to poke their noses into the mine.'

'And how would we do it?' asked the second to have spoken. The first two turned to the third – the one in the well-filled, red, velvet cloak.

'Like our forebears before us, for that is our calling,' replied the one in red.

'You mean a trial and if found guilty… death?' asked the first. The third nodded.

'But what are they accused of?' asked the second. 'It was by accident that they stumbled on our assembly. They have not done anything wrong. No… no, that's not going to happen.'

'That is for us to decide,' dismissed the third.

'But… but you cannot; it is unfair,' protested the second.

'So what is your suggested alternative? We let them go free?' asked the third.

The two others fell silent.

'In that case, let us proceed,' stated the third.

'What?' exclaimed the second. 'You are prepared to go ahead without having the defendants present? What kind of fair trial is that?'

'You are beginning to tire me,' snapped the third. 'If you are unhappy, then you must leave.'

After a moment's hesitation, the second replied, 'I will stay, but let it be noted that I objected to this indiscretion.'

'Then let us begin,' instructed the third. 'Read out their names.'

Holding the guest book, the first read out the names of the four Americans. 'Charlie White and his brother Mason White, who are both descendants of mine owner Josiah Pendeen; Grace Brown, heritage unknown; and Lily Taylor, heritage also unknown.

'How do the defendants plead?' asked the third, who was acting as judge.

'Not guilty, Honourable Judge,' declared the first.

'That is impossible,' replied the Judge. 'The four came here uninvited. They are at least guilty of trespass. I therefore commit them all to be executed.'

The second jumped up. 'That's ridiculous, preposterous even. You're not serious? I mean, surely you can't be suggesting we turn to killing just because we've been discovered?'

'But it is not just their discovery of us,' asserted the Judge. 'If the one who may have seen us talks to others, as he no doubt will, it will bring many here and, eventually, it will threaten that which we have fought to protect.'

'Fought to protect? We haven't done any fighting. Don't talk such poppycock.' The second's voice was raised. 'There's nothing we could do about it, anyway. It's not ours to keep.'

'Then why did you join us?' the first asked, his voice calm.

'Because of history and tradition, not to commit cold-blooded murder,' blurted the second. 'When I returned alone from Australia having seen what families from our great county had done for that nation, I was proud – proud to be Cornish – and I wanted to maintain our county's identity.'

'But not proud enough to kill to protect it?' asked the Judge.

'Of course not – why would anybody? And who gives you the right to sentence others to death? You're just like the rest of us, not some superior being.' He turned to the first. 'Are you going to listen to this, and take this… this… crap? Is it you who will be executioner?'

The first did not reply.

'I thought not,' sneered the second. 'You're no different to me. Poncing around in a cloak is one thing, but playing the Grim Reaper… no.'

'Enough,' shouted the Judge, standing up. 'If you are not with us, then you must leave now.'

Under the cover of the hood, the second was surprised. He'd not expected expulsion. 'But… but… but how will I return? The river is in flood and the truck will not be back until dawn. With my prosthetic leg, I cannot walk to the bridge.' He shook his head. 'Come on, you're not serious about killing… are you?'

The silence of the other two told him they were.

'Oh for fucks' sake. Enough of these games.' He threw back his hood, revealing the face of a man in his sixties, his skin weather-beaten, his fair hair cut short. 'I have no intention of leaving until I have transport.'

'Then I will have to assist you,' said the Judge.

The second man had no time to avoid the blade of the twelve-inch dagger the Judge drew from under the long, red cloak. The tip tore through the second man's throat, ripping an inch-deep, six-inch-wide gash. Blood spurted over the table as the man, wide eyed, his jaw drooping, stared in total disbelief at the Judge. He slapped his right hand to the wound, trying to stem the flow of thick, metallic-smelling liquid. His mouth made a gurgling sound as he sucked blood into his lungs. In an attempt to prevent himself from falling, his left hand grabbed the back of his chair. Although only staying upright for a few seconds before his knees buckled, it was long enough to catch the eye of the first man whose hood had lifted when he'd leapt back in surprise at the Judge's action, revealing a thin, gaunt face with a thick, manicured moustache and thinning dark hair.

In between his bouts of gurgling, the second man managed four words. 'How could you let…?' he pleaded. His question unfinished, he crashed to the floor.

'What the hell have you done?' asked the first man, keeping his distance from the Judge.

'It was necessary; the same as it is necessary to carry out the sentence on the four upstairs,' the Judge replied.

* * *

Light from the rising sun shone through the gaps in the canvas top of the ex-military Leyland Daf truck. It's 5.9 litre engine roared as it splashed through the ford, deeper than usual after the heavy rain. The hard suspension did little to cushion the blows of the tyres as they thumped through the potholes, causing four of the five occupants laying in the back to roll violently around, at times crashing against the solid metal legs of the side seats. However, the fifth felt no pain and unlike the other four, had not been gagged and bound.

Still drugged, Charlie, Grace and Lily had been wrapped in blankets before the three men who had returned in the truck had carried them down the stairs, unceremoniously lifted them, then tossed them into the back of the truck. Mason, who'd been dressed but unconscious after being struck with the well-aimed fist, went in next. The dead man with the short hair followed, blood still dripping from his throat.

The men who had done the carrying had not challenged the Judge when they were given their instructions. They were paid well to ask no questions, but merely to drive the truck and set up the pub for the monthly meetings, making the surroundings hospitable and comfortable for the twenty or so attendees. However, it was the first time they'd taken on board such an unusual cargo.

'If that's what they want,' said one, shrugging his shoulders, 'then who am I to query an order?'

His colleagues had merely grunted; their promised bonuses were already mentally spent. All three worked as lorry drivers and weren't particularly well paid, so a bit extra meant they could improve the heating and lighting system in the industrial unit they co-owned, resulting in a large increase in the amount of cannabis produced.

The Judge, with cloak removed, and the man who had agreed judgement sat in the cab with the driver, whilst the other two sat in the back with the Americans and the corpse.

The truck had stopped just before the ford to allow the men to wheel the two scooters, the four helmets attached to the handlebars, into the deep pool a few yards downstream. As they sank, a small slick of petrol floated to the surface; its circles of various colours expanded to the size of a car tyre before gently elongating in the current and flowing away.

The next time the truck stopped, one of the men jumped out of the back and opened the wooden gate, shutting it as soon as the truck's tailgate was clear. He climbed back in, bracing himself in anticipation of the heavy jolting the rutted track would provide. The engine snarled and smelled hot as the driver gave it full revs in second gear, being keen to get up the slope and out of sight as quickly as possible. Reaching the derelict mine buildings, he did a one-hundred-and-eighty-degree turn, reversed fifty yards and switched off the ignition. Hidden behind mature trees, which had once just been bushes growing on the drystone wall of the mine's sett, no one passing by on the road would see them; not that there would be many motorists at this time of the morning. It was also too early for quarry lorries arriving to take on their first load of the day.

The three employees peeled back four rolls of loose turf covering the wooden boards. Once lifted, the boards revealed the shaft descending into the darkness below. A deceased local builder had regularly used it for several years to tip rubbish stripped from renovated houses, but, after the builder's death a year ago, a domestic appliance repairer from St Austell had been treating it as a way of avoiding council recycling charges. Aware that no one had claimed ownership of the land, he was confident his late evening visits had gone unnoticed. As far as he was concerned, his infilling was merely rendering the shaft safer.

'Right, in they go,' instructed the Judge from the window of the cab.

'But—' began the man who'd also been at the trial.

'But what?' interrupted the Judge.

'But four are still alive,' protested the man who'd just spoken. 'What if they manage to get out?'

The Judge huffed. 'Even with many years of fly tipping by our late friend and comrade, we know the adit to be clear of rubbish. I cannot see anyone surviving a fall of at least two hundred feet.'

One of the lorry drivers turned to his colleagues. '"Twon't be the fall that kills 'em, but 'twill be when the poor buggers hits the bottom.' The three laughed, instantly ceasing when they saw the Judge's scornful expression.

'I pay you to work, not to be a comedy trio – now get on with it,' said the Judge.

'Yes, your worship,' replied one of the three.

The body of the dead man went in first, then – one by one – the Americans were unceremoniously dragged to the edge of the shaft and pushed into the black hole. There was no sound of them hitting the bottom, nor the irregular sides of the hewn-out granite hole.

'You three will come back later with shovels,' instructed the Judge. 'Dig up some earth from the pile of 'deads' and throw it down on top – just in case anyone starts prying around with torches. It's unlikely, but you never know.'

'Yes, your worship,' acknowledged the one who'd replied before. 'And may we keep any missed ore we find in them?' he muttered, as the thought of trying to get a shovel into the sand-and-slime waste that had lain undisturbed for over one hundred years offered little appeal. His sarcasm went unheard.

'One question,' said the driver as he climbed in beside the Judge. 'What if the police come looking, as they'll be duty bound to do?'

The Judge smiled. Turning to the man still dressed in his black cloak, with the hood covering his face, the Judge said, 'I think we can leave that to you, Chief Inspector Breock, to sort out, don't you?'

Riled that his identity had been revealed to the driver, the chief inspector didn't openly protest but merely looked away. The revelation was a clever move by the Judge, one that meant the judge wasn't the only one to know the policeman had become entangled in what had suddenly escalated from harmless gatherings into the concealing of murders. Therefore, should he ever need to deny his involvement, it would no longer be one person's word against another.

As the truck had trundled its way to the mine, Breock had considered how best to avoid any full-on murder inquiry. Covering up the death of the four Americans wouldn't be straightforward, but he was sure he could concoct some story during the investigation about them not wishing to return to their own country. Regarding Herbert, the other hooded man killed by the judge, he lived alone and, as far as the chief inspector knew, had few friends; in fact, he was certain he didn't have any at all. It should, therefore, be easy to lay a trail suggesting that, due to his loneliness, Herbert had returned to his mining roots in Australia.

However, having someone like Smithy, the driver, aware that the head of the local constabulary was an accomplice in what was basically a mass killing wasn't sitting comfortably with him, even if Smithy and his mates were also accessories to the crime. In the morning, he would have to see what his neighbourhood bobbies knew about the three lackeys.

Starting the engine, Smithy allowed himself a brief smile; knowing that a top copper was involved in murder might prove quite useful in the future. Letting up the clutch, he threw Breock a quick glance – he was sure they would soon become great friends.

THIRTY-ONE

17th June 2013

ETHAN

'How the hell did you end up crashed in the hedge?'

On the way to Hingston, Claire had stopped her car at the junction where Ethan had left the road. He was unable to answer her question. He shook his head.

'I don't know, Claire. Perhaps I tried to escape from the pub, drove too fast and misjudged the bend.'

'Or perhaps you were drunk.' She got out of the car. Looking up and down the road, she told Ethan to get out. 'Okay, is it me? Am I missing something?'

'Sorry?'

'Ethan, the road is virtually straight. I'm no Lewis Hamilton, but I would have said the only way I could leave the tarmac is if I fell asleep or possibly misjudged turning into the junction; however, in either scenario, to end up there...' She pointed to the damaged hedge. 'I wouldn't have been racing away from where you say the pub is, rather I would have been driving towards it.'

His bewildered expression told her that had never crossed his mind.

'So what the hell was I doing?' he asked.

'I wish I knew the answer. And this woman you say helped you out – where did she come from?'

'I don't...' Ethan screwed up his eyes. 'I... I... swerved. She walked out in front of me.' Opening his eyes, he crossed to the other side of the junction, opposite to where he'd run off the road. 'She came out of the hedge... came out of here.'

'But there's no gate; how could she have come out from there? For Christ's sake, Ethan, you really have lost it.'

'You're wrong, Claire. I can see it clearly now.' He waved his arm in the direction of St Austell. 'I was coming from there, and going to turn right down the lane towards the pub. She stepped out from nowhere. I had to straighten up, else I would have hit her.'

'If that's true, then where were you coming from?'

Glued to the spot, he closed his eyes again. He could see the faint words 'Fine Ales & Quality Wines' written on the side of a building, the pebbledash tired and cracking; a car park, its gravel surface weed ridden; some beer casks, perhaps stacked neatly at one time but now lying on their sides, their ends pointing in different directions; and 'J.A. Devenish & Co. Ltd' was written on a small sign on what was presumably the rear entrance to a pub.

'The conniving bastards. They tried to fool me. They probably drugged me and dumped me in another closed pub's car park, thinking that when I woke up I wouldn't remember The Hung Drawn & Quartered. The conniving, fucking bastards,' ranted Ethan. He stared at Claire. 'But I did remember – well, subconsciously – and I came back or was on my way back.'

'That's all very well, Ethan, and possibly feasible, except that you lost two days,' reminded Claire.

'True. God only knows what happened. Perhaps I was still dead to the world.'

'And the woman?'

Ethan shook his head. 'I don't know, Claire, but as sure as hell it wasn't Jenny Woodbury...' He hesitated, before adding, 'But, on the other hand, if Linda Jones can be fooled by someone impersonating her husband, then perhaps she and her late husband were fooled into thinking their daughter was dead. After all, they said they didn't see the body.'

'So who did?'

He shrugged. 'I don't know that either, but Linda Jones might.'

* * *

There was no one home at the Joneses' house, although the key was still under the mat. Having checked there was nobody in the back garden, Ethan had let himself and Claire in. The photos were no longer on the sideboard, neither were they in any of the drawers. There was no sign of Ethan's kitbag in any of the rooms. Yanking open a kitchen drawer, he grabbed the two rechargeable torches – both appeared to be fully charged. He ran out of the house.

'Lock the door behind you,' he shouted, opening the passenger door of the Range Rover.

'Yes, O Master,' replied Claire. 'I'm here to serve.'

Three minutes later, he barked another order. 'Right, low ratio – or whatever these new-fangled gearboxes have – and not too fast.'

Despite the heavy rain the night Ethan had stumbled on The Hung Drawn & Quartered, the ford was yet to return to its usual full depth. The Evoque had no trouble making it through, much to Claire's relief.

'There, I told you it's not just a "Chelsea tractor",' she had great delight in declaring as they headed towards the pub.

Like at his last visit, the outside of the former pub suggested a neglected and unwanted building. The inside was no different.

'Leave the doors open, just in case,' whispered Ethan.

'In case of what? This shithole hasn't been used for years,' moaned Claire, wiping a cobweb off her hair. 'You can't have drank or stayed here.'

Ethan felt she was right and yet something else told him this was where he had come, drank beer and whisky, ate chicken and chips from a plastic basket, gone to bed with the barmaid, and then… then what? Instinctively, he rubbed the back of his neck.

The light from the torches revealed nothing more than he'd seen the last time; however, with the batteries full of life, he suggested they look upstairs.

Claire opened the door to room two. Fortunately, she didn't automatically step inside. There were no floorboards, and the joists were obviously suffering from woodworm, as there was dust in small piles on top of the ground-floor ceiling.

Room three was the same.

'And you reckon you stayed here?' she whispered, the atmosphere causing her to lower her voice.

'I see where you're coming from,' acknowledged Ethan, 'but I was in room five, I think.'

'And you expect that to be any different?' mocked Claire. Ten seconds later, she had to eat her own words. Room five was furnished, decorated and water ran from the taps in the en suite, albeit cold.

There were nine bedrooms, but only rooms five and nine were furnished.

'I don't like this, Ethan – it's all a bit weird.'

'You can say that again, Claire, but at least you might believe me now.'

He took her into the empty lounge bar and restaurant. Like the majority of the bedrooms, it had fallen into disrepair. He looked around, searching for answers. About to leave, he was drawn to the stainless-steel sink. He bent down to look underneath it.

'I was sick in here; I'm sure I was.' He saw Claire pull a face of disgust. 'There's no pipe. I remember it dripping onto the floor and then…'

'Then what, Ethan?'

He straightened up. Shaking his head, he replied, 'Nothing. Somebody must have cleaned it up.' He rubbed the back of his neck again. 'Perhaps it will come back to me.' He sighed. 'Anyway, let's have a look in the kitchen.'

In what had no doubt once been a fully functional commercial kitchen, all that appeared useable was a deep-fat fryer, two stainless-steel worktables, the sink and a relatively new microwave. A large American-style fridge was empty, but clean inside. On one end of a worktable sat a wooden cutlery tray containing various knives, spoons and forks. A dozen or so plastic baskets were piled on top of each other on the draining board. The bain marie with overhead lights was covered in a layer of dust, as were the six-ring gas stove and dishwasher.

'I wonder what's through there?' asked Claire, opening a half-panelled, glazed door into a conservatory. 'Ethan, come and see this,' she exclaimed.

Leaning against an end wall, was the pub sign Ethan had seen when he'd first arrived.

'Yuck, that's sick,' sneered Claire. 'Who the fuck wants something like that?'

Also in the conservatory were two 47 kg, bright-orange, Calor Gas cylinders, one of which was connected to a floor-standing boiler the other to a pipe feeding through a hole in the kitchen wall, probably having originally been for the gas hob. Two portable generators were sitting at the opposite end to the sign.

Back in the kitchen, Ethan picked up a propeller-like gadget attached to a cordless drill from one of the worktops. On the front of the propeller was a plastic cup with lid. Moulded on the lid were the words 'The Cobweb Maker'. On the side of the cup, written in black pen, was 'Property of Truro Film Studios'. He switched on the drill; the propeller began to whirl, making a very loud, metallic clattering. He quickly switched it off.

'Claire, I told you I was here, didn't I? And I can tell you how they changed the appearance of the pub.' And then quietly to himself, 'But why leave it all open? And what the fuck's it all about?' There was no response from Claire. 'I said I was here and I did stay here.'

Still no reply.

'Claire?'

Silence.

The conservatory was empty. A back door by the sign was open. It led into what was once no doubt a car park, roughly the size of half a football pitch; however, much of it was now given over to nettles and bramble, save for an area big enough to park a couple of cars or, judging by the deep tyre-tread marks, a large truck.

'Claire, it's not a good idea to explore without...' He mouthed the last word – her torch was lying on the ground, still switched on. Grabbing it, he shouted, 'Claire, where the hell are you?'

He heard a vehicle accelerate away. Running around the side of the building, he was confronted by double, five-bar, wooden gates. A chain and padlock ensured he had to climb over. By the time he reached the front of the pub, there was no sign of a vehicle. He rushed over to Claire's Evoque. Wrenching open the driver's door, he swore. 'Fuck it.'

The offside front tyre was flat, as were the other three; the sidewalls had been slashed with something exceptionally sharp; the three-inch gash in each one, clean and straight. He held his head in his hands. 'No, no, no, no, no... Please not Claire as well.'

'I tried to warn you.' The voice came from behind him.

'Claire?' he exclaimed. He'd only turned ninety degrees when he fainted.

THIRTY-TWO

The room was lit by a candle; it's flame flickered in the slight draught from the open door. It was the only light, early evening having been replaced by night. Ethan was sitting on one of the public bar's window seats, his legs stretched out on a chair. A dampened beer towel rested on his forehead.

His vision slightly blurred, he began to make out the face in the shadows. Jenny was sitting opposite him, an arm's length away. She was wearing the same clothes as the day she'd rescued him from the hire car: a short-sleeved, pink blouse; ankle-length, tight-fitting, white jeans; and pale-pink trainers. Her hair was in a ponytail.

'Jenny?' he asked.

She nodded.

'But your parents said you were dead – killed in a car crash.'

'Not killed – murdered.'

Ethan sat up, catching the towel as it slid off his brow. Her words didn't sink in. 'Is Claire here – please say she is?' he begged.

'I'm sorry, she's not.'

He remembered the car speeding away. 'Then where is she?'

Jenny stood up and walked over to the fireplace. She deliberated before answering. 'Where those who walk uninvited into this once-hospitable-but-now-evil place always end up – Wheal Hingston.'

The mist was beginning to clear. He rubbed his fingertips against his forehead. 'I don't understand. She's been taken to Wheal Hingston, you say you were murdered and… and I'm still here, but I wasn't invited either.' His head was just about back to normal – at least as normal as it had been over the last few days. 'I don't wish to be fucking rude, but you sound to me as though you're talking absolute bollocks, if you'll excuse the expression,' he sneered. 'How can you have been—'

She cut him off. 'That's fine; believe what you want. You either choose to believe or you don't; however, whichever choice you make, the ending's the same.' She returned to her seat.

Where have I heard that before? he asked himself.

'What the hell do you mean "the ending's always the same"?' he shouted. His failure to remain calm had no effect.

'What I said. We cannot change destiny. We will all die, some sooner than others. All we can do is heed what others say, as you should have heeded my warning. Had you listened, your friend Claire would have still been here.'

He looked her straight in the eyes, which – in daylight – he recalled were deep blue.

'When you say "here", do you mean here in the pub or here in the sense of ali…?' He couldn't bring himself to say it.

She met his stare for a moment longer, then rose to her feet.

'It is unlikely you can save her, unless—'

'Unless what?' he interrupted, anxious to know how much hope there was in that 'unless'.

'Unless they do not risk going to the mine tonight. People are home from work. A vehicle seen driving across the field might be questioned. The local council has put an end to the fly tipping that went on in the shaft and our... I mean their local councillor is above corruption. If she hears of it, she will report it.'

'So if not the mine, where then?'

'Where you saw the light, the light you should not have ignored.'

He frowned. 'The adit?' he asked. 'But there was no light; it was a reflection.'

The candle had burned to its base on the cardboard beermat and was beginning to flicker more rapidly. Before he received an answer, he was in darkness and alone.

* * *

His torch was on the table. Checking it still worked, Ethan stumbled out the front door.

'Jenny... Jenny... where are you?'

A frantic dash around the back of the pub confirmed she was gone, unless she was playing one of her 'hiding in the bedroom' tricks.

Sod it, I haven't got time to play games, he thought.

He ran off in the direction of the ford. He had no idea how long it had been since he'd heard the vehicle drive off with Claire, but if Jenny – whoever Jenny was – hadn't been lying, then there may still be time to find Claire alive.

Staggering along the uneven riverbank, the light from the torch beginning to fade, he reached the plank bridge. To his right, he heard voices approaching from the track on the opposite side of the river to the adit, together with what he guessed was the clatter of cartwheels on the stony surface. About fifty yards away, he saw the beam from a powerful lamp lighting up the air – first one way then the other, as it swung to and fro.

For a moment, he considered confronting whomever was drawing nearer, but then a flashback of a lifeless Roger falling on him after the gunshot told him it probably wasn't the wisest move. He backed off into the shadows and crouched down behind a large lump of granite, then watched as three men, one inside the drawbar, hauled and pushed a two-wheeled handcart over the planks and up to the adit entrance. Although the majority of the light from the lamp hanging from the front of the cart shone forwards, skywards and sideways, it was still sufficient for Ethan to see Claire's prone body laid out on the flatbed. He couldn't be sure, but it looked as though her hands and feet were bound, and a gag tied across her mouth. There was no sign of any movement.

Ethan could hear them talking, but not clearly enough to make out every word they were saying.

'The Judge says we're to give her another dose and then leave her not too far in,' said the man pushing the drawbar.

'Must admit, I wouldn't mind giving her a dose meself,' said another.

The three laughed.

'Now, now, Smithy,' replied Harry, the man in the drawbar. 'If the Judge got to hear of it, there'd be trouble. Killing is one thing, but shagging a sleeping a woman wouldn't go down well.'

'Could go down on her instead, then,' said Smithy.

'Not sure she'd like that very much, not with those teeth,' joked Harry.

As Smithy bared his remaining two front teeth, the third man snapped, 'Enough. The sooner we gets this finished, the sooner we can go for a pint. Now then, give me a hand.'

The three men carefully lifted the body off the cart and carried it into the adit.

'Here, Harry, pass me that lamp,' instructed Smithy. 'The Judge wants her alive, so we'd better keep her arse out of the water.'

Lowering Claire into a sitting position against the adit wall, Smithy undid the gag. Claire let out a sigh and half opened her eyes. 'Quick, pass me the flask, we don't want her to see us.'

'Huh, what difference would that make? Likely she'll be dead before the end of tomorrow,' said Harry, unscrewing the top of a small hip flask and passing it to Smithy.

'Hold her head back and mouth open.'

After half the flask's contents had been poured down Claire's throat by Smithy, he retied the gag.

'I thought they said no more killing,' said the third called Len.

'Apparently so,' acknowledged Smithy, lighting a rollup he'd had behind his ear, 'but I guess they weren't bargaining on Roger Jones threatening to tell all. Had he not got so friendly with that journalist chap, then the Judge wouldn't have had him shot.'

'I should have shot the interfering journalist as well, I says, then us could have carried on without more hassle,' said Harry.

'We couldn't. Others knew where he was – would have come looking, as her did.' Smithy nodded towards Claire. 'Keeping him drugged for three days whilst the river level dropped so we could tow out his car should have put him off the scent.' He took a long drag on his 'rollie.' 'Trouble was, silly bugger came back for more.'

'So why isn't he here with her now?' asked Harry. 'Once bitten, twice shy and all that.'

'Good question, Harry, but same reason, I s'pose. You'll have to ask the Judge. The phone call said there was a white car, but us was only to take the woman. Anyway, whatever the reason, let's get out of here.' He threw down the stub of his half-smoked cigarette.

* * *

'Damn sight lighter without her on board,' said Harry as they pulled the cart across the bridge and up the other side of the valley.

'Pretty maid, though,' replied Smithy.

'You think anything with tits and a fanny's pretty,' sniggered Len.

'Fair point, Len,' agreed Smithy. 'Just as long as they moves.'

'You've changed your tune,' sniped Harry.

Their laughter shrank into the night.

THIRTY-THREE

As much as he shook her and lightly slapped her cheeks, Ethan couldn't wake Claire.

'Claire, c'mon, for God's sake.' Eventually, he gave up. 'Right, miss, I'm going to have to carry you.'

But where to? he thought.

He untied the scarf they'd used as the gag, and undid the thin, blue rope around her wrists and ankles. Holding the torch in his mouth, he bent down and lifted her over his left shoulder, the same way he'd carried many of his team mates in the football training sessions. Fortunately, she was much lighter than them, but, even so, he knew he wouldn't get far without several breathers. Leaving the adit, he looked to his left and right.

Where do I go? The Joneses' house? Even if they're still out, they'll be home sometime – then what? The pub? I could go back there, sleep over in one of the furnished bedrooms and in the morning? I'll worry about the morning when it comes.

He took a couple of steps, then stopped.

On the other hand, what if the three men who dropped off Claire also go there? Once they realise she's no longer in the adit, the pub will be their first port of call – won't it?

He looked back at the adit.

Perhaps they'll think Claire has woken, released her ties and run off – there's always the chance that they'll spend time looking in the adit and the surrounding area. Meanwhile, I could... I could... I could do what, exactly?

A tingling sensation shot up his left arm.

Call the police? What would they say? 'It's that nutter from London again, Sarge. You know, the one who said a woman had gone missing. Now he's saying his lady friend's been kidnapped, but he's rescued her and he can't drive her car because all four tyres have been slashed. Bit far-fetched, sir, wouldn't you say?'

He shifted Claire to his other shoulder.

Okay, so I could go the pub, get up before dawn drive her car on four alloy wheels with no tyres, but the stony surface would soon cause the alloys to crack. So... then what?

With his eyes half-closed, he bit his bottom lip.

Call the RAC?

He smiled.

Call the RAC or AA. Not such a bad idea. They have four-wheel drives. They could bring out new tyres or get a tyre company to fit some. Brilliant, that's what I'll do.

He took another step.

But how do I call them? Easy, Claire's mobile.

With his free right hand, he tapped the pockets of Claire's jeans.

Nice bum, Claire!

There was no sign of a mobile. Her jumper had no pockets.

Fuck. Ah, perhaps it's in her car. Bound to be.

His optimism lasted seconds

Bollocks. What's the chances of a signal?

He felt an urge to drop Claire, and lie down beside her, close his eyes and sleep. However, accepting that it was him who'd dragged her into this mess in the first place, he still had to give them both a chance to get out, regardless of how small a possibility it might be. Although it seemed likely that Claire wouldn't have a problem sleeping anywhere in her present condition, returning to the pub where they could rest in relative comfort struck him as being the best option.

His confidence that he was making the right decision received a further boost when it occurred to him that her mobile was on a different network to his, so – provided it was in the car – he may be able to get a signal.

About to set off upstream, he hesitated; a sudden thought struck him. Despite their head start, he'd got to the adit before the men. Not having seen any vehicle on his way, there was obviously a different route to the pub; perhaps it wasn't shorter, but was possibly easier. Shifting Claire back to his left shoulder, he set off in the direction in which the hand cart had disappeared.

The climb up the slope took its toll on his back; a sharp pain shot down his left leg.

Shit, fucking sciatica. Sorry, Claire, I'm going to have to put you down.

He let her body slide down his chest to the ground and breathed a sigh of relief. Rubbing his side, he shone the faint beam of his torch around. The ground levelled off in the next few yards and, nestled into an area of wooded scrub, was a small door-less shed. It contained the handcart he'd seen earlier and nothing else save a couple of long-handled Cornish shovels and a pick. Off-road tyre tracks led away into a narrow lane. Sitting down on the bare ground beside the drawbar of the cart, he switched off the torch, drew a long breath and shut his eyes.

* * *

It hadn't been his intention to sleep, but, fortunately, he was awake before dawn. Shaking his head clear, he raised himself steadily to his feet. Sleeping in such a position hadn't proved to be a good idea – his back was aching and his neck was stiff. Claire was still out cold. The night air was mild, but, even so, her clothes felt damp.

'Sorry, my love, I didn't mean to leave you there for so long. Let's get you to the pub,' he said, kissing the top of her head.

Eventually, the narrow track joined the potholed road amongst a row of high bushes, and was, as had been the case for Ethan, easily missed. After a couple more rest stops, with his lower back feeling as though a hot poker was being driven into it, he finally reached The Hung Drawn & Quartered. From a distance, Claire's Evoque looked fine, but a closer inspection confirmed that the tyres were definitely flat and undriveable. Sitting Claire against the front wheel, he opened the driver's door. The courtesy lights revealed no phone in the centre console, door pockets or glovebox. The overnight bag in the rear contained just clothes and a toilet bag.

Shit!

He sat down beside Claire.

'Oh well,' he said quietly to her, 'it probably wouldn't have worked anyway'.

Getting back to his feet and bending awkwardly, he grabbed a lightweight, blue gilet off the backseat. He winced as the pain shot down the back of his thigh.

The entrance doors to the building and to the public bar were as they'd left them – wide open. Carrying Claire in his arms, he manoeuvred her around the ninety-degree turn, then paused, surprised by what greeted him. A single candle on the corner table, beside which Ethan had earlier woken on the window seat, spluttered and shimmered in the draught from the door, intermittently lighting up Jenny's face. As she stared into the flame, her words were barely audible.

'Why have you come back?'

Being more concerned with making Claire comfortable on the window seat, Ethan didn't reply. Once he was happy that she couldn't fall off, he kissed her forehead and stroked her hair as he tenderly rested her head against the folded gilet. He closed the door and pulled up a chair opposite Jenny. Placing his elbows on the table, he cupped his chin in his hands. He took a while before acknowledging her question.

'And what else was I supposed to do?' he said, his voice calm and impassive. 'Was I expected to carry her all the way to St Austell?'

'You could have left her,' replied Jenny, her eyes still focused on the flame, which was steady and even now that he'd sat down.

'And is that how you treat your friends?'

Her attention lifted from the flame. 'I have no friends where I exist, just contacts.' Her eyes dropped back to the candle.

Exhausted, Ethan was in no mood to play games. 'Your existence being where?' he asked sarcastically.

Jenny held the palm of her hand an inch above the point of the flame. Ethan instinctively knocked it away.

'What the hell do you think you're doing? Are you stupid or something?' he yelled at her. His raised voice caused Claire to stir. Touching her shoulder, he reassured her. 'It's okay, Claire; there's nothing to worry about.' Satisfied she'd settled, he turned back to Jenny. 'So?'

She smiled. 'You really do not understand, do you?'

'Understand what?' he asked, frowning. He leaned back, disturbed by her response.

'I am no longer like you.'

Ethan leapt to his feet. 'For fuck's sake, Jenny, what are you talking about?' He paced around, shaking his head. 'Are you saying you're a ghost?' He giggled. 'Oh no… no… no, I'm not having that. There's no such thing.' His giggle developed into an irrational laugh, ceasing abruptly as he met her dispassionate gaze. 'You're serious?'

He saw by her stony expression that she was. He slumped back into his chair, his head in his hands.

'Don't you think I've had enough?' He sighed. 'Sarah's disappearance; my loss of memory; Claire's kidnapping; your father being killed; you hiding in the house before running away, then turning up here; and then…' He recalled what she'd said a few hours ago. 'Telling me you were murder…' He paused and looked up, a large smirk covering his face. 'I get it. The car crash. Your parents said you were killed, but they never saw your body.' He took time out, gathered his thoughts, eventually continuing, 'That's it. You fooled them into thinking you were dead. You're in on whatever's going on, aren't you?'

Jenny remained still, and was totally emotionless.

'Well? Aren't you?'

She didn't reply.

'I'm right, aren't I?' Ethan was desperate for an answer, desperate to be right. He was tired, hungry, thirsty and, above all, his mind was cracking. He needed solace, and, at the moment, the only person who could give him that had told him she was a ghost.

He considered risking the Evoque despite the punctured tyres, but common sense told him it would be unlikely he'd reach the river, let alone the sanctity of a town. Even if he did manage to make it, what then? Tell the police? He'd already considered that option and dismissed it. Adding a ghost to his story was not going to help.

It was hard for him to believe that, not many days ago, he'd been sitting in his office, editing the next issue of his magazine.

This time, he didn't knock Jenny's hand away when she held it over the candle. Instead, he just stared as the flame appeared to go through her hand without causing the slightest burn or pain.

'There is your answer,' she said, holding up her unmarked palm.

THIRTY-FOUR

'Yes, it was me you were trying to avoid when you swerved into the hedge. I was trying to warn you and trying to tell you not to go back. I waved my hands, but you didn't see me until it was too late. You looked dazed even before you hit the hedge.' Jenny pointed to Claire, still asleep on the window seat. 'You were drugged, like your friend. I took you back to my parents' house – I knew they were away. I thought if you had something to eat you would feel better – that you would be strong enough to leave.'

'The car – why did you have it towed away?'

'You had escaped once, or rather they'd let you go. If they knew you'd crashed and were still here, you may not have been so lucky a second time.'

'What do you mean "lucky"?' asked Ethan; his brain was already planning his next question.

Jenny answered in a whisper. 'The Americans didn't just disappear, Ethan; they're dead at the bottom of Wheal Hingston, just like my stepfather.'

He recalled that her stepfather had told him they'd been murdered, and he'd been told the same thing by Tristan Maw...

He couldn't remember the second name. He knew he had to ask the question, but – fearing the answer – it wouldn't leave his lips. He looked up at Jenny. She nodded. He jumped up.

'You're lying!' he screamed at her.

'I'm sorry.'

He turned away, trying to restrain his tears. Calmly, he asked, 'But how… how do you know?'

'It was her destiny.'

Finally, the tears ran down his face. Wiping them with the back of his hand, he faced her. 'Destiny. You and your fucking destiny. Is that all you can say?' He was hysterical and any sense of a false calmness was gone. 'I suppose you're going to say she was murdered as well… Was that her destiny?'

Jenny shook her head. 'No, she wasn't murdered.'

'What then?' shrieked Ethan. 'If she wasn't murdered, what then?'

Until now, Jenny had spoken to him without taking her attention away from the flame; however, before answering, she lifted her head.

'She followed in her father's footsteps; it was a choice she made.'

Shaking both fists above his head, Ethan blurted, 'For God in hell's sake, stop talking in riddles. Just tell me how she died.'

'She entered the adit following her father, who had managed to explore too far. They'd widened the hole to stop anyone else doing the same.'

He stared at her.

'What? You mean the adit where I found… the… trainers?' His face dropped; he'd forgotten about the trainers.

After Roger Jones had been shot, other things had taken over. Finding no body when he was accompanied by PC Fraser, he would have been ridiculed if he'd said anything about trainers going missing as well.

He should have told Claire, and he should have confirmed they were Sarah's size, but his mind was intent on investigating the pub. 'Shit,' he snapped.

As if to rub salt into the wounds, Jenny added, 'The light you saw was of another, a spirit who tried to save her own father and brother. She wanted to take you to Sarah, to where she lay at the bottom of the shaft. She wanted to make up for failing her family.'

Ethan ran his hands through his hair. His anger had given in to despair. He sank to his knees. 'Are you saying I could have saved her?' he mumbled between the heavy sobs that were engulfing him. 'You mean I killed her?'

'No, Ethan, your friend Sarah was already dying,' Jenny assured him.

'So… so what could I have done?'

Jenny smiled and reached out to him, gently lifting his chin. 'Hedra Roscarrow wanted to take you to her, not because you could save her, Ethan, but because Sarah wanted you with her when she crossed to another life.'

'But how did this Hedra spirit know?' he whispered.

She caressed his cheek. 'Unlike me, Hedra has no form. She exists only in the light of her soul. However, had she been able to, she would have recounted Sarah's last words.'

'Which were?'

Touching his lips, she replied, 'They were, "I'm sorry, Ethan."'

THIRTY-FIVE

11th June 2013

SARAH

Day passed into night, night into day, but – for Sarah – seconds, minutes, hours, days and even a week were all irrelevant. She'd resigned herself to dying in a way she could never have imagined. She loved the mines, and the excitement of exploring where men and boys had worked to provide for their families. Danger had never crossed her mind. When friends asked her if she was afraid of roofs collapsing or levels flooding, she'd answered, 'The shafts and tunnels were dug at least a hundred years ago, some much, much longer. If they were going to fall in, they would have done so ages before I go in them.' Her bravado would have been slightly different had she spoken to them after climbing from the adit into the level below. Her assumption that it was a recent collapse hadn't been correct, but it had been intentionally enlarged since her father stepped over the original two-foot-diameter hole.

'With regard to flooding, I always check the weather forecast, so – unless we have a storm like the one that hit the hill above Boscastle – there's no chance of getting trapped,' she would also say.

Like the Chilean miners, she'd eked out her food supply; the two chocolate bars had lasted four days, or rather what she had defined as four days. She allowed herself two fingers of the wafer biscuits each day – one in what she called the morning and one a few hours later. In truth, she'd consumed both in just over thirty-six hours.

She'd managed to drag herself to the side of the shaft and had licked moisture off the cool, granite stone, but water alone couldn't stem the pain from her ankle, which at times was almost unbearable.

I know what you said Dad, and I'm sorry I didn't listen, she thought.

Her father had always insisted on taking a first aid kit with him, including paracetamol.

'It's easy to bump your head, or to find the air stuffy and unpleasant. If you take tablets with you, then you can deal with headaches,' he'd reminded her several times, but she'd never listened; the same as she'd ignored his suggestion she take a toilet roll, 'Just in case you get caught short.'

She also hadn't planned for another eventuality – the start of her period. Whilst a toilet roll wouldn't have been a perfect answer to her feminine-hygiene requirements, it would have made life a little more comfortable, as it would have done when needing to defecate. She'd resisted for as long as she could, but eventually nature had won.

Getting into a crouching position had been a massive challenge, but – when the couple of waterlogged tissues in a pocket had ripped into tatters as soon as she'd wiped herself – her stubborn will to live had begun to wane.

Four days later, had her eyes been capable of opening, she would have seen the speck of light above her head increase in size. She would have heard voices exchanging words two hundred and thirty feet above, followed by the thuds and clomps as the limp body crashed and bounced against the walls of the shaft. Finally, she would have heard the eerie squelch of the trapped air discharging from the lungs of the thirteen stone five pounds of Roger Jones as he landed on her broken ankle.

However, Sarah Louise Jenkinson, aged twenty-seven years and three months, was aware of neither light nor sounds, for – on the 11th June 2013 – she'd passed to another life, in which – on the day before she left the one on earth – she'd prayed she would be welcomed by her newly worshipped saviour.

Even if she'd been alive, she wouldn't have known the dry spell would end and torrential rain soaking through the parched ground would turn the lower part of the adit into a fast-flowing stream, which would cause her deserted rucksack to roll over, dislodging her trainers and carrying them to where the flow would peter out into harmless puddles.

THIRTY-SIX

18th June 2013

ETHAN – THE HUNG, DRAWN & QUARTERED

After Jenny had told him about Sarah, Ethan had shrugged off her comfort and tried hard to regain some of his composure. Knowing Sarah had been in the adit all along, and that he'd neither followed up on the discovery of the trainers nor followed the light, were things he would never forgive himself for. It didn't occur to him that perhaps the reason Roger Jones was shot was a deliberate distraction tactic by whoever was attempting to prevent further exploration of the adit. Sitting back on a chair, he eventually managed to ask Jenny a question.

'So if what you tell me is all true, why am I still alive?'

'I cannot be sure,' she replied, 'but I believe the answer lies in the safe in the small office. I suggest you go and fetch the book in there; it isn't locked.'

Picking up the candle, he made his way to the small office that was just off the passageway to the kitchen, which doubled as a reception for guests. Seeing a key rack hanging precariously by one screw on its top, right-hand corner – the left-hand one having lost its grip in the soft wood of the partition wall – Ethan recalled something he'd asked of a young barmaid: '*Will that be for a double or a single?*'

Eager to find the book, he shook his head; there was little point in trying to place the words now. Time was moving on, and he feared the three men who'd dumped Claire in the adit would soon be returning to look for her.

Old papers lay scattered around, faded and torn. The glue in a roll of Sellotape had oozed its way to the spool's edges and attracted several flies; their partially decomposed bodies no doubt providing fodder for any spider lucky enough not to get trapped. On a period desk, various pencils and pens – entwined in dusty cobwebs – sat upright in a mug emblazoned with 'The Miner's Arms', the original name of the pub. The safe was on the floor below the rack.

As Jenny had told him, it was unlocked. He lifted out two A4-sized books: one was marked 'Guest Book' on the front cover, and the other – a much thicker book – was unnamed. On the shelf below, he noticed a small plastic tray containing no more than a few odd coins; he guessed it was the reason for there being insufficient change for a twenty-pound note. With the books under one arm and a hand in front of the candle protecting its flame, he made his way back to Jenny.

The only entry in the guest book was on the first page; it was dated 2nd June 2011:

C White and G Brown, Los Angeles, USA, Room 5
M White and L Taylor, ditto, Room 9

'The four Americans,' said Ethan, sitting down.

'That's right; two of whom, the White brothers, were related to Josiah Pendeen.'

'Is that meant to mean something to me?' asked Ethan, curtly.

'Pendeen was joint owner of Wheal Hingston when it was flooded, killing sixty-three men and boys, including a man called Kevern Tregunna and his two sons: Jory and Davith. Their three bodies were never found. Despite there obviously being gross negligence – mainly on the mine captain's part, a man called Pendogget – the three owners escaped scot-free. They then emigra—'

'To America,' interrupted Ethan.

'Yes.'

'The landlord told me. He was called... Tristan... Tristan... Maw—'

'Mawgan?' offered Jenny.

'That's right, and the barmaid was called Anne,' he shouted. Ethan was ecstatic. Tugging at the front of his shirt with both hands, he continued, 'And when I got dressed after... after... Oh, never mind that, let's just say I'd changed out of a shirt because it was soaked after visiting the mine, and yet – when you found me in the car – I was wearing it. There were creases in the arms: it had been ironed.' He grabbed hold of Jenny. 'I can see it all now. I must have been drugged, like you said I was when I crashed. I was kept for three days, probably in this very pub. God, it's all beginning to make sense. It feels so good Jenny... Jenny?'

He noticed her head was bowed. His eyes narrowed. 'You knew all this, didn't you?'

She didn't look up.

Ethan got to his feet. 'You knew everything that happened, didn't you?' he snapped. His raised voice drew a sigh from Claire, but she didn't wake. He continued, but in a more controlled and quiet manner. 'So if you knew, why the fuck didn't you tell me where Sarah was?' He cocked his head to one side, his gaze attempting to pierce deep into her mind. 'Is that why you ran away from the kitchen, so you didn't have to tell me? Was it?'

She looked him straight in the eye. Unperturbed by his aggressive attitude, she answered, 'I have already told you it was too late to do anything about Sarah, nor could I do anything once you were drugged. I may be what you term to be a "ghost", but that does not give me magical powers, neither does it make me visible to those who knew me before I died.' Still meeting his gaze, a gaze that was beginning to soften, she continued, 'I ran because you were beginning to remember, to remember what had happened to you, remember the people involved. You would have asked more questions... questions which, if I had answered, would have put you back into danger. I hoped you would leave. You had been let go once, but a second time?' She shook her head. 'At the time, I doubted it very much.'

Ethan sat down, his thoughts confused. 'But I went back anyway.'

'Yes.'

'And I am still alive.'

'Yes.'

'So why did they take Claire and not me?'

Jenny nodded at the second book.

He turned the cover. However, as far as he was concerned, the list of names and dates it contained might just as well have been an electoral roll; there was only one thing on his overloaded mind: the vivid memories of his first visit to The Hung Drawn & Quartered.

THIRTY-SEVEN

11th June 2013

ETHAN – THE HUNG, DRAWN & QUARTERED

With his journalistic curiosity temporarily overriding his need to find Sarah, Ethan had listened intently as the landlord now sitting opposite him, had related his tale about the curse. Whilst it made a good story, perhaps one that would be worth including in next month's publication, it was the follow-on part about how he held the mine responsible for the death of four American guests that he really found intriguing.

'They turned up one day in June two years ago; two couples. The two men – brothers, they were – had been tracing their ancestry; they said they were descendants of one of Wheal Hingston's owners, who'd emigrated to America. They wanted to see the mine for themselves, whilst they were over here on holiday. Unfortunately, they never used the return halves of their flight tickets.' This last comment drew a wry smile, as if he was proud of his morbid humour.

Acknowledging the landlord's wit with a slight raise of his eyebrows, Ethan asked the obvious question. 'So what happened to them?' Fully expecting to be told they'd died in a car accident or something similarly not unusual, he swallowed some beer and sat back. As he'd discovered himself, the Cornish lanes presented totally different challenges, particularly for anyone used to driving on wide, open roads whilst sitting on the other side of the car. However, his jaw dropped at the landlord's response.

'They were murdered, all four of them.'

Ethan slid forwards on his chair. 'What do you mean... murdered?'

'What it usually means: killed, slain, slaughtered.' The latter verb was delivered with half-closed eyes.

'Bit strong, isn't it? You know, "slaughtered".' Ethan was shaking his head, beginning to wonder if the landlord was an idiot after all. 'How do you know that?'

'Well—'

'Tristan, you're needed in the kitchen. Water's coming under the door again.' It was the barmaid. She was standing beside the table, hands on hips. 'I know you pay me, but I can't cope on my own with the bar and everything else.'

'Sorry... sorry, Anne, m'dear. I was just telling this gentleman about our American cousins; you know, the ones the police said had done a runner, but others suspect otherwise.'

'I know who you mean, but I'm sure he doesn't want to hear such an unpleasant story.'

'No... no, I'm fine. I'm really interested,' protested Ethan. 'Anything to do with mining; it's my sort of thing.'

'But I thought you came here looking for your friend, not to hear about tragic events? And anyway, it's not exactly a mining story, is it?' Anne might be of diminutive stature, and probably no older than eighteen or nineteen, but she wasn't one to withhold her opinion.

'I suppose not,' agreed Ethan. Whether it was her unassuming glamour or her stern demeanour that made him accept her observation so readily, it made little difference – the landlord had already departed.

'Now, may I get you another drink?' she asked, 'Or perhaps a menu Mr... er... Mr?'

'Menhennett, but please call me Ethan.'

'Okay, Ethan.' She stared out the window. 'It's still raining heavily. I can't see you crossing the ford, assuming that to be your car.' It was the only one parked outside. 'You'd need at least an old Land Rover or even a tractor, and no one this side of the river has either anymore. All the farmers moved out several years ago.'

'I see. So what exactly are you saying?' He was fascinated by her manner and, despite her curtness, he found her rather attractive.

'You will have to call off your search for today and you might consider staying over – we have rooms available. We could offer you a generous discount.'

'And how exactly will that help me find my missing friend?' Then, without thinking, he added, 'Will that be for a double or a single?' Anticipating a brusque reply, he stuttered, 'So-sorry. I... er... meant—' before being interrupted by a wink.

'Double, of course, Ethan. I wouldn't expect you to sleep alone.' Her smile had gone. 'Now then, as I said, would you like another drink, something to eat or perhaps both?'

'Both I think, please, Anne.' He passed her his glass. 'This is a very different type of beer – where's it from?'

'We brew it ourselves. Small breweries don't like coming down the lane with just one cask – they say it isn't worth it – and the landlord won't buy from the big ones, as he says they're too expensive. Consequently, we make our own.' Turning on her heel, she made off to the bar. Ethan watched as she caught hold of the long handle of the cask beer pump. Her slim fingers slid down it and up again before pulling it slowly towards her. She glanced across at him, smiled, then concentrated on filling the glass. Bringing it to his table, she remarked, 'I've given it plenty of head; I hope you like it that way.'

His cheeks felt on fire as he took the menu. 'Yes... yes, thank you,' he replied.

'I'll be back in a moment for your order.'

She disappeared through a door Ethan could just see led into a passageway, over which was a sign saying 'Toilets'. It was the same one the landlord had used, so he guessed it might lead to the kitchen as well. After gulping some beer, he let out a loud breath. As much as he enjoyed an occasional flirt, Anne's openness had made him uncomfortable. Holding the menu, he stared out of the window, just as a flash of lightening tore through the darkened sky. The dim lights flickered.

'Shit,' he exclaimed, instinctively drawing back. No more than four seconds later, there was a large clap of thunder. He looked across at the other customers. As far as he could tell, none of them had shown any interest in the events outside. They were all busy chatting; two or three were smoking. The distraction took his mind off Anne's obvious come-on.

It was a limited menu; in fact, a very limited menu.

* * *

Ethan lay naked on the bed, studying the drapes over the top of the bed, for he had no wish to move from his prone position. He turned his head to the left. In the semi-darkness, the red LED display on the bedside digital alarm clock showed 8.29pm. A small gap in the red-velvet curtains provided the only source of light. Turning his head to the right, he saw a double-fronted, freestanding wardrobe, probably made of oak. Next it to it was a half open door through which he could see a hand basin. He looked back at the ceiling; his head was throbbing.

Struggling to recall the events of the last three hours, his thoughts returned to Sarah, not just his search for her but also of Sarah the journalist, the girl who made him laugh at conferences, the girl he'd realised a day ago he fancied and the girl he now wished was lying beside him.

From the menu Anne had given him, he'd chosen 'chicken and chips in the basket', a way of serving a meal his graphic-designer friend's elderly father had once talked about over dinner in a local pub at home.

* * *

'It used to be 'chicken in the basket', 'scampi in the basket' or 'sausages in a basket', all served with chips. The baskets were even made of plastic, apparently, so they could be washed and used time and time again. If you were lucky, you may have had a pasty or a pork pie. Didn't even have burgers.' He'd then finished his pint before adding, 'But then, that's what pubs offered. They were drinking houses, not fancy gastro pubs with children shouting their heads off and running around out of control. Kids weren't allowed in, you see. Had to sit outside, with a bottle of coke and a bag of stale crisps.' He held his empty glass tankard up in front of him. 'Ah well, the good old sixties. Now, whose round is it?'

* * *

The Hung Drawn & Quartered's menu wasn't quite from the sixties, as – in addition to the three basket meals – it also listed various meat salads and jacket potatoes.

Perhaps it's a theme welcomed by the locals, Ethan had thought, finishing his beer.

Anne's offer of a large whisky 'on the house' was readily accepted, as was another.

'It's exceptionally generous of you,' he said. He sniffed its aroma. 'Hmm, that's a bit different. Do all your guests get plied with free drinks?'

Although she acknowledged him with a smile, her eyes remained strangely cold. 'Only those to whom we want to give special attention.' She ran her tongue around her lips. 'Nice whisky?' she asked.

'Very nice, once you really get your tongue into it. Very special.'

'It's distilled locally,' she informed him. 'It's quite unique.'

Had he still been wearing his journalist's hat, he would probably have corrected her grammar, but now – with a full stomach and alcohol induced acceptance of idle conversation – he enjoyed the drink without further comment.

'As soon as you're finished, I'll show you to your room. I've put you in room five... on the first floor.' She smiled, lighting up her unwrinkled, young face. 'I don't know why I say first floor, there aren't any others – apart from the ground floor, of course; I s'pose it sounds posher than upstairs, and less like an ordinary house. It's got a four-poster bed and a walk-in shower.' Despite her smile, her words lacked any emotion, unlike the way she'd kissed him after closing and locking the bedroom door.

* * *

'Shush,' she said, putting her hand across his mouth. 'We don't want anyone to hear, or I'll lose my job.'

Pushing him onto the bed, she'd jumped astride him and began undoing his belt buckle. Kneeling up straight, her eyes fixed on his, she slowly and deliberately undid the buttons on the front of her blouse. Sliding the sleeves over her shoulders, her delicate hands moved unhurriedly to cup her braless breasts. They were small, perhaps being no more than a 32b.

Letting go of her breasts, she eased her blouse down her arms.

Ethan reached up for her.

'Whoa there, big boy; not until we've both showered.' She leapt off the bed, her skirt slipping to the floor. 'Get your clothes off and follow me.'

He watched her barely G-string-covered, heart-shaped bum walk towards the bathroom, the door of which suddenly seemed to have moved further away. Not only that, she appeared to be unstable on her feet.

Clumsily, he undressed. Meaning to throw his t-shirt onto the back of a chair, he waved nonchalantly as it missed and fell on the floor. 'Bollocks,' he murmured as he tripped over the leg of his jeans.

'What are you doing, Ethan? Get off the floor and come in here,' She beckoned with her finger, her other hand rubbing the front of her G-string. 'I've got something for you.'

* * *

Now, as he lay on the bed alone, he had no recollection of what it was.

The clock's display had moved to 9.03pm before he managed to lift his legs off the bed. Shaking his head like a dog shedding water, he teetered his way to the window. Easing back a curtain with one hand, whilst holding his neck with the other, he took in the scene outside. Through the fading daylight and relentless rain, he could vaguely see the rented Mondeo; it was still the only car. Across the road was a four-foot-high stone wall and beyond that he could just make out open fields. He'd not noticed them when he'd arrived, as his total attention had been focused on the grotesque pub sign still swinging frantically in the wind.

Even the gloom was bright enough to make the throbbing of his head worse. Leaving the curtains open, he caught a vague image of himself in the mirror – the dull light did nothing to flatter – he looked like he felt. He could have carried potatoes in the bags under his eyes.

'Bollocks,' he exclaimed. The shout hammered another nail into his skull. 'Bollocks,' he repeated, only much quieter. He had a sudden urge to urinate. Sitting on the toilet, he sighed as his bladder emptied. His head in both hands, he tried hard to remember what had happened.

'I've put you in room five; it's got a walk-in shower,' she'd said, and later, 'I've got something for you.' And then he'd woken up alone.

He pressed the button on top of the cistern and turned on the handbasin's hot tap. Before the water splashed his hands, he took a hasty step back. Out of the corner of his eye he'd spotted his brown-leather toilet bag lying open behind the bath taps.

How the fuck did that get there? he thought.

He looked inside. It contained his toothbrush, toothpaste, disposable razor, shower gel, roll-on deodorant and the Hugo Boss *Pour Homme* eau de toilette spray Sarah had given him. It wasn't exactly a present. She'd won it in a raffle at a conference they'd both attended.

'It's no good to me,' she'd joked. 'I'm a Chanel girl, not that you've probably noticed.'

He had and it suited her. He remembered its gentle fragrance, how she'd smelled, how the softness of her hair had teased his cheek and how warm her thighs had felt against his when they'd smooched to 'Knights in White Satin'.

He needed to clear his mind and deal with the present. He shook his head and winced.

Shit, that hurt.

He picked up the bag.

I didn't bring this in… did I?

Turning off the tap, he went back into the bedroom. On the bedside table nearest the en suite lay the keyless fob of the Mondeo. On the floor was his kit bag, the one he'd been given when playing football for the mine team. A couple of changes of underwear were inside, plus a plain, blue t-shirt, but there was no sign of his wet khaki shorts and blue polo shirt, nor his tan loafers.

They must be in the car.

The clothes he was wearing, which he barely recalled stripping off, were slung over the back of an armchair on the opposite side of the window to the dresser.

Didn't I throw them on the floor?

His trainers were placed neatly in front of the chair.

Thankful the pneumatic drill in his head was being gradually replaced by a pickaxe – with the throbbing reduced to once every fifteen seconds, which was just about more bearable than once every two or three – he pulled on his t-shirt, jeans and trainers. The boxers he'd been wearing were also missing, but perhaps he'd taken them off with his shorts and polo shirt. He'd put another pair on once he'd returned from the bar.

He caught hold of the brass door handle. On tentatively twisting it to the right, his fear of having been locked in was immediately dismissed. Cautiously, he swung the door towards him just far enough to allow a look along the corridor; it was clear. He stepped out onto the wooden floorboards.

Edging his way towards the stairs – the fingertips of one hand dragging along an uneven, whitewashed corridor wall – he listened for any sign of life either on this floor or downstairs. It was silent; there was not even the sound of a chinking glass or a murmur of conversation.

The carpeted boards of the stairs creaked each time he warily placed the ball of a foot on them, and each time he did so he paused, listening for any hint of movement. Halfway down the stairs, where a landing made a one-hundred-and-eighty-degree turn, he waited for almost a minute, comforted by a false sense of security that if anyone downstairs had heard him, he still couldn't be seen; that is, until they reached the landing.

Finally, he stepped off onto the flagstone ground floor. He peered to his right, the direction of the public bar; it was in darkness. On his left, no light came from the small, eye-level window in the swing door of the kitchen. There was no one in the public bar, and no empty glasses on the tables. Tristan Mawgan and his staff were obviously conscientious when clearing up after service. Thinking some chilled water would help his recovery, Ethan lifted up the counter flap and reached down to the shelf containing mixers and bottled lager. Picking up a sparkling water, he paused. It was lighter than his subconscious had expected – in fact, it was empty. He tried another, then another – they were all empty; however, the half-dozen bottled lagers and ales were full, as were a couple of mixers

What the fuck?

He pulled the tap of a draught lager, but nothing came out, nor did it from the soft drinks' dispenser or the keg cider.

What was it Anne had said?

'We only have one cask ale, but I'd thoroughly recommend it.'

Perhaps she meant they only had cask ale and fuck all else. What the hell's going on?

He rested his elbows on the bar counter, his head in his hands. The pneumatic drill was starting up again.

Come on, Menhennett, pull yourself together. You've worked underground in mines for fuck's sake.

He took a deep breath. Forcing himself upright, he walked through an arch into what he assumed must be the other bar. When Anne had led him to the foot of the stairs via the passageway leading to the kitchen and toilets, he vaguely remembered passing a closed door marked 'Lounge Bar & Restaurant'.

'There's no one in tonight,' she'd remarked as they climbed the stairs. 'It's always quiet when the weather's like this.'

Standing behind the lounge-bar counter, he could see why. There were no tables or chairs, the walls were unplastered, the mortar between the original stones was crumbling, and – like the ceiling – in places was non-existent. Even in the poor light, Ethan could see what would have once been described as 'character oak beams', were now rotten and riddled with woodworm. As in the public bar, none of the beer taps worked, although one had a handwritten label on it marked 'Lager'. A pipe ran from the bottom to what he assumed was an adapter for fixing to a beer keg. There was no sign of a carbon dioxide gas cylinder. He managed a smile.

Pretty shit, flat lager.

Rather than being stacked with bottles, the shelves were bare, although one shelf contained an array of clean glasses.

His heart began working overtime, the resulting increase in blood pressure uniting the drill and the pick. He retched and threw up in the under-counter sink, unaware that there was no plumbing attached. His vomit dripped through the plughole onto the floor. Bent double, he sank to his knees, his neck providing an easy target for a short length of two-by-four.

THIRTY-EIGHT

January 1884

MONTANA, NORTH WEST AMERICA

It hadn't been easy for Tegen Tregunna following the death of her husband and two boys when Wheal Hingston flooded for the second time. Having no alternative accommodation, she reluctantly accepted the mine owners' offer – the ones whom she blamed for her loss – to let her stay in the cottage until another tenant was found. A collection amongst the mining fraternity had raised sufficient funds to pay for a few weeks' rent, and to buy nutritious food for her and her unborn child. However, when finally given a fortnight's notice to make room for Kenwyn Petherick, a working miner and his family, she moved in with the widow of a wealthy wool merchant. In return for a roof over her head and a small wage, Tegen helped in the kitchen and with cleaning duties. She was well looked after and, in late April 1883, Tegen gave birth to a healthy, six-pound-nine-ounce baby boy named Kevern after the father he would never know.

Still angered by the announcement that the three mine owners – Pendeen, Trethorne and Pollick – had been found innocent of negligence, and the fact that her son was suffering from asthma – which was not helped by the damp autumn air – Tegen made a big decision. Told by her employer's generous gentleman visitor of the money to be made above and below ground in the 'blossoming' copper mines of America, she borrowed the fare from him, and, in December, she and Kevern set sail for a new start, promising she would begin repaying the gentleman's loan as soon as she found work.

After an uncomfortable, forty-day sea and overland journey, and a testing three weeks searching for work – during which time they stayed in some dubious boarding houses – Tegen took a job in one of the hotels that had sprung up in various towns in Montana to accommodate visiting gold and silver merchants. The pay was more than she could expect to earn in her native land, and, as a chambermaid and dishwasher, she could keep Kevern nearby. She was also able to repay her benefactor in less than a year.

Many single Cornishmen had made the same choice to emigrate, and, two years after leaving Hingston, she remarried. When copper became a must-have commodity, due to the advent of electricity, she and her underground-mining husband saved enough money to open their own respectable guest house in Butte in The Rockies. There, Tegen gave birth to twin sons. Sadly, four years later – when Kevern was seven and his stepbrothers just three years old – her husband was hanged for murder.

Tegen kept the guest house going until she died in 1913. Kevern joined the army and, in 1918, served in the Great War before returning to America and marrying in 1920. He and his wife Geraldine had two boys, one of whom died childless whilst fighting against the Japanese in the Second World War, whilst the older boy survived and – after marrying – had a daughter and son. Kevern's stepbrothers, after a short spell with the Amalgamated Copper Mining Company, both joined the navy and died at sea off the coast of Papua New Guinea in a tragic collision with an Australian merchant ship.

THIRTY-NINE

18th June 2013

ETHAN – THE HUNG, DRAWN & QUARTERED

'Ethan… Ethan… are you all right?' asked Jenny.

Ethan was staring at the candle, the thumb and one finger of his right hand flicking though the pages of the book, whilst his left hand was rubbing the back of his neck.

'I said, "Ethan, are you all right?"'

'Sorry, Jenny,' he mumbled, 'My mind was elsewhere. What was it you said?'

'It doesn't matter.'

He stopped flicking and looked at the open page. 'What's this?' he asked.

'It's an alphabetical list of the names, dates and places of birth, and dates of death of all the miners, men and boys who died whilst working at Wheal Hingston.'

Absentmindedly, Ethan turned to 'R'. He ran his finger down the list until he reached Roscarrow:

Roscarrow	*Tomas*	*5th May 1717*	*Penryn*	*8th June 1749*
Roscarrow	*Peder*	*20th September 1736*	*Penryn*	*8th June 1749*
Roscarrow	*Hedra*	*4th May 1738*	*Penryn*	*8th June 1749*
Roscarrow	*Rosen*	*2nd February 1719*	*Helston*	*13th August 1754*

His finger paused on Hedra, and then he tapped it on Rosen Roscarrow's name.

'But why's this name here?' he asked Jenny, he slid the book around to face her. 'She died five years later according to this. And, anyway, how does this help me?'

'The list includes all relatives, both living at the time and born since.' She swung it back round. 'Look under "M". I think you'll discover why you are still alive.'

He turned to the page. However, before he had time to read the list of names, the sudden influx of light from the door swinging open distracted him. It was rapidly followed by the voice of one of the men who'd kidnapped Claire. 'Ha, there you are – I said you would be.' He was looking at Claire, whose eyes were now half open. He glanced at Ethan. 'No doubt he brought you up here.'

Then, in an instant, all colour drained from the man's cheeks – he was staring at Jenny. He took a step back. 'But... but... but you're dead. I saw you in the car. Your head... it... it was lying on the passenger seat. You were well and truly—'

Ethan took his chance. He'd wanted to have a go when they'd dropped Claire off at the adit, but taking on three would have been pointless; however, one was a possibility. Levering himself off his chair, he lowered his shoulders and drove the left one into the man's stomach, forcing him out of the doorway and into the closed lounge-bar door on the opposite side of the porch. The man's head struck the stained-glass half panel, smashing the glass. Unfortunately for him, the lead strips weren't so forgiving. Remaining in place, they retained large, pointed shards of glass – two of which penetrated the nape of his neck. Blood began to spurt.

Holding his neck with both hands, his eyes pleaded with Ethan. 'What have you done? What the fuck have you done?'

Ethan's jaw fell open. He'd reacted on impulse, intent on revenge for Claire, but – as the extent of the man's injuries sunk in – so did remorse. 'Oh my God. I'm so... so...' He wanted to say sorry, to rush forwards and attempt to stem the flow of blood, and yet... yet deep inside, something wanted this man to suffer. He couldn't be sure, but he thought it was the one they'd called Smithy, the one who'd said, 'I wouldn't mind giving her a dose meself.'

Recalling the words was enough to ensure that Ethan remained motionless, his remorse overridden by satisfaction. He watched as the man staggered out into the road and fell to his knees, the collar of his Tattersall shirt and the back of his leather waistcoat stained bright red. He saw the rays from the rising sun glittering off the pieces of glass in the man's neck and he laughed, louder than he'd laughed for weeks. As the man collapsed forwards, his head crashed onto the tarmac. Still kneeling, his torso twitched uncontrollably until it came to rest in a position as though he were worshipping his maker.

Ethan threw up; his own face was as white as the man's. Head in hands, he sobbed, quietly at first, then much more noisily, until, finally, he wailed. Like the body still oozing blood in front of him, he knelt down, his regret enveloping his soul. Despite what Smithy had done to Claire and, from his comment, the more serious thing he had done to Jenny, no one had the right to take another man's life. It was only when a hand touched Ethan's shoulder, the same shoulder that had condemned Smithy to death, that his bout of self-pity eased.

'Ethan, are you okay?' It was Claire, her eyes still learning to cope with the daylight.

Taking his hands away from his face, Ethan pointed at Smithy. She gasped. 'Oh my God, Ethan, what happened?'

Wearily getting to his feet, he explained. 'He was one of the men who kidnapped you, drugged you and left you in the adit. They were going to kill you, Claire, and throw you down Wheal Hingston's shaft, just like they threw down the Americans and the dead body of Roger Jones.'

'No, no, Ethan, that's ridiculous. Why would anyone do that?'

'To protect what they consider to be rightfully theirs.' It wasn't Ethan who had replied, but Jenny.

Hearing the commotion, Claire had stumbled out of the bar, groggy and disorientated. As the candle had burned out, she hadn't noticed Jenny in the darkness.

'And who are you?' demanded Claire, turning to challenge her.

'Jenny Woodbury,' she replied.

'Yeah, right,' acknowledged Claire, her senses returning. 'But you're dead; Ethan told me. Isn't that right, Ethan?'

'It is Jenny and she is dead,' he replied.

Claire shook her head. 'I'm sorry, Ethan, but you've totally fucking lost it. It's time we got you out of here and found Sarah.'

'I'm serious, Claire. The man over there...' he said and pointed to the body, which had now toppled over from its praying position and was lying on its side, 'drove his lorry into Jenny's car and decapitated her. I think that's right. Jenny?'

Jenny nodded. 'He drove into me deliberately. I was on my side of the road. He had to change his line to hit me. He'd been told to kill me.' She shrugged. 'He'd never seen or met me before; he'd just been told what car I drove and when I was expected home.'

'C'mon, you can't think I would believe such a load of crap,' sneered Claire. 'I mean even if I accepted you were dead, which I don't, then why would someone want you killed?'

'Because – like you, Claire – I knew too much.'

FORTY

Jenny confidently reassured Ethan and Claire that the other two men wouldn't follow for some time, saying, 'They all work for a haulage company and won't all have the same days off. Smithy would have been expected to deal with Claire on his own. He probably left his vehicle nearby, otherwise we would have heard its engine. It's unlikely any of the descendants will do the dirty work.'

She then instructed Ethan to dump Smithy's body at the rear of the pub and cover it with anything he could find.

'The key for the padlock on the gate is hanging on a nail in the conservatory,' she told him.

Although at first reluctant to do what she said, he eventually saw the sense in it. Left out the front, Smithy would be immediately spotted from a distance by anyone who came looking for him. Hidden at the back, it maybe some time before he was found, which would give Ethan and Claire more time to make their escape.

Grasping Smithy's limp legs, Ethan slowly dragged the lifeless corpse, face up, trying to avoid contact with its wide-open eyes, which seemed to be studying him as he strained and tugged it along. It would be obvious, from the pool of blood on the tarmac and the broken window, that some altercation had taken place, but – at least, with the head wound already congealing and leaving a barely noticeable trail as the skull bumped and jolted along the ground – it might appear initially that the blood's owner was still alive and may have wandered off.

A ripped, moss-encrusted tarpaulin that Ethan found discarded behind the conservatory acted as a perfect shroud. After locking the gates, Jenny then suggested that the three of them go back inside. Fetching a candle from behind the bar, she lit it with a match from a box in her jeans pocket and, for Claire's benefit, did the same demonstration with her hand in the flame that she'd done for Ethan.

At first, Claire pooh-poohed it, saying that Jenny obviously suffered from 'congenital insensitivity to pain', but – once she realised the flame was actually passing through Jenny's hand – she agreed that there was a possibility her new acquaintance was in some way different. She then listened to Jenny's explanation of why people were prepared to kill to protect their secret, as did Ethan.

'It all started several years ago, not long after this pub – which was then called The Miner's Arms – was the only building remaining in Hingston. In 2009, two local amateur historians – both descendants of one of those who had died in one of the two Wheal Hingston flooding disasters – decided the tragedies and those lost in them should never be forgotten, hence the book.'

It was still lying open on the table.

'Once word got around,' continued Jenny, 'other descendants also wanted to be included. From there, a type of family-tree social group was formed, and the obvious place for meetings was The Miner's Arms. Unfortunately, apart from a few tourists in the summer, they were the only ones who patronised the pub. So, like many others, it closed a year later and the group disbanded.'

'You told me it had been used as a filmset,' said Ethan.

'That's right. It was used by the BBC for some fictional mining TV series, so that's why it still looks like a complete building from the outside.'

'And why the inside has false bottles on the shelves and disconnected beer pumps?'

'Right again, Ethan. It's also what gave the group the idea of reforming, and this time using the pub as an exclusive, secret meeting place. They decided to restore two of the bedrooms, in case anyone had to stay over, perhaps if they were too ill to travel or possibly too drunk.'

'Or drugged.'

'Not the original intention, Ethan,' countered Jenny.'Anyway, during the time since the group had originally disbanded, three members had developed a somewhat more sinister motive.'

'How do you mean "sinister"?' asked Claire.

Jenny sighed. 'Well, in Cornwall, there are people who believe stannary law should still apply to the county.'

'Yeah, but that's been going on for years – no one's ever got anywhere, though, and I would imagine they never will,' said Ethan.

'You're right, Ethan,' acknowledged Jenny. 'But those people belong to the passive organisations, the ones who just want to revive and maintain the Cornish language and heritage, want the freedom to lobby more effectively in Parliament for extra funding for Cornwall, or even genuinely believe that Cornwall should have total independence from much of UK legislation. Unfortunately, the three I am talking about are—'

'Extremists who are prepared to kill?' interrupted Claire. 'Surely nothing, not even independence, is worth that?'

'It depends on what they are trying to protect and how valuable it is,' replied Jenny. 'I said the whole group decided to reform, but, regrettably, the three members also formed a splinter group – it meets after the main group's evening social events have ended and the members have gone home. You see, in late 2010, something was discovered in the adit by one of them who'd just returned from abroad, which – shall we say – is extremely valuable.'

'You mean silver?' said Ethan.

Jenny shook her head. 'Something even more valuable.'

'Surely you can't be talking about gold?' said Claire

Jenny shook her head again. 'No, I'm not. I'm talking about diamonds.'

'Ha, that's ridiculous,' scoffed Ethan, managing a short laugh. 'They don't exist in Cornish mines. C'mon, Jenny, I'm sorry, but that's total rubbish.'

'So why are these people so keen to ensure the Duchy of Cornwall doesn't learn about what they've discovered?' Jenny queried.

'Because the mineral rights belong to it, I suppose,' said Ethan, 'but that could apply to anything, tin, copper, tung—'

'Correct,' said Jenny. 'But would that be worth killing for?'

'Probably not,' accepted Ethan, shrugging his shoulders.

'And it's why, a year ago,' continued Jenny, 'having been surprised by the visit of the four Americans, the three persuaded the whole group to agree to bulldozing the ruins of the other buildings to make Hingston less of a deserted-village attraction. At the same time, they deepened the ford, ensuring that the place was virtually inaccessible. Obviously, those who didn't know about the diamonds assumed it was to ensure their secret meetings weren't disturbed by someone who might turn up unexpectedly. The fear was that they would report them to the council, leading to a ban on using the pub due to something like health and safety issues. Also, they were told that, without a licence, alcohol couldn't be sold, not that anybody ever actually paid on the day of the meetings. Unfortunately for you, Claire, Ethan brought you here and, like him, you discovered their secrets.'

'Hmm.' Claire rubbed her chin; she was finding it hard to believe what she was hearing. 'And have you actually seen these diamonds?' she asked Jenny.

'In the adit… past where the roof of the level below caved in. Had your friend Sarah not chosen to climb down into the level and become trapped, she may also have seen—'

Claire held up both hands, her palms patting at the air. 'Whoa, whoa, whoa.' She looked at Ethan. 'Trapped? Am I missing something here?' Turning to Jenny, she asked, 'You're telling me Sarah is trapped in the mine and we aren't doing anything?' She grabbed Ethan's arm. 'Ethan, you knew, and we're sitting here talking to this… this… so-called ghost about make-believe diamonds?' Pushing her chair back against the wall, with its feet scraping noisily on the slate floor, she got to her feet. 'Right, let's go.'

Ethan's head was lowered, avoiding her eyes.

'Ethan… are you coming?' enquired Claire.

He didn't move.

'Ethan are you…' She froze, the truth having hit her. She stumbled back and crashed into her chair.

Ethan tried to hold her hand, but she knocked it away.

'Don't touch me,' she shrieked at him.

Sliding to her knees, she leaned forwards and started pummelling his thighs with both fists.

Accepting he deserved her anger, Ethan made no effort to fend her off. 'But I didn't know for sure until after you were kidnapped… honestly,' he argued.

'You bastard… you fucking bastard.' She was screaming hysterically. 'You knew she was trapped and you let her die.' Getting to her feet, she burst into tears. 'How could you do it? I thought you were better than that, but you're just a fucking bastard.'

He saw the hatred in her eyes. He'd never seen her like this. 'Claire, I swear there was nothing I could have—'

Five minutes later, his cheek was still burning from the final slap she'd given him before running out the door and rushing to the Range Rover. He'd been slow to react, her sudden departure totally unexpected. He'd shouted to her not to drive the vehicle and that the tyres were flat, but she either didn't hear or decided to ignore him. She'd hit the throttle hard; in fact, so hard that the four thin layers of rubber were already shredding as they struggled to make purchase on the overgrown tarmac. Eventually gripping, sparks flew off the alloys as she sped away. There was no way of telling how far she would get, but he hoped she would quickly realise it was a waste of time, stop and choose to walk back. Sadly, it wouldn't be an option.

FORTY-ONE

'So, what now?' asked Ethan.

He was sitting on the ground, leaning back against the post, which – when he had first seen it – had sported the pub's swinging sign. Now, like on his subsequent visits, at the top were just the frame and two hooks. He'd considered chasing after Claire, but if she'd managed to keep the Range Rover moving, she might have crossed the ford and already be on her way to wherever she'd decided to go. His best guess was the police station, but that was miles away and there was no chance she could travel that distance. *She could walk, I suppose*, he'd thought to himself.

'You've got to leave, Ethan. As I've said already, you might not get another chance,' replied Jenny. She was standing over him.

'What, just leave, forget everything that's happened and do nothing about it? Surely, like me, anyone could just turn up think the pub was still open,' protested Ethan, 'and end up like the Americans, your stepfather and you, not to mention those who might try to explore the adit.'

'That cannot be your concern.' Jenny dismissed his objection. 'And, anyway, as I just told you, Hingston isn't that likely to be visited anymore. Since it became uninhabited twenty years ago, it's never appeared on any maps. As far as I know, it doesn't come up on any satnavs either, like the one in your hire car.'

'But it was on my 1960 map, which means—'

She laughed. 'And how many people are as sad as you and still refer to maps that old?'

'I can't be the only one. Although, it's unlikely I suppose,' he conceded.

'Also, don't forget that the ford is usually about three feet deep and impassable to ordinary cars, even standard 4x4s. Anyone on foot would need waders, which is not something normal people carry around. Two-wheeled transport wouldn't fare much better either,' said Jenny, trying to reassure him. 'Remember, you found it after a rare lack of rain resulted in the level falling. There's little chance of it occurring again for ages.'

'And the small plank bridge?'

'I suspect that will be taken up after recent events. I doubt it's ever been a problem before; it's too far off the beaten track.' She sat down beside him and touched his arm. 'Ethan, other than the splinter group, these people aren't murderers, so don't try to spoil it for them. A few are old miners from South Crofty, who had continued the work of previous generations until it finally closed in 1998. They want to reminisce and talk about the possibility of it reopening. Others just want to meet, perhaps having lost their spouses; have someone cook old-style pub grub; and drink old recipe beer from one of the small breweries run by Tristan Mawgan, which is served by a couple of his staff. They just want to relive the good old days they had at The Miner's Arms. Several are young – with their great, great grandparents having been tut men, tributers, bal maidens or even adventurers – but, whoever they are, they all have a connection to Wheal Hingston, and all want to drink to the memory of those who worked and died there. Mining wasn't just an industry; it was a way of life, a community. You must know that.'

He did. It was part of the article he was writing on the train from London.

The way Jenny spoke made everything sound so plausible, so innocent and so quaint. But six people had been murdered, plus Sarah had lost her life. Claire would also had died if Ethan hadn't saved her.

'And the three – the ones who are prepared to kill – what about them?' asked Ethan

'They are now only two, and I believe that their time is running out,' replied Jenny.

'Destiny again?'

She smiled.

Ethan was confused. He felt inadequate, unusually lacking in self-confidence, and both mentally and physically exhausted. He studied her closely. 'But how do you know all this?' he asked. 'I mean, I know you were killed because you were aware of what was going on, but how did you know?'

She took a deep breath. 'Because I was involved at the beginning.'

Ethan frowned. 'But I thought you only started living with your parents when you got divorced two years ago.'

'I did, and that's when I found out about the ones who'd discovered the diamonds. They wanted to keep them, although they didn't and still don't have the ability to mine them. I did not agree with their principles, but I knew everything and was judged to be a risk.'

'And that's when they faked the accident?'

She nodded.

Ethan began picking at the fluffy head of a dandelion, which, having forced its way through the tarmac, was now ready to distribute its seed.

The two of them sat in silence for over a minute, before Ethan finally asked, 'Were you one of the historians?'

'Yes, I worked at the County Records Office in Truro,' replied Jenny, staring unblinkingly straight ahead. 'It's why I was keen to form the group; that and the fact my parents lived near Wheal Hingston. My husband and I lived in a cottage in a small village on the outskirts of Redruth. He bought me out, which is why I moved back here.'

'And the other founder?'

'Bill Kerslake, who's the one who towed away your hire car.'

'But he's dead,' said Ethan. 'Your mother told me.' There was no surprise in his voice and no disbelief, just weary acceptance.

'We keep in touch.'

At any other time, her comment would have been funny, but this wasn't any other time and, anyway, Ethan had no energy to laugh.

'He will have told the hire company where he left it,' added Jenny.

'Thank you,' He pursed his lips and blew away the remaining dandelion seeds. 'So, who are the three or, rather, the two?'

'It's best you don't know. There is still a chance that if you run, they will not pursue you.'

Ethan turned his head towards her. 'Why? I know about what goes on in the pub, I know about the diamonds – not that they are necessarily aware of that – and I know they killed Roger.' He shrugged. 'So why would they even consider letting me go?'

She touched his face. 'Because they have already given you a second chance.' She saw his puzzled expression. 'Look, Harry Quinn, who's a friend of the dead man under the tarpaulin, is a crack shot. If he had been instructed to kill you as well as my stepfather, he wouldn't have missed.'

'So, that still doesn't answer why.'

'Come with me.' Getting to her feet, she offered Ethan her hand.

He took it, grateful for her assistance. Dusting off the back of his trousers, he followed her inside.

She lifted the book and pointed at the name Ethan Menhennett. 'Menhennett was the married name of a Cornish woman called Tegen Tregunna – it belonged to her second husband. She emigrated to America after losing her first husband in the Wheal Hingston flooding of 1883. Sadly, her second husband was hanged for the murders of the three owners of Wheal Hingston in an act of revenge for his wife, but before he died, she bore him two children. She was your great, great, great grandmother.'

'Well, I'm fucked,' he acknowledged, rather indifferently. In his current state, he was finding it hard to cope with any more. 'So, I'm actually related to an old mining family. Life is full of surprises.' Shaking his head, he huffed. 'I suppose you're now going to tell me it was always my destiny to be involved with mining – you know... sort of preordained – and, consequently, the reason I'm still alive.'

'No, Ethan, I'm not going to tell you that,' she replied, ignoring his sarcasm, 'but something else might explain why you are still alive.'

'Which is?'

'There is another from that family line who is also still alive.'

'What?' His indifference had immediately disappeared. 'And who is this person?' he demanded.

But before Jenny had time to answer, the sound of an engine approaching caused Ethan to lose his attention.

'It must be Claire – she's coming back,' he said and ran outside.

* * *

'It's best we go inside, don't you think?' It was an instruction, not a question. The man in the black cloak, who had climbed down first from the cab of the truck, pointed the small handgun at Ethan.

'Do I have a choice?' asked Ethan, backing slowly towards the porch.

'Not really,' said a second voice. It came from the person in the red, hooded cloak. Unlike the one in black, the red hood was covering this person's face.

Once inside, Chief Inspector Breock waved the gun at the table with the candle. 'I see you've been making yourself comfortable. Are you alone?'

Ethan glanced at Jenny, who was sitting in the window seat. He raised his eyebrows.

Shaking her head, she mouthed what he thought was, 'No, they can't.'

He recalled she was seen only by those who didn't know her before she died.

'Currently, but I'm expecting my friend to return. She's gone for the police.' It was a longshot and sounded like a well-used line from a movie, but what else could he say? 'They'll be here at any moment.'

'And is that the lady in the white car?' asked the one in red. This gentle voice was familiar to Ethan.

'Er… yes,' replied Ethan tentatively and uncomfortably. His eyes moved swiftly as he glanced from one person to the other. Something told him he wasn't going to like what he was about to hear.

'Then we have good news, but, unfortunately, we also have bad news,' said the man in black. 'The good news is that the police are already here. Let me introduce myself; I'm Chief Inspector Breock.'

Ethan collapsed onto a chair. It didn't take a genius to work out the bad.

'What have you done to her?' His bravado was now fear. 'I said, what the fuck have you done?'

'Your friend's driving skills…' the chief inspector said, rubbing his chin, 'shall we say, weren't of the highest level.'

FORTY-TWO

18th June 2013

CLAIRE

Learning that Sarah was dead was more than Claire could take – she had to get away, have time on her own, have time to take it all in and, more importantly, to call the police. She'd heard Ethan shouting about the tyres, but she'd specified run-flat tyres when she'd ordered the Evoque.

'If you get a puncture, madam, it means you can carry on driving for a few more miles, which will hopefully be enough to get you home,' the salesman had told her. Unfortunately, he hadn't told her that a puncture did not include slashed sidewalls. Her archaeologist husband had no interest in modern cars, instead preferring his restored Morris Minor, and his knowledge of tyre design was restricted to cross-ply and radial.

Claire had travelled no more than one hundred yards when she realised there was something seriously wrong with the way the Evoque was handling, regardless of the horrendous scraping noise coming from the wheels. She knew she should have stopped. The tyre-pressure-warning lights were on, but they went unnoticed – she had one objective and that meant she had to keep moving. Learning of the loss of Sarah was like losing a daughter.

* * *

They'd had many a conversation, sometimes on the phone, sometimes by Skype and Facetime, and occasionally face to face. Unbeknown to Ethan, Sarah had often asked Claire for advice about life in general, advice about what was fashionable in London and, above all, advice about her feelings for Ethan.

'But he's ten years older than me – what if he doesn't want children?' she'd asked Claire as the two of them sat huddled and inebriated in a corner of a nightclub during last year's Christmas party. 'And, even if he does, he'll be nearly fifty when they're still at primary school.'

Claire had laughed. 'One step at a time, young lady; you need to see how you get on first. I know he likes you, but he was very much in love with his wife, and he's finding it difficult to get over her. Also, you have to remember it was only a year before she died that he lost both his parents in the car accident. He'd had a tough time before he moved to London.' She saw Sarah's face drop. She reached across and put her hand on her knee. 'Don't worry, he'll notice you soon, and, regarding the age gap, it's nothing. He might run a tough business, but he's still young at heart. Now, then, let's have another vodka martini.' She nodded towards where Ethan was standing at the bar, talking to his northern journalist. 'After all, he's paying.'

As well as Ethan not knowing Sarah had feelings for him, he also didn't know that Claire had helped her out with money a couple of times.

'Pay me back when you get your next big scoop, but don't tell Ethan,' she'd said as she transferred some funds into Sarah's bank account. 'We can't have you looking like a pauper when you go for your interviews with the hoi polloi.'

* * *

Willing the Evoque around a corner, she pulled the steering wheel hard to the right, broadsiding the vehicle. Broken stone, loose tarmac and shards of alloy flew out over the beat-up, white Toyota pick-up parked in the middle of the road.

'A stupid fucking place to park, you dickhead,' she exclaimed as she narrowly avoided hitting the massive, chrome bull bars. She guessed it belonged to the now deceased Smithy. It had large, oversized tyres and wheels, no doubt to enable it to cross the ford.

Worried she wouldn't get going again if she stopped, she revved the engine – the rev counter hit six thousand, straining the normally quiet engine to its absolute limit. Fighting to keep going on the grass verge, all four wheels were still spinning manically when the khaki-coloured Leyland Daf struck her full on the passenger's side. She hadn't seen it coming, nor had she bothered to put on her seat belt. As the truck pushed the Evoque back towards the hedge, her door burst open, flinging her out. The truck stopped. Getting to her feet, she looked up at the cab. The two occupants stared back. She saw the red-hooded figure nod to the driver and, knowing what was about to happen, Claire's bladder emptied its contents. As the warm sensation spread down her legs, she heard the engine note rise. Loss of control of her sphincter wasn't the only muscle her brain was powerless to command. Instructions telling her legs to react didn't get a response. Within seconds, pushed by the truck, the Evoque slammed her against the trunk of an unforgiving, long-established oak tree.

Blood spewing from her ears, through bulging eyes, she saw the face of the red-hooded female. It was grinning... a sickly, contented grin. Claire tried to shout, to curse her killers, but – being penetrated by sharp, pointed ribs – her lungs had already let out their final gasp. As the truck reversed, Claire slid between the trunk and the buckled lump of metal that had ended her life.

'Put her in the back,' instructed the woman. 'Then, once we have found my nephew, you can take them both to the shaft.'

FORTY-THREE

ETHAN

Ethan's first reaction on hearing Claire was dead was to swear and curse at Linda Jones. He'd recognised her voice and expressed little surprise when she'd eased back her hood. However, deep inside, he felt sick, sick with how easily he'd been fooled by her, even to the extent of believing she had dementia.

'You fucking bitch; how could you do it? How could you kill her?' he shouted at her, before – on placing his elbows on the table – his head collapsed into his hands. His second reaction was to break into loud, drawn-out sobs.

'She didn't deserve it,' he gasped in the gaps amongst his tears and deep breaths. 'She came to help me and Sarah. She wouldn't have said anything about your cosy group of dissenters or whatever you call yourself.'

'Huh,' objected Linda, 'We're hardly dissenters.' She glanced at Breock. 'Rather, we're two people fighting for what we believe is rightfully ours; wouldn't you say, so Chief Inspector?'

Breock nodded.

'And don't be so stupid as to think she wouldn't have gone running to the police. You said yourself, that's where she was going,' she continued.

Ethan laughed through his tears. 'Some bloody rights movement. It takes more than two people dressed up as monks to change things.'

'There will be others,' replied Linda, remaining calm. 'It requires time to convert the uninitiated, but we will get there. We need strong, committed followers, unlike the wimp who wanted to save our four American brethren.'

Sitting upright, Ethan wiped the back of his arm across his face. 'Brethren? How can you call them our brethren? They were just four tourists who wanted to visit the sight of an ancestor's workplace and you murdered them. You don't kill brethren.'

'Oh, they were brothers all right,' asserted Linda. 'Unfortunately, two of them were related to one of the despicable mine owners whom I hold personally responsible for the death of Tegen Tregunna's first husband and two boys.'

'But that was over a hundred years ago, and, anyway, what's it got to do with you? It's not as though you were... related... to this... Tegen woman?' As Ethan spoke, he recalled what Jenny had said and he'd begun to realise who the other person was. 'You mean you are also a Menhennett?' He went to stand up, but the barrel of Breock's pistol suggested it was in his best interest to remain seated. 'She emigrated. You can't be – I mean, Roger said you grew up in Cornwall...' He paused and grabbed the top of his head. 'Hang on, how come he wasn't involved?'

Linda pulled up a chair. Lifting her cloak above her waist, she sat down at the end of the table. Out of the corner of his eye, Ethan watched as Jenny rose from the window seat and, without looking at him, left the bar.

'Put the gun away, Chief Inspector; I don't think my nephew is keen to go anywhere just now.'

Breock did as he was told and sat where Jenny had been seated.

Linda pushed the still-open book at Ethan. 'Yes, I'm a Menhennett.' She pointed at her name on the page. 'Linda Alexandra Menhennett, born 18th July 1950, and sister of Bruce Kenneth Menhennett, born 16th August 1948.'

She saw Ethan's jaw drop. 'That's right, Ethan, I'm your aunt.'

Unable to speak, Ethan stared at the entries in the book. Finally, he managed to say, 'That makes... sorry, made, Jenny my cousin?'

'Correct,' agreed Linda. 'I came to England when I was sixteen – I wanted to travel the world and get away from home. I got a job in a bar in London and met a man called Jeremy Lee. I then stupidly got pregnant, so I married him, had Jenny and then, six months later, got divorced, but I kept my married name. He was a nasty piece of work. He knocked me about when the baby wouldn't stop crying – and said it was my fault.' She shrugged. 'As if. Anyway, I got what I wanted. Being married and with child, I couldn't be kicked out of the country. However, I wanted to be as far away from him as possible, so I moved to Truro as a housekeeper. I brought Jenny up on my own. When Roger retired to Cornwall from his practice in Farnham, we met at Cornish language lessons and... we eventually married. It was Roger's first time.'

In the light of the candle, Ethan saw Linda's eyes were watering. However, her tears, even if they were genuine, weren't enough to arouse a sense of family loyalty in him. 'And Roger wasn't involved?' he asked.

'He was at first, but with no historic ties with Cornwall, his heart wasn't in it and he soon lost interest,' she replied, with her sadness evaporating.

Amazed at her hypocrisy, Ethan shook his head in disbelief. 'And you had him shot because of that – why for heaven's sake?'

She sighed. 'He began to learn too much, so... it was simple. The same as my daughter, sadly; not that I thought much of her after she said she wouldn't join us.' She was totally matter of fact, like a clerk in court reading out the charges against a defendant. 'If only Roger hadn't started poking around in the adit, and instead had concentrated on his gardening, it wouldn't have been necessary.' She smiled wryly. 'Mind you, his books on the effects of drugs came in very useful; it kept his nose out of my business, providing – of course – he drank his cocoa.' She exchanged lingering glances with Breock. 'Isn't that right, Chief Inspector?'

'And the occasional cup of daytime tea, my darling.'

Linda returned the policeman's blown kiss, watching Ethan as she did so. She saw his look of disgust. 'Sorry, nephew, but a younger man has so much more to offer.' She laughed.

'And Roger's books presumably provided you with the knowledge to formulate the drugs used on me?' asked Ethan.

'How astute,' she acknowledged. 'And on the Americans,' she continued. 'Poor Roger, he was so gullible. He thought I was actually interested in chemistry when I started probing him for more detailed ingredient information. He even believed me when I fooled him into thinking I had dementia.' She smiled at Ethan. 'It's so useful when covering one's tracks and excusing one's behaviour, don't you think Ethan?'

He didn't. 'And the non-working telephone?' he asked. 'Was that your doing?'

'Just like your father, you're very quick to learn. It was a terrible shame about his accident by the way,' She spotted Ethan's raised eyebrows and held up her hands. 'No, no, no, no. I might have hated him as a teenager, hence why he probably never told you he had a sister, but no... no, of course I didn't kill him and your mother. I'd already moved to England by then. My father – your grandfather – told me how they died. It was something to do with an oil tanker when they were driving on a freeway. It jack-knifed in front of them, I understand. Oh, by the way,' she said and reached under her cloak, 'here's your mobile. I took it from your kit bag when you were... um... sleeping.' She offered it to him but then dropped it on the table. 'Sorry, I forgot to say that the battery's dead. I also took your clothes, which I trust you appreciated were washed and ironed before being returned.' She wasn't expecting thanks and didn't get any.

Ethan had known the facts of his parents' deaths, but – with his current state of mind – it wouldn't have surprised him to have learned that his Aunt Linda had somehow orchestrated it. He sat back. 'You've got it all sorted; you even got Tristan Mawgan to stand in for the late Roger – photographs and all.'

'Ah, I did wonder if you'd recognise him.' She gave him a smile, which Ethan was now finding arrogant, contemptuous and repugnant. Before answering, she reached out for Breock's hand. 'Such a nice man, Tristan. I met him three years ago, before this gentleman got involved. He used to be an actor, but he runs a small brewery now – he's always drunk though, which makes him talk too much. His girls have to remind him to keep things to himself.' She squeezed Breock's hand. 'He's a good lover too. We had several days out, hence the photos. Oh, his wife Beverly works in the local archive office – she's a very useful lady to know. She keeps me in touch about any busybodies snooping around.'

Ethan stared at the candle flame; there was no more than a half inch of the candle to go before it would be extinguished. Perhaps it was what prompted his next question. Without looking up, he asked, 'So what happens to me now?'

Linda let go of Breock's hand. She sighed.

'We gave you two chances to leave unharmed, and twice you've come back. Unfortunately, Ethan, you don't get a third one.' She smiled her sickly smile. 'However, the good news is…' She paused, obviously relishing the moment. 'You will be in the company of four fellow Americans, my late husband, the lily-livered Herbert, your dear friend from the Range Rover and I can only assume – bearing in mind the pink trainers left in the adit, which, incidentally, I removed on my morning walk before Harry shot Roger – you will also be joined by the girl you were looking for. After all, it was a very big hole, and not one that you would want to fall in.'

'And all to keep the diamonds from the Duchy,' sneered Ethan. 'You are very sick people.'

Linda rubbed her chin. 'No doubt Roger told you about them.' She turned to Breock. 'I am somewhat relieved his death was worthwhile.'

'Indeed,' acknowledged Breock.

Ethan didn't tell them Roger hadn't mentioned diamonds, just silver.

'Now then, Linda,' continued Breock, 'Presumably it will be easier to load a dead body onto the back of the truck, not that I expected to ever need to use this.' He stood up, intending to withdraw the pistol from his trouser belt under his cloak. However, the butt got caught in the buckle. As he lifted his cloak to sort it out, Ethan chose his moment.

The edge of the oak table around which they'd been sitting struck Breock full in the face as Ethan used what little strength he had left to lift and tip it over. Instantly, there was a loud bang, followed by a scream of agony from Linda. She was clutching her stomach. Breock hadn't put on the pistol's safety catch and the trigger had caught in the buckle's prong. Ignoring Linda, Breock was frantically brushing the flames off the lap of his cloak. Unfortunately for him, his usual heavy, satin cloak, which may have resisted the flames, was at home, so – when he'd received the message from Linda to tell him Smithy had not reported back – he'd put on the cheap, polyester cloak over his uniform; it was the one he kept in his car and only used for outdoor ceremonies if it was raining. Normally, whichever cloak he wore gave him a real sense of importance and status, something that his six-foot-four-inch height no longer provided within the realms of policing.

However, now he would have gladly traded every ounce of status in return for wearing only the force's uniform.

The cloak had ignited as soon as the candle flame had touched the inflammable material, and flames quickly engulfed his front. As Ethan ran for the door, Breock's face was beginning to blister. He fell back against the boarded window – the boards of which were made of dry, woodworm-damaged wood that had been torn from floors in the restaurant and upstairs. Dropping onto the window seat, whose cushions had been made years ago from non-flame-retardant cloth, offered no resistance to the intensity of the heat. Even before Ethan had reached the truck, the pub was already well alight. Above the sound of the crackling wood, he heard desperate pleas for help, pleas which – as he climbed into the cab – had already begun to weaken and fade.

He studied the controls. He'd never driven anything as big or as old as this before, but he guessed the principle must be the same as a car. He turned the key. The engine turned over, but didn't fire.

Shit, he thought.

He tried again – there was not even a cough.

Glow plugs, it must have glow plugs.

He scanned the array of warning lights that had come on. One looked like a coiled piece of wire. He waited – it went out. This time, when he turned the key, the engine spluttered, then fired up. He crunched the lengthy gearstick into what he hoped was first. About to release the clutch, out of habit, he glanced in the central mirror. Through the small window in the back of the cab, he saw Claire's blood covered body lying face up on the floor of an otherwise empty load area.

Transfixed, he stared at the woman he'd known for years, who understood him better than he understood himself, and a woman who had a husband and two young children. Winding down his window, he shrieked, 'You bastards, you didn't even have the decency to cover her up. May you burn in he...'

Intent on getting away, he hadn't noticed how quickly the fire had spread. But now, as he'd turned to shout, he watched as flames leapt out of the first-floor windows, shattering the glass as they curled up the front of the building. Realising there was no longer any hurry to leave, he pulled the gearstick into neutral. A broad smile of satisfaction gave him the appearance of a madman, an impression further enhanced by the yelp he let out, when – cloak in shreds and the remains of her hair blackened – Linda Jones lurched from the porch. She was holding her stomach. Seeing Ethan, she reached out one arm, mouthed something inaudible, took a couple more faltering steps, then collapsed in a smouldering heap. Finally, part of a course of burning straw from the thatched roof, which was now flaring like a petrol-ignited Guy Fawkes bonfire, struck her on its journey to earth. She didn't move.

'It was what you deserved,' muttered Ethan, wrenching the gearstick. 'You and your policeman friend.' Hitting the throttle, he let up the clutch – the engine stalled.

'Fuck,' he exclaimed.

He turned the key. The starter motor whirled, but got no response from the engine.

'C'mon, you fucker – you're just flooded, that's all.' He tried again and again, but there was still no reaction. He slammed both hands on the oversized steering wheel. 'Shit, shit, shit, sh…' He didn't finish his last curse.

Turning his head to the right, he stared in disbelief at the barely recognisable, scorched face of Chief Inspector Breock, whose left hand was now tightening its grip around Ethan's neck, with its finger nails digging deep into his windpipe.

'Get off, get off,' screamed Ethan. He grabbed Breock's wrist, but – for somebody whose face was no longer defined by eyelids, nose nor eyebrows, and whose teeth were the only indication of where his mouth had once been, the policeman still had tremendous strength. Whilst Ethan struggled to wrestle free, Breock's right hand reached for his hair, pulling Ethan's head towards him.

Poking two fingers into Breock's protruding eyeballs, Ethan managed to break the policeman's grip and seized hold of the door handle. Using his right shoulder, the one he'd employed to break into the Joneses' bathroom, he rammed it against the door. He yelled in agony as a debilitating pain shot down his arm; however, the force was enough to dislodge Breock's foothold on the lorry's step, and he careered backwards, taking a clump of Ethan's hair with him.

Trying hard to ignore the tortuous stinging in both his shoulder and scalp, Ethan turned the key – the engine roared into life. Shoving it into gear, he pressed his foot down hard on the throttle, disregarding the protest from the overrevving pistons. Gently, he raised the clutch pedal, determined not to stall. The truck shot forwards. He yanked the wheel to the left, the effort increasing the excruciating trauma affecting his right-hand side. He felt a bump from the rear wheels and heard a muffled howl above the noise generated by the clatter of the unbridled diesel.

He allowed himself a wry smile – Breock and Linda Jones would not be harming anyone again.

FORTY-FOUR

ETHAN – THE ESCAPE

Steering with one hand wasn't easy. Power assistance may have been helpful for someone with the use of both hands, but, for Ethan, that luxury didn't exist. He managed to get the truck into second gear, but pushing the stick into third was beyond his ability. Double-declutching may have helped, but it wasn't something Ethan knew how to do, nor had even heard of.

'It's okay,' he said aloud, perhaps thinking of Claire, 'there's no rush, second will be fine.'

Driving past her wrecked Evoque, Ethan tried to look away, not wanting to witness how painful her death might have been.

Reaching the ford, he slowed down from his twenty-mile-per-hour progression and braced himself as the front wheels dipped into the water. They thumped against the stone bottom. Out of the corner of his eye, he saw Claire's body jolt forwards, then backwards, as the hard springing did little to soften the blow. He pressed firmly on the throttle – there was no way he was going to risk another stall.

He had no idea what he was going to do once he got to the quarry road. Not all coppers would be bent, but, after his encounter with PC Fraser and the desk sergeant, he couldn't be sure how much influence Chief Inspector Breock had locally. His best option would be to go to the police in Plymouth; a different county should be safe. He must also ring Sophie at his office – she must be frantic to know what was going on.

For a brief moment, he felt relieved he'd made a decision, which would explain everything, make it all seem okay, mean he could go back to work and carry on as if nothing had happened. His relief didn't last long.

Who are you kidding? he thought.

Doubts began to set in, doubts which made him shift in his seat and doubts which made sweat run down his brow.

He had a dead body in the back – how was that to be explained? Perhaps he could say he found her in her crashed vehicle and he was taking her to hospital, but she died on the way.

Once the bodies of Breock, Jones and Smithy were found, how could he prove he wasn't to blame?

He would also have to say that he suspected there were six bodies at the bottom of Wheal Hingston's shaft – perhaps he'd be suspected of putting them there.

And what was he doing in Cornwall in the first place? If he were genuinely looking for a missing work colleague, why didn't he report her disappearance sooner?

And what about Claire's husband – who would tell him his wife was dead, dead because of her boss' stupidity?

But they were doubts that, in just a few minutes, would become totally irrelevant; at least for Ethan Menhennett, born 19th May 1976 and died 18th June 2013.

Reaching the junction where he'd crashed his hire car, Ethan slowed down, recalling what Linda Jones RIP had said about the speeding lorries, and where Jenny Woodbury had met her end. Trying to avoid changing into first, he edged cautiously forwards. Crossing the faded, white line marking the T-junction, he looked to his right then to the left. About to look right again, he sensed the engine was going to stall.

Bollocks, where's first?

It was no more than just a glance at the gearstick – the sort of glance any driver might make to check which gear they're in, or to check the heater or radio's controls – but even a glance eats into time and, during that time, things can change. For instance, the concrete lorry that hadn't been there when Ethan had first checked left would have been if he'd looked again.

The two men in the cab were discussing their anticipated profit from the forthcoming sale of their cannabis crop, cannabis, which – until the early hours of that morning – they'd been sampling with friends in the back bar of The Horse & Groom. Unlike the passenger, the driver didn't see the khaki-coloured Leyland Daf truck stopped halfway across the road.

'For fuck's sake, look out, Harry!' shouted Len.

Harry slammed on the brakes, but his drug-diminished reaction time meant the stopping distance of a six-wheeled lorry travelling at fifty miles per hour, its fourteen-cubic-metre tank full of fresh concrete, was longer than the gap between it and Ethan; it smashed into the Daf.

Ethan never saw what hit him; with his head still down and his one useable hand turning the ignition key, he was manically trying to fire the stalled engine back into life. He also hadn't noticed the temperature gauge was in the red-zone, driven there by the high-revving, second-gear journey from The Hung Drawn & Quartered. In fairness, he couldn't have known the worn wiring on the starter motor was overheating and shorting, causing sparks to leap from the positive terminal to the diesel-and-oil-soaked side of the cylinder block, as the persistent key turning shot twenty-four volts into the motor's armature.

The impact drove the Daf into the same ditch where Ethan had involuntarily 'parked' the Mondeo. The concrete lorry followed it, then summersaulted into the field beyond. Three of the four occupants of the two vehicles were still alive until the corroded fuel pipe on the Daf leaked diesel over the already burning fluid on its engine.

A passing bus driver was able to get Harry and Len out of their crushed cab, but the paramedics he called knew it was unlikely either would recover from their skull fractures, and – later that day in hospital – their prognosis was confirmed. As for Ethan, the fire had already spread to the fuel tank under the rear floor of the Daf.

'I did my best,' the bus driver told the paramedics, 'but it was impossible; it was too hot. I'm so sorry.' In tears, he gratefully accepted the comfort of PC Fraser, who attended the scene.

Claire's body wasn't found until the fire brigade said it was safe to approach the burned-out shell. A missing person's check found that her husband had reported her disappearance, saying she had told him she was going to Cornwall, but hadn't told him why or where. She was identified by her dental records, with a DNA check of what was left of her bones proving inconclusive.

* * *

Linda Jones, Chief Inspector Breock and Smithy were found a week later, after a full-scale police search.

On being declared unsafe by a structural engineer, what was left of The Hung Drawn & Quartered was demolished.

The ancestors of those who died in Wheal Hingston moved their meeting place to Tristan Mawgan's brewpub in Treworthy. In addition to the miners, bal maidens and adventurers, they would also toast the health of Linda Jones and Chief Inspector Breock – two fine, upstanding citizens who must have died fighting to save the pub, as its heritage had meant so much to them.

The bullet wound that killed Linda was 'allegedly' missed by the pathologist, who stated the cause of death was apparently due to smoke inhalation and ninety-percent burns, the same as Breock, whilst Smithy's death was attributed to being struck by falling glass and masonry.

No mention was made at the inquest of Harry driving whilst under the influence of drugs. Harry and Len were declared 'unlawfully killed'.

The handgun found in the ashes was discreetly returned to the Police Armoury by PC Fraser.

A woman called Beverly told anyone who asked that Roger Jones must have left his 'not so monogamous' wife and gone back to Surrey.

Finally, the four Americans were still on the run, and as for Sarah Jenkinson, the missing person's case remains open.

EPILOGUE

7th July 2014

'Ivy Cottage is so quaint, Gerald; we must buy it.'

'What are your thoughts, Mr Sinclair?' asked Nikki, the young lady from the estate agent.

'I quite like it,' I replied, looking at my wife Connie as I spoke, 'but it'll depend on the price.'

* * *

Perhaps if Connie hadn't been so keen, I wouldn't have been either. We'd only been married six months. Winning the jackpot on The National Lottery meant we were able to give up our proper jobs in personal finance, tie the knot and move from Coventry to Cornwall. We were both in our early forties, and the thought of leaving the regulation and compliance of a world we'd known for the last fifteen years held so much excitement.

'We can grow our own veg, and keep chickens, perhaps even goats and sheep,' said Connie, as we held each other after making love on our wedding night. 'And I can have a couple of horses and learn to ride. It'll be great fun. We'll need some land, though.'

No doubt it was the usual vision shared by many townies when the excitement of a life of self-sufficiency beckoned, before discovering what hard work it actually entailed. Fortunately for us, with seven million quid in the bank, no children and no surviving close relatives, we could always buy ourselves out if the going got too rough.

We'd been an item for thirteen years, since one year after our practices joined forces to compete in an ever-changing business world. Selling the firm proved easier than expected – it was possibly too easy, when I looked back – but I'm a great believer in fate, to the point where I accept that our lives are mapped out from the day we're born.

* * *

It turned out the price was right – a quarter of a million pounds – which was a mere drop in the ocean, as far as we were concerned.

'It's exceptionally good value for this size of property,' said Nikki, 'Apart from the quarry, which you don't really hear down here, unless the wind's in the wrong direction; it's a very quiet area. It's been empty for roughly twelve months,' she informed us. 'It's only recently that someone came forwards and instructed us to undertake its sale. Both the previous owners died – well actually it was in the wife's name.' Nikki didn't say how they died. 'A close family friend inherited it. He owns a local brewery and just wants rid of it. He says there are too many memories for him and his wife to live here. Apparently, their friends lost their daughter in a nasty road traffic collision.' She shrugged. 'So I suppose you can understand it.'

'We could do with some more land though. An acre's not really enough. Do you know of anything up for sale nearby?' I asked.

'Er… not really. There's a lot of horse owners around here, and anything that comes on the market tends to get snapped up…' She paused, thought for a moment, then said, 'It's possible you might be able to buy the field by the quarry. It's been empty for years, I believe. It used to be treated as a bit of a dump, but the council put a stop to that. It needs a lot of work to get it back up to scratch, though.' She smiled. 'I can recommend someone who could do that for you; however, the only thing is that it's not clear who owns it.'

So, we bought the house, and then – being unable to find out who the land Nikki had told us about belonged to – we took the bull by the horns, instructed Nikki's brother (who happened to be an agricultural contractor) to clear it and we moved in Connie's two newly purchased thoroughbred horses. In the meantime, we continued to search for land we could legally buy, so that if anyone challenged us and we were evicted, we would have somewhere to go.

One thing Nikki hadn't told us was the field was home to the ruins of Wheal Hingston, a Cornish copper mine; however, the engine house was barely visible under a coating of thick ivy and brambles. In addition, in one corner of the field – just beyond the ruins – I discovered there had once been a pond.

'It's an ideal area for pigs,' Nikki's brother told us. 'I could fence off a bit, dig out the pond and you'd have a freezer full of pork for the winter.'

We took his advice and, in the spring of the following year, we bought three saddleback weaners.

* * *

Life in our new home was wonderful, at least until I began to get bored of cutting grass, trimming hedges and – for five months of the year – feeding pigs. We made a few friends, although it was obvious that it would take time for us to be accepted as anything other than 'foreigners', or 'furriners' as the locals called us behind our backs. We had to drive to a pub, as the one in the derelict village in Hingston had burned to the ground, not that we ever tried to cross the ford to see it. However, Connie was happy learning to ride, and then, one day as I sat watching her trot around the field, something drew me to the old mine buildings, which – until that moment – had never interested me.

'I'm going to look into its history,' I told Connie that evening over supper. 'Next year, I might even see if I can tidy it up a bit, clear the wall around it as well.'

I thought researching it would be simple, but – after finding nothing on the internet and being given no information by Beverly who worked in the archive office in Treworthy, I visited the County Records Office in Truro. All that was there were maps of the tunnels, or levels as they're called, and the dates the mine was in operation. Consequently, I decided I'd forget the theory and wait until the summer to start tearing the ivy off the walls.

During the winter, I bought every book I could find about the Cornish mining industry and, in May 2017, I began my project. By the end of the month, the granite walls were clear, the ivy leaves were beginning to drop from the full height of the chimney and I felt very smug with what I'd achieved.

Late evening, I would sit beside the ruins on an old, plastic outdoor chair, barbecue a few sausages made from the butchered pigs, and imagine what it would have been like to have worked at Wheal Hingston – to have gone underground, the darkness lit only by a candle, in hot, airless conditions. It was on one such evening, the 6th June, that I met a man called Ethan and a woman called Jenny.

They sat with me, told me about how the mine had flooded twice, and how many men and boys had lost their lives; they told me how four Americans had gone missing after searching for their ancestors.

I enjoyed the chat, but, as they got up to leave, Jenny looked me straight in the eye. The setting sun was directly behind her and the light gave her a weird sort of translucent aura – almost ghostly, I would tell Connie when I got home.

'Be careful, Gerald,' said Jenny. 'The mine is cursed – do not try to open the shaft.'

I laughed, but neither she nor Ethan shared my humour.

With that, they turned away.

'It was strange,' I said to Connie. 'I bent down to pick up a plate and when I looked up they were gone. They would have had to sprint to get to the gate that quickly.'

'Hmm,' she replied. 'No more Scotch for you tonight.'

The next day, after a full hour of scratching around for the shaft, I eventually found it under some thick clumps of grass. Until Jenny had mentioned it, I had not the slightest intention of searching it out, let alone seeing if I could open it. But her comment had made me curious, like telling a young child not to do something, knowing full well it would be the very next thing they would do.

I tugged at the grass – a large piece came easily away. Underneath was a wooden board. Removing more grass allowed me to lift it. The stench was revolting, like the smell from a dead animal rotting in a hedgerow. It was then that I was forced back by a massive swarm of bluebottles, all eager to escape from what had presumably been their breeding ground.

Desperately brushing the six-legged pests out of my hair and off my chest, I slammed the board down. Hopeful I'd cleared off all the buzzing stragglers, I fetched the piece of leftover wire stock fencing I'd kept from when the pig enclosure was built. I circled it around the shaft's entrance, planning that tomorrow, I'd buy some posts from the timber merchants in St Austell and secure it properly; however, for me, tomorrow never came. I did not see the twelve-inch square cut piece of granite slide off the top of the bob wall as I tugged at a thick piece of ivy that ran from the ground to the top of the wall.

Strange, I thought, giving it a good heave. *I'm sure I'd cleared everything from here.*

* * *

From the centre of the engine house, I watched Connie faint when she found me at just after 8pm that evening. My head looked like a tinned tomato squashed under the granite. When she came round, I called to her, but she didn't hear me. I saw her curse as she realised that, as usual, she had no mobile phone signal, not even one that would have connected her to any available network when dialling 999. She ran to the gate, no doubt to use the landline at home. It was another fifty minutes before the paramedics arrived, their task being to simply confirm I'd been dead for several hours, killed outright by a building that I had lovingly partially returned to its former glory.

Three weeks later, Connie led the horses away, and over the next few months – with the pasture no longer grazed or topped – the weeds and the brambles slowly began spreading their unwelcome leaves and stems over every inch of the field.

The ivy has also started its insatiable climb up the walls and chimney of Wheal Hingston, gradually hiding the beautiful stonework of the masons, who – over one hundred years ago – erected this magnificent edifice. However, unlike those masons who freely wander the earth as they please, the spirits of those who died in the 1749 and 1883 disasters can only walk or crawl along the tunnels they dug fathoms below the surface in order to produce the minerals their country so badly craved, a country led by those who regularly betrayed them.

I am not alone – though each day passes in the same way as the one before – for I share my afterlife with Sarah, Roger, Herbert and four visitors from America. However, we have nothing to say to each other, for we each have our own thoughts, thoughts which we keep close to our minds and hearts.

I have never again seen the two who called themselves Ethan and Jenny, nor would I want to, for had it not been for them...